HERMAN
STEUERNAGEL

The Greatest Pub In The Multiverse

THE GREATEST PUB IN THE MULTIVERSE

Emma

Fifteen years ago - In a London Not at All Like Ours

It was on her eighteenth birthday that Emma Corvus decided she wanted to be a bartender.

She was the youngest of her friends and the last to hit that milestone society arbitrarily declared was the age one became an adult. The only way to celebrate such an event, according to her friends, was to take her to the dodgiest London tavern they could find.

Emma smirked at the insistence. They had trained for years to become Hunters of the Cursed—the king's task force that oversaw the removal of witches, monsters, and magic from the kingdom. It amused her that there were those among them who thought certain areas of the city were unsavory.

Of course, each of them could easily hold their own against any attacker the city's most dangerous districts could produce. Moving to the outskirts of their protected area was more a matter of convenience. Besides, in these districts, the king's guards, no matter how well equipped and capable, would be ridiculed, harassed, and perhaps worse. Even the most well-trained Hunter could still die from a knife they didn't see coming. It wasn't worth the effort in any normal circumstance.

And it wasn't humans with their name-calling, sticks, and stones who would cause them the most issues in Westminster. It had been long known that this sector was overrun with magic —despite being mere steps away from the palace and all the king's anti-magic decrees. The king had intentionally contained the problem to this area of the city. Most of the magic users and dark creatures had gone into hiding, but they still didn't like soldiers poking around their territory.

The Tipsy Thames pub wasn't deep into the restricted area and rested right on the riverbank of its namesake.

The booth seating creaked beneath her. With a drink in one hand, Emma let the other hover over the spot where her daggers were hidden. Truthfully, despite everything, there was no true threat here within the tavern's walls. She likely wouldn't need the daggers, but they provided a sense of comfort all the same.

Was there such a thing as an emotional support knife?

The Tipsy Thames might not have been all that dangerous in the scheme of things, but it was a bit of a tired building with paint flaking off the walls, grooves carved into the tabletops, and more dust and grime than Emma imagined was healthy. But most importantly, it was a place where other Hunters wouldn't be sticking their noses into their celebration.

Emma and her friends could have a drink on their own terms here.

At least, that's what Emma's friends Monica, Nate, and of course Liam, had in mind.

They'd trained to be Hunters for six years already—ever since the day she and Liam were pulled off the street. Even then, at the age of twelve, Emma had been skilled with a knife, and when she'd thrown one between the eyes of an ogre who came crashing into their village, the Hunters who'd arrived to slay the beast were in awe of her untapped potential.

"Not everyone has the stomach for this," one of the soldiers had said.

To her, it had been nothing more than a reflex. She'd done what was necessary. Living on the streets as a child had forced her to harden her emotions.

Although she had a soft spot for Liam. The two of them had watched each other's backs for longer than she could remember. It had been them against the world, and she refused to go with the soldiers without him by her side. Whether it was because they saw his potential as well, or because she was too skilled to leave behind, she never determined, but both of them were recruited right there and then and neither had looked back since.

Liam gave her a wistful smile as he slid a mug of ale across the table. "Happy birthday, Em. I guess you're allowed to drink now."

Emma rolled her eyes. They'd been drinking ever since they were thirteen. Even if they were all underage, nobody at the tavern would have stopped them. But the Hunters had strict rules, and even in a bar on Westminster's outskirts, it was best not to get caught breaking any before their first mission.

Though that hadn't stopped them thus far.

The list of Hunter rules stretched longer than a nightfang serpent, but some were more punishable than others. Though not always enforced, there were at least three rules that warranted immediate dismissal: No underage drinking. No pocketing relics from the witches or monsters you hunted. No sexual relations between Hunters.

Well, they'd managed to keep one of those rules.

She raised an eyebrow, lips curving into a playful smirk. "Does that mean I'm allowed to sleep with you now, too?"

Liam nearly choked on a mouthful of ale, and some of the golden elixir spilled over onto his hand and into his lap.

Their companions, Monica and Nate, howled with laughter as Liam tried to clean the mess.

Neither of their friends knew she and Liam had been

secretly visiting each other's bed chambers. Liam obviously knew better. It was a risky joke, but Emma decided his reaction had been worth it.

Her relationship with Liam had grown more intimate over the past year. It started out as a bit of experimentation. They'd practically grown up together. But one night turned into two, and now they were in each other's chambers every other night.

It'd become a game of sorts, as one of them would need to sneak around the night watch to avoid being caught. It was a challenge that made it all the more exciting.

But it wasn't as if this sort of thing didn't happen all the time. In fact, from what Emma gathered, it happened so regularly that the superiors often looked the other way.

The real trouble came when you had to choose between saving your lover or a village in danger. Too often a Hunter would choose their bedmate, and they'd both have to face the consequences. Those were usually dire.

They knew they wouldn't be able to keep doing what they were doing forever, especially once they were in the field, fighting for the freedom of the kingdom. But as long as they remained in London, it seemed like a bit of harmless fun.

Emma swallowed. Harmless, except recently, she'd realized she had developed feelings for him.

If she thought about it, the feelings had always been there, masked under the guise of friendship, of loyalty. As the two of them had gotten older, this grew into attraction. And though they'd never discussed it—to the point of awkwardly avoiding the topic—she was pretty sure he felt the same way.

Well, they'd managed to hide it this far, anyway.

"I need to take a piss." Monica stood and gave Emma a wink. "I know it's your birthday, but don't drink my ale."

Emma rolled her eyes.

"I'll come with you," Nate said. "We'll let these love birds figure themselves out."

Liam groaned.

"I wonder if they're doing it?" Emma wondered out loud as she watched her two friends head outside in search of the latrines.

Liam's fingers tightened around his glass, knuckles whitening. "What did you go and say that for?"

Emma tilted her head, snapping out of her humorous mood to match Liam's serious tone. "Are you mad? It was a joke."

"A joke that bears true. We can't go around announcing that we're sleeping together. Especially not to Monica and Nate."

Emma was dumbfounded. They'd never had a problem joking around before. "I would have said the same thing to Nate. Hell, I'd say it about Monica, if they opened themselves up to it like you did."

Liam stewed, glaring at his ale as though it had committed a heinous act against his mother . . . And Liam didn't even know who his mother was.

This wasn't the carefree Liam she knew.

"What's going on?" she asked. "Something's happened."

"I didn't want to say anything. Not today."

Emma slid her glass to the side and gripped Liam's wrist, applying enough pressure to be painful. He tried to pull away, but she held on. Liam was strong, but so was she.

"Well, a bit late for that now. You can't act like a shroudling and then pretend nothing's wrong. Tell me, what happened?" She took another sip of her ale.

"They know."

Emma's stomach sank and the ale in her mouth went bitter as she fought to swallow it down. "*Who* knows? How much do they know? Who did you talk to? What's going to happen to us?" Her thoughts raced faster than she could voice them. They had been pulled off the streets and raised for the role of

Hunters. If they got kicked out now, she didn't know what would happen. Nothing good.

Liam lifted his hands placatingly. "This is why I was going to tell you tomorrow. I didn't want to ruin your birthday."

Emma squeezed his arm and gritted her teeth. "*Tell* me."

"Captain Becker approached me after training today. He outright asked me if we were fooling around."

Fooling around? Maybe that's what it was to Liam. Maybe that's how it started, but it had grown to something more. Hadn't it?

"He had me trapped. I couldn't deny it. You know how Becker is. He'd see right through any lie I'd tell him. Don't worry though, he said he's not going to do anything. Not this time. His exact words were 'I was young once, too.' Then he said it needs to end, or he'd be forced to let the Lieutenant know."

"Prick," Emma muttered.

"He could have done a lot worse," said Liam. "Even if they didn't kick us out, we're lucky we're not out there cleaning the latrines."

Emma sighed as she let go of Liam's arm. She reached for the hilt of her dagger instead, feeling its comforting presence beneath her cloak. "So, what are we going to do, then?"

Liam looked around the tavern uncomfortably. Since when had he gotten so skittish? "What do you mean, what are we going to do? We have to stop, Emma."

"Stop? You want . . . you want to stop?" Emma hadn't been sure what she'd expected Liam to say, but it hadn't been that.

Liam blew out a breath and shook his head, clearly exasperated. "We knew this had to end eventually. We can't be Hunters and be involved with each other. Command will be sending us out soon. You know what the consequences are if we mess this up out in the field. I won't let that happen. Not to you."

Emma gritted her teeth. "I know the risks, but that's my decision to make."

Liam's eyes were moist with held back tears. "What, you want me to face the firing squad instead? Look, we knew what we were signing up for. We were just having a good time, right? Don't make this more difficult than it has to be."

Emma pursed her lips and glared at the man who sat in front of her. His brown eyes gone distant as he sipped his drink. "You truly think that's all this has been?"

He shrugged as he averted his eyes, doing his best to look at anything other than her. "It has been. Hasn't it?"

"I don't believe it." Emma shook her head, fighting back tears. "I don't believe that's all it's been."

Liam met her gaze then. Conflict raged behind his eyes. There was still something more there. Something he wasn't telling her. Or was she imagining it?

"Maybe in another lifetime," he said. "I wish things were different, Em, but . . . you know what would happen. We've worked so hard to get here. We'd be risking our positions as Hunters. We'd be risking our lives. I'd rather have you as my best friend than not at all."

"As Hunters, we'll be risking our lives every day," she said.

"It's not the same, and you know it."

Emma's thoughts raced. Why had she let things get this far? They had told each other after that first night that it could never be anything more. He was right. They had both known going in that it couldn't last.

But that didn't stop her from feeling the way she did. It hadn't stopped her from wishing for more.

Her mind reeled, desperate for the conversation to go in any direction other than the one it was headed. Toward its inevitable outcome.

"Then we run away," she said.

Liam lowered his head. "Keep your voice down! That

would be treason, and you know it. We can't just abandon our post and think everything will be okay. It doesn't matter how we feel. I'm not going to put your life in danger."

"Maybe I don't want to be a Hunter anymore. Maybe they'll let me go." Her gaze flitted up to the woman behind the bar.

Emma hadn't caught the bartender's name. She stood behind the bar with kind eyes and a smile that could light up the dingy old pub she worked in. Her focus was on the patrons who were sitting in front of her, laughing with them as they sipped their ales—exhausted men and women who sought escape from their everyday lives. Their tired eyes and sagging shoulders led Emma to believe they were likely tradespeople who had worked long hours and needed a break. This bartender was the one making that possible. Giving them a chance to get away from whatever harsh realities life had thrown at them, to be an outlet for them to voice their concerns and have a listening ear who cared. If only for a little while.

The bartender might not have been a hero, but she was free; not merely a droog for the kingdom.

"Do you know how much the kingdom has invested in us? You'd never be granted leave," Liam continued. "The Hunters took us in, raised us. We're indebted to them for life. Besides, what would you rather do, Em? I know we were young, but do you remember what life was like before this? That wasn't living. We were barely surviving."

She sighed as she tore her thoughts away from the bartender.

Liam was right, her life was not her own. Not now anyway. Sure, the Hunters had pulled them off the street, given them the security of food, a roof over their heads, and trained them to fight. All they had to do in exchange was help the king eradicate the world of magic and witchcraft.

"We can only do our best with the circumstances we're

given, Em," said Liam. "I am not willing to risk everything we've been given."

Emma's insides tore open. She wasn't willing to settle for this, but she knew, at least for now, she didn't have a choice. However, something told her that one day she'd run away from it all, start a new life as a bartender, and live life on her own terms.

Even as she thought it, it seemed like such a stretch of her imagination.

Perhaps in another lifetime.

She wondered what choices would have to be made to live that life, and if she could ever hope to see her dreams realized.

One thing was clear. Nothing was happening tonight.

Emma stood just as Nate and Monica strolled back inside.

"Where are you going?" Monica asked.

"Somewhere else. Anywhere else."

Part One
O'Sullivan's Pub

James

Cuanmore, Ireland - Present Day
In a World Much Like Ours

James O'Sullivan hadn't even stepped out of his ride share and onto the cobbled footpath in front of his family's pub, and he already knew he didn't want to be there.

There was no piece of him that still called this place home. Maybe there never had been.

Forget that, he thought. *There never was, and there never will be.*

Rain drizzled over the sign that bore his last name. It waved in the breeze, faded as it always had been, creaking gently as its hinges complained of the movement. The sign had been there as long as he could remember and likely hundreds of years before. Sure, it had been remade and repainted more times than he could imagine, but for as long as anyone knew, there had always been a sign that read *O'Sullivan's* hanging over the door of a pub on this very spot in the sleepy town of Cuanmore.

Family legacy or not, it could all burn as far as he was concerned.

His father had already brought it partially to ruin. Why shouldn't he finish the job?

It was obvious in the fading evening light how much the building had deteriorated since he'd left a decade ago. Faded paint chipped off the green windowsills, which were covered with spider webs and piles of dirt. Mossy patches grew within the cracks of stonework, and the bricks themselves had dulled and become sullied to the point where the rain did nothing to enhance their shine.

It was an unironic reflection of what had happened on the inside ever since his mother died.

O'Sullivan's Pub had been a cornerstone in Cuanmore for centuries, maybe longer, and it had only taken his father ten years to run it into the ground.

In typical Irish fashion, James was already soaked to the bone. He didn't even try to shake off the rain; it matched his mood.

The car, a small silver European model—James had never been good with car names—sped off as soon as he'd gotten out, winding its way through the narrow Irish streets as though it had somewhere important to be.

But that was the thing about Cuanmore. There was *nowhere* important to be. Just a sleepy village that hadn't changed in James' thirty years and likely another four hundred before that. He eyed the cobblestone streets that meandered unevenly past quaint buildings and thatched cottages constructed before his grandfather had been born, and for some reason were still being built as though no other ways had been invented to build a home since the Ulster Rebellion. It was a marvel they were equipped with electricity. Some found it quaint, but to James, it was drab and antiquated.

He didn't want to be here.

As he thought the words, the rain lifted suddenly. James inhaled deeply, filling his nostrils with the earthen and mossy scent left behind by the fresh Irish rain. For a moment, his sour mood lifted. Perhaps there were some things he *had* missed.

Somewhere nearby a robin chirped an evening song, and farther out, the crash of waves upon the rocky shore roared. He couldn't deny there was a type of magic that existed here. Apart from the nosy neighbors, traditional songs, and generations of sheep farmers, there was something to be said about being removed from the traffic, hustle, and concrete towers of the city.

James sighed and shook his head, burying any thoughts that might have suggested this place held any sort of nostalgia. Being slightly closer to nature didn't change the fact that this was a location locked in time. It was a sleepy village where nothing ever changed, and the only type of adventures were the ones found in stories.

After his mother had passed, even the stories had fallen silent.

James had left Cuanmore for a reason, and he hadn't intended on returning. As such, this would be a quick visit. He'd deal with whatever legal mess he had been summoned for and be on his way back to Canada. Back to the life he'd built for himself.

He gripped the handle of the front door, taking a moment to admire the craftsmanship of the old oaken design. He'd been away for so long, yet the place was so oddly familiar. Time was a funny thing. No matter how much of it passed, a small town like Cuanmore could be frozen, as though it hadn't experienced any of its effects.

Out of habit, he pulled on the door and met resistance. He supposed not everything was the same. For the first time in his memory, the door was locked. The only other time he could remember the pub being closed was after his mother died. Now with his father gone as well . . . he wondered if this door would ever see the bustling of customers cross its threshold again.

He punched in the code his sister had sent him in advance then tried his luck again. Warmth and light greeted him as the door swung outward. The smells of the fire in the hearth, cooked stew, and oak furniture rushed from within. This was the smell of home.

Or at least, the home of his youth. There was no place for him here. Not anymore.

James stiffened, preparing himself for an onslaught of memories he'd rather not revisit. Not to mention guilt trips from his sister Kathy. If it hadn't been for her insistence that matters involving their father's estate had to be dealt with in person, he'd never have made this journey in the first place.

"James!" Kathy reacted so quickly to his entry that she must have been standing by the door, awaiting his arrival. She wrapped her arms around him in a full embrace. "It's so good to finally see you!"

James returned the gesture with as little enthusiasm as he thought he could get away with. Not that he didn't get along with his sister, but the two of them had grown apart in the last decade, and he had a difficult time feigning enthusiasm.

"It's good to see you too, sis," he said. "It's lashing rain out there. Let me at least come in and shake off."

"I was worried you'd decide not to come."

It was hard to ignore the excitement on her face. It only made James feel like a troll for not reciprocating the feelings of joy at seeing his only sibling—his only living family member.

That thought struck harder than he'd expected.

"I won't say it hadn't crossed my mind," he said. "But we have a break in projects at work, so I don't know when a better time would have come along."

James studied his sister's face. Had it really been ten years? Wrinkles hugged the edges of her eyes, and there was a lightness to her red hair that he didn't remember being there when he'd left. Though, in the dim tavern lighting, it was tough to see much more than the dark bags under her eyes. She hadn't been sleeping. Of course, he knew the lack of sleep was due to dealing with their father's untimely death and the handling of his affairs alone.

Another twinge of guilt tugged in his chest. Not only had he neglected to fulfill the role of eldest sibling in handling all of this, his younger sister had been burdened with the entirety of the task.

James cast the thoughts aside. He'd made his choices and wouldn't make himself feel guilty over them.

"Well, you didn't make the funeral, so I didn't know what to expect," Kathy said with more than a tinge of accusation.

So much for a lack of guilt.

If Kathy had intended to get a reaction, she didn't let it show. Instead, with a tired smile, she waved for him to finally come in. "You may as well dry off. I know you've been traveling all day. Let me pour you a pint." The tiredness didn't stretch beyond her face. With the way Kathy hopped behind the bar, arms raised halfway in the air with excitement, James would have thought she hadn't aged a day.

James sighed and scratched the back of his head. "If it's all the same to you, I'd rather head to my room. I've been in planes and airports for the last twelve hours."

"Normally, I'd agree that it'd be best to get some rest first," she said, "but there are things here that will need your attention, and I know you haven't given yourself enough time to properly process and deal with them."

"Surely it can wait until morning?" he asked.

Kathy scoffed. "Knowing you, you probably went and booked the first flight you could out of here, didn't you?"

James blushed. "I leave Sunday."

"Yeah, figures." Kathy scoffed again, but that didn't stop her from filling a mug with a dark stout and placing it firmly on the bar top. "You couldn't plan to spend a few days here with your sister? I haven't seen you in eleven years!" She placed a hand on her hip and furrowed her brow. "I'm the only family you've got left now."

"It's only been ten," James corrected, though he knew that wouldn't help in shifting his sister's mood. He decided to change course quickly. "I'm sorry, but you know how I feel about this place."

"Aye, that you don't belong. But that's the problem, James. You don't feel like you belong anywhere. That's why you've been bouncing around the world since the day you were able to leave. Now, sit down. We've got a few things to discuss before you take off and I never see you again."

James swallowed and tried not to mention the fact that it was a real possibility.

Kathy pulled the tap over the second glass mug. Dark liquid ran against its side and foamed as it hit the bottom.

"It has been a while since I've had a real Irish stout," James admitted. The drink brewed anywhere else never tasted quite the same.

Kathy slid the glass across the counter as James pulled up a stool.

"Well, don't get your hopes up. This stuff's piss."

James cocked an eyebrow as he took a swig from his mug. He winced. "Dad was serving this to customers? Where did he even get this stuff?"

"Dad let a lot of things go," said Kathy. "He just couldn't be bothered."

"I noticed the exterior could use a little TLC."

"A lot of things could use a shit ton of work." Kathy sighed. "It's like he'd just given up."

"He had," James said. "Ever since Mom died."

"I always expected he'd work through the grief." Kathy took the seat across from him. "He never did. I guess he never will. At least he's with her now."

James scanned the pub. A fine layer of dust coated everything. Behind the bar, James spotted his dad's pipe lying on the back counter, as though he had just left it there and expected to return and retrieve it.

James had been estranged from his father for years, but seeing his father's pipe resting on its tray as it always had . . . it was the first time he felt a pang of loss.

Seriously, who smokes a pipe anymore? James had never seen anyone else with the habit. It was odd that a small token could make him feel a way that nothing else had.

He breathed in deep, fighting back sudden emotions he didn't realize existed in him. "What do you suppose will happen to the place now?" The question came out of his mouth before he realized he was going to ask it. He didn't want to know, didn't care to know. Growing up, he had always assumed Kathy would take over, but she had become a partner in an accounting firm. There was no way she'd have the time.

Kathy dropped a file folder next to his drink with a thump, pulling him from his weaving thoughts. James cleared his throat and shook off any emotion that lingered near the surface of his mind. He didn't have time for that.

"Well, that's why you're here." Kathy's lips curled into a smug smile, the way they did whenever she was about to intentionally make him upset.

James' stomach dropped; he gripped the handle of his mug tighter. Whatever this was, he was sure he wasn't going to like it. "What's this? You said I needed to sign a couple of things to tidy up the estate. This is a book!"

Tentatively, he lifted the corner of the manilla folder to reveal the first page.

Timothy O'Sullivan Last Will and Testament

"Why is it so thick? Surely Dad didn't own this much stuff!"

"The bulk of it is the deed to this building," Kathy said. "While you've been doodling your little video games, I've been sorting through this, trying to make this as seamless as possible. But Dad never liked to do things easy."

"Pfft." James blew a puff of air through his lips. His father had made it a condition of the will that he sign it in person in front of an Irish executor. If he hadn't, James wouldn't have come home at all. "Don't I know it."

"You know nothing," Kathy snapped.

"If he did, he wouldn't have made me come all this way to sign a few papers."

"I'm fairly certain Dad knew this was the only way to get you back here."

"What are you talking about?" The words came out before he'd meant to say them. He knew exactly what she meant.

"Don't give me that. You could have at least shown up for your own father's funeral, James! You two might not have seen eye to eye, but he was a good man and a good father."

"He was until Mom passed," he said. "Then he was barely a man."

"Yeah, and instead of stepping up and helping, you left us! You left *me*! Here alone to pick up the pieces of a family that had fallen apart."

"We were *kids*. It should never have been on us to carry our adult father through his grief. If anything, he should have been helping *us*."

Kathy sighed. "Maybe at first. But you've been gone a long time, James. You can't fault Dad for mourning the loss of Mom. She meant everything to him." Kathy lowered her voice, the bite in it gone, and breathed another heavy sigh. "We're old enough now that you should understand that. But I don't think you've handled your own grief yet. Not for Mom and certainly not for Dad."

James waved a hand dismissively. "Whatever. Can I just sign whatever I have to sign? I'll say hello to the lads tomorrow and be on my way." He moved to flip the pages of tome that had been dropped in front of him. It was only then that he noticed that the pages weren't all the same. The top page was white and crisp, but as the document progressed to the bottom, there was an evident yellowing to a deeper brown among the pages.

"What is this anyway?"

"Like I said, it's the deed to this place." Kathy let out a tired sigh. "You had to come here because Dad left the pub to you. Though, other than centuries of misogynistic tradition, I can't for the life of me fathom why. But whether I like it or not, you are now the owner of O'Sullivan's Pub."

James

Kathy pursed her lips, bracing for whatever reaction James might have.

He wasn't sure what she was expecting. It wasn't as if he was going to lash out or throw his stout across the room. Bursts of anger had never been his style.

Panic attacks, on the other hand, he was all too familiar with.

James held his mug in mid-air, steadying his breathing, trying to ground himself so that the sudden rocking of the entire pub didn't send him into a tailspin. Centering himself was the only way to keep his emotions from overtaking him altogether. His mouth still hung half open as his brain struggled to digest the news.

Of course, this was a possibility he should have been prepared for. But it hadn't once crossed his mind that his father, who hadn't spoken to him in years, would have ever conceived that the family business should be passed down to the last person on earth who wanted it.

"There has to have been a mistake," James said. "Is this an old copy of the will? I could see maybe when we were kids that he might have left it in trust to me, but now?" He let the question hang, hoping Kathy might fill in some of the blanks for him, a gotcha, or tell him she was only having him on.

"He updated it three months ago," she said, her face dead-pan. "*I* tried to talk him out of it, but he wouldn't have it any other way. He said it was your birthright. Every eldest male in the O'Sullivan line has inherited this pub from their father. It's been an unbroken line for longer than we have records. He said he wasn't going to be the one to throw that away simply because you had some growing up to do."

Kathy sighed. "I guess he supposed you'd eventually come around, James. I also imagine he believed he had a lot of years ahead of him. There's a lot of history in this pub, in our O'Sullivan name. It was important to him that it remained that way. If it gets passed to me, the owner is no longer an O'Sullivan."

James waved her off. They'd both been told the stories of their family. Centuries worth of publicans and barkeeps. Who knew how many of them were true? His childhood had been filled with many tales, both real and fantastical, and often the two blended together. There was no telling how much of the pub's history was accurate, and how much of it had grown into legend over the years.

What he did know was that he did not want to be stuck in this backwoods town, with its archaic cottages and nosy neighbors. That was why he left in the first place, so Cuanmore would not be his lot in life.

Besides, he'd already chosen his path. His hand reflexively went to the top of his portfolio bag as he thought about his work. Regardless of how he felt about this place, some of those childhood memories had made their way into his artwork. The magic within his mother's stories had always inspired him. The day-to-day of managing a pub, though? That wasn't for him.

"Why didn't he *ask* me?" James groaned. "Hell, why didn't he just *tell* me?"

"Maybe he was waiting for the right time. Maybe he wanted you to call."

"The phone works both ways," James snapped but immediately regretted it. He didn't mean to get so worked up. The man was dead, after all. It didn't matter if he'd even wanted his father to reach out . . . he never could now. "Anyway, it doesn't matter," he continued. "If you want it, you can have it."

Kathy laughed. "As much as I appreciate the sentiment, I can't run a pub, James! I'm a full-time accountant. I'd be willing to help with the financial side of things if you'd like. Heaven knows I've been doing that for Dad all these years. I could pitch in until you get your feet under you. But like it or not, this is your burden to bear."

"I've built another life as well, Kath. We've just signed on for a huge project with GameCore."

"What, your little video game doodles?"

James glared at his sister. "Like running a pub is some heroic quest to save the world? You might not like what I've chosen to do with my life, but it's nothing to scoff at. I'm doing something I love, and I'm making a lot of money doing it."

This was neither the time nor the place to fight with her about his chosen occupation. Aside from his physical portfolio, his tablet sat on the bar next to him. On it were hundreds of sketches he'd created. The truth was, he couldn't have asked for a better position. He had moved across the globe to take a job as a character artist for a small house game designer that contracted to the big game houses. For the past three years, their sole contract had been with GameCore, the leading developer of console and PC games in North America.

"Running a pub is nothing to shake a fist at, either," Kathy said. "It's something both Mom and Dad were always passionate about. Believe it or not, it helps people escape their every day."

James shook his head. "That's all well and good, but it's not for me. If neither of us wants it, we'll sell the bleedin' thing. I'm sure the building alone is worth a decent amount, even without the crumbling business attached to it. If someone were to put some effort into the place, I'm sure it could shine again."

Kathy shook her head. "It's not that simple. There's a clause . . ."

James' phone buzzed in his pocket. He pulled it out as a force of habit more than anything. The screen flashed the name and photo of his project lead, Trevor Gimble. The image of the full-bearded man in his early thirties wearing sunglasses and a goofy grin against the Vancouver skyline was one James hadn't seen in a long time.

Trevor was a classic millennial—he texted, messaged, or emailed—he never called.

James held up a finger. "Sorry, sis. It's Trevor. I've gotta take this one."

"This is kind of important," she said, hands on her hips. "Surely they can go without your doodles for a couple of days?"

He ignored the remark about his artwork for the second time. "They should. If he's calling me now, it's got to be important." He let his thumb hover over the answer button. "I won't be long."

James stepped toward the back of the pub away from Kathy, though with the room as silent as it was, there wasn't going to be any privacy.

"What's up?" James answered.

"Hey buddy, how are things?" Trevor's voice sounded a bit . . . strange. James supposed it could be an effect of the long-distance connection, but there was a hollowness to it that was unsettling.

"As good as can be expected. Been reconnecting with my sister for a few minutes. What's going on? It's midnight, and I just got . . . here." He'd nearly said home but stopped himself.

Trevor's job title was technically project manager, but

really they were both character artists. Though, he handled more of the administration and left a lot of the actual design to James, which James didn't mind at all. He would have rather polished lawn mower blades with a toothbrush than worry about administrative work.

It was odd for Trevor to call him at all, but if anything, this call had to be about the illustrations he'd submitted right before he left. A few character sketches for their latest project, *Apex Predators: Humanity's Last Stand*. He had rushed to meet the latest deadline for the villains of the story—a race of highly evolved, highly militarized tigers that had mutated and were attacking Earth's cities. It was like Teenage Mutant Ninja Turtles except instead of turtles the mutants were tigers, lions, and bears, and instead of sarcastic, pizza-loving, crime-fighting teenagers, they were beefy bad guys.

These had been the characters James had been waiting to draw his entire life. Hell, he *had* been drawing them. In his old room above the pub, there would still be old drawings of tiger-inspired warriors. His muse had always been the stories his mother had told of wars fought in fairytale lands. Lands of epic heroes and adventures, tales of magic and myth that captivated James' imagination and set him on the path to become the artist he was today.

But what could be so important that Trevor would be phoning him now? Were the illustrations that bad? Did he get too complacent? Maybe in his excitement he missed some requested specs that had been required. That hardly seemed a warranted reason for a late-night phone call, unless they needed an update before the end of the Vancouver working day.

"*Dude.*" Trevor exhaled the word in exasperation. There was definitely an uneasiness in Trevor's voice, one that James only heard when his project manager was under a tremendous amount of stress.

"What's going on?" As far as James knew, everything had

been going great twenty-four hours ago. Trevor had been the one pushing James to take some personal days—something James almost never did. Trevor wouldn't be calling without something having gone catastrophically wrong.

In the split second before he replied, James' mind sifted through possibilities.

GameCore didn't like their sketches, and they have to redo them, pronto.

The deadline was shifted from next month to Tuesday and he needed to spend the eight-hour flight home trying to draw on an airplane tray table.

The project had been scrapped and now they were developing a game about pink fuzzy unicorns.

Something within James told him it was worse than that. So much worse.

"I'm so sorry to do this now and over the phone. But I thought you should know as soon as possible, so you could make plans . . . or whatever."

"Make plans? What are you talking about? GameCore didn't like what we sent? They were based on the mock-ups they approved last week."

"I know, I know. This isn't about that. They were actually blown away by what you did . . ." He paused as though unsure of how to continue.

"They loved the illustrations . . . but . . ." James waved a hand that Trevor couldn't see in a circular motion, encouraging him to spit it out.

"But . . ." Trevor let out another heavy sigh. "GameCore is declaring bankruptcy. They've canceled all projects that are in early-stage development. I wanted you to hear it from me instead of on the news."

James' mind emptied of all thought as it scrambled to find a way to cling to the meaning of Trevor's words.

"I . . . I don't understand, Trev. GameCore's one of the biggest in the industry. How's that possible?"

"Yeah, well, remember the whole CyberRenegade fiasco?"

How could James forget? Last year, the company released a game well before it was ready. They did so to appease their board members, despite protests from the developers. The game was so buggy that it backfired. Ninety percent of users demanded their money back. The company had already sunk millions of dollars into a game that was unplayable. If they had waited six more months, everything would have been fine, but the board and shareholders were looking at quick dollar signs instead of user experience.

"Well, it turns out they fudged the numbers, made it look better than it really was." Trevor was almost to the point of hyperventilating. Apparently, he'd been worked up over the news for some time already.

"They made it look . . . better?" James couldn't believe what he was hearing. "I thought they lost thirty million dollars. How could it be worse?"

"Try a hundred million. News got out this morning; their stock plummeted. Now they're being investigated for fraud. There's no way they're getting out of this in one piece."

"Damn." James let his gaze wander the pub, his mind at war over which bit of the day's news to be most anxious about. Not knowing what else to say, he let Trevor continue despite knowing exactly what was coming.

"Yeah, damn is right. Listen, I'm so sorry to lay this on you, on top of everything else you've got going on right now. But without GameCore, we don't have work. All our eggs have been tied up in one basket."

James' heart sank as his suspicions were confirmed. This couldn't be happening. This gig was the one job he'd ever cared about. Before this, he was drawing his own comics with the hopes of selling them on crowdfunding platforms. Without GameCore, they didn't have a client.

He struggled to find breath. Darkness edged in on the periphery of his vision, and he gripped the nearest bar table as though it might save him from a sinking ship.

"So . . . you're letting me go?"

"What? No, I don't want to let you go. But you may as well spend as much time as you need with your family because I've got literally nothing for you to come back to right now. But that doesn't mean we're done. There are hundreds of companies out there. We've built up a good portfolio over the last few years, but you know how these things go. We submit a proposal today and it could be months until we land something."

"Months?"

"*Maybe*. I'll do what I can to get us something sooner. I've got to eat too, you know? Don't worry, the company's got enough money to pay us both for a few months before we need to really be concerned. I'll call you again when I have something promising."

"Right," James said in a daze. "Shouldn't I be there helping look for something?"

"Hey, you've got your own shit to deal with. And this is why I handle the admin work, right? But by all means, if you spot a lead, don't hesitate to let me know. All right, man? But otherwise, let me connect with my network. It will all work out; it always does."

James ran a hand through his thick, dark hair and let out a sigh. "Right . . . I guess let me know if there's anything else I can do."

"Don't worry. I will. And I'm sorry, again. Not just for this, but, well, for your dad as well. Seriously, use this time to spend with your family. I'm sure they'll be happy to have you around for a bit."

James hung up the phone, not even sure whether he said goodbye or not. He didn't move from the table he had leaned against, but Kathy still noticed his conversation was finished.

"Everything okay?" she asked.

"It looks like you get your wish," he replied. "I'll be staying here a while after all."

James

Sunlight streamed through the window of James' childhood bedroom, its beams bouncing off dust hanging in the air before hitting old posters and childhood sketches that still clung to the wall.

It took James a few moments to orient himself as he opened his eyes and did his best to remember where he was and why he was there. Lately, when he found himself in this room, it was because he was having a nightmare.

Not this time. This was real, and the nightmare had only just begun.

James groaned as he rolled over, rubbed his eyes, then pulled off his sheets. Remnants of his past surrounded him. If it weren't for the state of the rest of the pub, he would have been surprised the room had remained untouched for so long.

His best memories in this room were of the stories his mother used to tell him of men and women in fantasy worlds who were pulled from their sleepy towns and forced on an adventure. Stories of hope in which dwarves, elves, and magicians would band together despite whatever differences they held. Of talking tigers that walked like men and wielded weapons of great power. Of magic and mystery. His old drawings displayed all of these, some of the work he was proudest of still hung here, framed with care. Other sketches had been tacked on the wall haphazardly—he'd switch these up whenever he came up with something new or one of his mother's stories piqued his interest. The drawers of the wooden desk in the corner were still filled with old sketchpads and notebooks, with memories that were both familiar and foreign.

Like something he remembered from a dream.

His eye caught on a particular sketch above the desk. It could have been the precursor to one of the sketches he'd submitted for Apex Predator. A tiger, except not. Standing on two legs, its arms outstretched as though ready to pounce on the person observing the image. Its orange and black-striped head sticking out of what could have been a military uniform. James grabbed it off the wall and pulled it closer to examine. The stories his mother told of a war between the mutant tigers and other mythical races were always some of his favorites.

Those stories were what had helped him escape the dreary village of Cuanmore, that helped him dream of other worlds and adventure. Of becoming more than what this town could offer him.

That was why he left: he'd set out in search of adventure.

As much adventure as could be found in the real world, at least.

The thought snapped him back to reality. James sighed. He had no intention of staying any longer than he had to. But with nothing waiting for him back in Vancouver, he had no excuse to rush back.

Maybe a few more days wouldn't hurt. If he had to sell the pub, he could use some extra time to get things in order.

Kathy would be thrilled.

A whiff of a familiar smell drifted into his room. At first, he thought it was the building's old oak wood, which did sometimes release a pleasant odor. This was something different, though. Something better.

Bacon, he realized.

That perked his senses, and more smells filtered through the floorboards. There was a sweetness to the smell, like fresh baked bread, in addition to the distinct scent of tea.

Someone was making breakfast.

He hoped it was someone other than Kathy. The woman might have been good with finances, but she was a horrible cook.

James took his time getting ready. As much as the thought of bacon appealed to him, he realized the grime of airports and airplanes still clung to him.

The small tavern housed a single bathroom a few doors down from his room. In the past, the home would have doubled as an inn, and guests would have shared the space. He made his way there, pulled off the last of his remaining clothes before turning the shower knob. He waited a few thoughtful moments before stepping in. Cold water hit his skin, jolting him from his sleepy state. He had forgotten that the old building didn't have much in the way of heated water.

Which was just as well. It kept his shower quick. Once he was done, he put on a set of slacks and a jumper from his suitcase before making his way down to the kitchen.

"There's the sleepyhead now!" an older woman's voice shouted to him before he could see who it belonged to. Though he didn't have to.

"Moira!"

A longtime family friend, Moira ran a deli down the street. Her sandwiches were always to die for. She had a sharp tongue, a knack for spotting trouble before it started, and an uncanny ability to make you feel like a fool without saying much at all. But beneath the gruffness, she was loyal to the core. If you earned her respect, she'd defend you like one of her own, even if she complained about it the entire time.

She was also the mother to his childhood best friend Liam, so she served as sort of a third parent over the years. Both families had essentially grown into one.

As a kid, the woman had seemed ancient, but it appeared she hadn't aged at all in the last decade.

Moira sat next to Kathy at the 'family table.' It was the one that sat between the main door and the bar, where they had often sat as a family before the tavern had opened. There was an old cookhouse toward the back of the inn that had been designed for family meals, but they had opted to use the large space of the pub before customers arrived. It also meant they had room for friends and neighbors like Moira to drop by and visit.

Moira stood from her seat at the table as James descended the stairs. She was a slender woman in her late fifties, with a no-nonsense air that seemed to cling to her like the flour dusted on her apron. Her dark brown hair, streaked liberally with gray, was always pulled back into a messy bun at the nape of her neck, though a few stubborn strands invariably escaped to frame her sharp, angular face. Her eyes were a piercing hazel; sharp and watchful, as if she were always half-expecting someone to knock over a jar of pickles or sneak a bite of something before paying for it. She wore her usual practical attire, a plain shirt, rolled-up sleeves, and a flour-dusted apron, and looked like she'd just come from running her deli, which she probably had.

James couldn't help but grin as he approached. "You haven't aged a day, Moira! Are you the one making the entire place smell divine?" He embraced the woman who stood a foot and a half shorter than him.

He stole a glance at the table to see a full spread of breakfast foods. Alongside the bacon, there were of course potatoes, soda bread, fruits and preserves, and a wild variety of pastries and treats.

"If you mean the rashers, then yes." Moira smiled, reaching up to cup a hand over James' cheek. "If it's pastries you're smelling, you'll have to thank Rudy."

Rudy had been a mainstay in Cuanmore for as long as James could remember. The old German baker lived on top of his bakery and had filled James' childhood memories with more sweets than he probably should have eaten.

"I suppose nobody in town will go hungry as long as the two of you are around." James laughed, though he was mostly serious. There was enough food on the table to feed a small army.

"I tried to stop them," said Kathy. "But you know how things are with these two."

Moira squinted. "Well, I know you, Jim. You probably haven't eaten since your plane left Vancouver."

James wanted to deny the accusation, but his stomach growled in hungry protest. "You know me too well." He laughed again. "Where is Rudy, anyway?"

"Well, he does have a shop to manage," Moira said. "We can't all sleep the day away, you know?"

James looked at his watch. It was nearly eleven A.M. "The time difference must be messing with me. I'm surprised you waited so long to have breakfast ready," James said as he grabbed a plate and started loading it up.

"Are you kidding?" said Kathy. "Moira's had this here for hours. She finally decided to throw the rashers on because she thought the smell would draw you out. It looks like it worked."

James couldn't help but grin. "Thanks, Moira," he said, grabbing a seat at the table.

"Some things never change, lad. Food was always the way to win you over." Moira returned his smile. "I'll be sure to bring

Rudy by later for a visit so you can say thanks before you head back. He'll appreciate seeing ya."

"I'm looking forward to seeing him," James said. "It sounds like I'm here for a bit, at least."

"Ah!" Moira lit up and looked at Kathy with widened eyes and lifted eyebrows. "That's wonderful news! So you will be taking over the pub, then?"

James exchanged a nervous look with his sister. "Uh, not exactly . . . I think I'm going to—"

"We have to finish discussing the terms Dad laid out, Moira," Kathy said. "James and I haven't been able to discuss everything yet."

"Oh, goodness! And here I am invading your family time. I'm so sorry." Moira stood and started collecting her dirty dishes.

"Don't be ridiculous! You're practically family," said James, and he stuffed another bite of bacon in his mouth. "I'm g-ad you s-opped by."

"No, you just got here, and you and your sister have lots to discuss."

The tavern door opened, letting a ray of late afternoon sunlight stream in.

The silhouette of a figure filled the doorway, a man of moderate build and above average height. "Do I smell rashers?"

"Liam!" James stood and moved to embrace his old friend. They patted each other on the back. Liam was tall enough that James barely reached his armpit.

"Leave it to Liam to smell food from down the street," Moira quipped.

"There's plenty here," said Kathy. "Help yourself."

"I can't believe you two have been apart for all this time," Moira said, crossing her arms. "When you were kids, you were inseparable."

"He's outgrown this town, Ma." Liam grabbed James and

ruffled his hair. "He's pursuing his dreams in the big city. Isn't that right, Jimmy?"

James scrambled to get out of Liam's playful grip. "Well, that *was* the plan."

"James lost his job," Kathy interjected. James shot her a glare. He wasn't sure he wanted all of Cuanmore to know that yet. But now that Moira knew, it would be a matter of hours.

"I haven't *lost* my job," James corrected. "Just a contract. I'm on a bit of a break."

Moira uncrossed her arms. Despite her usual crusty exterior, there was a flash of concern in her eyes. "Well, whatever the reason, we're happy we get to see you again. Aren't we, Liam?"

Liam had taken a bite of croissant just as his mother asked. Unlike James, he swallowed his mouthful before answering. "I don't know about you, but I came here for the food."

"Pah!" Moira rolled her eyes, her son's sarcasm going straight over her head. "Your friend comes all this way, and you're going to talk to him like that? He's never going to come back."

"That's right," said James with a grin. "If I never set foot in Cuanmore again, it will be all your fault."

Liam chucked a piece of croissant toward James' head. The toss was halfhearted, though, and it slapped against his shoulder. James grabbed it before it fell and popped it in his mouth.

"Hey now! No throwing food," Kathy scolded. "Moira, Liam's just joking. Of course, he's here to see James."

Liam grinned. "That's right! I came down hoping James would have whipped up a few of his famous morning Hemingway Breakfasts."

"It's too early to be drinking," Kathy said.

"I took the rest of the day off," Liam said. "I figured Jimmy wouldn't plan on being here long. Besides, it's nearly noon! Consider it brunch."

Kathy sighed. "Moira, you may as well stick around. But James, we really need to finish talking about the pub."

James nodded. "Of course, but we may as well make a cocktail here for old time's sake." He winked at Liam, who let out a chuckle.

"Boys." Moira rolled her eyes. "They never grow up."

Hemingway Breakfast

Drink Recipe

Ingredients:

- 2 ounces white rum
- 2/3 ounces lime juice
- 1/2 ounce Falernum syrup
- 1/2 bar spoon orange marmalade
- 3 dashes angostura aromatic bitters
- 1/4 ounce absinthe
- Ice

Directions:

1. Place a coupe or martini glass in the freezer to chill 15 - 30 minutes prior to preparing the cocktail.
2. Rinse the glass with absinthe and set aside.
3. Fill a shaker with ice and combine the white rum, lime juice, falernum syrup, orange marmalade, and bitters.
4. Shake vigorously for about 15 seconds until the shaker is chilled.
5. Double strain the mixture into your chilled coupe or martini glass.

James

Unlike Liam, Moira couldn't take the full day off, so she decided to return to the deli.

"Can't be lazy all day," she said. "No matter who's in town." She gave James another hug before heading on her way.

"Can we please finish discussing the pub now?" Kathy asked the moment the door shut behind Moira.

"Sure." James took his drink and set it on the table, grabbing a chair.

"Do you want me to leave?" Liam half stood, ready to go at the word.

"Don't be silly," said James. "You've been as much a part of the family as any of us. There's nothing that we'll discuss here that isn't for your ears too."

Liam nodded and sat back down, though his eyes were still filled with trepidation.

"Now," James continued, "how much do you think we can get for the place? Cuanmore might not be as bustling as it used to be, but I think with a little bit of effort, this pub could still be as popular as when Mom was running it."

Kathy and Liam exchanged a quick, worried glance. It was almost so quick that James missed it. But he realized there was something Kathy hadn't told him yet—something she had already discussed with Liam.

His offer to leave was a nicety. Liam already knew what Kathy was about to tell him. And James had a sinking feeling he wasn't going to like whatever it was.

"I had wanted to tell you this last night, but we didn't get to finish our conversation." Kathy said. "We can't sell the pub, James."

James expected a bit of resistance from his sister and could understand her sentiment. But it wasn't practical to hang on to a pub neither of them wanted.

"Listen," James said, "I know this pub is a family namesake or whatever. But I have no interest in sticking around to run it. You said yourself that you don't have time for it either. All I ever wanted growing up was to get out of this place. I don't want to end up stuck back here. We both have other careers, other lives."

He might have been without a job at the moment—*without a contract*, he reminded himself—but that would change soon enough.

Kathy shook her head. Her face had hardened, and James couldn't tell whether she was more worried or frustrated.

"No, I mean we *can't* sell it. There's a clause in the will. We are not legally able to sell O'Sullivan's, the building, the name, or any of its fixtures, for one year after Dad's death."

James almost let out a laugh. "You've got to be joking. How can a dead man stop us from selling the business?"

Kathy raised her hands in defense. "I was just as flabbergasted as you. But I've talked to multiple lawyers about this already. Apparently, it's been a clause on the property that goes back as far as we have paper records. Which is a very, very long time. There is no way out of it."

James scratched the back of his neck as he tried to piece together the implications of what his sister was telling him.

"Does the pub have to remain operational for that time?" It wouldn't be ideal, but maybe they could shutter it and wait.

Kathy nodded hesitantly. "The clause specifically states that the pub needs to be fully open to customers for twelve months before a sale. Otherwise, all proceeds go to charity."

James pursed his lips and ran his tongue over his teeth as he processed the information. "So, we have to run the pub for at least a year if we want to see any sort of inheritance?"

"Essentially, yes." Kathy nodded. "Dad had some savings. I think it's what he got from Mom's life insurance. But everything else he owned was tied up in the pub."

"Bleedin' hell." James let his gaze wander around the family pub that he now legally owned. The tavern he'd grown up in. Suddenly everything appeared a lot more dingy than it had the night before, and that was saying something. Shelves needed to be cleaned and organized. Old boxes stacked in the corner had to be put away. Mismatched glassware hung from hooks and was shoved into crannies on shelves where it never should have been. Dust covered absolutely everything.

Liam rested a palm on James' shoulder. "I've already spoken to my mum about it. I'm going to help out here any way I can. She's got things under control at the deli, and we've got capable enough staff that I don't need to be there most of the time. Hell, I'm mostly in the way as it is."

This was like a bad dream. He wanted to scream. But mostly he wanted to hang onto the table to keep the room from spinning.

"So, my choice is between running a pub I don't want for a year, or closing it until we can sell and we get nothing from the transaction. There's got to be some sort of loophole."

Kathy grimaced and shook her head. "I know it's a lot, but this thing is ironclad. I won't blame you if you decide to let it all go, but it would be a bit of a shame."

James groaned. "I can't believe Dad did this to me. He knew I never wanted anything to do with this place."

"I'm not sure it was entirely his choice," said Kathy. "I've been going through the paperwork for weeks. This clause has been and will remain in effect for as long as anyone from the O'Sullivan lineage owns the property. I think he probably could have worked out a way for me to inherit the pub, but even that would have been a lot of extra effort and legal fees. I think he hoped you'd find a way to deal with it."

"Can *I* transfer it to you?" He was stretching and he knew it. But there had to be a way for him to get out of this.

"Unless you die first, you can't until a year is up. But I don't want it any more than you do."

"But at least you *live* here!" The words came out more of a growl than James intended. This wasn't Kathy's fault, and she'd already been through enough with all the effort she'd put into figuring this stuff out. He tried to compose himself before continuing. "You could hire someone else to manage and run the place. Even to do that much I'd have to uproot my life and move back here."

"Look, I know you're not in the best of situations. But maybe this timing works out well for you. You said yourself you have at least a few months until Trevor gets you a new project to work on. Why don't we work on getting things sorted and running until then? After that we can figure out something, maybe get some extra staff to help out."

James grunted and then shot back the rest of his drink.

"And I'm more than happy to help take care of the financial side of things," she continued. "Dad maybe didn't have a lot of customers, but he didn't have much for expenses either. We've got a decent budget to help us get this place up to spec."

"I'll be willing to help manage," Liam said. "You guys have been like family to me, and I know your dad helped my mum get the deli up and running when she first came to town. It's only fair that I help you out too. You don't have to pay me if you can't. I've got enough woodworking projects ready to go that will pay the bills."

"If you're working here, we'll pay you," said Kathy. "The pub may be in rough shape, but it's not broke yet. But this is all up to James. Nothing can happen without his say so."

James wanted to dig in his heels and head back to Vancouver on the next flight he could board. But he wasn't the only one who would be affected by that decision. The pub was worth a fair sum, and Kathy deserved her share of the inheritance as well. And like Kathy said, he was out of work for at least a few months anyway. As inconvenient as it was, maybe the timing couldn't be better. His insides flopped just thinking about having to stick around, though.

His childhood best friend and his sister eyed him with the hesitant stares of parents who had just told their child Santa Claus wasn't real. Unsure if he was going to throw a tantrum or burst into tears.

Honestly, he wanted to do both.

Three heavy knocks on the front door of the tavern saved him from the spectacle of doing either.

"I'll get that," James said, relieved by the distraction.

It was getting close to noon. Somebody might be looking for a bite to eat for lunch. Most locals and certainly all regulars would know that the pub was closed, but it wouldn't be odd for the occasional tourist to stop by. James had assumed the pub would remain closed indefinitely, now it seemed that might not be the case.

The thought gave him pause.

Am I really considering staying?

He shuddered at the thought and tried to push it as far back in his mind as it was willing to go. At least for the moment. Hopefully, whoever was at the door now would provide a satisfying distraction.

Someone pounded on the door again. It wasn't a polite steady knock; the wood pulsed inward on its hinges from the force of whoever was banging on the other side.

"Bleedin' hell," Liam muttered. "Is it a bleedin' ogre? And what the hell did you do to piss him off?"

James hoped this was a hangry tourist who had no sense of common courtesy.

James unlatched the bar, turned the lock, and swung the door open.

At first, it seemed as though nobody was there—nothing but the street stretched out before him.

"Ahem." A deep male voice cleared his throat, prompting James to look down.

Standing in front of him was a very short man. He was no taller three feet, with a dark thick beard, wearing a woolen vest that could be part of a Victorian period costume with the chain from a silver pocket watch hanging from his breast pocket. He smoked a pipe with one hand and had his other arm casually behind his back.

All he was missing was a top hat and monocle.

James struggled to keep his face from contorting. There was no way this fellow had been responsible for nearly breaking down the tavern door.

"Can I help you?" James asked hesitantly. "I'm sorry, but the tavern is closed due to a death in the family. I don't know when we will be opened again." *Or if.*

"Actually,"— James was struck by how deep the man's voice was for his small stature, and it carried a thick local accent, but one that seemed a touch off— "I'm here to speak with James O'Sullivan."

"Er . . . that's me," said James, completely bewildered as to how this stranger at his doorstep could possibly be looking for *him.*

The man peered up at James, raising a bushy eyebrow

while squinting. He blew a perfect "O" of smoke from his pipe. "Ah, well, I suppose it has been a long time. You *have* gotten taller. A pity, I was hoping you wouldn't have."

"I'm . . . sorry? Have we met?"

"Ah!" the man said, chewing on the tip of his pipe. "Yes, of course!" The pipe disappeared from the man's hand as if it had never been there.

Likely into his sleeve, James thought. He must have blinked and missed the movement.

The man reached out a hand for him to shake, and James grabbed it on reflex. His grip was firm and hard, and very disproportionate to the hand's size.

"I'm sorry, I don't remember you," James said.

"I suppose that was by design. You were quite young. The name's Michael Flick. I was a friend of your parents. I'm quite sorry to hear about your father. We drifted apart after your mother passed."

"Thank you. To be honest, so did we." James awkwardly paused before saying, "I am very sorry that I don't remember you, Mr. Flick, but would you like to come in? The tavern is closed, but I'm sure an old friend of my parents is always welcome."

Michael lifted a hand. "Ah, you're a good lad. Much like your mother. You look like her, you know? But that won't be necessary. I only came here to give you something, and then I must be off."

"Give me something?"

Michael moved his hand in another swift motion and held up a metal orb. It was about the size of a grapefruit, but it appeared large in Michael's hand. Hollow on the inside, the intricate works of silver, gray, and gold metal wound themselves in a delicate pattern. There were markings around it, both inside and out—symbols James couldn't decipher.

James held out his own hand and gripped the top of the ball. The metal was cool to the touch.

Michael didn't let go.

"I was to bring this to you after your father passed. He couldn't bear the responsibility of it with your mother gone. Did he happen to tell you of The Pint and Portal?"

"The Pint and . . . Portal?" James said the words slowly, unsure if he'd heard correctly. Something about it made the hair on the back of his neck stand on end. James almost let go of the trinket as though shocked by a static charge. "He most certainly did not."

Michael let out a long heavy sigh. "Aye, well, seeing as your father wanted nothin' to do with it after your mother left, I shouldn't be surprised. I suppose the burden on you might be all the heavier because of it. But I have no right to keep this from you. It belongs to the owner of the pub in this realm, and I guess that's you now. The key's yours. Just remember, The Pint and Portal has always been a place of refuge for all who find it. Your father never wanted to be keeper of the gate, but we aren't always the deciders of our own fate. Oftentimes, that's a good thing."

Michael let go of the orb, releasing its full weight. James almost dropped the thing. It was much heavier than he'd anticipated, but he managed to regain his grip and brought it up to have a closer look at the intricacies in the design.

It was mesmerizing, like one of those illustrated illusions where a path never actually ended but morphed into another. The inside, which was visible through the cuts in the design, held some sort of engravings, though from what James could see, they were nothing more than meaningless shapes and patterns.

"What do you mean a key?" he asked, his gaze never leaving the sphere. The object and the man's words sparked a trove of questions. "What is The Pint and Portal? Where can I find it?"

But when James looked up, Michael was gone.

James

James shut the door and wandered back to the table with the newly acquired orb in his hands. He wasn't sure why, but there was something about the object that was mesmerizing. He couldn't put his finger on what that was.

"Who was that?" Kathy asked as James sat.

He set the ball on the table with a light thud. "Michael Flick. Claimed to be a friend of Dad's. Does that name ring any bells?"

Kathy and Liam both shook their heads.

"How about something called Pint and Portal?"

Both looked at him blankly.

"It was so bizarre. He was a short man, maybe three feet tall. Full beard, wearing a costume that made me think he might have come from a play down at the park. He said *this* thing was the key to The Pint and Portal. That Dad was a gatekeeper, and now it's been passed on to me."

Kathy and Liam looked at each other. James couldn't mistake the concern that rested on their faces. "Are you . . . sure, James? That banging was so loud we thought for sure it was an angry drunk."

"You think I'm making it up? That I just pulled this ball from the airport gift shop for a laugh?"

Liam and Kathy exchanged another glance.

"Fine," James said, holding his hands up, palms faced outward. "I admit that would be something I'd do when I was younger for a good laugh. But I'm being dead serious!"

Liam's brow hadn't gone down since James came back into the room. His voice was slow and placating, as though he believed James was having a mental breakdown. "Nobody's accusing you of making anything up. But you've got to admit, that's a strange story." Liam reached over and picked up the ball. "How is this supposed to be a key to anything?"

"Your guess is as good as mine." James shrugged. He opened a palm, and Liam tossed the orb back to him. James caught it but had to use his left hand to support the weight. "Anyway, I guess it doesn't matter. I'll ask Moira or Rudy about it later. This guy said I was a kid when he last saw me, so maybe they'll remember him."

"Rudy was going to drop by in a bit," said Kathy. "You could probably ask him then."

"You don't think there's actually something to it? Do you?" Liam asked. "Pint and Portal, you said? What could that even mean?"

James waved a dismissive hand. "Who knows, probably an inside joke. This guy was different though. Gave me an unusual vibe."

"Because he was short?" Kathy asked. "James, that's—"

"No! Of course not." James frowned. "Not at all. It was the way he spoke. His accent seemed local, but a shade different than it should have been. I don't know how to describe it any other way. And this orb too, something's off about it . . . I dunno." He shook his head like he could dislodge the thoughts. "It's probably jet lag getting to me. Let's forget about it for now. Anyone else want a coffee? Or maybe something stronger?"

James made his way behind the bar in search of a coffee mug. He set the orb down, making a mental note to check if

Rudy or Moira knew anything about it. Those two had been closer to his parents than anyone.

Behind the bar, a mismatch of glasses had been lined up along the shelf. Not a single one of them was the same. A few bore logos of beer companies, others had chips and scratches along their sides. Many were discolored. James didn't think a single pair matched.

"Dad used these glasses to serve customers?" James asked. "How many generations have these gone through?"

"What's wrong with them?" Liam asked.

Kathy gestured dismissively. "You know how Dad was. If it worked, he didn't replace it. Mom wasn't much better. You could check the storage room. Who knows what Dad kept back there. It would be nice to have a few more." She paused. "That is . . . if you're planning on sticking around?"

The question made James realize coffee was definitely not strong enough. He grabbed the least offensive looking beer mug and held it under the closest tap, pulling the handle and allowing a dark stout to slide down the side.

"It seems I don't have a lot of options, do I?" James set his glass down to let it rest. He watched the head settle as he attempted to sort through his thoughts. Was he really considering this? There was nothing in this place for him. How many nights had he laid awake dreaming of leaving and starting a new life? He'd done exactly that. He liked his life now, mostly. Sure, it wasn't the grand adventure he'd dreamed of, but he wasn't a kid anymore. Magic didn't exist, and adventures weren't real. But Cuanmore was a sleepy town at the edge of nowhere, and it didn't hold any excitement.

Vancouver at least held something for him. It was a bustling city, with nearby mountains, a thriving arts scene, and the odd celebrity sighting.

It was also bleedin' expensive, and he could sure put some of that inheritance to good use.

"Dad put me in a tough spot. I don't have anything else going on right now, so I'll help get things running again around here, for now. Once Trevor secures a new contact, we'll have to figure things out. But if I'm going to do this, I'm not willing to just carry on as Dad had. If my name's on the front of this thing, I want it cleaned up in here." He gestured to the glasses. "We get matching cups, we clean up pieces of the building that are falling apart . . ."

"You're worried about cups?" Kathy said. "You've been running away from this place for your entire life, and cups are what's going to make the difference for you?"

"We should bring the lot to the thrift store," James said, ignoring her and pulling out each glass one at a time. "Start fresh. This is insane. Every single cup here is different!"

"It's a cozy Irish pub." Kathy grinned. "This isn't one of your fancy Vancouver bars."

"I'm not asking for fancy," James said. "I just want it to look like we care."

"Oh, so you care now?"

James waved her off. Liam sat grinning like a mischievous schoolboy.

As he right as well should. I can't believe I'm actually considering this.

He grabbed his stout again and topped it off before taking a sip. He nearly spat out the brew.

"And bleedin' hell, we get a beer that's drinkable! You said Dad didn't have many customers? It's no wonder! Is this even Irish? I've never had a beer this bad!"

"He moves to Canada and he's suddenly a connoisseur of the finer things." Liam chuckled. "Listen here, fancy pants. If all it was going to take was delicate china and hipster beer, we could have wooed you back a long time ago."

James frowned and brought his mug over to Liam. "Take a sip of that, then tell me who the fancy pants is."

Liam's grin widened. It was the same devilish grin he wore as a kid right before he got the both of them into trouble.

"You're overreacting." Liam grabbed the drink and took a deep swig. His eyes went wide before he turned his head and spat the beer out.

"Hey! No spitting on the floor!" Kathy scolded.

"Holy hells! Jimmy, you weren't kidding! Damn, where *did* ol' Tim get this stuff?" Liam wiped the remnants off his mouth with the back of his hand. "We've got a few breweries set up in town since you left. I'm friends with a number of them. You remember Adam? He took over Cuanmore Harbour Brewing after his dad passed. Why don't we head on down there this afternoon and get something better we can pour? This is a travesty."

Liam caught Kathy glaring at him and rolled his eyes. "Oh, would you quit lookin' at me like that, Kath? I'll clean it up!"

James chuckled. "I might have been gone a while, but I know what a good stout should taste like!"

Another rap at the door stilled the table.

"You think that's your leprechaun again?" Liam ribbed. "Come back to give you another magical trinket?"

"That's offensive," said James. "Let's have none of that."

Liam's face reddened. "You're right. I'm sorry, James. But you have to admit, your story sounds a bit daft."

James knew exactly how he sounded. He grunted as he stood. "Never mind, I'll get the door, again."

"I'll come with you this time," Kathy said, standing and following James across the bar. "If it's another strange encounter, I want to be there for it."

James shook his head, but decided it was for the best. Kathy could either corroborate his story or confirm he was going mad.

"Great idea," said Liam with a smirk. "I'll stay back here and tidy up a bit."

James opened the door again, fresh sunlight greeting him as he did so.

It was not the same figure who stood at the door this time. It was a face that James recognized but couldn't say he was too happy to see.

"Mr. O'Malley." James stuck out his hand. He'd grown up being taught to be polite after all. "Didn't expect to see you here. Pub's not open. You probably knew that."

Mr. William O'Malley was the owner of The Cursed Dragon, the rival pub a few blocks over. There had been no love lost between their two families, and James could wager the man showed up on their doorstep after more than offering his condolences.

The older man stood there, giving Kathy a cursory glance before examining James. O'Malley ignored James' outstretched hand, leaving him hanging. His tweed coat, frayed at the cuffs, hung open to reveal a vest and a neatly knotted tie. It was the same old-fashioned sort of attire he'd always worn. His face was weathered but familiar—deep lines carved into his cheeks and forehead, a roadmap of smiling, laughing, and frowning. His once-dark beard was now mostly gray, trimmed neatly around his jaw, but his eyes . . . those sharp, piercing blue eyes hadn't dulled one bit.

"Well," O'Malley said at last, his voice a low, gravelly rumble, "are you gonna invite me in, or have you forgotten your manners while you've been away? I always thought the Canadians were supposed to be polite."

James exhaled and finally lowered his hand. "Mr. O'Malley," he said, "it's been . . . a while."

"Aye, that it has," O'Malley replied, stepping inside without waiting any longer for an invitation.

James exchanged an uneasy glance with his sister, but neither one of them was assertive enough to ask the man to keep out.

O'Malley looked around, his eyes sweeping across the room as if cataloging every detail. Then he turned back to James, his smile softening into something almost kind. "Ten years, give or take. I heard you were in town. Thought I should visit and pay my respects to your father. A pity you couldn't make it to the funeral."

James furrowed his brow. "Is there something I can help you with? This really isn't the best time . . ."

"It's as good of a time as any," O'Malley said with a gruffer tone, as he stepped closer to James.

James had to refrain from waiving his hand to dissipate the smell of pipe smoke.

"I can't imagine it's been easy," O'Malley said. "Coming back after all these years. And under these circumstances, no less."

James crossed his arms. "I really haven't had a chance to tell yet."

"James only just arrived last night," Kathy said. "We have family matters to discuss."

O'Malley pursed his lips. "This will only take a minute. I think this is worth hearing before you get too far in any of your decisions. Now, your father was a good man. Stubborn as a mule, but he knew how to run a pub. At least, he once did. This place has seen its share of history, though, hasn't it?" He gestured vaguely toward the walls, the floor, the air itself, as though the building might answer him. "But history only gets you so far. These old places take their toll. On a man, and on his wallet."

James's eyes narrowed. "What are you getting at, Mr. O'Malley?"

O'Malley turned to face him fully, his hands slipping casually into the pockets of his coat. "Ah, you're a grown lad now. You don't have to be going on with that 'Mister' stuff. Call me William. And I'm saying that I know what it's like to keep a place like this going. The long hours, the repairs that never end, the money that leaks out the cracks. It's a hard life, James. And you've been gone a long time. I reckon you've made a name for yourself elsewhere, haven't you? A life outside all this?"

James didn't answer. He didn't need to.

O'Malley took a step closer, his voice dropping. "I came here to make you an offer. A fair one. Let me take this place off your hands."

"The pub's not for sale," said Kathy firmly.

"Now, now," O'Malley said. "Don't be so hasty. I'll see to it that it stays open, that it keeps serving the locals like it always has—better than it has in recent years. Your father's legacy—your family's legacy—will stay intact. Kathy can focus on her firm. James will be free to go back to Canada, to whatever it is you've been doing. No strings, no burdens."

James stared at him, his mind churning. The offer was tempting, he had to admit that much. But it didn't matter, according to what Kathy had said, he couldn't sell the pub. It was his now, whether he wanted it or not, at least for a year.

Plus, his father and Mr. O'Malley never saw eye to eye. James didn't believe in an afterlife, but if there was ever a reason his father would come back to haunt him, he was sure selling the pub to O'Malley would be at the top of that list.

He forced himself to keep his expression neutral. "That's a generous offer, O'Malley," he said carefully. "But this isn't any other business. It's my family's pub. My father poured his life into this place. I can't just hand it over."

O'Malley's smile tightened, his eyes narrowing slightly. "It's not handing it over, lad. It's ensuring it survives. Places like this don't run on sentiment. They run on hard work and money, both of which I've got in spades. Be smart about this."

James straightened, his arms falling to his sides. "I appreciate the concern," he said, his tone firmer now. "But I'm not in a position to sell."

Finally, Kathy, who had stood silent the entire time, spoke up. "Really, Mr. O'Malley, we're still sorting out Dad's will. This is not the best time."

For a long moment, O'Malley said nothing, his eyes boring into James like he was trying to read between the lines. At last, he gave a small, curt nod. "Suit yourselves," he said, his voice colder now. He turned toward the door, his boots echoing through the empty room.

James followed him as he opened the door and let the late morning air spill inside. O'Malley paused on the threshold, glancing back over his shoulder. "You've both got your father's stubbornness, I'll give you that. But don't let it blind you. Pride doesn't pay the bills."

James met his gaze. "We'll manage."

O'Malley grunted, pulling his coat tighter around him. "We'll see. If you change your mind, you know where to find me. In fact, feel free to come down to the pub. First round's on me, in memory of your old man."

"Thank you, Mr. O'Malley. Good day to you."

James

"What a langer!" Kathy growled as the door closed. "Showing up practically the moment you've arrived, trying to twist your arm into selling the family business?"

James waved her off. "He's always been a dose. I'm not going to pay him any mind."

"I wouldn't pay him any mind, Kathy," Liam agreed. "He's always been a meddler."

"Still," said Kathy, shaking her head, "the nerve!"

"I need to take my mind off of all of this," James said. "I'm going to rummage around in the storage room. Maybe Dad was keeping a set of glasses back there that he was saving for a special occasion. Have you seen anything in there, Kathy? Or were you just guessing earlier?"

"Guessing," she said, her face still flushed from the encounter with O'Malley. But the change in conversation at least provided a momentary distraction. "Come to think of it, I don't think I've ever been *in* the storage room."

James paused. "You're kidding, right? You've been helping Dad with things here since I left."

"Pfft," she scoffed. "I helped him file his taxes. I didn't do any bar stuff. He wouldn't let me. Said I had more important things to be doing. And we weren't allowed in there as kids."

"Makes sense. I've never been in there either." James shrugged. "But we may as well see what kind of mess Dad left us with."

The door to the storage room sat within a recess behind the bar. He hadn't thought much of entering it in the past—any cleaning supplies were found in a broom closet across the room. If James or Kathy had helped clean the pub in their youth, that was where they got the supplies they needed.

The door was, not surprisingly, locked. But it only took James a few minutes of scrounging around drawers and cupboards to find a very old-looking key that fit perfectly in the door's keyhole. James turned the key with a satisfying click and pushed through, past the "Employees Only" sign that hung on the front of it. The wooden door squeaked on its hinges, the result of years of neglect, and his hand fumbled against the wall for a few moments to find a light switch.

A small dial controlled the lighting on a dimmer. A quiet hum filled the space as half a dozen lights illuminated. One or two flickered and popped before burning out completely.

Despite there being numerous bulbs, their yellow iridescent hue left much of the room in shadow and gave the items resting on the shelves a more sickly look than they likely deserved. The smell of dust, old cardboard, and sawdust wafted from the space, and James wondered how long it had been since anyone had entered.

"It's more spacious than I was expecting," he thought out loud.

"It's huge!" Liam agreed.

He had assumed he'd be entering a closet. What lay before him was a substantial room. He wondered if the space had at one point been a bedroom or perhaps a reading room.

Shelving lined three walls, and a stack of large boxes practically covered the back. All but a small stretch of brickwork had been covered by boxes, trinkets, and crates. A desk, a few old tables and a couple of old barstools had been scattered around the room.

James couldn't help but wonder how many centuries of crap had been piled into this room only to be forgotten over time. Many of the boxes were constructed of faded and sagging cardboard, stacked on top of and alongside rustic wood crates.

"Any luck?" Kathy called from the other room, but her curiosity must have gotten the better of her as within a moment she was at James' side peering in.

"That's far more stuff than I was expecting." Her voice lowered in defeat. "We've got a lot of work to do if we want to know what's in all of those."

James nodded. He wondered if his parents knew what was back here. The layer of dust over top of them suggested they hadn't been opened in an exceptionally long time.

He supposed that, no matter what, they'd have to clear out this storage room eventually. Whether they sold the pub tomorrow or a year from now they couldn't have a buttload of crap hanging about.

"Well, no doubt there are glasses packed away in here somewhere. We may as well get to work."

Silence filled the room as the three of them stopped and stared at the mess for a solid minute.

"Does this need to be done right now?" Kathy asked.

"I'm not even sure how to get started," said Liam. "Are you sure we shouldn't do the beer tasting first?"

James could still feel the buzz of the Hemingway Breakfast, and he suddenly found a renewed energy. What sort of secrets were locked away within these piles? It would at least be something to take his mind off things.

"I'd really like to know if we're buying new glasses or not. Let's spend a couple of hours digging through this stuff first. Later this afternoon, we'll head down to the brewery and see our old friend."

"We've got more than one, you know." Liam crossed his arms. "I don't think we should rule any of them out."

James rolled his eyes. Liam wasn't going to be satisfied unless he saw him shitfaced by the end of the day.

"One stop is probably enough for now. But it would do the pub well to have some options."

"Glasses, beer options . . ." Kathy smirked. "For someone who doesn't plan on sticking around, you suddenly have a lot of opinions on making things better around here."

James frowned. "I already told you, if I'm going to be forced to make a go of it, then I'm going to do it right. If nothing else, it will be easier to sell a pub that's making money than one that's losing it. But don't goad me about it or I'll throw my hands up and just leave you to deal with the mess. We both know I don't want to be here, no need to make a show out of it."

Kathy humphed but nodded. She knew when to quit pushing his buttons. What he needed right now was a distraction from how his life had seemingly fallen apart overnight.

"Liam, why don't you start on the back wall. Make a pile that is obvious junk. Old flyers, old cords, aprons, stuff that we'd never foreseeably use again. Set a second pile for things that might be collectibles, maybe things we can use as decor. Old photos or posters. There's a lot of history to this place. Maybe we can use some of it to attract tourists."

There weren't a lot of tourists that came to this part of the country, remote as it was. But James had seen how out of the way locations could gain popularity because they were charming or eccentric enough to garner attention on social media. Anything that stood out as unique might be of interest. Their pub was old, even by Ireland's standards. It had mostly flown under the radar, but if they managed to capture the right element, perhaps they could use it to their advantage.

James gave his head a shake. *Opinions indeed.* Kathy was right. But if they could turn this old pub around maybe it could run without him being here physically to manage it. It would take more than a few weeks, but with Liam and Kathy's help, it might be doable.

"Kathy, take this wall here." He pointed to the left. "I'll take the one on the right."

They all got to work in their respective spaces. James brushed off his hands, eyeing the mountain of boxes in front of him. "I guess we tackle this one box at a time."

He grabbed a box closest to him and grunted. It was heavy and it jangled as he moved it. Straining, he pulled it over to an old desk. He flipped open the lid, revealing a mess of old cutlery. Some pieces were bent, none of it appeared to match. If it were silver, he maybe could have understood, but at least the bulk of it had been crafted out of a dull gray metal.

"Great," he muttered. If this was any indication of what was stored, they were going to spend a lot of time tossing things.

The afternoon wore on. A lot of what James encountered was the same: tangled extension cords that looked older than he was, rusty bar equipment—bottle openers, corkscrews, and the like. He thought he'd found something when he pulled out a box that was filled with stacks of plates, but upon closer inspection they were all chipped and scratched.

So far, he had a large throw away pile and only a few items in the stack of things to keep.

He had also started a third pile of things that were mysterious and . . . odd. Though they were probably no less useless than his first pile. There was a small case of jars filled with something. They appeared to be pickled, but he couldn't begin to explain what they contained. He probably should have tossed them, but a rainbow of colors, almost iridescent in the dim storage room lighting, swirled within them, piquing his interest. There was a heavy padlocked chest but no visible keyhole. That could prove interesting. Then there was a short staff made of a dark wood that was almost black that held carvings of mesmerizing geometric patterns.

James was starting to wonder if this endeavor was worth the effort. The boxes loomed over top of him, seeming never ending. At this rate they'd be doing this for weeks.

"Take a look at this," Kathy called from her side of the room.

For the first time in over an hour, James looked over at her. His sister had crafted similar piles, though she hadn't made as much progress. One pile appeared to consist mostly of old moth-eaten tablecloths. From the look of things, Kathy had taken each one out to inspect before deciding to discard it. Knowing his sister, James imagined she was hoping there would be at least one that was salvageable.

He groaned inwardly. She was as bad as his parents. He was going to have to resift through her piles to make sure she wasn't hanging onto any trash.

Kathy had a box propped open on the floor and was sifting through its contents. "What do you make of all this?"

James peered over her shoulder. The box seemed to be filled with documents, some yellowed with age while others appeared to be made of something other than paper. Old parchment maybe? Vellum?

"What are those? Old maps?" It was hard to see in the dim light of the storage room, and he wasn't familiar with the materials cartographers used, but one thing he did know was that some of the items in that box had to be very, very old.

"They are, but . . ." Kathy carefully leafed through a few then pulled a stack out before setting them carefully on a coffee table next to her.

Liam had found an old lamp somewhere and turned it on. The light coming from it was no less yellow than the rest of the room, but it allowed him to direct some of the light so they could see what they were looking at.

"It's the strangest thing. They're maps of made-up places," Kathy said.

James looked at the parchment she was holding. It looked like an old, albeit rough, map of Ireland to him. "What do you mean? It's just old."

"No, it looks that way, but this parchment feels new. It's soft and flexible. Not rough and dry like I'd expect. But that's not even the strangest bit." She unrolled the map a bit more. "This *looks* like Ireland, but look at the names."

James crouched to get closer, squinting to read the scripted text. "Hibernia," he read aloud. "Didn't some of the Greek and Roman maps call Ireland that?"

Kathy nodded. "I think so, but what about this?" She pointed to a larger piece of text that James had missed. It outlined much of the northern coast of Europe and included England, Ireland, and stretched as far east as Denmark (which the map had named Kalmar). The large text read "Lancastria."

That wasn't one James had heard before, though he wasn't a geography scholar.

"That is a new one to me, but kings were rewriting boundaries all the time back in the day. Maybe someone at the museum could help us."

Kathy shook her head. "I'm pretty sure I would have heard some of these names before, but this isn't the only one."

She pulled out more maps from the stack and laid them out on the coffee table. "These maps don't even have consistent land masses. Look at this one! It has Ireland connected to the UK in one solid block. Others look like they're of completely different territories, but I don't recognize any of them. Some are written in languages I've never seen!"

James studied the examples Kathy had laid out, and it was only a small sample of what was in the box.

What stories did these maps hold? He could imagine a day in his family's past where sea travelers would stop in Cuanmore and rest when the building also served as an inn. He could see the appeal of collecting maps from faraway lands. Maybe one of his ancestors had as much of a bug for traveling as he did.

Maybe they too had felt stuck in this pub at the edge of the world. Perhaps they dreamed of faraway lands, living vicariously through travelers' tales. Hell, who knew if all the maps were real? There was every possibility that someone made up maps for the sole purpose of telling tales and selling dreams of exotic places.

"I say we bring them down to the museum. I'm pretty sure back in the day a lot of those traders would make up stuff—books, maps, paintings, anything to sell to some gullible dreamer. It appears we had a map collector in the family."

"I've found something over here as well." Liam didn't appear to have any interest in the maps. His back was turned to them, his arms crossed over his chest, and he leaned back, looking up at something. "Wasn't that the name of the place the fellow at the front door was asking about?"

James followed his friend's gaze. Liam had whittled his stack down, revealing a piece of the wall just beneath the ceiling. A stack of discarded boxes sat beside him. Based on the logos stamped on the cardboard, these were put here much more recently, maybe packed away by his father.

That wasn't what caught Liam's attention, though. Visible above the stack was a wooden sign, with engraved lettering surrounded by a decorative design.

Pint and Portal.

James

"Let's get the rest of these boxes out of the way." James didn't wait for the other two to move—he got straight to work. Starting at the top, he grabbed a box and handed it to Liam, who set it down on the floor. Then James grabbed the next and the next.

His heart pounded ferociously. He didn't know what exactly the sign meant, but he couldn't believe it was a coincidence that they uncovered it right after Michael appeared on their doorstep. The two events had to be related. Another box moved and James noticed a horizontal seam marked in the stone wall.

"I think there might be a door frame here," he said.

"I hate to burst your bubble," said Kathy, "but it's not like there's going to be something else behind a door! Frankly, I'm surprised there's enough room here for this storage room. If anything, it's going to lead out back."

Rationally, James knew that, but something within him screamed that there was more going on here. There was a secret something called Pint and Portal, and now he *had* to know what it was.

What exactly was this secret? Why had their father gone to such lengths to hide it? Maybe it had been a meeting room for the town leaders. Or perhaps a speakeasy for wealthy out-of-towners.

"It's probably just a fire exit," James admitted, pausing to catch his breath. He wasn't used to moving boxes all day. He wiped a bead of sweat from his forehead. "But do you remember when we were kids? Mom and Dad used to actually have fun with the pub! The Pint and Portal might not be anything, but whatever it is, it's a piece of who they used to be." James shook his head. "I miss the magic this place had when Mom was around."

Kathy let out a breath. A sad smile formed on her face, and she rested a hand on James' shoulder. "They did have a lot of fun back then, didn't they? They were always the life of the party."

Pint and Portal.

Suddenly some of what Michael Flick had said returned to him. "'Your father never wanted to be the gatekeeper' . . . What do you think that meant?"

"Maybe your folks were part of a DnD group." Liam laughed. "Maybe this was like their secret clubhouse."

James nodded. That would make what Michael had said make sense. The strange orb that he claimed was a key could have been some sort of prop. He stepped to his pile of oddities and picked up the black staff he'd found. Did they dress up for their campaigns as well?

"You might be on to something," he said.

Kathy laughed. "Did we just never realize what massive nerds our parents were?"

"Of course! That would explain a lot." James' eyes lit up, his excitement building. "The stories Mom told us! They were filled with elves, quests, and dark worlds. She must have been telling us kid friendly versions of their campaigns! Michael must have been one of their players. Dad was never the storyteller that Mom was, so once she was gone, Dad had no interest."

"It would also explain the maps." Liam stroked his chin as he put the pieces together. "And some of the clothes Kathy found. James, I think you're onto something."

As James wondered if there might be any evidence of their campaigns, a small book resting on a nearby shelf caught his eye.

It was a leatherbound journal, its surface worn smooth by time and touch. A slender leather cord wrapped around it, securing its secrets with a simple knot.

He reached over, picked it up, and unbound the tie.

"You're getting distracted." Kathy smirked. "Just like when we were kids. Can we deal with one mystery at a time, please?"

James ignored her and leafed through the pages, skimming fragments of the handwritten text inside. It was definitely his mother's handwriting—he'd recognize it anywhere. There were pages missing. Jagged edges remained where some had been torn out.

James was a slow reader, and he knew he'd have to study the words it contained later, but his excitement was reaching a new fervor. There was a single phrase written on the front page in large, printed text that was hard to miss.

Before realizing it, he was reading the text out loud. "*The Pint and Portal: A haven for the lost. A home for the found.*"

Kathy and Liam both stared at him wordlessly.

"What are you on about?" Kathy asked.

He shut the book and held it up in one hand emphatically. "This is Mom's journal! I bet this holds details of their campaigns."

Kathy pinched the bridge of her nose with her forefinger and thumb. "Are we going to move these boxes? Or are we going to read old books?"

James nodded. Kathy was right, of course, he was getting

distracted. He'd have to unravel this mystery one clue at a time and not all at once. He tucked it into the back pocket of his trousers.

"I'm going to grab the orb. If we do find more of their game equipment, I'd like to get the whole set together. Later, I'll go through Mom's notes and see if we can learn anything else about their campaigns."

For the first time since he arrived, he was excited. He had dedicated his adult life to developing games. His mother's stories had inspired the characters he created, and to think they might have been the byproduct of games *she* had played, of stories his parents and their friends might have told. For whatever it was worth, he was learning things about his parents he'd never been privy to before. Things they had passed on to him without him realizing it.

He had only been gone a minute, but by the time James returned, Liam and Kathy had already cleared away the bulk of the boxes beneath the sign, pushing them out of the way.

"You're not going to believe this," said Liam.

James studied the wall behind his friend. It was made of the same stonework as the outside of the pub. Large, smooth, flat stones had been arranged to form the outline of a massive door, creating a distinct frame. The space within the frame was filled with the same type of stone as the surrounding wall with no deviation in color or style. It was as though the door had been deliberately sealed, yet the craftsmanship made it appear almost indistinguishable from the rest of the structure.

The sign reading Pint and Portal, hung silently above as though mocking the blocked path.

Whatever the reason was for it, this entryway had been sealed for a long time. It was certainly not something his parents had constructed. But . . . why? Had they hung the sign above the doorway as a joke?

Perhaps that was what this was, an inside joke they had

built a game out of. James tossed the orb a few inches in the air before letting it fall back into his hand absently.

"You think this used to be an exit?" It was the only thing that made sense . . . kind of. The stonework suggested the wall was built like this, but why make it look like there could be a doorway, only to seal it shut during construction?

"That's not all." Liam lifted a hand to the stonework beside the outlined shape. "There's an indent here."

It was hard to see it within the dark stone with the shadows of the room cast over it, but indeed there was a small patch of smooth brick, made of the same stone as the empty frame that held an indentation. A half-sphere shape that was the perfect size to fit the orb he held in his hand. Symbols etched into the surrounding circular frame matched the ones carved within the orb's interior.

"You don't think this is what Michael meant?" James stepped forward. Liam and Kathy stood silent, both as bewildered as him.

There was no mistaking that the orb was meant to fit into this space.

"He said it was a key," James thought out loud. "But that can't mean . . ."

He slid the orb into the space and the wall seemed to suck it inward, like a vacuum grabbing onto something. Of its own volition, the orb twisted, and a piercing blue light filled its hollow interior.

"What the . . .!" Liam stepped back, his eyes widening.

The lighting flickered as a light breeze swept through the room, shuffling old papers onto and around the floor.

James was too shocked to do anything but watch the display unfold.

The stones within the doorframe . . . shifted . . . as though they were melting.

The effect lasted only a moment and soon the rock within

the door's frame had disappeared altogether. The air stopped moving and the lights stopped their flickering.

A swirling blue and violet mass had replaced the rock within the frame.

James, Kathy, and Liam had all unconsciously moved closer together. Each of their mouths hung agape.

Liam moved forward with slow, calculated steps, afraid something was going to jump out of . . . whatever it was.

"Don't get too close!" said Kathy. She reached out a hand, but she held back, frozen in place. Whether out of fear or plain shock, James wasn't certain, but he felt it too.

Could this really be happening? A metal ball set in a stone wall had somehow caused this to appear. Maybe it was an illusion, a trick of the eye. If it was, he had no way to explain it.

"Keeper of the gate," James whispered. He took two steps forward, joining Liam at the threshold of the spectacle. "It can't be . . ."

Kathy's voice quivered. "Please don't do anything stupid."

"Michael said Dad hadn't wanted to be keeper of the gate and that we don't always get to choose what fate has in store for us. What if . . ." What if what? James couldn't get a hold of his thoughts. It was too surreal to believe. "What if this is some kind of gateway?"

It sounded far too fantastical to be true. Too *magical*. Magic and fantasy, they were the products of the stories that his mother would tell him as a child.

Not real life.

Was this more than some light display for an elaborate campaign?

His eyes drifted to the sign above the door. Whatever Michael had been talking about, this was it.

James took a deep breath and stepped into the portal.

James

Kathy screamed, but the noise muffled as James plunged into the murky substance that filled the doorway. It felt like plunging into a cold, viscous barrier—not wet, but with the weight and pressure of walking through a waterfall. Kathy's cries warbled, distorted, and lengthened. He'd have sworn the sensation of the encounter took his breath away, but he wasn't exactly sure he was breathing.

Before he could figure it out, he was met with warm, stale air and the distinct, musty smell of old wood and dust.

The gateway, or whatever it was, lay open behind him.

Kathy's voice was still there, but it was distant and fuzzy. Like there was a bad connection during a video call.

It was hard to focus on his sister's voice. The room he'd entered was dark, yet there was enough light coming in from somewhere to illuminate the spot where he stood. A thousand tiny blue balls danced above him, casting a blue glow upon the space before him.

Not the back alley. Not anything he'd expected. He wasn't sure what exactly he'd expected, but it was certainly not this.

A sprawling room laid out before him. Blue light danced off a long bar top that wrapped around an intricately carved floor to ceiling cabinet in the center of the room that was filled with an array of dusty glass bottles. At least, James thought the cabinet went from floor to ceiling—in the dim light it was hard to tell how high the room stretched. A wooden banister hinted that there was a second floor. Not to mention that the wood plank floor reached far into a room that was much larger than all of O'Sullivan's pub.

James didn't know what to think. He'd stepped through a hole in the closet of his family pub and ended up . . . in another pub? One that bore only a passing resemblance to O'Sullivan's but was incredibly larger.

"The Pint and Portal," he whispered. Not a DnD guild or quest. He fumbled for some sort of explanation that made rational sense and came up empty.

A large wooden bar dominated the space before him; a centimeter or two of dust coated the bar top. Wooden stools with green cushions were lined up against it.

The room was mostly dark, save for a strange glowing that appeared from the small blue orbs that hung over the entire pub, providing just enough illumination to see by. Tables, dozens of tables, were spread out through the open space, stretching deep into dark corners of the back room.

Kathy's shouts entered his perception again as they grew louder.

". . . going to get us all killed." Her final words came out loud and clear as she appeared a few steps behind James, exiting the gateway. The luminous surface stretched and contorted around her frame. Liam appeared behind her.

She stopped her protest as she got a glimpse of where she was. "Where the hell are we?" Her tone switched from panicked to awe.

"Some sort of speakeasy," Liam suggested. His lips were pursed in a surveying frown. The man gave the pub an intrigued once over, nodding as though what they were looking at was the most natural thing he could have expected to find.

"One hell of a speakeasy," said James.

"Why do you think we never knew this was here?" Liam's voice was hushed, almost breathless.

"I'm more concerned with *how* this place is here." James looked back toward the gateway, then to the pub again. "There's no way this could fit behind the pub! We should be into the backside of Rudy's. Hell, this space looks bigger than Rudy's. And what exactly did we walk through?"

"It's hard to tell anything with how dark it is in here," Liam muttered. "There's got to be a light switch in here somewhere." He moved to the edge of the wall beside the gateway to begin his search.

Another blue light caught James' eye immediately to the side of the gateway. The orb that he had placed in the wall in the storage room had appeared here as well.

Liam found a set of switches on the side wall, as well as a large lever. Without question, he flipped the switches, grabbed the handle of the lever, and pulled it up with a *thunk*. Clicks and a dull hum accompanied a series of bright overhead lights cascading through the pub and illuminating tables, chairs, old posters, pool tables, darts, and a sturdy hardwood floor. The blue glow paled in the new luminescence and faded into obscurity.

This pub had to be at least four or five times the size of O'Sullivan's. The bar itself was about three times as long. A wooden staircase in the back spiraled up toward an unseen second floor.

The walls had been constructed of an intricate stonework that did not match that of O'Sullivan's. The stones were larger and flat.

Everything was covered in the same coating of dust as the bar, giving the entire place a dull look. It hung in the air, having been kicked up by whatever breeze the gateway must have made when it opened.

James took two steps forward, letting the enormity of what they'd uncovered sink in. Or at least, he tried to let it sink in. He had no idea where he was. Never in his wildest dreams had he expected to find something like this hidden in the back of his childhood home. If he hadn't been staring at it, he would have said it was impossible.

The faint sound of voices came from the gateway behind them, and the surface of it shimmered.

With no idea what to expect, James, Liam, and Kathy all tensed. It sounded like someone else was coming through.

It only took a moment for the surface to be broken and a large, aging man in a baker's apron with graying bushy eyebrows and a thick mustache stepped through.

There was a wide look of wonder in his eyes, but it didn't match the level of bewilderment of James and his allies. It was more the look of someone who had returned to a familiar place after a long absence.

It had been years since James had seen the man who stood before them. Rudolf Schäfer, or Rudy as everyone called him. Originally from Germany, he was the best baker James had ever encountered, either in Cuanmore or abroad. Even now, Rudy held a plate of what looked to be his famous apple cinnamon strudel.

Behind him, Moira appeared, worry painted across her face.

"What are you kids doing here?" she asked. "How did you get the orb?"

James didn't know how to answer her, so he ignored her for the moment. "Uncle Rudy!" He opened his arms and embraced the larger man in the tightest bear hug he could muster. "It's so good to see you!"

"Yes, good to see you too," Rudy said. He held James out and took a good look at him. "It looks like you haven't been eating enough in Canada. There's nothing on your bones!" Rudy poked at James' ribs with his free hand.

James smiled. "They don't make strudel like you do." He nodded to the plate. "I can't say I haven't missed your baking."

"Of course not!" Rudy exclaimed. "Nobody makes a strudel like I do. I have to cut it though. I'm sure there's a knife here somewhere."

"Em . . ." Kathy said and cleared her throat. "As nice as strudel would be right now, could someone explain to us where the hell we are? What is happening?" Her eyes darted back and forth as though unsure where to focus. James had only seen his sister like this a handful of times. She was normally steadfast and unshakable, but she was clearly rattled now. He couldn't say he blamed her.

It was Moira who stepped to Kathy and placed a hand on her arm. "Now dear, it's all right. I guess your father never explained any of this to you?"

James and Kathy both shook their heads slightly.

"Mum, what's going on?" Liam said. "You *knew* about this place?"

"Of course I did," she said, her attention never leaving James. "And I'll tell you kids the same thing I told your mother. A place like this isn't natural. It's best that you don't mess with things you don't understand. Your father figured that one out."

"Are one of you going to explain it to us?" James was growing exasperated. "*Where* are we?"

Rudy rested a heavy hand on his shoulder. "This is The Pint and Portal. The greatest pub in the multiverse." The baker's gaze drifted to the wall on the far side of the room, longing in his eyes.

James and Liam exchanged an uneasy glance. "What does that mean, exactly?" James asked, afraid of what the answer might be.

"Grab a seat," said Rudy. "This might take a while."

Emma

Cuanmore, Hybarn — Present Day

It seemed strange to find comfort in a cozy tavern that had nearly been destroyed.

Emma Corvus stood entranced by the remnants of a pub she once knew and wondered how long O'Sullivan's had sat in this world abandoned.

Abandoned? Emma nearly let out a laugh in spite of herself —in spite of the heaviness of the place. The pub had been completely leveled like most of the world she'd seen since she arrived.

She wiped her forearm across her brow, though she supposed the action did little more than smear ash across her forehead. It was hard to get away from the soot that hung in the air and clung to every surface. Even the scarce water she'd managed to find had a slimy film on it. It couldn't be safe to drink, but she had a choice of taking her chances with soot and grime in the oily liquid and maybe find her way off this version of the planet or dying of thirst.

When she began hopping between worlds two years ago, she never would have imagined there could have been a world with so much damage, where every building was reduced to nothing more than rubble and ash. Then again, she could never have imagined that there were other worlds at all.

Other worlds. It was amazing she'd grown so accustomed to the idea.

How much her life had changed since she'd been a witch hunter, a Hunter of the Cursed. A member of the king's army who traveled throughout the kingdom, ridding it of magic users and magical creatures.

That was before she had discovered she possessed magic herself. An ability that allowed her to, for lack of a better description, speak with drinks. It was a bizarre twist of fate when she found out. Forced to abandon her post and run, after becoming the very things she hunted, she'd also had to abandon the man she'd convinced herself she'd one day end up with.

It was that chain of events that had led her to discover the device she held now. One that would transport her to alternate Earths where different versions of histories had played out.

Her previous companions may have been ready to settle somewhere, to stick to one world, but she hadn't finished exploring. With the blessing of its creator, she'd taken the device and carried on with her travels.

For two years, she'd hopped between realities, each shaped by a different outcome of Earth's past decisions. She'd seen great wonders, learned impressive drink recipes, and had one grand adventure after another.

Demon Box, as it had decided it wanted to be called, was both the key to her travels, and her only companion. A sentient machine who opened portals to other worlds and allowed her to travel between them.

At least, until she'd dropped it.

When the portal to this world opened over a pile of rubble, she'd stumbled, and the device went flying and landed on the corner of a rock. Emma had been lucky she hadn't broken a leg doing the same thing.

While Demon Box retained its ability to offer nonstop

sarcastic comments, its ability to bend space and time had been crushed.

If only it could have been the sarcastic comments that had been damaged, Emma thought, not for the first time.

You know I can hear you? Demon Box quipped back.

That was the other thing—her magic allowed the box to read her thoughts and vice versa. Its creator, Professor Aldrich, had installed a voice synthesizer so it could communicate with anyone, but it typically chose to communicate with Emma silently.

In some ways it was a blessing, like when others were around. She got all sorts of funny looks and death threats when people realized the box she held could talk. But often she wished she could get the voice out of her head.

"Well, Demon Box," she said out loud, "I think this might be another dead end."

Do you have to say 'dead'? Demon Box groaned in her mind. *I thought we could have a nice relaxing evening for once.*

Emma sighed. "If we can't find a way off this world, I'm not sure we'll have a relaxing evening ever again."

It had been a long shot, traveling as far as they had in search of some last vestige of civilization. Coming here had been her last-ditch attempt at holding onto hope. Cuanmore had been the town where her journey began.

It was here that she'd met the professor who had built Demon Box in the first place. It was here where the first portal to other worlds had opened. Perhaps, amidst all the destruction and ruin, there would be a way off this world.

The town she'd entered was known as Cuanmore, at least in her version of it, and it was located in the province of Hibernia. In other worlds, it was situated in a territory known as Ireland. Here, there was no way for her to tell if it had been called either. She hadn't spoken to a single soul since she'd arrived.

She hadn't seen another human, though a few tattered footprints remained. Emma could still make out the outline of a crumbling O'Sullivan's pub. The second floor was gone, leaving the main floor open to the elements above, three and a half of the building's four walls still stood, and tables and chairs were set up as if there had been patrons only days before.

Like every other village and city they had passed on their journey through this cold, lonely world, the scars of whatever attack had besieged this place seemed both fresh and ancient.

"Who goes there?" a gruff voice shouted from within the pub's rubble.

Demon Box whirred.

Emma whipped a dagger from beneath her cloak and held it at the ready as she silently told Demon Box to keep quiet.

To Demon Box's credit, it did what she asked.

After weeks of lonely solitude, this was the first soul, other than Demon Box, willing to communicate with her. But in a world as broken as this one, it was equally likely that he could be friend as foe.

Maybe not equally, she thought grimly.

"Who's asking?" she called back.

A short, portly man emerged, climbing over the half-destroyed wall.

No, not a man.

Emma was no stranger to non-human races. In her old life, she'd encountered magical creatures of all kinds: ogres, fairies, dragons. But this was something she'd only ever encountered in legends and folklore.

A dwarf.

As if ready for battle, the dwarf gripped a battle axe, taller than himself, in both hands with a confidence that betrayed both the gray hair that hung over his shoulders and his short stature. His face was grizzled with a lifetime's worth of wrinkles and age spots; despite that, his body was built out of pure muscle, evident even under the tired and scorched armor he wore.

The dwarf squinted at her, his face contorting as though trying to determine if what he was seeing was a mirage. "I'm Tarvo." He hesitated a moment before lowering his axe, weighing his words before he spoke. "You're . . . human?"

"Human?" A woman's voice echoed from behind the rubble.

From within the pub's shadow, a set of scrutinizing eyes gawked at her then disappeared.

Tarvo stood firm, ignoring the woman, his gray eyes still evaluating Emma. "It appears that way," the dwarf replied. "I never thought I'd see the day."

Emma didn't lower her dagger, but the dwarf's shoulders relaxed, and he lowered the butt of his axe to the ground and leaned on it like a walking stick.

"Come on in then. We don't have much, but this is as safe a haven as any."

Emma didn't loosen her grip on her blade as she stepped through the remains of O'Sullivan's pub. She had no way to know if it was called that on this world as the tavern's sign had long disappeared, but there was no mistaking this had been a version of the same place she'd visited many times before.

"No one's going to hurt you here, miss," said Tarvo. To prove his point, he rested his axe against the wall then replaced it with a gnarled dark wood staff.

"That's yet to be determined," another dwarf male growled from the shadows.

A third dwarf emerged. A woman with a face smoother than Tarvo's, indicating she was far younger in years. Her hair, though matted and tangled, was thick and dark, and she wore a sullied burgundy dress with a faded yellow sash tied around the waist. She possessed less muscle build than the elder dwarf, and a hollowness in her eyes suggested it had been some time since she'd had a proper meal.

"Easy Ha'dran." Tarvo's voice was steady and firm.

Ha'dran stepped forward. His brow creased, a scowl painted across his face. "Don't 'easy' me, old man. Inviting strange creatures into our home. That's a good way to wind up dead."

"She's human," Tarvo said. "Not Tíogar Mór."

"Human?" Ha'dran squinted as he stepped forward. "Bog water! You want me to believe she's some tale come to life?"

"How many times have we been through this?" Tarvo asked. "You of all people should know that there is truth behind most of those tales."

"Yes, yes." Ha'dran rolled his eyes. "I know the stories. I don't care what fantasies you chased in your youth, there's no such thing as humans, not anymore. You have to wake up to *this* reality. It doesn't matter if she's Tíogar, dwarf, or pretends to be human, we can't just be taking in any lark off the street."

"Then how to you explain her?" Tarvo pointed his staff in Emma's direction. "She's not one of them. And she's certainly no dwarf."

"Skinny, is what she is." Ha'dran grunted. "Maybe she's fae. Either way, nothing good can come of letting her stay."

Emma half expected Demon Box to chirp a cheeky agreement, but the box rested silently in her satchel. She sent the device a silent word of thanks.

"Listen." Emma sheathed her dagger. If Tarvo decided to attack her, the old dwarf might give her a run for her money, but he at least seemed to be on her side in this exchange. The other two seemed haggard enough that she likely could best them without a blade in hand. But she'd do better if she could defuse the tension in the room. "I'm not looking to cause trouble. I'd hoped to find a place that had escaped whatever calamity had befallen this world, maybe discover a way out. But it appears even the far reaches of this land have been destroyed."

"Nothing escaped the Tíogar Mór," the woman huffed. "Send her off! If she's human, as you claim, I won't wake up in the middle of the night with her trying to eat my brain!"

Emma frowned. *Is that what dwarves thought humans did?*

Demon Box let out a silent chuckle.

"Gloria's right," Ha'dran agreed. "If the stories *are* true, everyone knows the destruction they caused." He turned to Tarvo. "I don't trust her; you shouldn't have invited her here."

"Human's do not eat dwarf brains, and they *are* real." Tarvo's voice was gruff, but his focus was not on the other two dwarves, it was squarely on her. "You said, *this world?*" A sparkle had lit his eye. "You're not from this reality then, are you?"

Emma's breath caught. It took a lot to catch her off guard, but never once, in any of the worlds she'd traveled through, had anyone guessed the truth. "How . . . how could you know that?"

"For one,"—Tarvo's lip quivered as though attempting to hold back his increasing enthusiasm—"humans, at least humans from this world, have not been seen in these lands for centuries. So, it only makes sense that if one is here, they've come from somewhere else. And two,"—the dwarf reached into a pouch that hung by his side and pulled out what appeared to be an ornately decorated silver ball—"because of this."

Emma had seen her fair share of talismans, but the orb that the dwarf held was one unfamiliar to her. The metal ball was not much larger than the palm of her hand. It was, no doubt, an object of magic; she could see it was inscribed with symbols from where she stood. Tarvo held it outstretched in his palm, allowing it to sit atop decades-old callouses and glint in the light of the setting sun.

"Here we go again," Ha'dran muttered, rolling his eyes. "That damned ball."

"What is it?" Emma was intrigued but didn't want to get her hopes up. The elder dwarf might have been the friendlier of the group, but that didn't mean he still had all his wits about him.

"It's our key out of here." Tarvo waved a hand toward Ha'dran. "I know you don't believe. But nobody asked you to follow me out here."

Ha'dran lifted his hands in defense. "Don't get me wrong, Tarvo. Gloria and I are grateful for what you've done. You promised a place of refuge from the Tíogar Mór and the wilds that have filled in their void, and you delivered. This ruin might not be the pub you remembered it being, but it's given us protection enough. There's plenty of fish nearby to keep us sustained, and enough liquor behind the bar to help us forget for a time."

Shadows stretched along the sides of the pub walls. Night was fast approaching. Emma wasn't too proud to admit she was grateful to see others alive and willing to share a little camaraderie with her; even if it was with dwarves who viewed her as suspicious. She'd spent nights braving far worse.

"Tíogar Mór? Is that who was hunting me in the streets of London?"

Tarvo inclined his head as if she'd said something of inter-est. Gloria gasped, and Ha'dran nearly choked.

"You're being hunted by them?" Fear flashed across Ha'dran's face "And you led them here? You fool!" He ran to the threshold of the building, frantically searching up and down the street, trying to spot anything out of place in the fading light.

Emma shook her head. "I lost them weeks ago. Nothing's been following me since I left the mainland."

"Relax, Ha'dran," said Tarvo. "They wouldn't have followed her for that long without attacking. There's not much left on this world for them. If they haven't left yet, they soon will."

Ha'dran grumbled with a wary eye still on the street beyond the tavern. He stood there for several long moments before he reluctantly stepped back to join Gloria, who had pulled up a seat at a table that was much too tall for her.

Emma had so many questions. "Who are the Tíogar Mór?"

"Predators," Tarvo grunted.

"Some say they were sent as a punishment for welcoming magic into our cities," Ha'dran said. "Others say they are the gods themselves, come to reset the world."

Tarvo shook his head. "They're no gods. From what little we've learned, they're beasts who travel between worlds. They're on the hunt and not afraid to destroy everything that rests in their path. Us dwarves fought our best for as long as we could. In the end it wasn't enough."

"Is that why there are no humans around either?"

"Despite Ha'dran's skepticism, humans once roamed these lands, though they disappeared centuries ago," Tarvo said. "Nobody knows why. That was long before the Tíogar Mór appeared."

"But I'm not the first human you've come across."

The glint reappeared in Tarvo's eye, but only for a moment. "You are not. Which reminds me, it's time to give this another try." He lifted the orb and gave Emma a wink before wandering toward the back of the pub to what looked to be an old stock room.

"What's he doing?" Emma asked, her voice lowered. She watched Tarvo step up to what used to be a doorway in the back. There was no longer a door, there was barely a wall to hold the wooden frame upright.

Ha'dran sighed. The dwarf seemed to have relaxed around her enough to take a few steps closer. He kept his voice to just above a whisper. "Tarvo has had a long and difficult life. And I would never be one to speak ill of him, so don't take this the wrong way. But he's not the same dwarf he used to be."

Tarvo set his orb in a small recess in the remaining wall, waited for a moment, as though expecting something to happen, sighed, then removed it, looking downward in defeat.

"Since we got here," said Ha'dran, "every evening as the sun goes down, he's put that ball into that recess. He waits for a moment, just like that. Every night he's disappointed."

"Disappointed? Why?"

"I'm no stranger to magic," Ha'dran said, "so it's not that I believe it's impossible, but at some point, you have to wonder if the old man is telling tales of his own."

Emma wasn't following. "Why? What does he say will happen?"

"He thinks that the orb will open a doorway. You heard him speaking of other worlds. His mind has been fried after years of war, and he believes he can open a portal to a different world. One where the Tíogar Mór never attacked."

Emma caught her breath. Could this be the answer she'd hoped for? What were the odds that the answer to leaving this world was in the city where she'd started long ago.

Could it be possible?

You talk to a sentient box that can do the same thing, and you're not sure? Demon Box spoke into her mind for the first time since they'd entered the pub. *Of course it's possible.*

It's also possible that Ha'dran's right: the imagination of a madman.

Yes, well, thought Demon Box, *anything is possible. Isn't it?*

Indeed it was.

"I mean, other *worlds*?" continued Ha'dran, unaware of her silent conversation. "Could you imagine something more farfetched?"

Emma flashed the dwarf a smug grin. "You're speaking to a human. So you tell me."

The dwarf moved his lips, his widened eyes indicating he hadn't expected that response. Before he conjured a response, Emma stood and made her way to where Tarvo had slumped against the wall in defeat.

"It's been almost twenty years," said Tarvo. Emma wasn't sure if he was addressing her as she approached, or merely thinking out loud, so she remained silent, letting the dwarf continue his train of thought. "I haven't seen him in almost twenty years," he repeated. "I should have never returned to fight this gods-forsaken war. I've wasted so much time that we could have spent together. Now either something has happened on the other side, or the gateway is too damaged to function. My world was destroyed, who knows how any of the others fared. And for what? Was all we did for nothing?"

He slid the orb from its slot in the wall. "I suppose I should be grateful for the time I did have with him. But for nearly two decades I've held onto the hope I'd see him again." Tarvo turned to face Emma—somehow he'd known she followed him. His expression sagged in defeat. "It's what kept me going during the darkest of days. Trust me when I say there have been many. And now? I just hope he's okay."

Emma didn't want to pry into who Tarvo was referring to. If the dwarf wanted to tell her, he would do so in his own time. So, instead she asked, "Why do you only try once a night? Perhaps it will work later in the evening, or earlier? Maybe—"

Tarvo lifted a large hand. "Six depths of the mines, it's no use. I could drive myself mad trying every five minutes and the result would be the same. Hell, I almost did. I suppose I was a fool for holding on to hope for so long. Even worse, I've dragged Gloria and Ha'dran into this mess. Got their hopes up that there might be an escape from all this."

Emma closed the distance between them but stopped short of resting a hand on his shoulder. Affection was not her strength, and she could only guess that dwarves were even less touchy-feely than she was. "From what your friends were saying, it sounds like this location has provided a place of refuge. Perhaps that's all that they've needed."

Tarvo shook his head. "The bar that rested on the other side of this gateway was different. It had been built to provide rest to the weary. A home to those whose adventures had gone sideways. People from all sorts of worlds would get together and find friendship and a good pint of ale."

Emma smiled. The old dwarf deserved a listening ear he could reminisce to. "What's the name of the pub?"

Tarvo raised an eyebrow as though unsure of her motives for asking. "The Pint and Portal," he said solemnly.

"I've been in a lot of taverns and bars in the last couple years," said Emma. "After a while they all seem fairly standard. Even this place, despite its missing walls and crumbling ceiling, is close to your typical public house. A functioning pub or tavern, well they'll have a few tables, chairs, maybe a fireplace, maybe some rooms to spend the night, and a bar with a barkeep and waitstaff, but that's not what keeps people coming back." Emma studied Tarvo's downturned face. There was no question the man was heartbroken. She wasn't sure there was anything she could say to ease his pain, but she carried on nonetheless. "Let me ask you this. What is it about that pub that made it so special? Aside from it existing in a world that hasn't been destroyed. What was it about that place that made you hang onto that key for years while you fought for your own world?"

Tarvo exhaled slowly. "This place . . . this place was special. It didn't matter who you were, or where you came from, they treated you like your problems mattered. The barkeep and owner, he was the nicest man, and his wife was a gem if I ever did meet one. They were human too . . ." When he continued there was a shakiness to his voice. "Then there was this baker; he'd bake the tastiest pastries you've ever had. I can still remember how they tasted all these years later. His name was Rudy. We made the decision for me to leave so I could fight for my world, but I never thought that if I lived, we'd be apart for so long . . ." Tarvo allowed his gaze to drift back to the door again. He sniffed lightly and tightened his lips.

"Exactly." Emma cleared her throat. She had expected his answer, at least the gist of it, but she'd not realized how awkward it would make things, or how emotional the dwarf might get. "It was the people there that made it special. Ha'dran and Gloria, I'm sure they wouldn't have complained about leaving for a place that wasn't falling apart or ravaged by war, but I don't think that's why they traveled with you all this way. They care about you. That's what friends do."

Tarvo licked his lips and nodded but seemed unconvinced. He leaned his back against the wall and slumped to the floor.

Emma reached out a hand. "Could I see the orb?" she asked.

The dwarf shrugged and threw it with an underhanded toss. Emma caught the sphere with ease and pulled it in for a closer look.

The orb was made of some sort of metal, that much was clear, but it was unlike any Emma had ever seen. Too light to be iron, too solid to be gold or silver. And despite Tarvo claiming to have carried it around for ages, there was no sign of rust or tarnish. In fact, it looked practically brand new, and in a world that was covered in dirt and grime, that was quite a feat.

What really made it unique, though, was the way it was formed. Bands of metal had been sculpted in a delicate pattern of flourishes and swirls. Through carved holes in the design, it was easy to see the orb was hollow. Its inside surface was smooth and carved with some sort of runes.

"Are these dwarven runes?" she asked, guessing that it had to be magic that would make such a gateway possible.

"No. They're an ancient magic," Tarvo said. "Older than dwarf or man. I don't know much other than that."

In contrast to the intricacies of the orb, the spot in the wall where it fit was drab and unassuming. If it weren't the perfect shape and size for the ball, she'd never have guessed that the two were related at all. She put her hand inside the recess, feeling its smooth surface. It was carved out of the stone itself but without blemish. It was as smooth as a marble slab.

Without thinking, Emma lifted the orb and placed it into the recess. She jumped and let out a gasp as something inside latched on and spun the orb a quarter turn. The orb's interior flared into a blueish-green ball of light.

"Is it supposed to do that?"

Tarvo was on his feet, his mouth open as he stood before the doorframe in shock. Where previously there had been nothing but the ruined street, was now a swirling fog of light filled with the same blueish light that engulfed the orb. A violent wind swept through the room, picking up dirt and debris as it tore around them.

"Gloria! Ha'dran!" Tarvo called, raising his voice above the noise. "Gather your things! The gateway has opened!"

James

Moira shifted through the portal for a second time, returning from O'Sullivan's with a bottle of Irish whiskey. Apparently, ale wasn't strong enough for the conversation they were about to have.

The rest of them grabbed a seat around the bar, and Rudy made his way behind the counter to face them, like he would an audience. "You've noticed the area of the pub doesn't quite fit with O'Sullivan's space, haven't ya?"

"It's pretty tough to overlook," James admitted.

"That's because this place doesn't exist in our reality," Rudy said. "Or in any reality—not really."

James, Kathy, and Liam exchanged uneasy glances. Moira slammed back a shot of whiskey and poured herself another. She pulled out four more shot glasses, filled those too, and passed them around.

"I don't think you're making any sense, Uncle Rudy. Between what realities?"

Rudy sighed. "To be honest, I've never quite wrapped my head around it myself. All I know is that our world isn't the only one that exists. Our . . . universe runs parallel to others. There are other Earths. Worlds where different choices have led to different outcomes. Worlds where magic exists, where there are men who fight wars with creatures you couldn't begin to imagine, and others who have known nothing but peace and security. Some of those worlds connect here, to this place. But this place is outside of any of them. It was created by a magic long forgotten. For some reason, your family was chosen as the caretakers."

"A curse is what it is." Moira nearly spat the words. "You should know better than anyone. It's nothing but asking for trouble."

There was a sadness in Rudy's eyes. "Lots of heartache, ya. But this pub also saved my life. It probably saved hundreds, maybe thousands of lives. And it's done a lot of good for you too."

Moira scoffed.

"Wait, wait, wait." Kathy lifted her hands. "What kind of half-baked tale are you trying to spin on us, Rudy? Is this some kind of joke? You're talking of magic and other worlds? Next you'll be telling us of leprechauns and fairies. I have to admit this is a pretty impressive setup. And I don't understand the glowing doorway we walked through to get here. But there has to be a logical explanation for all of this."

"Just because you don't understand it, doesn't mean it's illogical," Rudy said.

"Why don't you want it open, Mum?" Liam asked. The man seemed less concerned with the ridiculousness of the claim and more worried about why his mother had been upset by the notion of it. Which in some way made perfect sense.

"Always some sort of trouble coming though those gateways," Moira said. Whether she realized it or not, she'd waved a hand toward a side wall adjacent to where they'd entered. It was only then that James noticed a series of four doorways, each identical to the one they'd come through. Frames lined with stone, each with a smooth round inset, the perfect size for an orb. A small platform rested below each one, like a kind of landing pad.

"One night it's gnomes, the next its some paladin on their way to fight some evil. Then before you know it, that evil sneaks through because someone didn't shut the damn portal behind them. We were never meant to muck in the affairs of other worlds. If you ask me, each universe should keep its own problems to itself."

James didn't know what to think. *Gnomes? Paladins? Evil?* This was exactly the stuff of his mother's stories.

He was no stranger to the term "multiverse." He'd seen enough sci-fi and Marvel movies to understand how different decisions made can create alternate worlds, but he was having a hard time wrestling with the thought that a doorway to them all existed in the storage room of O'Sullivan's.

It was too ridiculous for him to believe.

"That's a bit dramatic," said Rudy. "You know there are wards in place to prevent anyone truly malevolent from coming through."

Moira pursed her lips. "Those wards aren't enough if the Tíogar Mór are able to drain their magic."

James was barely listening to their exchange. "So these people . . . from other dimensions, come through these gateways, and then what? They have a pint and go home?" James lifted his hands in mock surrender. "I'm sorry, but this all seems a little farfetched."

"That's precisely what happens," Rudy said before taking another sip of his drink. "The Pint and Portal serves as a refuge for weary travelers, for heroes. Those seeking to do good in the world. It's a place of rest for those who need it most. Whatever magic runs this place also decides who will be let inside. The orbs don't work for just anyone, and the magic of the tavern seems to control how many patrons are able to enter. Otherwise, I suppose we'd potentially get millions of customers coming through the gateways, and we wouldn't have the space." Rudy let out a hearty chuckle.

James took a sip of his whiskey. The smooth caramel and oak notes were the touch of familiar he needed to settle his thoughts. He let the warmth of it roll down the back of his throat and into his belly.

He couldn't shake off his encounter with Michael and how the man had called him the gatekeeper. He knew O'Sullivan's had been in his family for generations but . . . an inter-dimensional speakeasy?

He struggled with what question to ask next. It was especially challenging because he didn't know if he believed any of it. His brain was struggling with the reality of where his body sat. Instead, his thoughts spilled out in a series of questions.

"How did my family come to be the ones to run this pub? How long has it been here? Did my ancestors build this place? How did they set it up? Why—"

Rudy placed a firm grip on James' shoulder to stop the stream of questions from flowing. "Easy now. One question at a time. But the truth is, we don't know. We know that ancient magic created it. Your mother was always more interested in it than your father. But your grandfather didn't know how it worked, either. Your parents were in much the same position you are now. The only difference is that when your grandfather passed, this pub was still running. Your parents had already been helping in a limited capacity before then. Once they were on their own, your dad wanted nothing to do with it. However, your mother insisted they take over. Your father loved her so much that he carried on helping her. They learned what they needed as they went.

"For whatever reason," Rudy continued, "your pub, O'Sullivan's, in our dimension is the only one that controls the master key and switch. If your orb isn't set into the wall nobody else gets in. We don't know why it was set up this way, just that it is."

Kathy was shaking her head. "I've seen all of the financial records for the bar," she said. "Sure, the pub was making a lot more before Mom passed, but it wasn't enough to stock two bars. How did we fill the shelves? Where did all the money go?"

Rudy laughed. "Some of it from the shop. Some of it from other worlds. Some of it is magic. Most of the people who come through those portals have never heard of a Euro. So they pay what they can or make deals. Sometimes an adventurer is so grateful for the time they spend here that they bring barrels of ale in appreciation. Some of the ingredients will come from our world, sometimes we acquired things that were only available elsewhere. But like I said, this place runs on magic, so sometimes you find it has exactly the ingredients you need."

Rudy grabbed his plate of strudel and tilted it to the others. "Hah! If only I could be so lucky with my baking!"

James' head was straining under the weight of everything he was hearing. He pressed his thumb and forefinger against his temples in an effort to relieve some of the pressure.

"So, not only am I forced to get one failing pub up and running," he said, "I also have to run a second one—one that runs on . . . deals with parallel worlds and magic?"

"You don't have to do a damn thing." Moira stood. "Your father had the right idea shuttering this place. He should have tossed that orb away. That Micheal was always a troublemaker too. I don't know why your dad trusted him the way he did. If you know what's what, you'll do the same. I want to see O'Sullivan's do as well as any of you, but Pint and Portal? This place was better off forgotten." She threw back the rest of the whiskey in her glass and stormed through the gateway. The waves of the portal caused her outline to linger and expand like ripples in a pond.

"Don't mind Moira." Rudy looked at Liam. "No offense to your mom. I hate to say not everything always went as it should. Moira, like the rest of us, went through some bad experiences. She's never quite looked at this the same since." He let out a heavy sigh. "In a lot of ways, I can't say I blame her."

Liam frowned. "What kind of experiences?"

"Not my story to tell," Rudy said. "She'll tell you if she wants you to know. Some things made her paranoid of what might appear through one of those gateways, and what it might mean if they gained access to this place. It's best to remember that not everyone who came through those gateways had an easy life. Most didn't, actually. You throw people from other worlds or cultures with different rules into one room and misunderstandings are bound to happen from time to time. But that doesn't mean they were bad people. Some of them were only lost. Others were trying to find their way."

"Isn't that the same thing?" James asked.

A warm smile graced Rudy's lips. "No. Hardly ever."

A low, resonant hum rolled through the room, like the distant stirrings of a storm. It seemed to pulse in the walls and floor, a subtle vibration James could feel in his chest. Rudy's ears piqued, his head snapping up as his sharp gaze fixed on the four archways along the wall. James followed his line of sight just as a sharp blue light sparked in the second gateway from the left. It flared like a struck match before swelling and rippling outward.

Rudy's gaze darted to the switches in the corner of the room.

"You opened the gates?" He shouted the words as he stood, poised to run to the lever, but instead, he froze, his gaze focusing back on the new gateway forming. "That lever allows travelers to find us!"

"I was trying to switch on the lights." Liam's eyes darted from Rudy to the opening portal, back to the switch. "I can turn it off."

Rudy raised a large hand to stop Liam from standing. "It's too late. If you close the portal now, who knows what will happen to those coming through."

Concern crossed Liam's face as he paused, eyeing the swirling array of lights that was forming a new doorway.

Kathy gripped the table and pushed herself to a standing position. "Do we need to be worried?"

"Not likely." Rudy shook his head. "Unless they're thirsty."

Light expanded into a swirling vortex of light blue and green. Based on what Moira and Rudy were saying, James had no idea who, or what, he expected to come through.

Seconds ticked by as the gate formed and remained unchanged. Though the sight was a spectacle enough on its own. James was starting to think perhaps it opened by mistake; maybe nobody was coming through after all.

Then a shape emerged from beneath its surface, and a red-haired woman about the same age as him stepped through. She was dressed in a cloak and cradling a small black satchel under one arm. In her right hand she held a short dagger, the blade reflecting the yellow and blue of the pub's lights.

A gasp escaped from Kathy's lips.

It wasn't the dagger that shocked James, though, it was who came through the portal next.

Three short, stout people—one woman, with two long blonde braids hanging down the front of her, and two men. One was older, one younger.

James wasn't one to judge appearances, but he wasn't sure that they were even human. Both wore what he'd consider to be capes, and the older one had a weapon of his own strapped to his back. If he wasn't mistaken, it appeared to be a very hefty battle axe. Their faces were like rough leather—even the younger ones' skin was creased and worn. There was something very . . . familiar about them. Like something out of a Peter Jackson film.

"Are those . . . dwarves?" The words were barely audible, but he couldn't stop them from leaving his lips.

"Ya." Rudy's answer was barely more than a breathy whisper. "That's exactly what they are."

Emma

Emma's feet landed softly on a hard wooden floor. Her dagger rested easy in her hand. It had been months since she'd had to protect herself, but some habits didn't die. If it had been nearly two decades since Tarvo had traveled through the portal, there was no telling what might be on the other side.

Despite Demon Box's protests, she saw her one, and maybe her only, chance to get off a world that had come completely undone, and she had to take it.

You never listen to me, Demon Box complained. *We could have ended up in the fiery pits of a volcano, or far worse.*

"Far worse?" she asked with an eyebrow raised. "I already have to put up with your whining."

In truth, there was no telling if this pub Tarvo had remembered still existed, but they took that chance any time they'd traveled to a new world. The threat wasn't unique just because Demon Box hadn't been the one to open the portal.

If we didn't leave that world with them, Emma directed her thoughts toward her inter-dimensional friend, *we would have likely gotten stuck there forever, and you would never get a chance to be fixed.*

She got the distinct sense that Demon Box was rolling its

eyes, though it didn't have eyes, so she had trouble visualizing what it was broadcasting to her.

Of course, they hadn't landed in a volcano, they had landed . . . here. A pub—of course a pub, just as Tarvo had said. Every world she'd visited so far had its own version of O'Sullivan's pub in Cuanmore. Why that was, she'd never really bothered to question. Her assumption was the pub had existed for so long, the timeline would have had to split millennia ago for it to have never been built.

Even though they had left from the remnants of O'Sullivan's, wherever this was, whatever world it was, this pub wasn't the same one.

Tarvo had called it The Pint and Portal.

Her newfound dwarven companions, Tarvo, Ha'dran, and Gloria ran through behind her. The portal they had entered hadn't been all that different from the ones Demon Box created when it was functional.

My portals are a little less bumpy. The box's voice rattled in her head. *I think I'm going to be sick.*

Normally, Emma would have had a witty comeback for the conscious device, but for right now, she remained silent, letting her gaze and other senses take in the surroundings. The air in this place lacked the metallic char of Tarvo's world, and she was more than happy for the reprieve for her lungs. The smells were replaced with a staleness and layers of dust that suggested it had sat empty for some time.

Tarvo let out a heavy breath as a hint of a smile crossed his face. "It hasn't changed." The dwarf's voice was raspy with wonder. "It's just as I remember."

He seemed to break himself out of his trance long enough to turn and grab an orb from the wall beside the portal. At the same instant, the gateway winked out, leaving the space they'd entered feeling darker and dingier than it had a moment ago.

"Liam!" cried a portly, older gentleman who stood behind a table on the far side of the room. "Pull the switch!"

Emma held her breath as a younger man with black hair, a short beard, and piercing dark eyes stood from where he was seated and darted for the wall. The man pulled a large blocky switch down, and a hum that she had barely noticed now fell quiet.

Liam. How many years had it been since she'd seen the man? Since she'd seen *any* version of the man. Because of course this man wasn't, couldn't be, the Liam she'd grown up alongside. The man who she'd fought monsters with, who had become not only her very best friend but also the man she hadn't realized she was madly in love with.

Not until it was too late.

When she'd first started traveling between worlds, according to the code of the Hunters of the Cursed, Liam should have arrested her for possessing magic. Instead, he let her go. It was that day that she'd traveled through a portal for the first time. Out of necessity, she'd made new friends: Aldrich, the mad scientist and creator of Demon Box, and Vespa, the empathic fairy who wanted nothing more than to help people discover what they needed.

She'd seen several versions of Liam immediately after that, which made her think she'd have infinite chances to win him back. Each world being a variation of her own meant she'd encounter familiar people who had lived completely different lives. But over the last few years and countless worlds, she'd yet to see another man who possessed his face.

Now, here he was again. She wondered if she'd ever get used to Liam's features being attached to someone who didn't remember her.

"Tarvo?" The older man said the dwarf's name as he moved from behind the table.

Tarvo had finished putting the orb in his satchel as he looked up. His eyes were still in a half daze. "Rudy?"

Barely a blink exchanged between the man and the dwarf before both of them broke out in a sprint toward each other at a surprising pace given size and advanced age. Though based on what she knew of dwarves, Tarvo was likely far older than the man he had called Rudy.

The men wrapped their arms around each other in a deep and knowing bear hug. Tears streamed down both of their faces.

Wherever this place was, there was no danger here.

"I never thought I'd see you again." Rudy's face was wet and contorted with unrestricted emotion.

Emma had never imagined she'd see the dwarf cry, but rivers of tears flowed down Tarvo's face as well. He shook as he embraced the man.

Emma felt awkward staring, so she focused her attention on the others in the room. There were two people who stood alongside Liam in a daze. Both were around the same age as she was. A charming, if pale, man with little muscle on his frame, but not much fat either. And a woman who was so obviously his sister it was ridiculous. Other than the fact that she had reddish-brown hair and his was black, they were practically the mirror image of each other. Neither paid her any mind, however. Their attention focused squarely on the dwarves. Both Tarvo and the two who stood behind her.

So no dwarves in this world either, she thought. *Yet somehow, this man knows Tarvo.*

The older men clearly needed a moment, so she slid past them and toward the other three humans. She glanced back to the two dwarves who looked as dazed as anyone else. They hung back in the shadows, obviously as stunned to see more humans as the humans were to see dwarves.

Tarvo had seen humans before, but not ones from his own world. That much was clear now. Still the question remained: Who were these people, and how did they have the power to travel between worlds?

Perhaps like her world—the world she left years ago—this one possessed great magic. She shuddered. Were its magic users gathered up and arrested here too?

In her kingdom, the penalty for the mere possession of magic was death. A punishment she helped arrange far too often.

She let out a sigh before catching herself again and hardening her resolve. She couldn't let her guilt consume her. Emma pushed the painful memories aside; she wasn't going to deal with those now. Her fingers danced along the hilt of her dagger though as adrenaline coursed through her.

It's safe here, she assured herself. *A space where a man can unabashedly embrace a dwarf with tears in his eyes was a special place indeed.*

Emma wondered if she'd ever find herself in a place where she'd be able to live; a place she could call home. It had been a long time since she'd thought she could stay in one location. At the very least, she needed a break in a world where she wasn't on the run, and after spending more than enough time in a world that had been all but destroyed, she needed some reprieve.

She reached out with her magic, and it was like embracing an old friend. There was magic here at least, not like on some worlds she'd encountered.

Her magic was limited to influencing alcohol. For some reason, the frequency of her abilities was restricted to drink, and to the crystals that Demon Box housed. While other magic users mastered fire, water, wind, or some other element, she controlled drink—an ability that lent itself well to bartending, but not much else.

Which was fine by her.

For a pub, the bar was relatively dry. There were some bottles that rested on a shelf behind the bar. She allowed what was there to leave an impression on her mind. Let the alcohol speak to her as it often did. From what she could tell, it had been left untouched for over a decade, probably for as long as Tarvo had been away, but what had been left unopened was still drinkable and of good quality. She let her consciousness drift from one bottle to the next. Each had many stories to tell, though she didn't dwell on any one of them. These were merely impressions. But one thing was certain, this was no ordinary pub.

Those impressions, in combination with the layer of dust that coated everything, made it clear that this place had not been open for business in quite some time.

"Where are we?" She voiced the question more to herself. She didn't think anyone was close enough to hear her.

Don't ask me, Demon Box quipped.

Emma rolled her eyes. For a moment she'd forgotten the companion she held.

I wasn't, she silently answered.

Sure, sure. I suppose I'm forgettable, Demon Box whined. *Why bother with a lonely device when you have dwarves, humans, and other meat sacks to keep you warm?*

"Please, miss," Rudy said. "You won't need your daggers here." The older man held his hands up in a placating fashion. It was only then that she realized she still held her dagger at the ready.

She looked at Liam and the other two in the corner who had situated themselves behind their table and chairs as though that might offer them protection if she decided to strike. Though, she could tell from their stances that they had no experience in fighting, outside of perhaps a bar brawl.

So, this Liam had not been trained as a competent fighter.

Emma sighed and sheathed the blade. She couldn't help but concede that part of her was slightly disappointed. She'd prefer if the man could hold his own if ever faced with the anger of some wretched beast. Though, these days she'd much rather swing a drink than a knife.

"So this is The Pint and Portal?" she asked, not to anyone in particular. It was substantial in size; Tarvo wasn't wrong about that. But he had mentioned it to be a lively and welcoming place, and aside from the five humans and three dwarves, this pub was vacant. "It doesn't appear to be open."

"It's not," the young man beside Liam snapped. While he didn't look like he'd fare well in a fight against . . . well anyone, he certainly had an attitude about him. The young man crossed his arms and leaned back, scrutinizing her and her party.

"The pub's been closed for many years," Rudy said more gently. He clasped a hand on Tarvo's shoulder. "The kid hadn't left the pathways open for more than a few minutes. I can't believe the luck that you happened to open the gateway at the right time."

"He's been attempting it for months," Ha'dran spoke, stepping out from the shadows. There was a lightness to his voice that Emma hadn't heard before. The younger dwarf stepped forward with a swoosh of his cape and a half bow toward the humans. "He spoke of the grandness of this place. The crowds that would gather from worlds I couldn't imagine being real. To be honest, I thought he was mad. I didn't believe his tales."

"I may be mad,"—Tarvo grinned—"but this place is real."

Ha'dran continued, ignoring the older dwarf. His face was earnest. "It seems you already know Tarvo. My name is Ha'dran, this is my partner, Gloria. When animals were plentiful throughout the plains, she could make a mean Parlock stew, else she was a fine server in many a fine Hybarn pub. Before I became a soldier, I was a traveling magician. I performed in pubs across all seventeen of the Dwarven territories, including for Queen Aleyna herself. I could tell stories with the best of them, draw crowds so large establishments would need to turn dozens away. We would gladly exchange our services for a safe place to sojourn. Perhaps you'd like a display of what I can do?"

Ha'dran outstretched his arms, palms facing each other, paused for a breath, then separated them quickly. A streak of flame burst from the center of his palms as he did so, expanding up and down but contained as though within a glass column.

One of the younger men gasped. The woman shrieked and her brother let out a noise not unlike that of a strangled cat. Even Tarvo appeared startled by the display.

Emma pulled her dagger out once again on instinct, holding it up at the ready.

Ha'dran's a mage?

The only one who seemed unmoved was Rudy, who held up his hands in earnest, moving toward the dwarf. "Easy, friend. Magic is not so common for these folk."

Ha'dran's face went red. Emma couldn't tell whether it was from embarrassment or anger. Maybe annoyance. But he quickly shook it off and lifted his hands in placation "My apologies. I didn't mean to offend. I'm able to tone down the use of magic when I tell my tales as well if it's going to scare instead of delight."

"I think that's all a little premature," said Rudy. He gestured a hand to the man who stood next to Liam. "This is James. He's just inherited this place and"—Rudy took a look toward James, whose eyes were wider than some soldiers' shields—"as you might guess by the expression on his face, he's been a bit overwhelmed by everything that's occurred today. It might be best to save your stories, for now."

Emma pursed her lips. There was more happening here

than Rudy was saying, but perhaps what he had said was enough. She suspected that Ha'dran's earnestness was nothing more than desperation to remain somewhere that offered the appearance of comfort and security. How long had they lived amongst the ruins of a destroyed empire? This perhaps was the first chance the dwarf had seen to return to what might be a normal life.

Yet something about the entire exchange threw her off guard. The dwarf's eagerness might have been excitement, but she'd learned to read people during her time as a Hunter. Ha'dran's sudden bravado could be masking something he didn't want to reveal to the humans, including her.

"Inherited?" Tarvo asked, his voice softening. "So you're Tim's son?"

"Aye," replied James.

Tarvo looked at Rudy with a heaviness in his eyes. "Does that mean . . .?"

Rudy simply nodded.

Tarvo looked down and shuffled his feet. "I'm so sorry, lad. Your pa was a good man. The best, actually. What of Shay?"

James' head tilted at the mention of the name.

"My mother died when I was young," he said.

Rudy nodded. "Tim closed the portals right after you left." A look of trepidation crossed his face. There was something he was holding back.

"I see," said Tarvo.

As much as the vague catching up was intriguing to Emma, she was more worried about what the pub's status meant for her and her companions. If she were forced to return to the waste-land of the last world, she'd be stuck there without a way to fix Demon Box. This might be her only chance.

"If we're not welcome to stay, are we to return the way we came?" she asked. "I don't belong in the world we came from."

Tarvo grunted in agreement. "The world we came from is a

wasteland. We'd be returning only to suffer a slow, agonizing death."

"I think James and I should have a discussion in private," Rudy said cautiously. "For now, please, if you all have a seat, I'll see if we can scrounge up some passable ale, and I've brought enough strudel for everyone."

Emma

Emma took a sip of the ale Liam had brought to their table. It wouldn't have been a bad brew in half the worlds she'd been to.

"Sorry, this is all we've got at the moment," Liam said. His cheeks were flushed, as though he was embarrassed to be serving it.

Emma considered using her magic to improve it, but after the reaction Ha'dran had received, she decided she'd hold off on exercising her abilities until she knew more about the world they were in.

It's best if you remain quiet here as well. She directed her thoughts toward Demon Box. *We don't know what kind of reaction they'd have to a talking sentient device.*

Fine, I'm never allowed to talk. You know, I find it rather insulting.

These folk seem pretty jumpy around magic, Emma said. *It's best we don't spook them more than necessary.*

I'm not magic. I'm a sentient piece of technology.

If you want to test that theory out, be my guest. But don't expect me to save your circuits if they decide to set you aflame or smash you to bits with an axe.

There was the briefest of pauses before Demon Box replied. *Point taken.*

It wouldn't be the first world where its ability to speak had gotten it into trouble.

Emma had taken a seat with the dwarves. The other humans seemed to have their own matters to sort out, and everyone, other than Tarvo, appeared to be on edge.

"This is the glorious bar you were so anxious to return to?" Gloria had been mostly quiet since they'd arrived. She kept her voice low as she outstretched a hand, gesturing at the rest of the pub. "I grant that it's large, but this pub hasn't seen greatness in years, maybe decades. Never mind the thick layer of dust, this ale is stale. And there are no customers. It's no wonder either, they hardly want us here. We may as well return home for the welcome we've received. Have you ever seen someone react the way they did to poor Ha'dran? That was a dazzling performance, and they reacted like he had threatened them!"

"Not all worlds possess magic," Emma said before pulling another swig of her drink. She wiped a small bit of froth away with her index finger. "He startled them, that's all. To be honest, I was a little surprised as well."

"Bah!" Ha'dran spat. "I've traveled the world and never found a place where my magic didn't delight and entertain. I've never been so insulted in all my life!"

"Yes, but this isn't *your* world," said Tarvo. "In truth, this isn't any world. But for these people, magic is not something that exists. Not in the way we think of it."

"What do you mean?" Emma asked. "This isn't any world?"

"It exists as a space between," Tarvo said. "There's nothing outside of these walls. It doesn't exist in any reality. It is a reality on its own."

Emma looked around the pub. There were no doorways, no windows, only the soft glow of yellow lighting that seemed to come from nowhere and everywhere at once.

Between worlds.

Emma had to admit she was struggling to grasp that one.

Anything she'd ever known existing between worlds was a brief chasm of colors and lights before appearing on the other side of a portal. It all happened in the blink of eye, and she'd never considered that there might be something that existed in between.

"That doesn't excuse that this place looks like it's been through its own apocalypse," Gloria muttered. "Even the pub we just left didn't have so much dust in it, and half the walls were missing!"

The dwarf woman wasn't wrong, but Emma had never been one to sit and complain about something. She slid her stool back and stood before making her way behind the bar toward a large two-bin sink. She pulled on the hot water tap and allowed it to spit and sputter as it worked air out of the pipes. She tried not to think too hard about how a place that only existed between the fabric of time and space had running water.

Emma had lost count of how many worlds she'd visited since she left her home a few years ago. Though she knew Demon Box had cataloged all of them. Some worlds had magic, some hadn't. In some worlds, running water would have been seen as sorcery. Emma had slowly grown accustomed to expecting the unexpected.

But something else gnawed at her. She could lie to herself and say she didn't know what it was, but she knew.

Ha'dran and his magic.

It wasn't the fact that he possessed magic that bothered her —though that had been a surprise. What was making her insides churn was how she responded. That her immediate reaction to magic was to reach for her dagger.

Even though she hadn't been a Hunter of the Cursed for years, and even after years of knowing she held magical powers herself, her instinctive reaction to the display was one of violence. She tried to push the feelings of guilt down as she often did. All she needed was a bit of a distraction. Cleaning could provide that.

She found a small waste bin as well as a small handheld brush. She grabbed them along with a cloth that she moistened under the running tap.

"What are you doing?" Gloria asked as she returned to the table.

Emma got to work right away, using the brush to push the dust into the bin. Then she took the wet cloth and wiped down the table as best she could. It would likely take another round with a cleaning solution to make sure it was properly clean, but this would make a difference.

"You're cleaning for them?" Gloria shook her head. "Why?"

Emma smirked. She had worked for more than a handful of bars throughout her journey. Her main goal was to learn how to make cocktails as best she could, but in working any bar there was always a substantial amount of cleaning involved. Some of the barkeeps hated that part of the job, but Emma found it relaxing—a way to focus her thoughts and clear her mind.

"When I was a Hunter," she said. "I used to relish the time it took for us to travel between towns. At first I thought what I liked about it was seeing new lands. But after traveling for a few years, I realized that it was the quiet time I enjoyed. Sure, seeing different places, hearing stories from different parts of the kingdom were enjoyable too, but when you're tracking and fighting magical beasts there's not much time to reflect. When I started working bars, I realized that those same quiet moments could be found in simple acts, like cleaning, wiping tables, polishing glasses, or sweeping up at the end of a long night of chatting with patrons. There's a type of meditation that it can provide."

"Bah!" Ha'dran waved a hand. "What good has meditation ever done anyone? A waste of time."

Emma smiled. It was a sentiment she might have once

shared. "You'd be surprised at how much better you can perform other tasks after you've had some time to pause. Especially if you're working with magic. Meditative focus will allow magic to flow through you unobstructed by your own troubles."

"Still," Gloria muttered. "These humans have not bothered to clean their own pub. I'm sure as hells not going to do it for them."

Emma sighed. That was likely another sentiment she might have shared while she was a Hunter. "You heard what Rudy said. The fellow there has just taken over this place. And I'd gamble from the look on his face that he knew nothing about this inter-dimensional business before now."

"What does that matter?" Ha'dran asked.

"Well," said Emma, "before I came along, how many humans had you met?"

"None," Ha'dran said. "If it weren't for Tarvo, I don't know if we would have believed that we were seeing a true human in the flesh."

Tarvo sat reclined in his chair. His eyes were almost closed as if he were ready for a good night's sleep. But he nodded anyway and stroked his white beard absently with his hand.

"Exactly," said Emma. "I'd bet a mine full of copper that they've never seen dwarves before either. Give people a little grace and understanding, and I think they'll surprise you in the end."

Ha'dran puffed air between his lips. "Surprise you with a dagger between your ribs. Our stories are full of humans and their ways. Vicious and greedy. Would do anything to make a quick profit. Us dwarves stayed hidden in our caves for centuries, minding our own business, guarding the mines, so that humans didn't strip them dry and interrupt the Great Balance."

"The stories are mostly truth." Tarvo opened his eyes and leaned forward. "But not the entirety of things. Some humans were evil, sure, but so are some dwarves. These humans"—he gestured to the table where the humans sat, still deep in their own conversation—"are some of the finest folk you'll ever meet."

Gloria scoffed.

Emma decided to let it be for the time being. If Tarvo couldn't convince them, she sure wouldn't. And she'd wager she'd not convince James and Liam of their intentions either. The best she could do would be to help out and be a friend to all. She thought back to when she'd first discovered her powers and befriended a fairy. She had been convinced the sprite was going to walk her off a cliff.

"Either way, unless you'd rather go back to your world and sleep in the sulfuric rain, this is the best place we've got to be right now. I'm going to do what I can to get it up and running so it stays that way."

"Waste of time," Ha'dran said. "I'm sure we'll be on our asses back through that portal before nightfall."

"Emma is right," Tarvo cut in, his eyes still half shut. "They may be wary of us, but we'd be the same way if a handful of humans showed up on our doorstep."

"Bollocks," cursed Gloria. "We trusted Emma from the moment she arrived."

Emma couldn't help but laugh. "A few hours ago, you were afraid I might eat your brain!"

Gloria looked startled then thought for a moment. "You still might, I suppose."

"If it weren't for me, you'd have chased her off," said Tarvo. "Give them time. It will all work out."

Emma decided her role in this conversation had taken its course. She took the bin and the brush and began making her way from table to table, brushing the thick layer of dust off the tables and chairs. It seemed whether they be human or dwarf, people were always suspicious of someone who was different. She wondered if there was any way around that.

She looked at the group of humans who sat talking in the corner amongst themselves. Her eye was drawn to Liam. His hair was similar to how it had been on her world—dark and wavy, not quite reaching his shoulders. His eyes were still the same piercing green and he was as handsome as ever.

She had to force herself not to stare.

He's not my Liam, she reminded herself. No matter how he looked, he wouldn't share the same past. She couldn't help but let out sigh as she brushed another coating of dust into the bin.

Hunters of the Cursed. That's what they had been. It seemed like it was so long ago, but in reality, a few years was hardly any time at all. Not after a lifetime spent hunting magical creatures, arresting any they came across who possessed even a sniff of magic.

The Kingdom of Lancastria had also been afraid of what it didn't understand. Everything they'd done was because King Brampton believed magic users posed a threat to his reign.

How many innocents had she sent to the dungeons because they were seen as being different? She'd been so indoctrinated to believe that men and women traded their souls to gain unnatural powers that she had never stopped to question whether magic had indeed been a curse. She'd never asked why the king was so vehemently opposed to magic and its users. Not until she'd realized she held a magical power of her own.

In the scheme of things, having the ability to manipulate alcoholic drinks was a minor magic to have—one she maybe could have hidden. But it was magic all the same, and it had taken her a long time to accept the fact that she was not, in fact, cursed, as she had once believed.

Now that she could finally accept the magic within herself, she had to come to terms with what she had done to other magic users in her old life.

"Thank you, miss . . ."

Emma had been so lost in her own thoughts, she hadn't noticed the man walk up to her. She started slightly, and it took her a moment to realize Liam was waiting for her to introduce herself.

This Liam had never met her. Did she exist in his world? Had they yet to cross paths? Or was this world like most she'd encountered where there was no other version of herself.

"Emma," she said. "My name is Emma Corvus."

"I'm Liam," he said with an outstretched hand.

Emma swallowed before she grabbed it. She was expecting this man's hand to be soft. Those in worlds with more technological advancements typically were. Though his skin wasn't as rough and calloused as the Liam she'd known, those hands had known their fair share of work.

She met his eyes, expecting, or maybe hoping, to find warmth within them. But they were filled with an uncertainty that Emma hated to admit was more than a little disappointing.

"It's no trouble, really," she replied. "I like to keep busy."

His lips tightened, and he nodded. "Well, that I can understand. I'm much the same myself."

Heat rose in Emma's chest. She did her best to push it down. "Has James decided anything about whether we can stay or not?"

Liam's face darkened only a smidge. "James is having a tough time right now. He's got some decisions to make, but this" —he looked around the pub with no less uncertainty than the dwarves had—"this is a lot to take in."

"It's not for you?" she asked.

"Doesn't matter what I think. If this is what keeps James around, I'm all for it. But he'll need a bit of help seeing how much he needs this."

"Keep him around?" Emma asked. "He doesn't want to be here?"

Liam shook his head. "His dad just passed, and James never expected to inherit it. And that's speaking only of O'Sullivan's; we didn't even know this place existed until an hour ago."

That explains a lot, Emma thought.

"That's only part of things." Liam's gaze wandered around the space. "Though admittedly the more bizarre part." He paused, his eyes landing on the table of dwarves. "Maybe I just haven't processed everything yet, but what I do know is my friend needs a hand. His family did a lot to help my mum when she first came here from London. If I can help him, I'll do what I can."

"It sounds like you're a good friend, willing to jump in and help in a tight spot."

"It's what we do in Cuanmore. Besides, with or without magic, running a pub sounds a lot more interesting than working a deli or building tables. I think it's about time I start thinking about what I want to do with the rest of my life. Ya know? If I can help James get this place up and running, it'll feel like I've done something productive with my time."

Emma nodded. She knew exactly what that was like. "If it helps, I'm a bartender. I have a way with mixing drinks. I'm happy to offer my services for the time being for a place to stay and food."

Liam grinned. "If he decides to give it a go, we'll be needing staff. I'll be sure to let James know."

Some of the most fascinating men and women to have come through the portal were the dwarves who arrived with Rudy when he returned.

We were doubly excited to have him back. First, because we never expected to see him again—he'd slipped through one of the portals when we weren't looking and disappeared for nearly a year. His return was a shock, but of course, we were ecstatic to see him alive.

Even more thrilling, though, was the fact that he hadn't returned alone. During his journeys, Rudy had met someone—a rough-around-the-edges dwarf named Tarvo, who seemed as amazed to learn that humans were real as we were to discover the existence of dwarves. And Tarvo wasn't the last. Soon, more dwarves began arriving, drawn by the portals and the promise of a new connection between our worlds.

The dwarves, as it turns out, are in the middle of a magical renaissance of sorts in their world. Unfortunately, with any great awakening of magic, there always seems to be someone eager to twist it for their own dark purposes. This time, it's a mage. (Why is there always a dark one?)

Despite their gruff exteriors, the dwarves we've met so far have big hearts, and they're surprisingly generous. They never hesitate to toss a silver or gold coin our way in exchange for a night of ale, and I won't deny it's been good for the tavern.

It sounds like Tarvo will be with us for a while. Rudy, ever the dreamer, has plans to finally open the bakery he's always talked about, and Tarvo is all too eager to help him get started. The two of them seem to fit together like the gears of a clock, and I can only hope this is the beginning of a new life for them both.

James

James pressed his palms against his face.

"I don't even want to run O'Sullivan's. Now you're telling me I've inherited *two* pubs?" His thoughts spiraled; it was too much for him to filter. "We're between dimensions? How does this work? How am I supposed to staff both? How do I stock a bar that doesn't exist on any normal plane of reality? I don't know the first thing about running a normal business, never mind one that holds . . . magic . . . or whatever this place is. Where do I even start?"

He sucked in as much air as he could fit into his lungs, his mind scrambling to find anything meaningful he could hang onto.

Kathy leaned forward, resting her elbows on the table. "Okay, James, deep breaths. Losing it isn't going to solve anything. And for the record, you're not doing this alone. You've got me, remember?"

James dropped his hands and gave her a tired glare. "Yeah, well, you weren't exactly jumping at the chance to run the pub either."

"Not by myself," Kathy admitted. "But I'm willing to help. Between the two of us, we've got years of experience at O'Sullivan's. Multi-dimensional whatevers aside, this is just another pub, right? We can figure this out. It would help if you'd stop panicking long enough to think straight."

Easier said than done, thought James.

Rudy rested his chin on his finger. "Kathy's right. You're not in this alone, James. And those are all very good questions. I know this is overwhelming, so let's take things one at a time. Let's start with setting up the pub. I know a thing or two about running a service business. I've got extra staff, and a few casuals I can call in to help at O'Sullivan's. If you and Kathy can train them on the bar, I can train you to manage them."

James tugged his hair. "I won't claim to be an expert at running the bar, but between me and Kathy we should be able to help them work the till and pour pints."

Kathy smirked. "Speak for yourself. I've been pouring pints since I was tall enough to reach the taps. You're the one who always got stuck cleaning glasses."

"Thanks for the reminder," James muttered, though a faint smile tugged at the corner of his mouth.

"I won't speak for her, but despite her misgivings, I know Moira will help out if you need. She's nervous about magic, but she was always loyal to your parents. If everyone pitches in, it will be enough to get you started." Rudy nodded. "One step at a time, James. You're not as stuck as you think."

James shook his head. That wasn't what he'd meant, but he knew Rudy was trying to be encouraging, so he let the thought slide for the moment. "As nice as it is for you to offer, I can't ask you to give up your time and staff to help us out, though. This is our problem to deal with; I don't want to be a burden on anyone."

"Nonsense. Your dad was good to me when I first arrived in Cuanmore. It'd only be right for me to return the favor."

James sighed. That did take a bit of the pressure off. If he *was* going to run the business, at the very least he'd have some help. But as his eyes wandered around the space, he couldn't help but feel like it wasn't enough.

"That's very kind of you, Rudy. But that only solves half my problem. What about this place?" James waved an arm at The Pint and Portal.

"Your father left the pub to you, and that includes The Pint and Portal. He wouldn't blame you if you decided to leave it closed. Hell, he knew he wasn't up to it without your mom. There's nothing to say you can't do the same as he had—keep the portals closed and focus on O'Sullivan's for the time being."

"For what it's worth," Liam chimed in, "that woman there, her name is Emma. She claims to have bartending experience. And those dwarves seemed ready to help as well."

"There are rooms above," said Tarvo. "There always seem to be enough for those who need. It's part of the pub's magic. If you're okay with it, they would be able to stay there as long as needed."

Dimensions. Portals. Dwarves. How was he supposed to make this sort of decision?

He looked at the newcomers who were leaning in together, talking among themselves at a table in the back corner.

"And what happens to them if I refuse?" he asked. "It sounds like wherever they came from has been ravaged by some sort of war."

Rudy's chest expanded as he inhaled a long breath. "If I'm honest, that's part of why your dad never reopened this place. It's hard knowing that you can't help everyone. There are far more problems out there that you can hope to solve. But if you're able to give them a space where they can forget their troubles, even for a little while, you've at least given them that."

"But if I decide not to reopen it, they all go back?"

"They've got to go somewhere." Rudy's gaze lingered on the table. "Even if you keep this place open, people will have to return home. No matter what's waiting for them there. But it also wouldn't be the first time people ended up taking refuge in another world. You've just got to be careful not to set a precedent. We can't let refugees from all over the multiverse start to migrate into our world. Or into each other's. This is a pub, not a train station. Your mother always spoke of a balance between worlds that shouldn't be disrupted. But it's a hard line to draw when you begin to care about the people who show up night after night. But that's not a decision that needs to be made today."

James took a long swig of his ale. It didn't matter how terrible the drink was—it dulled the edge of his nerves. Somewhat, at least. His thoughts still churned violently, crashing like waves against the sharp rocks of his mind.

There was too much to process, far too much to accept. This pub belonged to him now. He was supposed to run a bar that existed between dimensions. The absurdity of it all weighed on him, yet he couldn't shake the feeling that he had no choice.

He was stuck.

And being stuck was the one thing James had sworn he'd never let happen. It was the very reason he'd left Cuanmore in the first place.

"Balance?" Kathy chimed in. "How much difference could a few people make?"

Rudy hesitated for a moment, as though weighing his answer. "The ancients set up this place as a refuge for heroes and those looking to bring hope into their worlds. Think about that for a moment. What if someone who is meant to be the hero of the story decides life would be easier for them on another world? Or if the hero from one world becomes another's villain? These other worlds are quite different from each other. There's a natural order to each place and a path each one has taken."

"How do we know all this?" James asked. "Who are these 'ancients' and how do we know what they intended?"

"Your mother went to great lengths to try to uncover some of those secrets." Rudy gestured to the book James still clutched. "I see you have her journal. You'd do well to go through it and learn what you can."

"I just found it," said James. "I've only had a chance to read one entry."

Rudy nodded. "We made a lot of difficult choices back then. It's never easy sending a person back to a world filled with hardship."

"So what are we going to do about the dwarves? Do we allow them to stay?"

"Them being here for now won't hurt anyone," said Rudy. "If you're considering running this place and they're willing to help, you may as well take advantage of that. I'll chat more with Tarvo; maybe he can take me back to survey the damage on their world. Maybe there's something else we can do to help them."

James let out a sigh, his gaze falling on his mother's journal that he'd set on the table. He picked it up and turned its soft leather case over in his hands.

"It's a lot to take in." Kathy sat down and placed her own mug of ale on the bar top.

James nodded.

"But hey, you get the adventure you always wanted."

The comment snapped James out of his storm of thoughts. "Adventure? This?"

Kathy's face hardened. "If you would stop focusing solely on the negative, perhaps you'd see that."

James crossed his arms and leaned back. "It's hard to see the positive in any of this. All my life I've fought to get away from this place. I feel like a cat that's being dragged to a bath, and I can't seem to escape the stranglehold grasp around me."

"I've always said it'd be easier for the cat if they'd quit trying to claw their way free." Kathy set down her glass and leaned forward. "Maybe you're looking at this the wrong way. You're so focused on being in Cuanmore, in being back at your childhood home, that you're missing what's right in front of you."

"Which is?"

Kathy let out a short laugh. "James, bleedin' fantasy-world dwarves practically fell out of the wall! A woman with daggers taped to her hip is talking to Liam about working the bar. You've been drawing creatures for your stories and games for as long as I can remember. Now they're standing in front of you, and you're sitting in the corner having a good cry."

James uncrossed his arms but only to grab his mug. There was truth to what Kathy was saying. Though, part of him was fighting against it. Running O'Sullivan's was one thing. But this?

"If it's true that The Pint and Portal served travelers from different dimensions, think of the stories that will flow through here," she continued. "Ha'dran offered to do just that. You could experience something nobody else has been a part of."

He tried to see Kathy's perspective. Truly, this was all surreal, and was more than he could have hoped for. Did it matter that he had to move back to his childhood home to go farther than he'd ever imagined possible? Maybe he could have the chance to visit those worlds . . . to meet peoples and creatures he had known only as the stuff of fairytales and legends.

But that was just it. He wouldn't be visiting these places; he'd be stuck at the bar hearing about them.

Once again, he found himself stuck in his parents' pub, with no brighter prospects than the promise of a story of faraway lands.

James ran his hands over his mother's journal again, flipping over the pages. His mind was too distracted to focus on the words, but he knew within them lay at least some of the answers he sought.

"Why do you think they never told us?" he asked Kathy. "I mean, I know I haven't talked to Dad in years, but you saw him almost every day. How did this not come up?"

"I've been wondering the same thing myself," she replied. "Part of me thinks it must have had to do with Mom. He was never willing to talk about her, right up until the end. But realistically, how do you casually bring up that there's a magical pub on the other side of your storage closet?"

"Both of you were quite young when the pub was running," Rudy said with a distant look. "It wasn't right to get you all mixed up in this."

"It was one hell of a secret," James said and took another sip from his mug. "If he knew we were going to take it over eventually, he should have at least said something to us."

"I agree. But people handle trauma in different ways," said Rudy. "And there were valid reasons for him to shut the doors on this place. It was probably easier for him to not think of it again."

"Didn't help him much, did it?" James asked. "That's why O'Sullivan's suffered as well. Whatever hole was left by Mom chewed right through that portal. It slowly gnawed at him until there was nothing left."

"Well, don't let the same happen to you." Rudy replied.

It took all of his effort not to roll his eyes. The truth was, it didn't matter what he thought. He had no job, no savings. The only funds he had access to were tied to O'Sullivan's. He had to admit The Pint and Portal at least made the prospect somewhat intriguing, but still . . . that almost made it worse. James couldn't help but shake his head. He was right where he had never wanted to be—stuck in Cuanmore.

His gaze wandered again to the newcomers on the other side of the pub. Tarvo and Ha'dran had their heads together whispering. The red-haired would-be assassin, Emma, had spent a bit of time doing some cleaning, wiping dust from tables and chairs. But now she was seated again between the two dwarves. None of them looked any more certain of where they were than he was.

It was hard for him to sort through all the thoughts he had. This pub, Mr. O'Malley, his parents, his lack of job prospects, his lack of options.

Kathy was right about one thing, he was curious as hell to see what else would walk through those portals, and he couldn't have dreamed up anything as interesting as a gateway to other worlds in the back of his parents' pub. If he was stuck here, he may as well find out what other surprises it held.

He gripped his mom's journal and flapped it in front of him. "What the hell," he said. "I don't know the first thing about any of this, but I don't have anything else going for me right now either. If this pub was important to Mom, I'm willing to give it a go. If it doesn't work out, we'll shut it down. We'll get started first thing tomorrow."

James raised his glass over the center of the table. "To The Pint and Portal."

Rudy returned the gesture. Liam and Kathy did as well, though more hesitantly.

As the others joined the toast, he couldn't help but think he was making a huge mistake.

I've decided to make a record of our journey running *The Pint and Portal*. Every day is a brand new experience, and I want to keep track, for the sake of James and Kathy, of everything that we've experienced, and give them a guide for the day when they inherit this place. Hopefully by that time they've grown, and we've already been able to share these experiences with them in person, but life can be unpredictable, and should the worst happen, I want them to at least have a glimpse into this part of our lives.

I always struggle at where to start these things. A blank page is such an intimidating thing. I could start when I met Timothy, why the portals are so important to me, or how he first learned of it. But I think those are all stories best saved for a future entry.

The most important place to start is when we first took over.

Initially, Tim didn't want anything to do with *The Pint and Portal*. "What was wrong with O'Sullivan's?" he wanted to know. The local pub was filled with good people, enjoying good craic, and taking refuge from their everyday lives.

"That's what a pub should be for," he'd said, everyday people facing everyday problems. Not a bunch of adventurers who were fighting dragons, searching for MacGuffins, or rescuing princesses. How, as he put it, was he 'bleedin' hell supposed to relate to that?'

However, I think he always knew my thoughts were different on the matter. The magic of the ancients was important to me, as was the pub's purpose. *The Pint and Portal* was never just about pouring pints, or traveling through portals (see what I did there? I'm sooo clever). What it was about, at least to me, was ensuring that each of the men and women who came through those gateways had a place of safety where they could take a load off their shoulders, even if for a night.

These were people who had been tasked with saving entire worlds. What better, more honorable mission could we serve?

After much persuasion, Tim begrudgingly agreed on the condition that we don't involve the children, at least not until they're grown. There was no telling what kind of trouble could pass through those gates, and it makes sense. There is magic that's supposed to keep ill intent from entering the place, but I couldn't imagine one of them wandering through a portal while we weren't looking. We'd never find them again. Plus, they are not yet old enough to understand to keep things hush from those outside our circle.

So for now, we'll keep them in the dark, or at least keep the adventures we hear from our patrons confined to the realm of bedtime stories.

James

The scent of fresh bread and roasted coffee drifted up the stairwell, but it did little to lift the heaviness in James' chest. He trudged down the stairs, his thoughts clouded by what had happened the night before and what it all might mean for him and his future.

When he reached the bottom, he found Rudy already at the table, a steaming mug in hand. Seated next to him were Emma, Kathy, and Moira. The four of them were exchanging pleasantries, but it didn't seem like any of them were engrossed in their conversation.

"Where are the dwarves?" James asked as he sat. "And Liam?"

"Tarvo, Ha'dran, and Gloria are in The Pint and Portal," replied Emma. "They'll likely be staying there for the time being. It's as safe of a place as they've ever known and there's a comfort there that they're not in a rush to leave. Especially after what they just suffered."

"It was that bad?" James asked.

Rudy's voice lowered when he spoke. "It was. But that's a story that would be best told by them if they're up for it."

"There was pretty much nothing left." Emma shook her head. "It was amazing they had been able to figure out where the doorway was. It was surrounded by nothing but a pile of rubble."

"That sounds terrible," said James. "But who are the Tíogar Mór?"

"You've already heard some of the stories," Rudy said solemnly. "Your mother always enjoyed retelling some of the tales we heard in the pub."

James' eyes lit up. "I knew it! I'll be right back." He jumped up and ran back upstairs to his room, ignoring the bewildered glances of the others. His portfolio rested on the dresser in his room; he grabbed it and barreled back downstairs just as quickly.

James took one of the pages out of the folio and slapped it on the table, struggling to catch his breath as he spoke.

"Is this one of them?"

The paper on the table was one of his most recent sketches. It was a digital illustration, but he'd printed it off to include with some of the rest of his work. On the page was an anthropomorphic tiger he had designed for Apex Predators. The character was dressed in military fatigues and very much resembled some of the sketches that were pinned to the wall in his room.

Rudy nodded.

"I never liked Shay filling your heads with those old tales," Moira said.

"These Tíogar Mór destroyed Tarvo's world?" James asked, ignoring Moira. "Using magic?"

"Some believe magic," said Rudy, "others think they're using advanced technology. You'll hear conflicting messages depending on who you ask."

Moira grumbled. "Come on now, enough heavy talk. You need to get some food in you after last night. It will help you feel better."

She had set out a spread of fruits: sliced apples and oranges, strawberries, blueberries, and bananas. Alongside them was a bowl of dip and a plate of what had to be Rudy's pastries. James couldn't mistake the jam-filled croissants of his youth.

James' stomach grumbled as the intoxicating smells washed over him. He wasn't going to argue. "Well, we won't know unless we try."

He crammed a bite of croissant into his mouth and washed it down with a swig of coffee. It was bitter and sharp, but it was exactly what he needed.

"So, what have you all been up to this morning? You can't tell me you've been sitting around the table waiting for me to wake up."

"Moira arrived with food only now," said Kathy. "Emma only just got out here as well. Liam was helping me clean a few things up before he went back to the deli. Mostly we were dusting and clearing out some of the junk. If you're serious about giving things a go, I suppose we'll need to get things in order."

James surveyed the pub. Perhaps the shelves had a little less dust on them, but otherwise he didn't think he would have realized anything had changed.

Perhaps he was still too distracted by thoughts of the Tíogar Mór and of magic.

Real magic.

The thought sparked another idea. He mulled over what Ha'dran had asked of him. If he was truly considering opening The Pint and Portal, then it might be worth having someone who could perform on stage. He'd have to talk to the dwarf. Perhaps a show was exactly what they needed.

"I suppose, we better start making plans then. There's lots of work ahead of us if we want to make a go of running two pubs."

"So, that's it then?" Kathy asked. "Are we making a run at this?"

James let out a slow breath. "I'm too curious to just leave it all shuttered. But we can't run anything in this state. I figure we should take a week to get things ready."

"A *week?*" Kathy's eyes went wide. "You don't think that's rushing it?"

"Not at all," James said. "Sure, Dad let things go stale, but it's nothing a bit of elbow grease won't fix. We've got the bones of it here. Rudy's willing to lend us some staff and help us find a few more servers. Maybe we can get the dwarves in to help paint and clean up. We can maybe put out some flyers. And we'll need better beer for the taps, obviously. For now, I think we focus on making O'Sullivan's presentable."

"That's a good idea," Kathy said with a nod. "While we're cleaning, we can make a list of anything else we need to spruce things up."

"Exactly," James said. "Let's set up a tasting at a local brewery to replace the piss Dad was pouring. I'll make sure we've got good stuff on tap before we open the doors again."

Kathy smirked. "Oh, so you'll treat yourself to a tasting while the rest of us are scrubbing floors?"

James laughed. "I'll take my lumps, don't worry. But if we're going to make this work, we need decent beer. I'll happily suffer through a few pints of the good stuff for the cause."

Kathy rolled her eyes but smiled. "Fine, as long as you bring back something worth drinking."

"Liam, of course, will need to come along," James added, glancing at Moira. "If that's okay with you?"

Moira looked up as if pulled from deep thought. "What? Oh, yes, of course. Liam's going to be around here anyway. I'll keep him for some projects that need to be done around the deli, but otherwise, he's yours."

Emma perked up at the mention of Liam's name. "Construction and a deli?" she asked. "Sounds like your son has a lot of skills."

Moira smiled. "When we moved here from London, my

husband started a carpentry business. He could build just about anything. I opened the deli to give myself something to do. After his father passed, Liam took on smaller projects to help us financially. He didn't have to, but he likes to keep busy."

James turned to Emma. "You should join the tasting with us. Liam mentioned you wanted to be a barkeep, so it might be good for you to get a sense of the options."

"She doesn't *want* to be a barkeep; she *is* a barkeep. She just needs a bar."

The entire table jumped at the voice that seemed to emanate from nowhere, each of them exchanging uncertain glances. Except for Emma who dramatically rolled her eyes.

"Quiet!" Emma hissed. "You're not supposed to be talking yet! Everyone can hear you!"

"Oh, right! Sorry," said the voice. "There are so many rules with you humans, honestly. I suppose I'll be relegated to spending the rest of this trip in the back corner? Or perhaps this fellow will also give *me* my own show on stage? *Behold the great and powerful Demon Box!* I would find that most entertaining."

Emma stared at the small velvet bag that sat beside her on the table.

Everyone else leapt to their feet and stepped two feet back from the table. Each looked first to Emma then to each other in bewilderment.

"What the hell was that?" James' heart was still racing from the shock of a disembodied voice interrupting their breakfast.

Emma sighed as she opened the velvet sack, pulled out a black box, and sat it on the table. Several blue lights pulsed from its glass-covered surface. It appeared to be a cube, about the size of a basketball, which was covered with a touch screen or some sort of interface panel.

"This is Demon Box," Emma said and scowled as she looked toward it. "And it *isn't* supposed to be talking yet."

"Very nice to meet you!" the box chimed as the lighting danced along its surface, ignoring Emma's rebuke.

"What is it?" Moira asked. "Not magic?"

"I am a quantum accelerator," the box stated as though it were the most obvious thing. "Designed to travel through space and time. Your guide to strange new worlds and parallel realities. Please check that your hands and feet do not get caught on the edge of the portal, I am not responsible for any accidents that may occur."

Emma sighed. "Before I ended up on Tarvo's world, this was what I used to travel between different realities."

Moira gasped. "You're a shifter? You're not . . ." She squinted at Emma, stepping closer as if trying to see her for the first time. Moira lifted her arm as though she was going to reach out and touch Emma's face, but Emma caught it so quickly James hadn't even seen her move.

"*Don't* touch me," Emma said.

"You're definitely not Tíogar Mór," Moira whispered. James couldn't tell whether it was a question, or if she was trying to convince herself.

"Don't they look like tigers?" Emma asked dryly.

Moira hesitated for a moment before she nodded.

James stepped toward the box. "May I?"

Emma nodded just as the box said, "Oh, please do. I *love* being manhandled by strangers."

James wasn't sure whether or not to laugh, but Emma rolled her eyes and gestured a hand at him to proceed.

The box was cool to the touch, its surface was indeed made of some sort of glass. He picked it up, inspecting it. There was a heft to it that he hadn't expected. It surprised him as Emma had been carrying the thing around with seemingly relative ease. He was sure his arms would have grown tired had he done the same.

"Put me down!" the box demanded. "If you couldn't tell

before, I was being sarcastic. The last thing I want are your greasy fingerprints all over me. Do you know how hard it is to clean them off this surface?"

"It talks well enough. Is it alive?" James asked. "Or is it just a computer?"

"Demon Box is very much alive," said Emma. "And it couldn't always talk. It used to communicate with me telepathically."

James tore his gaze from the Demon Box to meet Emma's eyes. "Telepathically?"

"Yes, but I was the only one who could hear what it was saying. In fact, the professor who built it didn't know it was sentient until I came along. Before we parted ways, he installed a voice synthesizer so that they wouldn't have to rely on me to communicate with it."

"Yes, what a dreadful day that was," Demon Box said. "The windbag wouldn't stop peppering me with questions. Can you tell me why you're conscious? What's the first thing you remember? Does it hurt when I poke you with this screwdriver? Blah blah blah . . ."

James raised an eyebrow at Emma.

"Yeah, it didn't take long for the professor to regret that decision."

"Well,"—James set down Demon Box—"would it be rude to suggest we leave the Demon Box in the inn for the time being?"

A muffled noise, like gears grinding, expunged from Demon Box. "Now listen here! I've spent most of my life stuck in a closet. It's bad enough the bartender shoves me into that black cloth every time she goes somewhere. Like I'm being kidnapped and my kidnapper doesn't want me to see how I got to our destination but—"

Emma grabbed the device with a single swoop of her arm and tucked it back into its bag, pulling the drawstring tight. It dulled the voice but didn't mute it completely. "I think that might be preferred."

"That's not fair!" The muffled voice strained through the bag. "What if I shoved you into a sack every time I grew annoyed with you—which would be a lot, by the way! I'm pretty sure you'd have me dismantled for parts and thrown to the bottom of the sea. Nobody would put up with a malevolent sentient device!"

James grimaced. Maybe the device had a point. "Are you sure it's going to be okay in there?"

"Demon Box is mostly bluster," she said. "Besides, it decided to continue with me rather than go back to its home world with the professor who created it. So it has to live with the consequences of those actions."

"Hmph," Demon Box grunted. "Just remember that if you ever want me to take you some place nice. You thought the last world was bad . . . I've seen worlds where humans never existed!"

"I'd prefer if we can keep details about Demon Box to ourselves for now," said Emma. "I haven't told the dwarves yet, and I don't think Liam needs to know yet either."

James shrugged. He didn't see what the harm was, but it wasn't his secret to tell. "You won't get any argument from me," he said. "I imagine Demon Box will end up being the one to decide who knows it in the end."

The others nodded in agreement.

"All right," said Kathy, as she stood and began to clear dishes from the table. "This has been enough weird for me to take in the last twenty-four hours."

Emma reached over and put a hand on her forearm. "It may be weird," she said, "and annoying. But Demon Box has been the best and only friend I've had in a very long time."

Kathy stopped and met her gaze. James thought she was going to tear Emma a new one, but instead she simply nodded.

"You're right," she said. "That was insensitive of me. This has just been a lot to take in. I've never dreamed of there being other worlds, other beings that I'd only thought existed in James' comics. Talking computers and the like. It's going to take some getting used to."

James supposed she was right. If dwarves, talking boxes, and who knew what else would be coming through that portal, he would have to reevaluate his definition of normal.

James

The week had flown by in a blur of activity, leaving James both exhausted and quietly optimistic about their progress. O'Sullivan's was finally beginning to feel like a proper pub again. Liam had gone above and beyond, even repairing the old bar top and crafting new shelves that gave the space a more polished look.

Ha'dran and Gloria grumbled endlessly about the state of the pub—Ha'dran muttering about "human neglect" while Gloria went on about "wasted potential"—but they threw themselves into the work all the same. Together, they had scrubbed years of grime from the walls, patched up cracks in the plaster, and helped to add some greenery to the space.

James and Tarvo focused on cleaning up The Pint and Portal, though to be honest, once the dust and grime had been scrubbed from the floors, tables, and walls, there was little else to do in the magical space.

Once the dwarves had finished, Rudy stayed true to his word. He sent over a couple of his staff to help with the heavy lifting and to start learning the basics of the bar—at least, the parts James and Kathy could remember. That was, until Emma arrived and quickly proved invaluable to their training.

After realizing she was no longer needed in the bar, Kathy

spent most of her time in the back room ensuring paperwork and accounts were set in order.

The pub's transformation was undeniable. The floors gleamed, the walls were freshly painted, and the musty smell of disrepair had finally been replaced by the faint scent of polish and paint. It wasn't perfect yet, but O'Sullivan's was beginning to feel like a place people would be excited to visit.

Now all it needed was beer worth drinking, and James, Liam, and Emma were on their way to satisfy that need.

Cuanmore Harbour Brewing was both familiar and foreign to James. As they entered the brewery, James grasped for faded pieces of memories that itched the back of his mind but came up short. Though the smells brought him back to days of picking up beer orders for his parents. Back when they served a good local Irish brew instead of whatever bog water his father had decided to serve since.

As he entered, the warm, yeasty scent of freshly brewed ale hit him, mingling with a faint tang of salt air that seemed to seep in through the cracks of the old stone walls. The brewery had a rustic charm, with timber beams overhead and walls adorned with nautical trinkets—coiled ropes, faded maps, and a polished ship's wheel mounted near the bar. A row of gleaming copper brewing vats lined a separate space that was enclosed behind glass behind the bar, their polished surfaces catching the dim glow of the hanging electric lanterns.

The floors, worn smooth by decades of footsteps, creaked under his boots as he crossed to the main counter. On the wall to his left, shelves displayed rows of dark green and amber glass bottles, each with labels of previous brews, showcasing the long history of the establishment.

Like most places in Cuanmore, the brewery had been around for ages. Not as long as O'Sullivan's, but long enough that it had become an integral part of the community.

For a moment, he stood still, taking it all in. The place felt alive. It was the kind of spot that welcomed wanderers and old friends alike, offering comfort in every corner.

Then he spotted the brewmaster. Adam Murphy was only a year older than James, the two knew each other in grade school, but James would have sworn the man hadn't aged one bit since he'd left.

"Well, if it isn't James O'Sullivan." Adam wiped his hands on a towel and reached out to shake James'. "I never thought I'd see your face back in Cuanmore."

"Neither did I, if I'm honest," James said, returning the gesture. "Though you're looking as good as ever. It must be all that stout keeping your youthful looks. Or have you made a deal with a fae creature?"

Emma went into a coughing fit, like she was choking on something she swallowed.

"You okay?" Liam rested a hand on her shoulder. James wasn't sure if that helped or made things worse as Emma turned a deep red, bordering on purple. She lifted two fingers, signaling that she needed a moment.

When she'd composed herself, she replied. "Yes, I'm okay." There was a question in her eyes, and James wondered if it had something to do with his comment about fae, but this wasn't the place to ask. Not in front of Adam. They couldn't be dropping hints about the portal around the other townsfolk. His parents had kept the second bar secret, even from their own children, for good reason. He wasn't about to change that anytime soon.

"You haven't even tried the beer yet," Adam smirked. "I promise you it's not that bad."

That earned a polite smile from Emma, and a chuckle from Liam.

"You're looking pretty decent yourself, James," Adam continued. "I'm sorry to hear about your da." He dropped his head slightly, with a worried look in his eyes that suggested guilt for not expressing the sentiment sooner.

A pang hit James' chest at the reminder. "It's okay." He lifted a consolatory a hand. "You know my dad and I weren't close. I'm sorry to hear about yours as well. I'm sorry I hadn't had the chance to say anything earlier. I haven't been back here in quite some time."

""Tis all right," Adam said with a forced smile. James could have sworn there was a tear in his eye though. "It's been a few years. The first one was the toughest. He always spoke highly of yours. I know Tim hadn't been the same since your mom died, but from everything my da spoke of him, he was a good man. Just one with a broken heart."

A different twinge flickered within James at that. He tried not to dwell too much on it. Was it guilt? He shook it off and decided it was time to change the subject. "If that were the case, he wouldn't have ever stopped serving your stuff. I still don't know what he's switched to, but it's bleedin' awful."

Adam smirked with tightened lips as though he wasn't sure whether he should laugh or not. "There were no hard feelings between us," he promised. "Times have been tough. The light faded from him, then from the pub, and so the customers stopped coming. He made decisions to keep the doors open. But you were there for a lot of it, you know how things were."

James shook his head. "I am learning that I honestly don't. I knew things hadn't been the same as they were growing up, but I had no idea it had gotten so bad since I left. Kathy knew more, but it seems he was keeping things even from her."

Liam snorted at the understatement.

If Adam noticed, he didn't show it.

"We're hoping we might do a tasting," said James. "Emma here's going to be the head barkeep." He almost added "of The Pint and Portal" but caught himself. He'd have to be more careful. "We'd like to start pouring your beers again. But it might be good to know what our options are."

Adam's face lit up. "I'd be happy to give you a volume discount. Give old O'Malley a run for his money."

James nodded. "I'm not opposed to a little friendly competition."

"Hah! Friendly. I said nothing about O'Malley being friendly. Thorn in your side is more like it."

James didn't want to get into O'Malley's conduct just yet. There was still a chance he'd need to take the old man up on his offer. "Well, what have ya got that we can try?"

"I've got a few right now that are on regular supply with enough volume to source out. Then I usually try to have two or three different beers that rotate seasonally. If you're willing to preorder in volume, I can make sure I've got enough to consistently have a couple seasonals you can keep on tap."

Adam reached behind the bar and pulled up a few trays of small tasting glasses. "I'm assuming all three of you are sampling?"

They all nodded, and Adam poured the first glass.

"I don't know what you have tried from us in the past, but since Da passed, I've done a lot of tinkering with our recipes. Tried to modernize them a bit. I still keep our mainstays unchanged, don't want to anger the regulars, but most of what we're trying today have been my recipes."

"That's what I like to hear," said James. "I want to have a few options that maybe our guests won't find elsewhere."

Adam smiled as he pulled the tap, and a yellow golden liquid poured into the tasting glasses.

"The lightest of these is our Shannon Sunset Pale Ale," said Adam. "It's fairly traditional, but it's got a touch of citrus and floral notes to it. It's our most popular brew, and kind of our 'new' flagship, if you will."

The Shannon Sunset Pale Ale glistened as the brewery lighting hit it. Floral notes wafted to James' nose. As he lifted the glass, new aromas of grapefruit and sea brine struck him.

James was surprised that it wasn't off-putting but instead was like the crisp morning feeling of walking along the shoreline.

Intrigued, he took a sip. Juicy tropical notes filled his palate, with the addition of citrus and light sea salt in a wave that danced along his tongue.

"This is incredible," James said. "You're not kidding that you've been playing with recipes."

A grin painted across Adam's face. "These aren't our fathers' beers."

Emma was staring at her pint glass, a puzzled look on her face.

"Something not quite to your liking?" Adam asked.

Emma startled as though she'd forgotten where she was and looked up at Adam with the same confused look. "No, that's not it. This is actually incredible. I'm not sure I've tasted anything like it. Do you do anything special to it?"

"Brewmaster's secret." He winked. "Now, let's move on to our Coastal Shadows. It's got a bit of citrus to it, which is unusual for a dark lager, but it complements the smokiness quite well."

Adam took three new tasting glasses and pulled a dark brown brew into each, setting them down in front of his guests.

"This isn't a stout?" Liam asked, holding his up to the light.

"Not yet," Adam said. "That'll come later. This is a smoked porter, and one I'm particularly proud of."

James grabbed his tasting glass and took a sniff. It was filled with aromas of roasted malts, caramel, and toffee. He took a sip, and smooth and robust flavors filled his mouth, coating his tongue with rich and sweet malt, and a hint of caramel. The porter carried a whisper of smokiness, like wood burning in a distant fireplace.

"You brew all of these yourself?" The way Emma spoke the words suggested there was an unasked question.

"I have a team of staff," Adam answered. "But I oversee each brew. There's a certain bit of magic I add myself."

Emma's head tilted slightly. "Is it something you learned from your father?"

"It's actually what separates these brews from what he did," he replied, but this time it was a little more cautious. "You seem to know your way around beers? Have you been in the industry? Is there something specific you're wondering about the process?"

"I've had a lot of beer, from a lot of different places." Emma flashed him a cunning smile. "I'm always curious about the process, and this is quite . . . unique."

Adam smiled. "That's what I aim for."

James had to agree. Though he didn't have the same breadth of experience as traveling to other worlds like Emma, he'd sampled a lot of craft beers across the United States, Canada, and Europe. He didn't think he would have noticed until Emma had pointed it out, but these beers *did* feel different. The quality was hard to explain, and it was more of a feeling than a tasting note. Each sip he took gave him a comforting feeling. As though he were drinking a warm hug. Like he was coming home.

Whatever it was, Emma had picked up on it quickly, and it left him wondering if he was just imagining things.

The three continued sipping, comparing their tasting notes. Both beers were ones he'd be happy to serve.

"Finally, the Night Stout."

Adam studied the third tap for a moment, hesitating. A smile touched his lips for only a brief second before a more pensive look crossed his face. He nodded to himself and instead of pulling the tap handle he crossed the space behind the bar toward a single tap that rested against the far wall. "Actually, since you're friends of the family, I'm going to let you try something I've been working on. It's still a variation on the Night

Stout, but I've played with the recipe a bit. I'm calling it the Nocturne Speciale, at least for now. Let me know what you think."

Instantly, James realized where Liam had gone wrong in calling the porter a stout. This brew was thick and creamy, and he could smell the notes of chocolate and coffee from where he sat.

"Shouldn't we taste them both so we can compare?" Emma asked.

"Sounds like you're trying to drink more," Liam jested.

Emma lifted a hand to her chest, opening her mouth in mock offense. "Who, me?"

All of them laughed.

"Don't worry," Adam said. "It'll only be fair to let you try both. So far, I've only shared this with close family and a few friends. It's a limited run. I'd probably have enough for you to carry a small amount at the pub, but it wouldn't be for long. It's got an ingredient that's a little hard to come by."

Adam pushed the glasses forward.

"We've really emphasized the sea salt on this one. The stout's natural caramel flavors give it a strong sea salt caramel taste on the palate. There's a balance of sweet and salty that took a long time to master. But it's like desert in a glass."

James took a sip. It was rich and velvety, the coffee and chocolate that were on the nose translated into the taste as well, with the addition of a lingering note of warmth of toasted oats. There was also an earthy note that reminded James of roasted mushrooms. Similar to the last two beers, the stout had a cozy aspect he had a hard time pinpointing. But he got the distinct sense that he was being wrapped in a warm blanket on a cool night. As though he were sitting in front of a fireplace enjoying the brew.

He closed his eyes, and the scene changed around him. Suddenly, James found himself sitting in a ski lodge. He knew he was still at the brewery, but there was another part of him that was more than convinced that he had just returned from a long day of skiing. An air of smoked cedar accompanied the notes of chocolate he'd been smelling with the stout. A fireplace crackled on the side of the room against a stonework wall that climbed up to the wooden ceiling. A fluffy gray rug lay in front of the fireplace that matched the heavy woolen blanket draped over him. Even though he didn't think this was the memory of a particular night, he knew this place well. He'd been here many times after ski weekends at Whistler. But it was more than a memory . . . it felt as though he were really there.

He could feel the warmth of the fireplace, the fibers of the blanket on top of him, vividly hear the crackling of the flames.

It was so real, for a moment he wondered if he had been here all along and Cuanmore had been the dream. He sunk deeper into the plush chair, feeling the cushions around him. That certainly made more sense. Here there were no portals, no dwarves, no magic.

He smiled at the thought. But he knew it was a passing fancy.

He opened his eyes. Blinked, trying to shake off the vision. But nothing changed.

A part of James began to panic, but it was a distant part of him, one that was far away in another place. Here at the ski lodge, there was nothing but comfort and relaxation.

A few more moments passed, and the ski lodge vanished as quickly as it had appeared. The comfy chair, the fireplace, the smell of cedar, all faded like a dream, and he was back at Cuanmore Harbour. The only remnants of the vision that remained were the smells emanating from the glass of stout he held.

Adam, Liam, and Emma were all standing around him, just as they had been a moment ago.

"What the blazes was that?" he said out loud.

"Pretty incredible, isn't it?" said Adam.

"Incredible? Was that real? I was transported someplace else entirely!"

Adam blinked in confusion.

Emma had a wide-eyed look that James was sure mirrored his own. Whatever that was, she had experienced it as well.

"It kind of takes your breath away, doesn't it?" Adam said.

Liam had a blissful look on his face, his eyes still half closed. He opened them fully and took a look at his glass. "Now that *was* exceptional. Makes me think of some of the good times we had as lads when we were younger. How is it that a beer can remind you so much of something from your past?"

James exchanged an uneasy look with Emma. The bartender shook her head slightly. Judging by the look in her eye, somehow, she knew what he saw. Or at least that he saw *something*.

He gathered she wanted him to keep it to himself.

But why?

Maybe so we don't sound completely bonkers.

"You look confused, James," said Adam. "Is something the matter? The few people who've tried this so far say it invokes a sense of nostalgia. But universally it gets positive feedback."

James gave Emma one last look and set his glass down. "I've never had anything like this before," he said. "It caught me off guard. Nostalgia, yeah, that's a good way to describe it. Something about it must have stirred up memories of my father."

Adam's face softened. "I'm so sorry, James." His mouth moved, searching for the right words to say. "I can see how that would be hard for you."

James raised a palm toward Adam. "Don't worry about it. The taste though, it's just incredible."

Emma

Magic.

There was no doubt in Emma's mind that magic had been brewed into the stout Adam had served.

She was back behind the bar of The Pint and Portal, getting the last of her prep done for the big opening. She'd sliced as many lemons and limes as she could before the citrus stung the callouses on her fingers. Syrups and herbs were all laid out and ready, and all the glassware had been set up and put in place.

There were still a few things she needed if she were to make the drinks she wanted, most notably a coffee machine. But there was plenty of time for that still.

The pub looked so much nicer than when she had first arrived. Gone was the dust and the grime that had coated everything. Gloria, Ha'dran, and Tarvo had done a great job in getting everything cleaned up and ready to go.

Soon James would walk into the pub, pull the lever that allowed the portals to access the tavern, and declare them open for business. She didn't know if there would be anyone who entered the pub at all. It had been closed for so long, would anyone come? It wasn't as though there were some inter-dimensional 'Open' sign that let people know they were back in business.

For the moment, none of that mattered. All she could think about was that stout.

Emma eyed the small keg from Cuanmore Harbour that they'd agreed to stock. They'd taken kegs of each of the beers they'd sampled, and an additional ale for good measure.

Most of Adam's beers spoke to her through her magic, just as she'd grown to expect from any alcoholic drink. Sometimes drinks didn't tell her much. There was nothing glaringly obvious that this ale wanted fixed. It was perfectly balanced, with the right amounts of hops, sweetness, and flavor to be content. That was rare in any world, but if she had been surprised, it had been pleasantly so at the brewmanship it revealed.

But she could *sense* that much at least.

It was Adam's experimental stout, the Nocturne Speciale, that was unreadable. And that bothered her.

Unlike most alcohol, the stout was silent and it refused to listen to her. She couldn't whisper to it to improve its flavor—though she had to admit, she didn't have to, it was nearly perfect already. But for the first time since she'd discovered her ability, she couldn't use it.

There was no doubt in her mind that some sort of magic had been used.

What she didn't know was if Adam possessed the magic himself—maybe a similar ability to hers. Perhaps he could talk to the beer and give it superior qualities. Perhaps he was able to cast a spell on it to make its drinkers *think* it tasted as good as it was. Maybe his magic was what prevented her from using her own. Or was there something else happening?

But the flavors and aromas of the brews, or even her inability to use her magic, weren't the strangest things about the beer.

James had felt it too. Emma had seen it on his face as soon as he came out of whatever trance the beer had put over them. But Liam didn't seem to have been affected in the same way. At least, he hadn't reacted at all the way he should have if he'd undergone the same hallucination—if that's what it was.

The stout had transported her. It was more than the nostalgia Adam had claimed. Was it a hallucination? She didn't think the beer had been laced with any sort of drug. But in the same way Demon Box transported her to other worlds, the stout had given her a glimpse of what had to have been another reality.

In it, she had been sitting at a candlelight dinner with Liam. Every part of her ached as she recalled the exchange. It had felt so . . . so *real*. He had looked lovingly into her eyes, in a way he'd never done in real life, not in any reality. Their table had been set up in what she could have only described as a magical forest. Fireflies had danced around them as his dark eyes bore into her. He had been enraptured by her.

She allowed herself to relive the blissful not-memory. How his rough and calloused hand grabbed her own, the eager look in his eyes that told her he wanted more. Not in the joking or crass way that the Liam in her world would often portray. This was a sincere, desperate, longing. Like he wanted to drink her in and would never be satiated.

Wherever she had been transported to couldn't have been real, despite it feeling as tangible as when she'd been awake in any world. But for that moment, at least, she had believed she was really there.

Regardless, she wasn't able to dive into the stout to find out why it behaved that way. It was as though an impenetrable film had been cast over the drink, and it pushed back on her magic, forbidding her to explore its secrets.

"I think we're about ready to go, don't you?" Emma jumped, jolted from the memory as Gloria stepped to the bar, oblivious to the fantasy she was interrupting.

The dwarf must have come downstairs while Emma hadn't been paying attention.

"I didn't mean to scare ya!" Gloria chuckled. "I was sure you heard me walking around. It's not like I'm exactly stealthy."

"Sorry, I was lost in thought," said Emma as she composed herself. "I'm just getting the last few details ready. How are you feeling?"

"As good as I ever have. Amazing what a few nights in a warm bed and a full belly will do. But ready or not those portals will be opening soon, and we'll be faced with whatever comes through."

Whatever comes through. The statement hit Emma like a box of empty whiskey bottles.

Was this really safe? The idea of someone nefarious stepping through lingered in her mind. Worse still was the thought of inadvertently allowing access to the portals and the worlds they connected to, with no way to stop it.

Gloria's face contorted in concern. "Hey now, Tarvo's told me that during all the years he had visited this place, nothing overly dangerous came through one of those gates. Plus, I've seen you handle those knives; I think you'll be able to protect yourself and us. And Tarvo might be gaining in years, but you better bet that he can still handle that axe of his. So don't start crying on me or nothing."

Emma's eye twitched at the insinuation. "Excuse me? I was a witch hunter for most of my life. I've hunted monsters you probably couldn't imagine. I am *not* going to cry."

Gloria shrugged, as she wiped at an already spotless countertop with her cloth. "Then quit worrying. This won't be anything we can't handle."

Emma swallowed. In truth, she didn't know why she was so nervous. Between the beer and the pub, something was making her uneasy. It wasn't the guests, those she could handle. There was something else.

"I don't know if I trust them, either." Gloria's words were a near whisper. So quiet that Emma wasn't even sure if she'd heard them correctly.

"What do you mean?" she asked.

Gloria looked surprised. Almost as though she hadn't realized she'd said the words out loud. She shook off her confusion and continued wiping the bar top.

"The look on your face. I know when someone is having doubts," she said. "I just . . ." She stopped the nervous cleaning, put a hand on her hip and looked at Emma. "There's something funny about all of this, isn't there?"

Emma did her best to keep her face neutral. Was the dwarf having doubts about James and the others?

She had to fight her first instinct to argue; she wouldn't learn anything that way. Perhaps if she played along, she could learn something. She painted as innocent of a face on as she could. "You feel it too?"

Gloria looked around the pub cautiously, as though checking to ensure the two of them were alone. Demon Box rested at the end of the bar, but he'd been quiet since she'd returned from the tasting. Emma wasn't going to do anything to disturb that peace. Though, she'd maybe have to ask the device if it had learned anything while she had been out.

Unless one of the humans had told her, the dwarf wouldn't have any way of knowing the box was sentient.

"There's something not right here," said the dwarf. "They might have Tarvo fooled, but I wasn't born yesterday, you know?"

Emma paused, weighing her words. Perhaps she could get a better sense of what the dwarves had been whispering to each other. "What do you suppose they're planning?"

Gloria set her foot on the narrow ledge that ran along the edge of the bar and leaned over. "I dunno. But I keep wondering if these humans are going to let us stay here?" she said. "We've been stranded here, plus they make us work for free? What if we decide we don't want to? Are they going to send us back to that wasteland?"

Emma frowned. "They've given us a place to stay and put food in our bellies. I'd hardly call that free."

"Aye, that's true, but then we're practically prisoners, aren't we? Tarvo says it's best if us dwarves don't venture out into the world beyond O'Sullivan's. Says we'd be best to stay away from places other humans can see us."

"You have to realize it's not as simple as opening the portal and heading into their world," said Emma.

"Why not?" Gloria huffed. "There's nowhere else for us to go."

"Do you think it would be easy for you to blend in?"

"Bah!" Gloria waved a hand. "I don't care what anyone else thinks of us. We won't bother nobody. We can mine the caves and hunt and fish the same as any of them can."

Emma had to hold back a smirk. "That's the problem. You don't know the first thing about what's out there." Part of Emma would have loved to see Gloria's reaction to the technology that existed in the world they were connected to. She knew the first time she'd seen any of it, it seemed to be nothing short of magic.

"Wait until you see the chariots that drive without horses, or the metal birds that fly them around from one city to the next—across oceans! They have boxes that tell them anything they could want to know, let them see any part of the world at any given moment. They produce lights at nighttime that don't get hot and never burn out."

Gloria paused, for the first time her hardened exterior dissolving. "Tarvo said their world doesn't possess magic. How could those things be possible?"

"They have an understanding of the universe that our

worlds have only begun to grasp. If Tarvo is to be believed, the Tíogar Mór didn't use magic either, and you saw what they managed to accomplish. The destruction they caused."

The dwarf furrowed her brow. "That raises another point. These humans plan to let anyone, from any world, come through those gates?"

"Same as any other bar," Emma said evenly, wondering where the dwarf was headed with this line of thought. "Anyone can walk in off the street."

"What if the Tíogar Mór walk through? They'd kill us all then take over the portals. They'd have access to other worlds."

Emma studied Gloria's face. Her large eyes were pleading with her. She was afraid. After all she'd seen in her world, Emma supposed it only made sense.

"From what Tarvo has told me," she said, "the Tíogar Mór can already travel between worlds. Why would coming to this place give them any advantage?"

That was the wrong thing to say. Gloria's face immediately hardened. "You're right," she said, shaking her head. "How silly of me. I sometimes let my imagination run wild. I just fear that others would suffer under those tiger bastards."

From what Emma could tell, Gloria was being honest about that at least. "Listen, I know that what they did to your world was horrific. I was there. I traveled through miles of devastation before I found you, Ha'dran, and Tarvo. But Tarvo seems to think that whatever ancient magic built this place won't allow for any with ill intent to travel through. It's meant as a place of refuge, and the door will only appear to those in need of respite."

"Tarvo is an old fool." Gloria nearly spat the words, but her eyes widened as soon as they left her mouth. "Sorry, I didn't mean that. Tarvo's a kind soul. Though, I hope not so kind that he trusts the wrong people."

To Emma's left, the portal leading back to O'Sullivan's

warbled and hummed, distracting Emma for a fraction of a second while James strolled in, rolling in one of the kegs Adam had dropped off. It was long enough for Gloria to stroll away, obviously finished with the conversation.

Emma eyed the dwarf, whose back was now toward her. What was she hiding?

Emma

After James helped Emma replace the beer kegs, there wasn't much left to do but plan some cocktail recipes for opening night.

The Pint and Portal was filled with the aroma of citrus cleaner. Emma wondered why the world connected to the pub insisted their cleaning products smell like food. It was nice to have a clean space to work in, but she hoped the scent would dissipate enough so that it wouldn't affect the drinks.

Smells fine to me, Demon Box chirped silently.

That's probably because you don't have a nose. Emma rolled her eyes.

Tarvo had disappeared somewhere with Rudy. Meanwhile, Ha'dran and Gloria sat bent over a table toward the back, whispering to each other. A couple of times Ha'dran grunted in discontent and Gloria sat dazed.

What do you suppose they're planning? She sent the thought to Demon Box. *I didn't like the direction Gloria's questions were headed when we were talking earlier.*

I have been meaning to mention, Demon Box said, *that I caught a whiff of a conversation earlier. I didn't hear the entire context—they were just walking by—but Ha'dran didn't seem very happy. Gloria was attempting to calm him down. All I could make out was that he said something to the effect of "going to burn the whole place down."*

Emma stopped what she was doing to stare at the box. "And you're only telling me this now?" She'd said the words out loud without thinking. She shot a glance toward the two dwarves, but they were so immersed in their own conversation they didn't appear to notice.

You haven't exactly been spending a whole lot of time with me this week, Demon Box said. *Though to be fair, if you were with me, I doubt they would have been talking close by me at all. They always seem to be on their own, whispering like they are now.*

Emma shook her head and risked another glance at their table. It seemed like a pretty damning statement. She'd have to tell James. Though there was the possibility they had been talking about something completely different. She didn't know Ha'dran well enough to assess if he might have said something offhand in jest.

Gloria had said something odd earlier to me as well, something about how she doesn't trust the humans here.

Of course, she didn't really know any of them either, but she realized early in her journey that she had to trust that people have the best intentions at heart, or she'd end up miserable and alone. That meant sometimes people would disappoint you, but the friends she'd made along the way had been worth it.

Right now, the only person she had known long enough to truly trust was Demon Box, and it wasn't a person at all so maybe that said something.

And yet, I'm the one you shove into a sack and leave behind when you go gallivanting around the city.

The box had a point. *If I promise to take you with me more often, can I get you to listen in on more of their conversations?* Emma asked silently.

Oooh, a spy mission? That sounds delightful and naughty.

Emma couldn't say she loved the idea of spying on her new friends. But their behavior was rather peculiar.

It's probably nothing, but I can't take the chance that they'd do anything to sabotage the pub. If something happened that I could have helped to prevent, I'd feel absolutely horrible.

Understood. Agent Demon Box reporting for duty. Put me in, coach. I'm ready.

I can't exactly carry you over there now, said Emma.

Sigh.

Emma rolled her eyes as Demon Box actually *said* sigh instead of attempting to imitate a sighing sound.

If only the Professor had provided me with wheels as I'd requested.

You won't get an argument from me. I'm the one who has to carry your heavy ass everywhere.

Hmph. Do you want my help or not?

Emma smirked. *You know I'd be lost without you.*

She thought it sarcastically, though she knew it was absolutely true. Not only did she depend on the little device to travel from one world to another, she'd grown emotionally attached. If the damn thing couldn't read her mind, she'd never say it to its face.

Well, it's nice for you to finally admit it, Demon Box quipped. *Now, haul my heavy ass over there. I've got official spy business to attend to!*

Not so fast. It will be too obvious if I drop you off beside them. We'll have to wait. Keep an eye on them from a distance as best you can for now, let me know if they do anything suspicious. But for the sake of the gods, be quiet about it.

Demon Box beeped but said nothing more.

Emma couldn't focus on Ha'dran and Gloria right now; she had to get ready for opening night. She reviewed the list of drink specials she had planned for the evening. Of course, she'd make anything that was ordered—assuming she had the ingredients. But these three drinks were what was on special, and she wanted them to be just right. She still needed a few ingredients to finish them off, but she had no doubt James or Liam could get them for her.

As Rudy had hinted, the bar seemed to provide whatever alcohol she needed. Whatever magic the space had been imbued with kept the bar well stocked.

It was like a dream come true. Any other ingredients, it seemed, she'd need to pull from elsewhere.

She'd decided to narrow the options down to three drinks. She had written out her ideas on a pad of paper she'd found behind the bar and stood back, assessing the drink options she'd chosen.

The first on the list was a take on an espresso martini, but she'd add gold flake to the drink as something extra special for opening night. She didn't want to just call it "Espresso Martini" though, so she erased the name.

"I'll call this one the Opener," she thought out loud. "If we don't allow it to get too sweet, it will fit the bill."

We still need coffee. So far, she hadn't found a machine to brew it.

She crouched down and began opening cabinet doors, but there was nothing that looked like it might have been a coffee maker of any kind. "Oh, this won't do."

"Is there something I can help with?"

She jolted upright at the sound of Liam's voice, standing so quickly that she nearly lost her balance.

How was it possible that this man was even better looking than when she'd last seen him? His dark hair shined in the magical light of the pub windows, and his brown eyes seemed to see right through her.

She must have waited too long to respond; that boyish grin

formed on his face, and he raised a questioning eyebrow. "What?"

"Oh, sorry," she said, scrambling to compose herself. "I seem to have a hundred different things on my mind. What I was looking for was a coffee maker. Ideally an espresso machine."

"You want a cup of coffee?" Liam asked. "I can grab you one from O'Sullivan's." He turned, as though he was going to hop through the portal right there and then to grab her a cup.

"Oh no!" she said, perhaps a little louder than necessary. "I don't mean for me. I would like to make a drink for the bar that has an espresso base to it."

It was only then that Liam looked down at the list of names she had on her pad.

"Listen, I don't mean to criticize, but I don't think this menu is going to do well. Opening Night? Wayfarer's Rest? Did James put you up to this? He's always talking about those fancy Vancouver drinks. I hate to break this to you, but I don't think you'll be selling any of these here."

Emma blinked. Was Liam questioning her menu? Though, the old Liam would have done the same. Always thinking *he* knew the best way to track down and slay whatever magical beast was wreaking havoc on a village. Or the best way to do practically anything.

"Oh?" she asked, with sass dripping from her voice. "And *why*, pray tell, would that be?"

"Look." Liam lifted his hands defensively. "I don't mean this to be insulting. I'm sure you make great drinks. I'm just trying to help. Take those dwarves for example, what are they drinking?"

Emma couldn't help but glance toward Gloria and Ha'dran, still leaned in together conspiratorially. She gritted her teeth at Liam's condescension and muttered, "Ale."

"Exactly! People aren't coming here expecting anything

more than ale and maybe wine. These drinks might do well in Dublin, but here? They just want a good pint. Hell, most pubs in these parts won't serve you anything but a good stout, and we've got a range of options from Adam on tap."

Emma glared daggers at the man. "Did you want to run the bar?"

"I wasn't trying to—"

"Look, if you want me to be here, let me worry about the drinks. If these don't sell, they don't sell. That's part of what this is about. But not everyone who comes through those gates will be dwarves or backwoods beer swingers. I've kept bar in countless worlds, so I think I have a pretty good grasp of what I'm doing. You can either help me get an espresso machine and the other ingredients I need, or you can get out of my way."

Liam tilted his head as though surprised by the buffet, but to his credit he didn't argue further. "Very well," he said. "I'll leave you to it." He made his exit through the portal.

Emma had to exhale several slow and steady breaths to calm her nerves. "Ale and stout," she muttered. "As if the only thing worth drinking is beer."

She tried to put Liam out of her mind for the moment. There was still a lot of work to do.

Emma found an old chalkboard leaning behind the bar. "This is perfect," she thought out loud. She proceeded to hang the board up on a pillar beside the bar and began to write down the drinks she'd come up with.

Opening Night Specials

1. The Opener – Espresso Martini with gold flake

2. Classic Tipperary Cocktail - Whiskey, vermouth, sweet chartreuse

3. Wayfarer's Rest - Rum, coffee, cinnamon, and maple syrup

Emma stopped to examine the menu items and only then realized that she had two coffee-based drinks planned. That was fine by her, as long as she could get that coffee maker. She would also need to find cinnamon and maple syrup.

She took a deep breath. Perhaps making the Tipperary Cocktail would take her mind off her argument with Liam. It was a simple drink that would give her a chance to breathe. Plus, she could provide a sample to the dwarves and gauge their reactions. It would be the perfect way to prove him wrong.

Only ale my arse.

Tipperary Cocktail

Ingredients:

- 1 1/2 ounces whiskey
- 3/4 ounces green chartreuse
- 3/4 ounces sweet vermouth
- 2 dashes bitters
- Orange twist for garnish

Directions:

1. Add Irish whiskey, green chartreuse, sweet vermouth, and bitters into a mixing glass with ice and stir until well chilled, about 25 rotations.
2. Strain into a chilled coupe.
3. Express the oils from the orange twist over the glass and serve.

Ingredients:

- 2 ounces dark rum
- 1 ounce cold-brew coffee
- 1/2 ounce cinnamon syrup
- 1/4 ounce maple syrup
- Dash of cocoa or walnut bitters
- 1 cinnamon stick
- Orange peel for garnish

Directions:

1. Prepare Cinnamon Syrup: Combine equal parts water and sugar in a saucepan. Add a cinnamon stick and heat until the sugar is dissolved. Let it cool and remove the cinnamon stick.
2. In a mixing glass, combine dark rum, cold-brew coffee, cinnamon syrup, maple syrup, and a dash of cocoa bitters.
3. Add ice and stir until well chilled and diluted.
4. Strain the mixture into a chilled coupe glass.
5. Express an orange peel over the drink and drop it into the glass.

Emma

"I tracked down an espresso machine for you."

Emma had barely stepped out of the backroom of O'Sullivan's when Liam came huffing through the front door of the pub, straining under the weight of a black and silver contraption cradled awkwardly in his arms.

"You . . . you what?" She hadn't even realized Liam had gone looking for one. When she'd told him to 'help or get out of the way' she'd assumed—quite reasonably, in her opinion—that he was opting for the latter.

His shoulder muscles bulged with the effort. They weren't as massive as the monster hunter's she'd once known, but something about the way they flexed made her pulse quicken.

She swallowed and rushed forward to help. Grabbing one end of the hulking machine, her hand brushed his in her haste. Sparks. That was the only way to describe the jolt that shot through her, lighting up her skin and sending a fluttery warmth straight to her stomach.

Goodness, woman, get a hold of yourself. You're not a schoolgirl.

She grunted as Liam shifted some of the weight to her end. It was heavier than it looked, and despite him bearing half the load, her arms strained under the awkward bulk.

"Thanks," he said, nodding at her, seemingly oblivious to whatever storm had ignited in her chest. He let out a relieved sigh, the strain easing from his face now that she had taken part of the burden.

"Where did you get this?" she asked, as they continued to move toward the storeroom.

"Rudy was here, and I mentioned you were looking for one. He had an extra that they never got round to setting up. He says we can have it."

"Rudy saves the day," Emma said, unable to keep the smile from her face.

"If he really wanted to be a hero, he could have helped to carry the thing."

Emma laughed. "He's a bit old to be lifting stuff like this, isn't he?"

"Don't ever let him hear you say that," Liam warned with a smirk. "It won't matter how many daggers you've got tucked away in that outfit."

Emma's eyebrow lifted. She'd known her fair share of grizzled old men—most were more bark than bite. Rudy, however, didn't strike her as one of those. That was more Tarvo's persona. No, Rudy was more like a cuddly bear . . . but sometimes those were the ones you had to stay on the good side of.

"He's tougher than he looks, is he?"

Liam nodded, all hints of amusement dissipating. "Rudy is the kindest soul you'll ever meet. You think he's giving this espresso machine as a special favor to me? Or James?" Liam shook his head. "He'd give the shirt off his back to anyone he saw in need of it. But don't mistake niceness for weakness. He doesn't like to talk about it, but he had a rough go of things before he came to Cuanmore. It made him as tough as nails, and he'll fight for those he cares for . . . and he doesn't like being reminded of his age."

Emma nodded. Most people didn't, especially as they felt their bodies slowing down.

"Well, still,"—steering the conversation away from Rudy—"that's no excuse to throw your back out."

Liam grunted. "Then how about less chatter and more getting this thing behind the bar?"

Emma had grown accustomed to the weight, and the two carried it through the portal to the second bar and set it down behind the counter.

"Thank you for tracking this down," Emma said once the machine was set up. "I realize it's not standard for most pubs."

"I'm sorry for giving you a hard time about it," Liam said, lifting a hand to scratch the back of his head. "James put you in charge of drinks, so if you want coffee and fancy cocktails, it's not my place to stand in your way. I was thinking about it, and truth is, you're right. Not everyone coming through that thing will be dwarves. Hell, I can't even believe there are living, breathing dwarves that came through with you. I shouldn't have shot down your drink ideas without letting them have a chance."

"Thank you." A thin smile creeped across her face. She let her gaze linger on him. It was still so hard for her brain to reconcile that this wasn't the same man she used to hunt magical monsters with.

"You know . . ." She swallowed. She'd tried so hard to push the memories down, but staring Liam in the face made it so incredibly difficult. "I understand how hard it is to see things through someone else's eyes."

"What do you mean?" Liam leaned on the bar, his dark eyes fixed on her.

How Emma had missed those eyes.

She tried to pull her thoughts together, but every time she tried to put what she felt into words, it either sounded wildly incoherent or wholly inappropriate. Her Liam had worked by her side, hunting down those whose only crime was possessing magic. But this Liam? What would he think of her? She'd ruined lives. She'd *ended* lives. She didn't deserve compassion from this man.

He couldn't know who she really was. Not yet.

"It's not important," she said finally, brushing the thought aside. "I'm sure there will be plenty of surprises for us in the coming days."

Liam's gaze drifted toward the portal that had brought her and the dwarves here. "To be honest, I'm not sure if it's something I'm going to get used to. I can't wrap my mind around all of this and what it means."

Emma frowned. Earlier, he'd sounded so sure of himself, almost eager to take it all on. Now there was a crack in that confidence, a hesitation she hadn't expected.

"That's a shift from earlier. Are you starting to have second thoughts about helping James run the place?"

Liam sighed. "Part of me can't believe James didn't bar up O'Sullivan's door the moment he found the portal. He never wanted to run O'Sullivan's. Never wanted to be stuck in this small Irish town. Even as kids, he wanted nothing more than to see the world and have adventures. He doesn't see it yet, but what grander adventure could there be than this?"

Emm could understand that sentiment. Once upon a time, the very idea of a portal to another world had been nothing short of magic.

"This might be the perfect place for someone who never outgrew the stories of his youth," Emma replied. "But I didn't ask about how James felt about it. I asked how *you* felt about it. You don't seem as fazed that there's a doorway to another pub in the closet of O'Sullivan's."

Liam shrugged. "I suppose I always figured there was more to the world than what we could see. The stories people tell, especially in Ireland—I always assumed magic has been here all along, just beneath our noses."

Emma raised an eyebrow. "I wouldn't have pegged you as someone who believed in magic. You strike me as someone more practical."

"Practical doesn't mean closed off." Liam smirked. "Some people would rather everything be explainable by ordinary means. But what's the fun in that?"

For a moment, Emma dared to allow herself to hope that maybe Liam would be accepting of her abilities. Did she dare open herself up to that possibility?

"I'll help out where I can," Liam continued, cutting through her thoughts. "I'm glad to have James back. His family helped my mum out more than I'll ever be able to repay. That's all that matters."

Emma got the sense he wasn't going to say more on the matter, so she let it rest.

"You weren't completely wrong though," she said. "People will expect us to have beer on tap."

"Thanks to Adam, we have a few options," he said. "Now let's see what you can do to give us some more options. Why don't you let me try one of those 'Opener' drinks?"

"Who knows," said Emma, "maybe you'll want to serve these on the other side of the portal as well." Emma stepped behind the bar and pulled out a martini glass. "Watch and learn," she said, grabbing a few ingredients from the shelves.

She frowned as she looked at the espresso machine. "Normally we'd use cold brew, it'd be much better. But espresso will work in a pinch. I'll prepare some once we're done so it'll be ready for tonight."

She brewed a quick shot, letting the dark liquid pool in a small cup before pouring it into the shaker. "Not quite the same smoothness as cold brew, but no one will notice once the glitter hits."

Liam leaned against the bar, arms crossed. "I'll admit, you've got me curious. I'm looking forward to seeing how this turns out."

Emma grabbed a small plate and drizzled a thin circle of corn syrup on it, then reached for a jar of glitter. She was impressed both had been behind the bar when she needed them. "First," she said, tilting the glass toward him, "you coat the rim. It's mostly for presentation—it makes the drink feel a little more special."

She dipped the edge of the glass into the syrup then carefully pressed it into the glitter, coating the rim.

"All right," Liam said, nodding. "I'll admit, that does look cool."

Emma arched an eyebrow. "Just wait." She grabbed a cocktail shaker and began adding the ingredients. "Two ounces of vodka," she narrated, pouring it in, "a shot of chocolate liqueur, one of coffee liqueur, and an ounce of coffee."

She shook the cocktail vigorously, the sound of ice clinking against metal filling the room.

After about twenty seconds, Emma set the shaker down and strained the golden-brown mixture into the prepared glass. The liquid settled smoothly, catching the light glinting off the glittered rim.

"Now for the magic." She caught herself and swallowed. "This isn't real magic, of course."

Liam's eyebrows twisted in confusion, but he didn't question her.

Emma pushed past her flustered feelings and grabbed a small jar of edible glitter. *Of course he wouldn't think it'd be real magic. Why did I say that?*

She mixed a pinch of the glitter with a drop of water in a tiny spoon, creating a shimmering suspension. Then, she swirled it gently into the drink. The liquid began to shimmer, tiny flecks of light swirling like stars in a nebula. This time she did reach out with her magic, just a touch, telling the drink to brighten the sparkle a bit.

Liam leaned closer. "That's . . . actually impressive. It looks like it's alive."

Emma grinned and reached for a bar of dark chocolate. She grated a few shavings on top of the drink, the curls landing lightly on the surface. With a little flourish, she slid the glass across the bar to him. "There you go. The Opener."

Liam picked up the glass and studied it for a moment before taking a sip. His eyebrows lifted as the flavors hit his tongue. "Damn," he said, setting the glass down. "That's really good."

Emma crossed her arms with a satisfied smirk. "It's smooth, a little sweet, with just enough bite from the coffee to keep it interesting. Perfect for someone who's looking for a drink that's different from beer or whiskey."

Liam took another sip then glanced up at her. "I'll admit, I didn't think you'd win me over with this glittery nonsense, but you've got something here."

Emma's smirk softened into a smile. "I'll take that as a compliment."

Liam tilted his head, raising the glass slightly in a toast. "To the Opener, and to whatever other surprises you've got up your sleeve."

Ingredients:

- 2 ounces vodka
- 1 ounce chocolate syrup or liqueur
- 1 ounce Kahlúa or coffee liqueur
- 1 ounce cold-brew coffee
- Edible glitter (for garnish)
- Ice cubes
- Chocolate shavings or cocoa powder (for garnish)
- Light corn syrup (for rimming the glass)

Directions:

1. On a small plate, drizzle corn syrup. On a second small plate, spread glitter.
2. Dip the rim of the martini glass into corn syrup, then into the glitter to coat the rim.
3. In a cocktail shaker filled with ice, combine vodka, chocolate liqueur, Kahlúa, and coffee.
4. Shake vigorously for 20 seconds.
5. Mix a small amount of glitter with a bit of cold water or simple syrup to create a glitter suspension.
6. Strain the cocktail into the prepared martini glass.
7. Slowly pour the glitter suspension into the drink, stirring gently.

8. Sprinkle a bit more edible glitter on top of the cocktail.

9. Optionally, add a few chocolate shavings on top.

James

James strode in through the portal, a bottle of sparkling wine in one hand and a tray of champagne glasses and what appeared to be a saber balanced carefully in the other. Liam and Kathy trailed behind him.

"Gloria," he called out as he navigated toward the bar, "could you get Ha'dran and Tarvo? I'd like to make a toast before we open the gateway."

Gloria nodded and scurried up the stairs, her eagerness suggesting she was either trying to be helpful or looking for an excuse to disappear.

"Can I talk to you for a moment?" Emma said, beckoning to James.

James handed the tray to Liam and Kathy. "I'll saber this once everyone's here, if you could get the glasses ready, and put the bottle on ice."

They nodded and got to work as James followed Emma a few steps away, far enough to be out of earshot.

"Is this about the beer at Cuanmore Harbour?" he asked. "I've been meaning to talk to you about that ever since we left, but with everything going on, I haven't had a chance. What the hell was that all about? It dwas as if I was transported to another . . ."

Emma held up a hand. "It's not about that. We probably *should* discuss that too, but there isn't time right now." She glanced toward the stairwell. "Demon Box overheard Gloria and Ha'dran having a heated exchange."

James reflexively looked toward the stairs then back to Emma. "About what? Did he . . ." James stumbled over the pronoun. "He?"

"Demon Box prefers to be referred to as 'it.'" Emma smiled appreciatively. "It didn't catch everything, but it did hear them say the words 'burn this place to the ground.'"

James pursed his lips. "That could be concerning, but it's hardly an uncommon expression. In fact, I'm pretty sure I had that exact same thought when I first arrived back from Canada. Are you sure he wasn't blowing off steam?"

"Normally I'd agree, but Ha'dran is a fire mage," said Emma. "He could be very capable of acting out such a threat. Plus, despite Demon Box having a flair for the theatrics, I don't think it would have brought the statement up if there wasn't some concern."

Emma continued, keeping her voice low. "Gloria also seemed to want to confide something in me. I played my hand wrong, and it caused her to back off. But she called Tarvo an old fool."

James nodded and lifted a hand to scratch his head. "So, do you think they are untrustworthy? We're kind of relying on them to help us for now, at least until we can get more staff. And we are sticking our necks out by keeping them here."

"That's part of what Gloria seemed upset about—that they're essentially trapped here. But I suppose as long as they're not venturing out into your world, they'll be where we can keep an eye on them. Hopefully that'll discourage them from doing anything rash—if they're planning anything at all."

"I appreciate that," James said. "Thanks for letting me know."

Footsteps echoing from the stairwell mimicked thunder rumbling.

"One thing I can say about dwarves," Emma added, "they don't step lightly."

———

James held a bottle of champagne in one hand, and a saber in the other. Was he really doing this?

Last week he had been sitting at home behind his laptop and a bag of Cheetos, minding his own business. Now he stood here, somewhere that was also nowhere. A pub that was between realities. His hands trembled slightly—he hadn't really tried to process that one yet. Never mind that he now was also seemingly having to deal with mind-altering pints of beer, a sentient, smart-ass computer that had the ability to travel through dimensions, anthropomorphic tigers terrorizing other worlds, and dwarves who wanted to burn the whole thing down.

Maybe they should. Then I can be rid of this nightmare.

His eyes met Kathy's questioning stare, and he wondered if somehow she could read his thoughts.

Sure, why the hell not? Everyone else had their secrets. Maybe she does too.

The inheritance, he reminded himself. He was doing this so they could split their inheritance. But surely they could split insurance money just as easily?

Of course, insurance wouldn't likely cover a building that existed outside of time and space—maybe he was out of luck on that one.

How the hell is any of this real?

He understood how he had ended up inheriting O'Sullivan's and being convinced to run it. That made sense to him. But The Pint and Portal? It had pretty much all spiraled out of his control, and here he was—holding a bottle of champagne, ready to celebrate its re-opening.

He cleared his throat; he had to rein his thoughts in, lest he spiral into a panic attack.

The dwarves, despite their arson-inspired leanings, had followed Gloria back downstairs. Rudy came down with them. The baker had a youthful glow as he stood behind Tarvo. Though nearly two feet taller than the dwarf, he looked perfectly at ease with their arms around each other.

Gloria was another matter. He wasn't sure if she was scowling, or if dwarf resting-bitch-face was especially bad.

Ha'dran was as unreadable as a stone. He stood with his arms crossed, but James would have sworn he was more nervous than anything. The dwarf was set to tell a story this evening. James insisted he didn't need to stay on stage for long. Ha'dran had said he wanted to do something to wow the audience. It was opening night after all; he wanted to make an impression.

Now the dwarf's fingers twitched, his weight shifted from side to side. Ha'dran had already shown that he possessed some form of magic—the ability to wield fire. James wondered how smart it had been to invite someone to perform magic, *real* magic.

I'm standing in a freaking magical pub. I'm surrounded by real magic.

Three pairs of dwarf eyes, and three pairs of human eyes met his. He stood there for a moment in a daze.

All eyes were on him, and he realized that his companions were waiting for him to say something.

"Err . . ." James stumbled.

What was he supposed to say? That he'd been brought here by forces outside of his control, to somewhere he'd never wanted to be, to do something he wasn't even sure was possible? It didn't matter what side of that portal he stood on. It seemed his fate was tied to Cuanmore, and everything was crashing in on him.

The thumping of his heart was so loud compared to the silent anticipation of his friends that he was sure everyone else could hear it as well.

Suddenly, all the air had been sucked from the room. He felt himself waver as the edges of his vision darkened and a churning in his stomach threatened to reveal the contents of his supper.

"It's all right, James," Rudy said. The man didn't move from his space beside Tarvo. But through his clouding vision, James could make out the creases of concern on his face. On *all* of their faces.

"Those of us here are your friends." Rudy raised a hand, finger pointed up with intent and shook his head slightly. "No, that's not right. We're *family*. We don't need a fancy speech. We all know this wasn't your first choice. Never mind the shock of learning of magic, dwarves, and portals. This was a legacy passed on to you by your father. And even though you weren't close, it still must be tough having lost him and having to face all of this without his guidance. But you've also discovered there was a side of your dad that you never got to know. One that you can never ask him about.

"I knew your dad a long time. He was a good man, and both he and your mom used this pub to help not just me, not just Tarvo, but many humans, dwarves, elves, gnomes, and all sorts of folk who walked through those portals in search of a pint of ale and a break from whatever reality they came from."

James lifted a hand to his cheek and was surprised to find it damp. Emotion overwhelmed him, and tears flowed freely. He fought to keep his composure, holding back the urge to completely break down.

He allowed Rudy's words to sink in and wrestled the reality of where he stood with the man he'd always thought he knew.

This was his father's legacy, and the man hadn't bothered to tell him about it when he was alive. He and Kathy were about to open portals to other dimensions, and his father had neglected to provide an iota of instruction, details, or advice. He had to rely on Rudy and Moira, and one of them didn't even want to open the damn thing.

His tears weren't from sadness—they were from anger.

He slumped down onto a barstool and breathed deeply.

For as long as he could remember, he wanted a real adventure. He had wanted the stories that his mother told him to be *real*. He never thought he'd get his wish, but he'd always assumed he'd at least be able to get *away*. Away from O'Sullivan's. Away from Cuanmore.

Everyone was still focused on him, a salvo of pity accompanying their gazes.

James cleared his throat and straightened. He didn't want their pity. There was no use in feeling sorry for himself. He had no other options, it was true. But he had made the decision to see this through, and he was going to do the best damn job he could.

Rudy was right about one thing. Everyone in this room, whether man, woman, or dwarf, had offered to pitch in to help him pull everything together, and for that he was grateful. Heck, even Moira, though not present at the moment, had agreed to help wait tables, despite grumbling about it.

James sniffed and cleared his throat. It might have been overwhelming, but he pushed through, knowing he was capable of more than he believed possible.

"Thank you all for everything you've done this week. I know it feels like we're flying by the seat of our pants. In most ways we are. Each of you has helped me to bring this pub and O'Sullivan's back to life. Rudy especially, you've basically been at our beck and call all week, providing us with staff, equipment, and advice."

Liam cupped a hand to his mouth to amplify his voice. "Don't forget the sweet buns!"

Everyone laughed.

"I have no idea what is about to come through those gateways, and I don't even know why I'm here at all, but I appreciate you having my back. If there's one thing I know, it's that I wouldn't be here without all of you." He felt the weight of his mother's journal in his back pocket and pulled it out.

"Maybe Mom and Dad didn't tell us about this place, but Mom seemed to think it was pretty special. Rudy seems to think it's special. Maybe it is. Maybe that's enough. My life seems to have given me no other options but to be here. But I appreciate you taking a chance on me, and I know my parents would as well."

James lifted the wine bottle and the saber, pointing it away from his friends. Whatever his misgivings, he was going to mark this occasion.

With everyone around him, for the first time since he'd returned to Cuanmore, everything felt as if it might be okay.

Stories of the Tíogar Mór are getting more frequent, and the pub's magic seems to be getting more erratic. I can't help but ponder that the two might be related.

I'm also ashamed to admit that I sometimes wonder if Tim and Moira are right, if we should close this pub and never speak of it again. But any time I think on what that means, on everything that The Pint and Portal has done for us, my heart mourns for the blessings that we would have never received without it.

We've all gained so much happiness, and we've helped so many people. Those we hold dear are only here because of this magical place. But if the portals were to fall into the wrong hands, I'm afraid everything might be lost for all our worlds.

Moira has insisted that the wards might not hold against their magic. Or worse: they might be attempting to siphon magic from the place for their own purposes—maybe even to weaken the wards. We have no confirmation that they possess magic. Yet with the recent power fluctuations, sudden breezes, and malfunctioning equipment, it's hard to argue. But Rudy and I are of the same mindset. The pub has been here longer than any of us could possibly know, and so far, its magic seems to know what it's doing.

This pub has brought so much good into our lives that I feel we must honor Tim's family legacy, if not for him, then for James, Kathy, and their children. The Pint and Portal must always be a haven for those of us who were lost, and a home for those of us who have been found.

I have been both, and I don't think it's fair to withhold that gift from others who might need it.

Part Two
The Pint and Portal

James

James had the honor of pulling the lever on the far side of the wall. He wondered how often during his formative years this switch had been open, allowing people from all sorts of worlds to roam on this side of their portal, steps away from his home, and he had been none the wiser. What sort of stories would his father have been able to tell him if he'd been willing to open up and share them with his own children?

A now recognizable hum erupted from the lever's box and filtered through the rest of the pub. It was not unlike turning on the lights in a gymnasium filled with old fluorescent lighting.

The seven of them stood in silence, expectantly watching the wall where the portals might soon open. Gray brick stood guard in silence.

"What if it's been too long?" Kathy asked. "What if they've all forgotten the pub is here?"

James shifted his weight. "Would that be the worst thing in the world?"

Rudy chuckled. He sat down and took a long sip of his ale. "They'll come."

His eye caught the chalkboard filled with drink specials. Perhaps he should start by learning some of the drinks Emma had dreamed up.

"Maybe while we wait Emma could show us one of the drinks she's concocted? It'd be good for us to know what we're serving up anyway."

"Don't you need to man O'Sullivan's?" Kathy asked. "I think one of us should be there."

"Rudy's staff have it under control for now," James said. That was part of the plan at least. "I'm sure they can manage pouring a few pints."

Kathy looked unconvinced.

"I can go," said Liam. "Make sure they don't need anything."

James caught a surprising flash of disappointment in Emma's eyes. Maybe he should allow those two to spend more time together.

"No, Liam," James said. "Stick around. It'll be good if you learn more of Emma's drinks so we can serve them in O'Sullivan's as well."

Emma was good at concealing her emotions, but James still caught the glimmer of excitement that sparked in her eye. Though he couldn't be sure if it was because Liam was staying or because she got to show off her mixology skills. Either way, she tried to mask it by slipping behind the bar and pulling out the barware she needed.

"That's fair enough," Liam said. "She already showed me how to make the Opener. It wouldn't hurt to learn a couple more. I can show the staff after. We can serve these cocktails in both pubs—give the Cuanmore residents something a little more special as well."

Emma shot a grin in Liam's direction from behind the bar.

There *was* something brewing between those two.

Each of the dwarves heaved themselves up onto the bar stools.

Kathy's gaze shifted from the wall where the dwarves' portal had appeared and back to the one that led to O'Sullivan's. "If it's all the same to you folks, I think I might head back. That paperwork isn't going to finish itself. And despite my faith in Rudy's staff, I'd feel better if one of us was on the floor."

Ha'dran, Tarvo, and Gloria let out loud noises of disapproval. Liam and Rudy joined along with quieter, but no less emotional, *awws*.

"You should stick around, Kathy." It was Emma who put the protest into words. "It's opening night, and you've been as much a part of this as anyone here. It would be good if you would celebrate with us."

Kathy took a longing look at the portal. She'd never been one for socializing, and James could tell that she was ready to call it a night before they even got started.

"We'd love it if you stuck around, Kath," he said. "But it's your decision. We'll all be here if you change your mind."

Kathy nodded slowly as she contemplated what to do. "Well, if it means that much to you, I'll stay." She bit her lip as though convincing herself of the decision. "At least to see if we get any customers."

The words had barely left her mouth and the lights dimmed slightly. A blue disc expanded onto the platform and wind swept through the pub. Leaves trickled out of the portal's mouth first, and James wondered if absolutely anything could wander through. What if wildlife followed whoever opened the gateway? He then remembered the orb that was the key to the doorway opening, and that relieved his worries slightly.

The eight stared at the portal, all eager to see who or what might be arriving.

"Hah! We're going to scare them away if we are all staring at them like this." Rudy lifted his beer mug to his mouth and swiveled in his stool slightly, but he didn't take his eyes off the portal either.

They waited for what felt like several minutes, but in

reality probably wasn't even sixty seconds. It was like they were watching for a pot of water to boil.

The workings of the portals were beyond him, their rules and limits still unclear. He hadn't yet figured out how far people traveled to reach the pub or what might happen if the gate closed too soon. There was so much about this inter-dimensional pub he'd inherited that remained a mystery. He wished he'd had more time to read his mother's journal. Inside of its pages might be the answers he sought.

Just as James was about to ask how long they should wait, three dazed-looking humans emerged from the portal and strolled through. Two women and one man, all clad in bronze-plated armor layered over thick, quilted clothing, as though prepared for both battle and cold weather. They were all shorter than he was but not as short as the dwarves. Bands of metal that encircled their temples like protective crowns and rose to a diamond-shaped plate on the front were inscribed with a peculiar symbol.

Each of them looked at their surroundings with confusion painted across their faces. The man looked back to the gateway, clearly baffled by the experience they'd just underwent.

I understand that feeling all too well, thought James.

It was only then that he realized, as the pub's owner, he should probably greet their first customers. He set his glass down and stepped toward the new arrivals.

Rudy followed behind him, hanging back, allowing James to take the lead.

"Welcome to The Pint and Portal! My name is James. I'm the owner." He outstretched a hand—he didn't know what else to do to greet these folks. But the woman looked down at his hand and frowned, almost with disdain.

"What is this place?" she asked roughly instead of taking his hand. The woman's accent was thick, and not quite like anything James was familiar with. Danish perhaps but not quite. "We found this orb at the back of an abandoned pub. It opened this portal, which led to . . . another pub?"

James nodded. "This is The Pint and Portal," he repeated. "It's a place of refuge for weary travelers and those in need. It's hard to explain, but we see visitors from many worlds."

At least we plan to.

The other woman grabbed the orb from its place in the wall and the portal winked out behind them. The three gasped. The man reached for a sword strapped to his back.

"Don't worry!" said James. "It closed because you removed the orb. You'll be able to reinsert it and return home whenever you'd like."

If they had to explain this to every patron who came through the gates it was going to be a full-time job in itself.

The man grabbed their orb from the woman with his free hand, looked at it with a frown and put it into a small leather satchel that hung from his belt. Like his companions, the man had a pale complexion and a small nose. His bushy eyebrows were light and blended into his light-colored skin, along with his thick mustache.

"I am Kira," said the woman at the front. She stood tall, her bronze-plated armor gleaming in the pub's dim light. The diamond-shaped plate on her headpiece was larger and more intricately inscribed than those of her companions. Similar to them, a fur-lined cloak was draped over her shoulders. Her gaze swept over the room before turning to those who had entered behind her. "These are my companions." She grabbed the second woman's hand. "This is Fredja, and he is Vidar. We are Sky Riders. We've ridden our dragons from the north in search of a magic that might help us in our fight against the Eastern Skraelith and their wyverns. They've been attacking our kingdom and are far too powerful for our dragons to counter."

Dragons, wyverns, riders, magic. James had to refrain from rubbing his temple. After the dwarves, he'd realized he needed to be prepared for just about anything to come through that gateway, but that was easier said than done.

"Please, have a seat," said Rudy. "We'd love to hear more about your travels."

The riders looked at each other skeptically then to the empty pub before them.

"We've just reopened," said James. "You're our first customers, so your first round of drinks is on the house. After that it's pay what you can."

They all sounded pleased at the sound of free drinks and didn't hesitate to move to the table where Rudy now stood.

"I'm interested," said Rudy, once the riders were seated, "if you were riding dragons, how did you manage to find the abandoned pub?"

It was a good question, and one James wouldn't have thought to ask. Not while his mind was still processing that these people were freaking *riding* dragons. Were they actual dragons? Or was it a name of something else?

"When you say . . . dragons," James blurted, not giving them a chance to answer Rudy's question. "You mean *actual* dragons? Like giant flying lizards in the sky?"

Kira and Fredja exchanged an uncertain glance. "Yes of course," Kira replied. "Surely you have dragons in this territory? Even if they are mostly wild?"

It was James' turn to share a glance with Rudy.

"That's a bit complicated," said Rudy. He went on to explain, very briefly, the pub and how it worked to the riders.

By the time he was done, their eyes were as wide as dragon eggs. Or at least the size James imagined dragon eggs would be.

"I knew it," Kira said, pounding her fist on the table. "This is where we'll find the magic we need."

"Uh," Rudy raised his hands. "It doesn't quite work that way. Think of this place as merely a pit stop on your journey. A pause in your story, if you will. We don't typically allow our guests to travel between worlds, nor to send each other artifacts. We don't want to become an inter-dimensional marketplace, nor to interfere with the conflicts any world may be experiencing."

"But this could be the key to defeating the wyverns once and for all!" Kira's voice rose with urgency. "Our ancestors spoke of tapping into magic from other realms—this is how we reclaim that power."

It certainly hadn't taken Kira long to accept the many worlds theory. Though, James supposed, if you were accustomed to riding dragons and wyverns, perhaps all other types of magic were more easily digestible.

"If you can learn something from one of the other patrons," Rudy said, raising his hands placatingly, "that's one thing. But this is meant to be a place of rest and respite. Each guest must fight their own battles."

James made a mental note to speak with Rudy about these rules. If his parents had established them, he wanted to understand their purpose—and if there were others he needed to know about. But if the rules weren't their doing, they were likely generational, passed down through the years as part of the pub's long history. Still, if following them meant turning away something that could help these people defend themselves, he wasn't sure he could justify that.

Fredja and Vidar started to protest, but Kira held up a hand to stop them. "We are Atlas Sky Riders. We are people of honor. If these are your rules, we will abide by them while we are in your realm. But if there is any way that we can gain knowledge that will help us, we will seek to do so."

Rudy nodded, satisfaction settling in his expression. Fredja's fingers drummed once against the hilt of her sword before falling still, her gaze fixed somewhere beyond Kira. Vidar exhaled sharply through his nose, his shoulders rising. Without a word, the two inclined their heads in a reluctant gesture of deference to their leader.

"So, if I may ask," said James. "If you were scouting the area, how did you find the gateway?"

"We'd been flying hard for nearly two days," said Kira. "But as good as our mounts are, they still need to rest. When we stopped, our companion Hector went off in search of supplies. He left three days ago and never came back. We went to search for him and happened to stumble upon an abandoned village and this pub while looking for him. We stopped inside hoping we'd find something that might still be drinkable. That's when we came across the orb and the doorway."

"We came through the portal hoping he was here," Vidar said. "But you said we were the first?"

"The dwarves came in a couple of days ago, but otherwise no one else for a very long time," said James.

Vidar cast his gaze downward but nodded as though it was what he'd expected. If any of the riders were surprised at the fact that a trio of dwarves stood before them, none of them showed it.

Of course, thought James, *they've got dragons, so why not dwarves?*

"We'll resume our search after a bit of respite here," said Kira. "Hector is resilient. If anyone can survive the unknowns of this terrain, it will be him. There is not much we can do now that night has fallen. It's better that we rest."

"We do have available rooms upstairs if you want to stay the night," said James. "Let us know and one of them can freshen them up for you."

"Nay," the woman said. "We need to camp close to our dragons in case the wyvern attack. We should have a few hours, but I don't want to be away longer than that."

"Can't your dragons fly? Wouldn't they be able to escape without you there?"

"Without us there, they might wait longer than is safe. We are bound to them, and if one of them is slain in an attack, we would lose our purpose."

"You've gone through a lot to try to find your companion." Rudy rubbed his mustache between his thumb and forefinger as though considering something. "You must be close."

"Hector and I are bonded," said Kira. "Much as we are bonded to our dragons. Connected through magic and fate. There cannot be a closer connection between two people. Beyond that, we're also tied to Fredja, Vidar, and their dragons through our pack bond. This connection strengthens our group as a whole, and it's only through this bond that our dragons will communicate."

"So you can sense where Hector is?" asked James. He had to admit his head was getting a bit turned around.

Kira gave him a questioning glance like he'd said the dumbest thing ever. "No, of course not. I *can* tell that he's still alive. But I'll admit, since we arrived here, the bond does seem extremely faint. But if we have traveled to a magical realm, as you claim, that would be expected."

Before James could question her further, Emma appeared at the side of the table alongside Gloria.

"Sorry to interrupt," she said. "But you were all promised drinks. This is Gloria, she'll be serving you tonight. My name is Emma, I'm the bartender. I wanted to introduce myself to start the evening off, and see if you'd be interested in one of our special drinks, on the house?"

Emma

Emma surveyed the dragon riders seated at the table, their gazes flicking toward her with a mix of curiosity and hesitation. She hated to interrupt their conversation, but they seemed a little unsure about being the first patrons in the bar. First impressions were everything, and if they left without a drink, she'd never get the chance to win them over.

The table eyed her expectantly. She'd memorized the drink recipes she'd planned for opening night, but none of them seemed quite fitting for this group. As she considered her options, the drinks behind the bar began to whisper to her—a soft hum at the edge of her senses.

It had taken her a long time to grow accustomed to alcohol speaking to her like this. Awkward to talk about, sure, which is why she rarely did. But she'd come to realize it wasn't so different from a fire mage speaking to flames, or a sky sorcerer bending the wind to their will. For some reason, she had the ability to connect with drinks—hear their voices, craft their recipes, even improve or manipulate their qualities at a base level.

Right now, those whispers told her these dragon riders needed something unique, something more personal.

"You asked if we wanted a special drink," said Fredja. "What did you have in mind?"

Emma smiled. "I have a recipe that I think might suit you and your companions. I call it a Sky Rider's Ascent. It's got floral and botanical notes with a bit of sweetness. The recipe is uniquely tailored to your group."

Kira and Fredja exchanged thoughtful glances, but Vidar merely scoffed. "A drink that tastes like flowers? No thanks."

"Vidar!" Fredja scolded. "You can't criticize it until you try it!" The Sky Rider's smile sweetened as her bright blue eyes met Emma's. "He'll have one as well. Thank you for the honor."

Vidar grumbled, staring at the table. "Yes, fine. I'll try one, but it's not what I would typically order."

Emma raised her palms in a gesture of reassurance. "If you don't like it, I won't be offended. I'll be happy to bring you a glass of whatever you prefer after, but I think you might be pleasantly surprised."

She turned to Kira. "And one for you as well?"

"Uh," Kira hesitated, her fingers tapping lightly on the table. Emma caught a flicker of uncertainty in the woman's otherwise confident posture. "I don't want to offend you, but I do not drink alcohol. I'm sorry."

Emma paused for a split second, horror filling her thoughts.

In all her years working in pubs, very few had offered non-alcoholic options. Water, maybe coffee or tea if you were lucky. But there was one pub she'd worked in that had done something different. They'd called them mocktails—mixed drinks without the alcohol.

They were just as flavorful as cocktails, but they didn't come naturally to her. Alcohol was the part of the drink that spoke to her, the part she could control. Without it, she had to rely on her palate alone. She'd practiced over the years, but in the mad rush of preparing for opening night, the thought of alcohol-free options hadn't crossed her mind.

"I'm the one who should apologize!" said Emma. "I'm afraid I don't have a large selection of non-alcoholic drinks to offer. Could I interest you in a coffee?"

"I would definitely take a coffee if you have some," replied Kira, her steady demeanor returning. "I wouldn't suppose you could make a double shot espresso with a splash of goat's milk?"

Emma couldn't help but smile. Luckily, she'd gotten that espresso machine, and she was thrilled she'd be putting it to use for the first customers of the day.

"I'm not sure about the goat's milk, but the espresso I can do."

Emma made her way back to the bar, doing her best to keep the smug look off her face. Liam was hunched over the notes she'd written down, reviewing her instructions on how to make the drink specials.

"Why do you look so pleased with yourself?" he asked, glancing up as she approached.

Well, she supposed she wasn't trying *that* hard. "Well, I thought I hid it a bit better than that."

"Not even close," Liam chuckled. "What's on your mind, then?"

"Actually, what the head rider wanted was a *coffee*." She emphasized the word, saying slowly to antagonize him. "A double shot espresso in fact."

Liam blinked, clearly caught off guard. For a moment, Emma had to remind herself this wasn't her Liam. This version of her old friend might not be used to her teasing, but after an initial pause, he shook his head and smiled.

"All right, all right!" He lifted his hands in mock defense. "You've made your point."

"Can you grind up a couple of shots of espresso for me?" she asked, turning serious again. "I'm going to get started on these drinks."

"Aye, aye, el capitan," he said, giving her a mock salute.

"Do we have any goat's milk, by chance?" she asked as he grabbed the canister of coffee beans from the counter. He popped the lid, releasing the rich, fragrant aroma of freshly roasted beans.

"Goat's milk?" There was more than a hint of incredulity in his voice. "What the hell kind of drinks are you making?"

"It's for the coffee," Emma replied.

Liam's expression shifted to understanding, and he pointed two finger guns at her. Emma had to refrain from groaning audibly. "Got it," he said. "I think I've got some back at my place, if you don't mind waiting a few minutes."

Emma glanced at the group of dragon riders. They were still deep in conversation with James and Rudy. A short delay wasn't likely to be noticed.

"Do it," she said. "While you're at it, you wouldn't happen to have any tea, would you? Preferably something blue or purple? There's chamomile tea back here, but I don't think that's quite what I'm looking for."

Liam raised an eyebrow. "You're not a typical bartender, are you?"

Emma smirked. "You have no idea."

"I don't have any," he said, "but Isabelle's shop might. She won't be open until tomorrow, though."

Emma pursed her lips; that would have to do. She'd have to pay a visit to this shop in the morning and hopefully find some alternative she could use for her drink recipes.

"That's fine," she said. "Just quickly grab the milk if you can."

Liam offered a two-fingered salute, opened the portal back to O'Sullivan's, and darted through.

Emma shook her head, watching him go. This was definitely not the same Liam that she'd trained with as a Hunter of the Cursed. Her Liam had been moody, brusque, and committed to his honor and his kingdom above all else.

This Liam, though? He was just as mischievous and equally handsome, but the differences between them stood out more than the similarities. This one hadn't been worn down by years of battle. He was light on his feet, quick to crack a joke, and . . . soft.

Part of what had attracted her to Liam in the first place was knowing he had her back in a fight. She hadn't faced a monster in years, but she wondered if that instinct still mattered as much as it once had. It wasn't as though she couldn't take care of herself—she could. But there was something comforting about knowing she wouldn't have to defend the man she was with as well.

The thoughts stewed in her mind as she gathered the pieces needed to craft the Sky Rider's Ascent.

She reached for the bottles of gin, maraschino liqueur, and lemon juice, and set each ingredient on the counter as she went. Two coupe glasses were slipped into the freezer to chill—if Liam took a few extra minutes to return, they'd have time to reach the perfect temperature.

Emma reached for the jigger before measuring two ounces of gin. As she poured, she glanced down at her hand.

Her fingers had once been calloused from years of training and fighting. Now, they were smooth and pink. She hadn't realized how much they'd healed. How could she judge Liam for not knowing battle when she'd not known it herself since her magic had appeared? A pang of disappointment hit her. It was like she'd lost a piece of herself without realizing it.

Emma was surprised to find she had to fight back tears. How could she mourn something she'd never wanted? Bartending had always been her dream; monster hunting had been a duty, not a choice. She knew that now. So why did she feel like she'd lost something important?

Emma forced herself to focus as she poured the clear spirit

into a cocktail shaker, the aroma of juniper momentarily over-taking the coffee smell that still hung in the air.

Next, she added half an ounce of maraschino liqueur, which would contribute a subtle sweetness and a distinctive cherry-almond flavor.

Emma scanned the shelves for crème de violette. It wasn't common, and she was somewhat surprised that it was there. It sung to her from the shelf, and she knew that it would add not only the unique taste of violets to the drink, but also the mesmerizing pale purple hue that would make this drink unique. The magic of the pub truly did provide. She poured half an ounce into the shaker.

She added three-quarters of an ounce of lemon juice to balance out the sweetness of the liqueurs and the botanical notes of the gin. But it was still missing something.

Emma opened her mind to the drink, and it told her exactly what it needed. Elderflower liqueur. She found it on the shelf behind her and added a quarter ounce. It was perfect! The added liqueur would complement the violet notes and add an extra layer of complexity.

She wove her magic, encouraging the different spirits to work with each other in harmony and unity to craft the drink she knew the dragon riders would be satisfied with. Ice rattled in the shaker as the mixture was added, and she vigorously shook it for half a minute until the metal chilled against her hands.

Knowing that she had a couple more minutes until Liam returned, she decided to get the espresso started herself. She pulled the grounds out from the grinder and tamped them into the portafilter, then turned the handle and locked it into the group head before placing an espresso cup underneath each spout. She hit the start button, and the machine came to life, humming and hissing as the water heated and ran through it.

The rich fragrance of the beans erupted from the spout, and

Emma inhaled the pleasing scent. There was nothing quite as satisfying as the smell of a brewing cup of coffee.

With that well underway, she grabbed the coupe glasses from the freezer just as Liam came barreling through the portal, a small bottle of goat's milk in hand and a sheen of sweat on his forehead.

"Did you run all the way there and back?" she laughed.

"What?" he huffed, clearly winded. "You told me to be quick!" He almost seemed offended that she'd asked.

"Thank you." She grinned, taking the milk. She hadn't expected him to take her so literally. "Everything's about ready. If you want to add that to the espresso, we can bring it out to the dragon riders."

She retrieved the coupe glasses from the freezer and carefully strained the shimmering, pale purple liquid into each one. As a finishing touch, she sprinkled edible silver flakes over the surface, which sparkled like dragon scales in the dim light of the bar.

"Perfect," she whispered. "This will do the trick."

The hum of the portal sprang to life again, announcing the arrival of more patrons. Emma straightened, ready for whatever —or whoever—came through next.

Sky Rider's Ascent

Ingredients:

- 2 ounces gin
- 1/2 ounce maraschino liqueur
- 1/2 ounce crème de violette*
- 1/4 ounce lemon juice
- 1/4 oz elderflower liqueur (such as St. Germain)
- Ice
- Edible silver flakes or silver pearl dust for garnish

Directions:

1. In a cocktail shaker, combine the gin, maraschino liqueur, crème de violette, lemon juice, and elderflower liqueur.
2. Add ice to the shaker and shake well for about 15-20 seconds until the mixture is well chilled.
3. Strain the mixture into a chilled coupe or cocktail glass.
4. Garnish with a sprinkle of edible silver flakes or silver pearl dust on top of the drink.

*Note: If you can't find crème de violette, you can substitute for Blue Curaçao, but the color won't quite be the same

Mocktail version:

Ingredients:

- 2 ounces butterfly pea flower tea, chilled
- 1/2 ounce lemon juice
- 1 ounce elderflower tea, chilled
- 3/4 ounce simple syrup
- 1/2 ounce vanilla syrup
- 1/4 ounce grenadine
- Ice
- Edible silver flakes or silver pearl dust for garnish (optional)

Directions:

1. Brew strong batches of butterfly pea flower tea and elderflower tea separately. Let both teas cool completely.
2. In a cocktail shaker, combine the butterfly pea flower tea, lemon juice, elderflower tea, simple syrup, vanilla syrup, and grenadine.
3. Add ice to the shaker and shake well for about 15-20 seconds until the mixture is well chilled.
4. Strain the mixture into a chilled coupe or cocktail glass.
5. Garnish with a sprinkle of edible silver flakes or silver pearl dust on top of the drink.

The simple syrup in this recipe helps to balance the tartness of the lemon juice and the bitterness that may come from the elderflower tea. To make simple syrup, mix equal parts sugar and water in a saucepan, heat until the sugar dissolves, then cool the syrup before use.

James

James' feet ached. The Pint and Portal had only been open for three hours, but it felt like he had been running around for days.

That's what I get for living my life at a desk.

After the Sky Riders, the patrons didn't seem to stop coming. Though, he realized that couldn't possibly have been true since there were still plenty of tables free.

While Liam had brought the Atlas Sky Riders their drinks, a party of men dressed in medieval-looking armor arrived. Then a group of women who were hiding from an oppressive state very hesitantly took a seat and asked if they would be able to stay at least for the night. Following that, another group of dwarves stumbled through, half a dozen of them.

James went around introducing himself to each visitor, hearing the barest bits and pieces of their stories and trying his best to explain to each of them where they were.

Gloria took kindly to the dwarves, and even Ha'dran stopped by their table to share stories of how their histories had diverged. It seemed Ha'dran and Gloria were excited to see dwarves again.

"It's not that the dwarves had been eradicated entirely," James overheard Ha'dran say with a note of sadness. "But it was pretty damn close. Most retreated back to the caves, and those left are so spread out, with so few resources, I'm afraid it might only be a matter of time."

"Dwarves are resilient," said one of the newcomers. "It may take a few generations, but your people will rebuild. I'm sure of it."

That seemed to buoy Ha'dran's spirits, and he continued to talk to the other dwarves with the excited enthusiasm of a man who hadn't seen his best mates in years.

The group seemed quite excited that Ha'dran would be telling his tales on stage later that evening.

Jovial laughs, clinking of glasses, and increasingly louder banter were beginning to fill the air.

"The energy in this place," said Kathy. "It's just like when we were kids, isn't it?" She allowed her gaze to wander around the room with the wonderment of a child observing an elaborate Christmas display. Captivated by what she was seeing, but unsure of where to look first.

"I don't seem to remember dwarves, gnomes, and dragon riders," he rebuffed.

Kathy's eyes narrowed as she took another look across the room. "Are there gnomes here? For real?"

James pinched the bridge of his nose as he grabbed a glass of whiskey off the bar and took a sip. "Table toward the back, colorful hats and all. I had a hard time understanding them, but from what I gather, they're on a quest to uncover a wizard's hat. Supposedly an heirloom that would protect their people from a maniacal tyrant who's been threatening their kind."

Kathy bit her lip. "Do you find it strange that everyone who comes in here has some sort of tragic backstory or they're on an epic quest? It's like we're getting the heroes of multiple fantasy novels all thrown into one place."

James looked at those who had already graced The Pint and Portal. He hadn't thought much of it, but Kathy was right. The

Sky Riders were trying to save their land, as were the gnomes. He hadn't spoken to the new dwarves for long enough to know what they were about, but whatever stories they were telling Gloria and Ha'dran seemed to be fairly epic.

"I don't know if it's that simple," he said. "These people don't seem like heroes to me. They seem like regular folk who have been through rough times and need a bit of a break."

"What if that's all heroes are?"

James thought about it for a moment. The people who fought their way to redemption in his mother's stories were often just that. Ordinary people who had been put in extraordinary circumstances.

Maybe that was why he loved them so much.

James shrugged. "Rudy had mentioned the portals only open for those in need. I think that's what we're seeing here."

His eyebrow began to twitch. The noise level of the pub had continued to creep louder, and it was now reaching an overwhelming level. James gripped the bar to steady himself.

"Maybe you should save the whiskey until *after* the night is done," Kathy said. She wasn't scolding her brother, but her tone indicated she wasn't exactly pleased either.

"I haven't had a drop yet," James said as he steadied himself. "But that's not a bad thought. Whiskey might be the only thing that gets me through the night. I'm not used to crowds like this. It's a lot to handle." He leaned against the bar. The night had only just begun. He was tired, in pain, and ready for bed.

Some adventurer I'd be.

Behind the bar, the espresso machine let out a low, angry hiss. The sound was sharp and insistent, cutting through the hum of conversations in the pub.

James stiffened on his stool, his head still spinning. *Why is it so loud?*

The hiss deepened, becoming a shrill whistle that grew

louder and louder. The sound clawed at his senses, rising to a pitch that made his teeth ache. The bar itself rattled, glasses trembling against one another.

"Is it supposed to do that?" Kathy asked, her wide eyes darting toward the trembling machine.

James wiped the sweat from his brow, heat prickling the back of his neck. "I really don't think so."

Behind the bar, Emma worked frantically. She darted from side to side, grabbing towels and trying to stem the deluge of water that was now cascading from the bottom of the machine. The towels were soaked in seconds, and a dark puddle spread across the floor, creeping toward her boots.

"What is wrong with this thing?!" she shouted, her voice strained as she fought against the chaos.

The whistle from the machine had hit a fever pitch, now accompanied by a rhythmic metallic *clunk-clunk-clunk* as the machine shook violently. Glasses danced precariously on the shelves, some toppling over and shattering on the bar.

James leapt off his stool, the dizziness that had plagued him moments before forgotten. His heart pounded as he rushed to Emma's side, nearly slipping on the growing puddle as he grabbed the nearest towel to help.

"Turn it off!" he shouted over the din.

"I did! It's not listening!" Emma snapped back, her eyes wild with frustration.

The machine lurched forward suddenly, the force of it knocking a stack of cups to the floor. James barely had time to process the movement before a loud *pop* erupted from its core—a deafening bang that cracked through the pub like a gunshot.

James flinched, instinctively raising his arms to shield his face. Shards of ceramic and metal shot outward, scattering across the bar. Half the pub's patrons jumped to their feet, the air thick with panic.

"Attack!" someone bellowed, and a dozen weapons flashed

in the dim light—axes, swords, and daggers unsheathed with metallic hisses. Even the gnomes pulled out small knives. Chairs scraped against the floor as patrons scrambled, their eyes darting toward the source of the explosion.

"It's all right!" Rudy's booming voice cut through the chaos, his hands raised in a calming gesture. "It's just a machine! *Everything is fine.*"

The pub quieted slightly, though a few disgruntled voices still murmured. Some patrons hesitated before sitting back down, weapons still clutched tightly in their hands. Others remained standing, their gazes fixed warily on the bar as though expecting the machine to lash out again.

James let out a shaky breath, his ears still ringing. Emma was desperately trying to contain some of the liquid that was still spreading over the counter and dripping onto the floor in a melodic drizzle.

"Could someone please get me a mop?" she called out to nobody in particular. Gloria made quick work of tracking one down.

Finally, the machine gave one last pitiful wheeze and fell silent.

Emma straightened, her chest rising and falling as she caught her breath. She leaned over the machine, her brow furrowed in disbelief.

James stepped back, surveying the scene. The countertop was littered with shards of ceramic, pools of water, and the remains of what had once been a functioning espresso machine. The smell of burnt coffee lingered in the air, mixing unpleasantly with the faint metallic tang of overheated machinery.

Emma let out a long sigh, tossing the sodden towel onto the bar. "Well, I guess I'll add 'fixing espresso machines' to my list of skills to master."

James stepped over to Rudy, lowering his voice. "You sure that thing was working before?"

Rudy nodded, his expression serious. "Ya. It's practically brand new."

James frowned, glancing back at the machine. It didn't make sense, but sometimes equipment malfunctioned. He rubbed the back of his neck, the tension of the last few minutes still lingering.

In the couple pages he'd skimmed through of his mother's journal, he did see something about malfunctions . . . it wasn't possible the two things were related . . . was it?

"Rudy, can I ask you a question?"

"Of course!"

"My mother mentioned in her journal that equipment and electricity started to act up. My dad and Moira were worried the Tíogar Mór were siphoning power from the pub to weaken the wards. Do you think that's what this is?"

Rudy cleared his throat and pursed his lips. "Listen, there's a lot to Moira's past that made her real worried about the Tíogar Mór. But this was built to be a place of safety. Trust me, you won't be seeing none of those tigers coming through these gates."

James nodded, but there was still something about the incident that didn't quite feel right.

The rest of the pub was slowly returning to its usual chatter, though James had to admit the conversations were a bit more subdued.

The uneasy silence was broken by the sound of chairs scraping against the floor. Kira stood from her table with the Sky Riders and the rest of her party followed suit.

"We should get some rest," she said, brushing a hand over the hilt of her sword. "If we're going to continue our search for Hector tomorrow, we'll need to be ready."

James watched the dragon riders closely; despite the respite they'd found at the pub, their slow movements indicated that they were all bordering on exhaustion. Their search was clearly wearing on them.

Emma abandoned the mess and crossed the room toward their table. Her hands were still slightly damp, but she moved with determination.

"Good luck," Emma said warmly, her voice cutting through the quiet hum that had settled over the pub. She dried her hands on the apron tied around her waist as she approached them. "Whether you find him or not, please come back. I hope to have something special ready for you next time."

"We will," Kira said. "Fredja and Vidar have been going on about your drink all evening. It was a smashing success!"

"I apologize for not being more open to it at first," said Vidar. "It wasn't what I was expecting. Very refreshing!"

Kira smiled. "I hope we get to try more of your delicious creations."

James swore Emma blushed as she granted them a final wave.

The three Sky Riders stepped up to the spot where they entered, Vidar inserted the orb back into the recess, and they were off again.

Dragon riders. James wondered what their lives were like. He tried to imagine the feeling of riding a dragon with the wind in your face, on a mission to try and save your people from some sort of other mythical beings.

Cold was the thought that came to mind based on the coats they'd been wearing beneath their armor. Riding a dragon high in the sky must be frigid.

Gloria appeared at his side, snapping him out of his daydream. "Whatever happened with the coffee machine is spooking the patrons," she said. "We need to do something so they don't leave. Machines aren't something many of these worlds have. They think it's witchcraft."

Behind him, the espresso machine had turned on and was hissing loudly. Emma was already behind the bar again, cursing a string of profanities that would have made a hip-hop artist blush.

Witchcraft. A few days ago, he would have rolled his eyes, but now? Why not?

Rudy was still at the bar, poking at the agitated espresso machine.

"It was working fine when I last used it," he muttered, scratching the side of his beard with one hand while the other twisted knobs arbitrarily, as though sheer persistence might bring it back to life.

"It's no big deal," said Emma, returning to the bar. "We'll take The Opener, and *the Wayfarer's Rest* off the board. There are a lot of other drinks I can make."

That didn't seem to appease the baker.

"I'm so sorry, James! Emma!" Rudy's gaze bounced between them. "If I had known it was faulty, I never would have leant it to you!"

James couldn't think of a time when he'd seen the baker so rattled.

"It's all right, Rudy. These things happen," James said, trying to sound reassuring. "Who knows, maybe something came loose while Liam was carrying it over here. He should have never tried to do it himself."

"Still." Rudy shook his head. "I'll make up for whatever damage it caused."

James scoffed. "Don't be absurd. You have done more than I can ever repay to help get this place running. Your staff are all but running O'Sullivan's right now. And despite the mishap, Kira seemed quite pleased that she had a non-alcoholic option. No harm done."

Rudy's shoulders slumped slightly, obviously unswayed by James' consolation. "I don't want to let your dad down. He did so much for me; if it weren't for him, Tarvo and I . . . Well, that's all in the past now. I need to know that I've done right by him."

James reached out and gripped Rudy's shoulder firmly. "Rudy, you have more than shown your appreciation. If it weren't for you, I wouldn't have stuck around for this long. Neither pub would be running. You're the only reason we've got enough staff for O'Sullivan's. You're the only reason I entertained the notion that dwarves were not something to freak out about. If you hadn't been here, I would've sent them straight back where they came from and spent the rest of the day hyperventilating through an existential crisis in an airplane bathroom on my way back to Vancouver.

"If any part of my dad wanted to see this legacy carry on, then you are the one he has to thank. Because I swear, without you, I wouldn't have even tried."

Rudy puffed out his chest and inhaled deeply. "You're right. I guess you're not the only one who's been a bit overwhelmed by all this."

"Why don't you sit for a bit?" James said. "You've been running yourself hard all evening. Hell, all week. You're not a young man anymore."

"Bah! Speak for yourself!" Rudy scoffed, waving the suggestion away. "I'm used to being on my feet all day. I've never felt better! You're the one who should sit."

James was almost embarrassed at how badly he wanted to do just that. Especially with the heavyset seventy-year-old baker bragging about his stamina. His muscles complained, his bones ached, and his feet were so sore he wondered how he would remain standing for hours to come. "I'll be fine," he said. "I'm still getting used to this."

Before Rudy could argue, Moira swept in, seemingly out of nowhere.

"Rudy, you know right well that this has nothing to do with the coffee machine!" she squawked, setting down a tray of empty pint glasses with a loud clink. She motioned to Emma for another round before planting her hands on her hips.

"Moira . . ." Rudy began. "Don't start this again."

"What is she talking about?" James asked.

"It's magic!" Moira said, her voice rising as she gestured toward the espresso machine. "'Tis why Timothy shuttered the pub in the first place. I told you not to open The Pint and Portal back up. This is only going to get worse."

"Moira, you agreed to help out—" Rudy started.

"And I *am* helping, aren't I? I promised Tim and Shay, and I'll promise James too. I'll stick around if you're stubborn enough to keep the portals open. But magic isn't to be messed with." Moira stomped off in a huff before James could get a word in.

"Don't you think she should be working O'Sullivan's instead?" Emma asked.

James shook his head. "She insisted on helping here. As long as she doesn't start scaring customers, I guess I don't mind."

"I'll talk to her," Rudy said, scratching at his beard. "She used to do this with your parents too. She means well—thinks that she can offer some protection if something *does* come through. But she doesn't realize we're not as young as we used to be, and it's not fair for her to dump her anxiety on you. Especially when we've seen no real threat here. Not ever."

Before James could respond, the room began to hum. A low vibration rippled through the air as the blue surface of a portal ballooned to life.

Glasses rattled on tables and ripples spread across the surface of an abandoned pint. The swirling light of the portal flickered and warped, its edges shimmering unevenly, as though struggling to stay intact.

"What now?" Emma asked.

James set down his whiskey and ran toward it; Rudy was quick at his side.

Something was wrong.

The portal buckled and swayed, its form twisting like torn fabric fighting an invisible wind. Its usual smooth, steady rhythm was gone, replaced by violent surges as though it were wrestling with itself.

James had to step back to get a full view of their new visitor. He had to be nearly eight feet tall, and stocky to match. "Welcome to The Pint and Port . . . al . . ." The words nearly died on their way out. It was only when the light faded that James saw who, or what, had strolled into the pub.

James' brain struggled to makes sense of who had just walked through as a hulking figure walked through with thick, green skin stretched taut over bulging muscles.

"An ogre?" James swallowed. The word had slipped out before he could stop himself, and his stomach twisted in dread at the thought that he might have offended the hulking figure.

The ogre didn't seem to care. His heavy shoulders rose and fell in a shrug, and without a word, he reached behind him, grabbed the glowing blue orb from the wall, and strolled toward the bar.

As the last vestiges of the portal waned, the lights around the room flickered. A large snap could be heard, then the lights cut out. The same blue orbs that provided faint light when they'd first discovered the pub gave the room some dim illumination.

Gasps erupted from one side of the room, laughter from the other. The faint blue glow of the enchanted orbs cast eerie shadows across the pub. But through it all, the ogre remained unfazed.

He didn't flinch, didn't pause, didn't even glance at the shocked faces around him. Instead, he calmly made his way to the edge of the bar, his massive presence commanding the room without so much as a word.

James' pulse quickened as he urgently scanned the room for Rudy. The baker was standing at the table of dwarves, who were surprisingly oblivious to the ogre's entrance. Ha'dran was guffawing at some unheard punchline.

"Rudy!" James hissed, his voice sharp.

Rudy blinked, finally noticing the dim lighting and the towering figure now occupying the bar. His eyes widened in confusion. Then, slowly, recognition dawned on his face, and he spoke a single word that cut through the noise of the bar.

"Hal?"

Emma

Emma inhaled deeply, steadying her trembling hands. The glass she was holding felt fragile in her grasp. For a moment, she thought she might drop it.

She'd seen monsters before, of course. Hunted them. Much more hideous, more grotesque, more terrifying than the one who marched toward the edge of the bar.

The thing that had stepped out of the portal was more man than monster, yet it still sent a jolt through her. This was an ogre—there was no mistaking it. She'd encountered them before, though only from a distance, in her kingdom where ogres were considered magic-born abominations, unnatural beings to be eliminated without hesitation.

Her breath caught in her chest, her heart twisting with a sharp pang of anguish. Ogres weren't just creatures she'd come across during her time as a Hunter. They were some of the creatures she had pursued.

"Six depths of the mines . . ." Tarvo whispered beside her. "It's Hal!"

The ogre turned his head slightly at the sound of Tarvo's voice, letting out a low grunt in response. If he recognized the old dwarf, there was no sign of it on his broad, impassive face.

Without breaking stride, he continued his slow march toward the corner seat.

"You *know* him?" Emma asked, unable to mask the disbelief in her tone.

Tarvo nodded with a grin on his face. Emma's thoughts were spiraling.

Across the pub, James stood frozen, his posture tense. Slowly, his shoulders eased, and Emma realized she wasn't the only one who had been put on edge by the ogre's sudden appearance. That made her feel a little less embarrassed, but guilt still gnawed at her insides.

She'd captured magical creatures like this one before. How many of them had been like Hal? How many hadn't been monsters at all? Any of them? All of them?

For the first time in her life, the sight of a strange, powerful ogre didn't make her reach for a weapon. It made her quiver. But not out of fear. No, the tremor in her hands came from the weight of what this meant—what it meant about who she was.

This giant with green skin and a physique that looked carved from stone was someone Tarvo knew by name. Someone who had a life, a history, a place in whatever world he called home. If she had come across Hal while she was in the field . . .

She stopped herself from finishing the thought. It was too horrible to consider.

She pressed her lips together to keep the emotions threatening to spill over in check. That was her old life. She hadn't known any better. She'd been trained to see creatures like Hal as nothing more than threats to eliminate. For years, she'd strived to convince herself that wasn't her fault. She'd been raised that way—indoctrinated into the life of a Hunter from the moment she could hold a weapon.

But now, watching Hal enter the room as a welcomed guest, those excuses felt paper-thin. Flimsy shields against the truth she didn't want to face.

The noise of the pub grew distant, muffled beneath the roar of her own thoughts. Her hands tightened around the glass, and she forced herself to set it down carefully on the bar before her trembling gave her away.

Emma exhaled, her gaze dropping to her hands. They looked soft and unscarred now, so different from the calloused, bloodied hands of her past. But the blood was still there, wasn't it? Invisible but no less real.

She swallowed hard, her mind circling back to the same question she'd been asking herself ever since she left her old life behind: Could she ever be anything more than the person she used to be?

Tarvo must have seen her mouth hanging open and felt the need to explain.

"That's Hal," he said. "He's a bit of Pint and Portal legend. From what we know, he was here when James' dad took over the pub, and he was around likely far longer than that. Ogres live a great long time, centuries even. But every day, Hal came in, and sat down at that very same seat, and ordered two double pints of ale. He'd sit there enjoying them until the pub closed."

Emma surveyed the ogre. She guessed ogres must have an extended lifespan compared to humans. If she had to guess, she'd say he appeared to be in his early thirties. But then, she had nothing really to base that on. The scuff of dark black hair on his head, the sharp lines of his jaw, the still-taut muscles bulging beneath his ripped tank top—they were all human-like. But there was the fierceness to him that left no doubt that, friendly or not, Hal was certainly an ogre.

"What's his story?" Emma asked. "I thought everyone who came here was a hero?"

"We don't really know," Tarvo said. "Hell, we're not even sure Hal is his real name. That's the thing about him, he don't say much. He just shows up, orders, and sits. Like clockwork."

"ALE," the ogre's voice boomed from across the bar.

Emma jumped at the sheer volume of the request. Most of the other patrons hadn't given him a second glance.

"He hasn't missed a beat," Tarvo chuckled. "Don't worry, his bark is worse than his bite, though . . . I don't think I'd want him biting me either. Say, pour one for me too, will ya?"

Tarvo crossed the space toward Hal and pulled up a stool next to him.

"Hal! How have you been, old friend? Can you believe how long it's been since this place has poured us a pint? My hair might be grayer than when you last saw me, but it's the same old me on the inside."

Tarvo carried on in an energetic monologue. Hal, for his part, listened in silence, occasionally grunting in response. He didn't seem disinterested, but he didn't contribute much either.

Emma might have even detected a hint of a smile.

Her heart sat heavy.

Hal sat calmly, yet her instincts screamed at her to reach for her daggers. Years of hunting had trained her to react this way, to see creatures like him as threats the moment they entered her space. It didn't matter that Hal wasn't doing anything wrong. The dark reflex was there, and she loathed its presence within her.

Emma bit her lip, forcing herself to focus on the task at hand. She didn't cry, not often, but as her mind spiraled back to the countless magical creatures she'd hunted, her throat tightened. She drew in a slow, steadying breath, trying to pull herself away from the deep pit her thoughts threatened to drag her into.

She poured a pint of Cuanmore Harbor ale into a glass, but as the amber liquid swirled to the brim, she realized the glass would be laughably small in Hal's massive hands. It would look like a teacup to him.

She was sure she'd seen something beneath the counter that might work. She crouched down and rummaged through the shelves until she found what she was looking for: a massive mug, triple the size of a normal pint glass. At the time, she'd thought it was a novelty item, but now she was certain it had been used for Hal-sized customers.

She polished the mug quickly and filled it to the brim.

Before she could serve it to the ogre, Liam appeared at her side. He kept his voice low, but there was a nervous intensity behind his words. "What are we going to do about this?"

"I know he looks a little unsettling, but Tarvo says he used to be a regular," she replied, barely paying him any mind. "They seem to be chatting up a storm. We don't need to do anything."

Though a quick glance in their direction confirmed that Tarvo was doing most of the chatting.

"Not the ogre," Liam hissed. Though, one nervous glance in their direction told Emma he was uneasy with that too. He threw his hands up in exasperation. "The lights! Haven't you noticed? We lost power the second he came in. I don't even know where to start looking to fix the issue."

"You're asking me about lights?" Emma set the full mug to the side of the counter. "Where's James?"

"I'm pretty sure this is a magic-user type of an issue," Liam responded.

Emma looked up at the softly glowing blue orbs around the room. She'd been so distracted by Hal's arrival that she'd hardly noticed the power outage. The patrons didn't seem to mind— the orbs cast enough light for everyone to see their drinks and enjoy their conversations, at least for now.

"Unless they run on gin, I'm not going to be of much help."

She watched as a trio of goblins rose from their seats, ready to leave. Instinctively, she knew what was about to happen.

"I think the lights are going to be the least of our concerns." She nodded in the direction of the goblins, just as one of them lifted their orb to place in the wall.

Liam followed her gaze as the sphere entered its place.

Nothing happened.

The goblin stared at the unresponsive orb, his confusion quickly giving way to irritation. He turned it over in his hands, inspecting it like it might suddenly reveal the cause of the malfunction. His two companions leaned closer, their high-pitched chittering like an anxious chorus of crickets. One of them jabbed a clawed finger toward the wall, while the other gestured animatedly toward the orb, their voices rising in a frantic, squeaky debate.

The lead goblin growled low in his throat, silencing the others. He tried again, lifting the orb and pressing it against the wall with more force, as though brute strength might succeed where finesse had failed. When nothing happened, he let out a frustrated yelp that turned heads across the room. His lips curled into a faint snarl, and his yellow eyes darted toward the bar, agitation flashing in their depths.

Emma tensed. That sort of agitation couldn't remain unchecked.

"You better say something," Emma murmured to Liam. "Or we're going to have a pub full of very upset patrons."

Liam shuffled nervously and cleared his throat before turning his attention to the room.

"Folks," he called out, striking a confident pose. "As you've likely noticed, we're having issues with our power. We're working on the problem and promise to have everything up and running as soon as possible. Until then, please have a seat, relax, and enjoy your drinks."

His gaze flicked to the goblins, whose irritation was palpable. "Unfortunately, the portals won't work until we've sorted it out," Liam added, his tone apologetic.

The goblins exchanged dark looks. The head goblin muttered something under his breath—probably a curse, judging by the tone—before gesturing sharply for his companions to follow. Reluctantly, they shuffled back to their table, their frustration evident in the way their claws scraped against the wood as they climbed into their seats.

Emma released a breath. For the moment, at least, the tension in the pub had eased. She grabbed three mugs from the counter and filled them with ale, the amber liquid swirling as the foam settled beneath the brim. Sliding them across the bar toward Liam, she reached out instinctively, her fingers brushing against his hand.

A warmth spread from his skin to hers, and she nearly yanked her hand away, but she wanted nothing more than to grab hold of it and never let go. She let it linger, though her pulse quickened like she'd been caught doing something she shouldn't.

When Liam turned to her, his eyes locked on hers—warm and soft, yet somehow piercing. It felt like he was seeing her in a way no one else did.

His hand shifted slightly, his grip tightening enough to keep her from pulling away. He opened his mouth, as though he wanted to say something, but no words came out.

Emma cleared her throat, breaking the spell. "The drinks." She nodded toward the three mugs she'd placed on the bar. "Bring them to the goblins. It'll keep them occupied for a bit, at least."

Liam blinked several times and let go of her hand slowly, as though trying to do so without her noticing. "Oh, right," he said, his voice flustered. "Good thinking."

I wonder what that was all about?

You humans are all alike. Demon Box had been so quiet she'd almost forgotten it was there. *Always making your feelings more complicated than they need to be. If you like him, just tell him! He obviously feels something for you too.*

Did he? Surely it was absentmindedness and nothing more.

It's not that simple, she thought to the box.

Of course it is. You make the sounds from your mouth. He'll make sounds back. I'll finally be able to speak out loud around him, and we'll end up being one big, happy family all making sounds together.

Emma rolled her eyes.

Sure, I'll just say 'Excuse me but you look like someone I used to slay monsters with in another life. I fell in love with him, I think I'm falling in love with you too. I know that slaying monsters sounds awful, especially when they looked like our beloved patrons, but don't mind that, I don't do it anymore.'

She inhaled sharply and cast another worried eye toward the ogre.

But there was something else about the thought that unsettled her.

Love? That seemed premature. She felt like she barely knew this Liam, yet she couldn't deny they had formed a connection of their own. Was it just because he bore the same face? This Liam was different in so many ways. Charming and considerate. She didn't think that she was ready to put herself out there. Not yet.

"ALE," Hal barked, louder than before, and this time there was more of a hint of agitation in his voice.

"Oh, right!" Emma grabbed the giant mug from the counter where she'd set it, hefting it with two hands, and carried it over to the ogre.

Sorry, Demon Box, I've got work to do. We'll chat later.

Sure, sure, I'll just sit here in the corner by myself and shed a tear. The moisture will probably fry my circuits. Perhaps then someone will pay attention to me. Or not. Maybe it will be an ironic end for this lonely machine.

You don't have tear ducts. Emma shot back. *But you have enough melodrama for the entire pub.*

"So sorry about the wait, fellas." She sat the mug down in front of Hal and rushed to grab Tarvo's as well.

The dwarf had a large grin painted across his face. So engrossed in his own stories, he hadn't even noticed his drink was taking an extra minute.

The ogre nodded with a grunt, in what Emma assumed was a gesture of thanks, and slid a paper note over the bar.

Emma picked it up and studied it. It appeared like any other bank note might have—in worlds that had paper money—but she couldn't make out the language, or numbers. She had no way to ascertain the value, but that was like most of the forms of payment she'd received that evening. James and Rudy had said it didn't matter, so she didn't let it bother her.

"I can't make change for this," she said.

Hal looked at her with a furrow in his brow and grunted, "Hmm? Ah!" He lifted a giant-sized hand as he waved her off.

"Hal knows the rules here probably more than any of us," Tarvo said. "You needn't worry."

She thanked Hal and deposited the note in her pouch, then moved back to continue with her work.

It's magic you know, Demon Box said, intruding on her thoughts once again.

Emma nearly choked. "What? The money?" She spoke the words out loud; thankfully she was out of earshot of the others.

Demon Box quietly groaned.

The lights. They're powered by magic, so whoever turned them off probably used magic too.

Emma reflexively scanned the room. *You think someone did this on purpose? Why would they do that?*

Demon Box chirped in the corner. *I don't know. I'm just putting pieces together.*

There was only one person in the room she was confident had magic. Her gaze fell upon Ha'dran. The dwarf still sat at a table with six newly arrived dwarves, but he wasn't really engaging with them. Instead, he was leaned back, an arm draped over an empty chair with a distant smile on his face.

James

James did his best not to panic.

If they couldn't get the power back on, the portals wouldn't open—meaning they were stuck here, outside of any known reality, along with some potentially very upset dwarves, gnomes, goblins, and an ogre. Well, the gnomes were still all smiles. He had the feeling that if they ever got angry, he wouldn't want to be anywhere near them.

Which was worse: being stuck in Cuanmore or caught in between realities? Of course, he knew the answer, and he tried to swallow the lump building in his throat.

All that was keeping him from launching into a full-blown panic attack were the patrons who were now relying on him.

No, that wasn't true. That was probably making it worse.

He did his best to center himself with the breathing exercises his therapist had gone over with him time and time again.

Shutting his eyes, he focused on breathing. Inhale. Hold. Exhale. This was just a small hiccup in the day. He could get through it—he had to get through it, so long as he could figure out how to get everyone home. The how was still painfully unclear, but passing out in the middle of the pub certainly wouldn't help.

It would have been so much simpler if he knew how exactly a magical pub had electricity in the first place. It wasn't as though it streamed in from his world. Though, if it did, he'd really be in trouble since the gateway to his own world had been shut off like the rest of them. There was no way back. Not even for him.

His gaze scanned the room. Dozens of dwarves, gnomes, and humans exchanged nervous stares. The goblins glared openly, and the ogre seemed unaware or uncaring that anything was amiss. The laughter and lightheartedness of the place had slowly taken a downward turn ever since the lights failed. The dim, blue glow of the backup lighting didn't help—it cast everything in a faintly eerie hue, making shadows stretch and dance in ways that set James' nerves on edge.

Gloria slipped between tables effortlessly with a huge smile on her face. James couldn't tell whether it was genuine or in an attempt to make the patrons feel at ease.

Tarvo, on the other hand, held no qualms about enjoying himself. He sat at the bar next to that ogre—Hal. Dwarves were one thing. Other than being more solid, bulbous, and hairier, they didn't really appear that much different than humans. The gnomes were peculiar but seemed ultimately cuddly. The goblins were . . . something else.

This ogre, though . . . he was more . . . James tried hard not to use the word "terrifying," even in his own mind, but it was difficult.

He'd never been one to judge others by appearances, but he'd also never expected those appearances to be eight feet tall and green. Tarvo seemed to be having a blast with the ogre, though. James knew he'd just have to try a little, to swallow his fears and realize that there would be people coming through those gates that looked nothing like anyone he'd ever seen up until this point. And that that was okay.

"I told you," said Moira, as she slapped her empty tray

down on the bar. "Opening this place won't lead to anything good. All of this? It's because of them."

Despite her protests about reopening The Pint and Portal, Moira had been an incredible help keeping the pub running smoothly. However, it seemed she had her limits of how nice she was willing to play.

"When you said to expect trouble coming through the portals," James said, "did you mean . . .?" He was unsure how to phrase it without sounding like he was accusing Hal of being dangerous, but he couldn't help his gaze falling back on the ogre.

"Hal?" Moira let a single 'Ha!' escape her. "Heavens, no! Hal may look like a monster, but he's as docile a man who'll ever take a seat. He don't say much and he keeps to himself, but he's a good egg."

James sighed with relief. If Moira was at ease with him, then there was certainly nothing to be concerned about.

"It's unsettling the first few times you see a new mythical creature," Moira continued. "But you get used to it, and you'll come to realize appearances don't mean much."

"Then what *did* you mean?" He couldn't help but ask. "Tarvo says that the portals won't let anyone with ill intent come through."

"Tarvo has a very selective memory." Moira snorted. "It's true the orbs won't work for someone who's outright malicious. But that doesn't mean a deviant can't slip through alongside them. The portal doesn't put up a barrier once it's open. For the most part, like attracts like, and we see good people. But every now and then, a troublemaker sneaks in."

Her gaze drifted toward Hal. "And just because someone's well intentioned doesn't mean they won't react if they run into something that scares them. Not all ogres are like Hal, you know. Some folks have had bad run-ins with ogres who weren't so docile. More than one person's tried to put a knife in his back."

James was apprehensive enough about running this place, and he hadn't even stopped to consider he might have to stop one patron from stabbing another in the back. That couldn't be tolerated. He looked to Emma, pouring beers behind the bar. The bartender carried those daggers beneath her cloak, but would that be enough?

"It's not knife fights you have to worry about, lad," Moira said as though reading his thoughts.

James shook his head, confused. "Then what? Why is everyone being so secretive?"

Moira sighed, her distant gaze clouded with unease. "Magic." She looked as though she wanted to spit at the word. "There are too many worlds with unpredictable magic out there. Try as you might, once those gates are open, some of it will seep into our world. The people coming through are fine, but the magic? It needs to stay where it belongs."

James frowned. "If we *can* get the gates open again. I have to admit, I'm more worried that none of us will get home."

"I tell you what, if there was ever a sign suggesting those gateways are best left sealed, you can take this as one."

James didn't believe in signs. But he did believe in not getting stranded outside of time and space.

"Does this happen often? Is it something I should expect to continue?" If this was something that happened with regular frequency, maybe he shouldn't let it alarm him so much.

Moira's scowl nearly caused James to step back. "It was happening more often right before they closed things for good. Sometimes signs aren't about some mystical intervention. Sometimes they're about common sense."

"Isn't this whole place built with some sort of ancient magic?" James asked. "Why would they create it if magic is dangerous?"

"Sometimes people only do something because they can, not because they've asked if they should." Her tone grew sharper as she spoke. "It was something your mother never understood—and she of all people should have. Whoever built this place created something so powerful that if the wrong people get their hands on it, it's trouble—not just for us, but the hundreds of worlds we have access to."

Her gaze grew distant, and a darkness fell across her face.

When she put it like that, the stakes suddenly felt impossibly high. This wasn't what he had hoped for when taking over a cozy pub. Suddenly, James wished he could talk to his mom, learn the full truth of everything that had happened back then. The journal she'd left behind had been maddeningly incomplete, written in fits and starts, with entire pages missing. It was like trying to assemble a puzzle when half of the pieces had been lost.

Perhaps there was still something he could learn from Moira. "What do you mean about my mother? Why her of all people?"

Moira's face puckered as though she'd bitten a lemon.

"Look, it's not just magic you need to be worried about." She leaned in, lowering her voice as she cast her gaze around the room. "I told Rudy I wouldn't say anything, but I don't think it's right to keep this from you kids. The *real* reason your dad closed this place was because of another threat."

James didn't have to be told what she meant. "The Tíogar Mór."

Moira nodded curtly. "They're conquerors. They possess a technology that allows them to jump between worlds. But it's not reliable. We were always worried . . ." Moira sighed. "Your dad and I were always worried that if they gained access to the pub, it would allow them to destroy more worlds than they already have. He made the tough call to close the portals, despite our friends fighting their own battles on the other sides."

Even though Rudy had already mentioned her worries, James' stomach dropped.

"Rudy and your mother never believed the threat was real," she continued. "But I'm telling you, these glitches in the pub's magic—it's them, they're trying to gain access."

"But I thought there were wards protecting this place," James said. "Shouldn't they keep them out?"

Moira nodded. "They should, and they have so far. But what if they can't hold? What if the magic isn't strong enough? What if whatever it is they're using can draw power from the wards themselves?" Her eyes shifted around the bar as though suddenly nervous.

"Then why are you here serving tables?" James asked. "Why help me at all if you think it's such a bad idea?"

Moira swallowed, her expression softening slightly. "I made a promise to your parents. I promised them that I'd help protect this place as long as I'm alive and as long as it's open. As much as I think reopening was a bad idea, we're still family. And I would hate to see anything happen to you, Liam, or any of your new friends. They're good people, and together you'll be stronger—just like your folks, Rudy, Tarvo, Michael, and the rest of us had each other when we were younger."

Something at the back of the pub caught her eye, and she straightened, picking up her notepad and pen.

"But look at me, I'm blabbering on while there are tables needing serving. Just please . . . think about it, James. Nobody will blame you if you decide running this place wasn't the right idea."

With that she stood and moved toward the bar.

Danger. Could the lights going out really be a signal that the pub was in danger?

He let his gaze wander the room, and Rudy caught his

attention. The baker was sitting at a table toward the back of the room, in the middle of a hearty conversation with a weary group of travelers. If there really had been something to worry about, wouldn't Rudy have told him? He wouldn't lie about something dangerous . . . but what if he were mistaken?

His mother's journal weighed heavy in his pocket. James didn't know what to make of Moira's warnings about the Tíogar Mór. Maybe they were behind the glitches; maybe Moira was being paranoid.

Either way, he was quickly growing tired of the secrets this place seemed to hold. Lights failing, the espresso machine breaking, and the portals powering down on opening night. Moira's unease with magic users. Ha'dran and Gloria whispering among themselves—and Ha'dran himself, a dwarf with the ability to use magic, and a pub with magic that was seemingly going haywire.

If magic *was* involved, he only really had one lead to follow—the one magic user he knew. Perhaps the only way he could tell if Ha'dran's magic was to blame for what was happening was to get him to showcase it in front of an audience. At least that way whatever he might be doing would be on full display.

It was either a brilliant idea, or a horribly awful idea. But he had nothing else to go on.

Decision made, James strode over to the dwarf table where Ha'dran sat surrounded by the dwarves.

"James!" Ha'dran called to him as he approached. The dwarf's face lit up. "This is unbelievable! How similar their world is to how mine used to be. But the Tíogar Mór never attacked theirs. The dwarves are living in relative peace and prosperity!"

James forced himself not to flinch at the mention of the Tíogar Mór. "Then what brings them here?"

"They're brewers themselves!" Ha'dran's enthusiasm was so

palpable that he didn't give the other dwarves space to speak. "They were just telling me about the quest they're on."

James's attention turned to the newer dwarf patrons. They couldn't have been more different from Ha'dran or Tarvo. Where those two carried the weight of their worlds on their shoulders, these dwarves looked as though they'd never known hardship. Their full, rosy cheeks and bright, sparkling eyes spoke of a life untouched by strife.

"A quest?" James asked, turning his attention to them. A smile formed on his lips. "Tell me more."

"Our ancestors spoke of a magic ingredient," said the dwarf seated closest to Ha'dran. He was rounder than Tarvo, with a rotund belly that shook slightly as he spoke. "They said it could be used to brew a beer unlike any other."

The second dwarf, his beard neatly braided and his voice rich with enthusiasm, continued. "The stories spoke of a door like the ones connected to your pub. But no one remembered where it was. In our world, it was overgrown, forgotten like much of the human lands. If it weren't for the written tales, we might never have found it."

"And your stories spoke of a magical brew?" James lifted an eyebrow. "In this pub?"

"Legend has it," said the first dwarf, "a beer brewed with this ingredient would send its drinker on a mystical journey. It would let them experience the happiest of experiences and a grand sense of nostalgia."

It took all of James' strength to keep his face neutral. "I see," he said. "And this ingredient was said to be kept here?"

"Not much is known," the dwarf admitted. "The legends say if we could find the gateway, we'd find the brew. So far, the ales we've tried haven't been what we're looking for, but the night is young! And there are plenty of options on the menu."

"Do you know what the ingredient was? Perhaps we could help you narrow it down."

Not that James needed to narrow it down. But what he *did* need to narrow down was what was in Adam's special brew, and how he had gotten a hold of this mystery ingredient.

The second dwarf leaned forward. "It's said that it's Tears of the Gods combined with a brewer who possesses an ancient magic. Some say it can only be made by the gods themselves. We'd always thought the gateway would lead to a holy place, a temple of some kind. Imagine our surprise when we stepped into what appears to be an ordinary tavern!"

James forced a laugh. "Well, I definitely wouldn't call this place ordinary, but gods? I'm afraid you won't find any here."

At least, he didn't think they would. Never mind ogres, did he have to worry about gods strolling through the gateways as well?

His gaze flicked to the bar, where Adam's cask of special brew sat, still untapped. If the dwarves were right and Adam was in possession of this magic, it would explain the experience he'd had.

"If I find more about these tears, I'll be sure to let you know. My name is James, I'm the owner of this place. Even if I don't know about this ale, you've come on a fortuitous night. This is the first night we've been open in a long time."

"I'm T'og," said the first dwarf. "Your friend here was telling us all about it. I'm certain this is the place our ancestors spoke of. It will only be a matter of time."

"And a matter of sampling all of your brews!" the second dwarf added with a booming laugh. The rest of the group roared in agreement, raising their mugs in a toast.

James cracked a smile, but inside his thoughts were reeling. He was sure Adam's Nocturne Speciale had been made with these so-called "god tears." But how had Adam acquired them? And he'd known the man practically his entire life—he was certain Adam didn't possess any god-like ancient magic. So what exactly was happening?

He pushed the mystery to the back of his mind. There were more immediate concerns.

"Ha'dran," he said, shifting his focus. "We need a distraction from this power outage. How quickly will you be ready to perform?"

The dwarf's smile turned mischievous, his eyes sparkling. "I'll need a few minutes to prepare."

James nodded. "Then get ready. I'm expecting your best show."

Emma

Emma passed Moira a pint glass. The woman stood beside the bar grumbling that James would have chosen *now* of all times to send the dwarf onto the stage.

"He's trying to keep our guests distracted," said Emma, "until we can figure out what's happening with the lights."

"I'll tell you what's going on with the lights," she said. "Magic! I told you and I told *him* that opening those portals would do nothing but allow troublemaking magic users through! And what does he do? Throws one of them up on stage! Magic is not to be trusted."

"What would you have him do?" asked Emma. "It won't hurt to keep people's minds off the fact that we're stuck here. Do you want Hal here to get so angry that he starts smashing things?"

Hal looked up at the mention of his name and grunted.

Emma smirked.

Moira sighed. "Hal would never do that. He's a gentle giant."

The ogre frowned. Though, it appeared more menacing than gentle. Emma let out a sigh of her own as her thoughts once again drifted to her past.

Over the course of the evening, one particularly horrendous memory had come to mind. While she had been a Hunter, her squad was ordered to follow up on rumors that ogres had been eating the locals' livestock—there had even been reports of them eating children. Her heart quivered at the thought. Maybe it had all been fear-based lies. Maybe the ogres had just been misunderstood.

"Mark my words" Moira continued, "it's magic behind this. Hopefully once it all gets straightened out, James will have the good sense to shut this place and focus on O'Sullivan's like his father did."

From the sound of things, he'd not really focused on O'Sullivan's either, Emma thought, but that was beside the point. Right now, she was more concerned with the woman in front of her and whatever was causing her to feel the way she did about The Pint and Portal.

"Someone must have done something with magic that really scared you, is that it?" Emma asked.

Moira's face went pale. "It's not natural, is all."

Emma recognized the look of someone who did in fact have a story to tell. "How about I mix you a drink. Something to help calm those nerves." A lot of bartenders might have poured a shot of whiskey or handed over a glass of wine, but Emma wanted to mix something special. Something that might ease Moira without her realizing it.

"It might take a few moments," Emma continued, grabbing a clean mug and setting it on the counter, "but I think we have some time before Ha'dran starts his performance. In the meantime, would you like to talk about what happened to make you dislike magic so much?"

Moira crossed her arms. "Not particularly."

Emma allowed a faint smile to cross her lips. So that was how it was going to be.

Maybe it was time to share a piece of herself. If Moira

wouldn't open up on her own, perhaps a little vulnerability would help.

"Have a seat," she said.

Moira looked unconvinced. She peered out at the room. "I'm needed on the floor."

Emma reached across the bar and rested a hand on Moira's arm. "You're officially on your break," she said. "So sit."

Moira pursed her lips, but didn't argue. She pulled up a stool and leaned against the bar, resting on her elbows.

Emma grabbed a teacup and pulled a bottle of Irish whiskey off the shelf.

Only Irish whiskey will do in this case, she thought.

Cautiously, she reached out with her magic—this drink had to be *exactly* what Moira needed. Plus, she had no other way to craft the concoction she had in mind without electricity.

Emma opened the whiskey bottle and measured a shot and a half and poured it into the mug before reaching for the kettle. The water inside it was room temperature, but Moira couldn't know that. She wouldn't calm Moira's nerves any if the woman knew she possessed magic herself. She added the water to the cup, along with a tablespoon of honey.

Emma scrounged around in the supplies. Even though she hadn't found the tea for the Sky Rider's drink, she was sure she'd seen some chamomile behind the counter earlier.

Who would've thought running an inter-dimensional pub would involve so much tea?

After a few moments of searching, she worried she was misremembering, but it didn't take long to find the yellow tin she was seeking.

"Are you making me a cup of tea?" Moira said, as she strained to peer over Emma's shoulder. "If I'm being honest, when you said a drink that would settle my nerves, I was hoping for something a bit stronger."

"Oh, don't worry," Emma said. "I also grabbed the whiskey."

Emma added the looseleaf tea to a tea ball and submerged it in the mug. Now came the important part. She reached out with her magic again, focusing on the whiskey. She wasn't entirely sure how her magic worked—she'd never bothered to figure out the exact science of it—but she'd learned that alcohol was . . . obliging. It would do almost anything she asked.

This time, she asked it to heat itself. Not a lot, just enough to warm the water around it. The strain was immediate; the substance was diluted, but she coaxed it gently. Slowly, steam began to rise from the mug.

"It's a good thing you'd heated that water earlier," said Moira, as steam rose from the cup.

Emma nodded. There was really no way to answer without straight up lying, and she didn't feel right about doing that either. Besides, she needed a moment to catch her breath before telling Moira what she'd intended.

"Now then, that will take a minute," Emma said, leaving the tea to steep, "and I promised to tell you a bit about me."

She took a deep breath and braced herself for whatever reaction Moira might have. There was no other way to say it than to blurt it out. "Did you know I used to be a witch hunter?"

Moira's eyes went wide, reflecting the blue glow that hovered above the bar. The transformation was so stark that Emma worried she had miscalculated. Surely the fact that she'd *fought* magic users would put Moira at ease . . . wouldn't it?

"You what?" The words came out hardly louder than a whisper.

Emma looked around to ensure Liam wasn't nearby; she wasn't sure how much his mother would reveal to him, but she didn't think she wanted him to know this part of her past, not yet.

"I haven't told anybody else yet. So, I'd appreciate if you would keep this between us." Emma took a deep breath. "But in my world, magic was illegal. Monsters had run rampant for centuries. Our king had decreed that magic was a scourge on the land and an abomination to the gods and to the throne. I was a soldier and belonged to a special task unit called Hunters of the Cursed. We traveled throughout the kingdom, slaying beasts and arresting anyone who appeared to possess a sniff of magic."

"So, you agree," said Moira. She said the words slowly, as though attempting to choose what she said carefully. "Magic is dangerous."

"Once I did." Emma nodded. "But I didn't join the Hunters by choice. I was an orphan." Emma stopped herself from adding *along with Liam.*

The Liam in Emma's world had never known who his mother was. Had never known the reasons she'd left him behind so young. She could have passed away due to illness or lacked the resources to feed another mouth. It wasn't an uncommon thing in the Kingdom of Lancastria.

But here, in Moira's timeline, she hadn't left her son, and there was no reason for Emma to reveal that there were some worlds where that hadn't been the case.

So instead, she continued. "I did believe that magic was evil while I was a Hunter. We were taught it was a curse on the land. We believed that by ridding the kingdom of monsters and magic that we were saving the world. But one day, something changed."

Moira let out a breath, and her shoulders visibly relaxed. "What was that?"

Emma paused. She wasn't quite sure she was ready to reveal *everything* to this woman. Especially someone who was so visibly shaken by the mention of magic. Someone who wanted to keep magic out of her own world at all costs. The mother of the one person she didn't want to find out about her past—not yet anyway.

Emma's mind slipped back to the last time she'd seen Liam. *Her* version of Liam. Back to when she'd first discovered she possessed the magical power to speak to and control alcohol. Ever since they were still in training and Captain Becker warned him about fooling around, he'd been a stickler for the rules. More than anything else, he didn't want to lose his position as one of the Hunters. Something had clicked in his brain, and it was as though his position became a safety net to never having to go back to living on the street again.

She supposed he hadn't been wrong, but it was more than stubborn determination. It became a part of him. As though it had no longer been possible for him to do anything but follow the rules. Some deep-rooted trauma wouldn't let him entertain any action that might send him back to the street.

That extended to Emma as well. The day she left her own world was the first time since they were eighteen that she'd ever seen him break a rule. He let her escape through a portal that Demon Box had created despite her possessing magic. Even though by every law and rulebook in the kingdom he should have hauled her back to London to be tried and executed.

On that day, there had been a look in his eyes that she had not seen since they were young: compassion. So much so that he was willing to break the rules to ensure that she lived.

Emma shook her head, bringing herself back to the present.

"I met some friends who taught me that magic by itself is neither good nor evil," she continued. "People can *use* magic to help, or they can use it to do harm, but magic is simply a tool. Just like a knife can be used as a weapon or as a tool; it's the same with magic."

"That's where you're wrong," said Moira. "Magic does possess a will. Some magic you encounter might speak in whispers, allowing its user to act as a guide, but other forms . . ."

Moira's lips drew tight as she shook her head slightly. "Some magic will take you in its grasp and refuse to let go."

Emma took the tea steeper from the mug and slid it across the bar. "Isn't it better to look for ways magic could be used to do good?" she asked. "Rather than being worried about all the things that could go wrong? Otherwise, you'll miss out on so many good things because you're always waiting for the worst."

"The problem is," Moira said lifting the teacup, "you don't know until it's too late. With magic there's always a price and it always collects."

Emma didn't believe what Moira was saying was true. Even though she'd felt magic tug on her stronger on some worlds than it did on others, never did she feel as though she was a slave to it. If anything, her magic had helped her come to terms with who she truly was.

Moira lifted the cup to her lips and took a sip. Her brow furrowed and she looked at the cup as though confused.

"Is there something wrong with it?" Emma asked.

Moira closed her eyes for a moment, apparently letting the warmth of the tea settle over her. "No . . . I don't think so," she said finally, and took another sip. Her expression softened, and a small smile replaced her stiff, guarded demeanor. She rolled her shoulders, relaxing a little against the bar. "This tea is quite lovely. It's not like anything I've ever had before."

Emma let out a long breath, relief washing over her. At least Moira liked the drink. Maybe it would be enough to help the woman take her mind off worst-case scenarios, if only for a little while.

"What do you call it?" Moira asked curiously.

"It's a Chamomile Hot Toddy," Emma replied.

Moira chuckled softly. "A good bartender knows what their customer needs. I'm impressed."

Emma leaned forward, studying her closely. "But there's still something bothering you about it, isn't there?"

Moira hesitated, her fingers tracing the rim of the mug. "I think," she began, "it's just been a long time since I've had a drink in this place. There are memories here—ones I had forgotten. Or maybe ones I didn't realize I'd left behind."

Her voice grew quieter. "This place is born of ancient magic, and I've always thought it was foolish to dabble with that kind of power. I disliked it then, and I dislike it more now that Liam's tied up in all this."

Emma stayed silent, letting Moira speak her thoughts.

"Since he was born," Moira continued, her gaze fixed on the mug in her hands, "I've done everything I could to keep him away from magic. From other dimensions. From all of this foolishness. Living on the other side of that portal was supposed to protect him from it." She shook her head. "When Timothy decided to shutter this place, I thought we'd left it all behind."

The entire pub, after all, was steeped in magic. It was woven into its very foundation. And Emma had come to believe that magic didn't always have to be something to fear. If she could be part of a place that used magic to help people forget their worries, to bring joy and comfort, then this was exactly where she wanted to be.

Still, she doubted she was going to change Moira's mind tonight. The woman's wariness ran deep, and Emma could sense the walls she'd built around herself. But maybe, just maybe, this was a start. If nothing else, perhaps she could plant the smallest seed of doubt—that magic wasn't always something to hate or fear.

Ingredients:

- 1 1/2 ounces whiskey or bourbon
- 1 tablespoon honey
- 1/2 ounce lemon juice
- 4 - 5 ounces boiling hot water
- 1 chamomile tea bag, or looseleaf tea
- Cinnamon stick and lemon wheel for garnishes (optional)

Directions:

1. In a mug, combine the whiskey or bourbon, honey, and lemon juice.
2. Pour the hot water into the mug and stir gently to combine all the ingredients.
3. Steep for 1 to 2 minutes.
4. Garnish with a cinnamon stick and a lemon wheel.

Tip: You can adjust the amount of whiskey, lemon juice, or honey syrup to suit your taste preferences.

Mocktail Version:

Ingredients

- 1 tablespoon honey
- 1/2 ounce lemon juice
- 7 - 8 ounces boiling hot water
- 1 chamomile tea bag, or looseleaf tea
- 1 /2 teaspoon ground cinnamon, or a cinnamon stick
- 1/2 teaspoon cloves
- 1/2 teaspoon ground nutmeg
- Lemon wedge (for garnish)

Directions

1. Brew the chamomile tea.
2. Warm a coffee mug or Irish coffee glass by filling with hot water. Let sit for a minute or two and pour out water.
3. In the same mug, add the honey, lemon juice, and spices.
4. Top off with the freshly brewed tea.
5. Stir well, add lemon wedge garnish and serve hot.

James

Ha'dran stepped onto the stage, a devilish grin on his face. James wasn't sure if the dwarf's good mood was because of the story he was about to tell, that he had gotten James' approval to use magic during the telling, or if there was something else the dwarf was hiding.

That was, until the table of dwarves burst out in a round of raucous applause and cheering.

The celebration took James aback. Apparently, the dwarves hadn't needed long to warm up to one of their own. He wished he had that sort of rapport with people.

The blue glow of the pub illuminated Ha'dran enough so that he was visible on stage. Shadows danced along his face while the blue orbs above him swirled in a circle, as if in anticipation of what he was about to do.

"Friends!" A bright blue flame exploded from the front of the stage. Several gasps rose from the crowd. The dwarves, however, cheered louder. The gnomes laughed and clapped in delight. Their laughter was so joyous, James couldn't help but smile.

He glanced around to see what effect it might have had on the other humans in attendance. It was strange to think that those who had crossed through a portal might be cautious of magic, but James was, and he knew Moira was too. Who knew how others might react?

However, his fears seemed to be misplaced. Between the pyrotechnic display of the dwarf and the high-pitched squeals of the gnomes, the rest of the humans in the tavern already had huge smiles plastered on their faces.

The one exception was Moira, who sat at the bar, sipping on a hot beverage with a scowl on her face.

Ha'dran stood still for a moment, letting the anticipation build. The raucous crowd steadily quieted as they waited, until the room was all but silent. The pub's blue lights dimmed, as if they too were waiting to see what happened next.

Then, with a sharp snap of his fingers, a flame sparked to life in his palm.

The fire danced and twisted, alive with a will of its own. It grew brighter, casting warm, golden light across the faces of the patrons. James leaned against the bar, his attention fixed on the dwarf. Ha'dran's grin widened as he held the flame aloft, and his voice boomed out, rich and deep, filling every corner of the room.

"In the land of Hybarn, there was a time when magic was the lifeblood of the world. It flowed through the rivers, whispered in the trees, and sang in the hearts of those who could wield it. But power such as this always breeds fear."

The flame split into two threads, one golden and vibrant, the other shadowy and dark. They twisted together like dueling serpents, hissing and sparking as they clashed. The crowd gasped as the dark thread grew larger, swallowing the light.

"In the midst of such a struggle, there are always two factions that emerge. One light and one dark. The lightness brings hope, but the darkness brings fear. Fear, if left unchecked for too long, will breed nothing but tyranny."

The fire surged before subsiding completely, and in its place rose the shadowy form of a towering castle. Its spires glowed red hot, as though forged in a furnace. Smoke curled from its battlements, and the faint sound of crackling flames filled the air. Ha'dran gestured, and the fire shifted, forming a figure atop the castle walls. The silhouette of a king, cloaked in shadow, his crown jagged.

"Bren, King of Hybarn, kept a tight fist on his reign through iron and fear. He could not abide the power of magic. He called it dangerous. Unnatural. He called those who wielded it traitors to the crown."

The shadows spread their tendrils from the stage out toward the crowd, and dark images of a village rose as though surrounding the shadow castle and its king.

The king figure raised his hand, and the newly formed village burst into a fiery inferno, its buildings crumbling to ash as quickly as they had risen. Sparks flew out into the crowd, harmless but startling, and James heard a few patrons gasp and pull back.

"And so began the Great Purge."

As Ha'dran spoke, the flames reformed, creating the shapes of villagers fleeing through the streets, their homes engulfed in fire. The figures were crude but unmistakable—men, women, and children running from soldiers whose swords gleamed like molten steel.

"But not all would bow to the king's will. Not all would let magic die."

The flames dimmed, the figures dissolving into embers. A new shape rose from the ashes: a dwarven woman cloaked in fire, her arms outstretched. Despite being made of shadow, it was clear the woman's face was sharp and defiant, her eyes flaming like two blazing embers.

"Princess Aleyna, daughter of the tyrant himself, turned her back on her father's throne. She joined the rebellion, wielding her forbidden power to protect those who had none."

The fiery figure of Aleyna stepped forward, her cloak trailing sparks like falling stars that flew throughout the tavern.

Ha'dran's voice softened. "She was a mage of unmatched power, a beacon in the darkness. But even a beacon needs a shield."

He paused, and the fire dimmed again before flaring back to life. This time, the flames formed the figure of another dwarf. Stocky and strong, he held an axe in one hand, its blade glowing white hot as if fresh from the forge.

"Tarvo was his name. A wanderer and a warrior. He had no crown, no title, no magic of his own. But he had fire in his heart and the honor of a man who had been born into legend. He swore an oath to Aleyna: to fight for her cause, to protect her people, and to bring the king's tyranny to an end."

The crowd erupted into cheers, mugs slamming onto tables in salute to the fiery dwarf. Ha'dran waited, letting the noise swell, before continuing.

James snuck a look over at Tarvo, who sat with the table of dwarves, hiding behind his drink. It might have been a trick of the mage fire, but James could have sworn the dwarf was blushing. He wondered how much truth there was behind the tale.

"Together," Ha'dran continued, "they led the rebels through the shadowed woods and across the bloodstained fields of Hybarn. The king's armies came, armed with steel and fear. But the power of Aleyna's magic and the fire of Tarvo's honor were a force no blade could match."

The flames surged upward, heating the air. They twisted and broke apart, forming the shapes of soldiers locked in battle. Lifelike sounds of war filled the pub—swords clashing, shields splintering, and arrows whistling through the air. Shadow Tarvo brought his axe down, scattering sparks with each blow. At his side, Aleyna unleashed her fire in a wave, consuming the king's forces.

"They fought day and night, their enemies falling one by

one. And when the dawn broke, they stood before King Bren himself."

The flames shifted again, forming the shadowy figure of the king. His claw-like hands reached for a sword that appeared to be made of pure darkness. Tarvo and Aleyna stood before him, their fiery forms burning brighter than ever.

"The king called them traitors. Heretics. Fools. But Tarvo stepped forward, his axe glowing fiercely, and said . . ."

Ha'dran lowered his voice, the fire dimming to a smoldering glow.

"'If you will not yield, then we will burn this entire place to the ground!'"

The fire exploded outward, a sudden burst of light and heat that filled the room. Shadows danced wildly on the walls, and the ground trembled beneath James' feet. The flames roared higher and higher before collapsing in on themselves, vanishing in an instant.

For a moment, there was nothing but silence. The pub was dark, save for the faint blue glow of its magical lighting.

"And that day," said Ha'dran, "Tarvo and Aleyna defeated King Bren, restoring peace and justice to Hybarn."

Released from the story's spell, the bar erupted into applause, cheers echoed off the walls.

Ha'dran stood at the center of the stage, his arms spread wide, a triumphant grin on his face. James shook his head, a smile tugging at his lips despite himself.

Then came a click and the electricity hummed to life and the lights were restored.

Emma

Emma awoke to thoughts of tea.

The light that crept into her room wasn't sunlight, there was no sun outside of this pub, but the windows somehow did a good job mimicking what both looked and felt like the sun's rays. However, when she tried to peer out the window, everything was a bright haze.

The bedroom was otherwise somewhat standard—if not more pleasant—than most tavern rooms she'd stayed in before. Her bed was sturdy, the mattress thick and comfortable. A small table stood beside it, holding a softly glowing lamp, filled with the same blue orbs that illuminated the bar when the power had been off. The floors were clean and covered by a gray-tone woven rug that added a touch of warmth to the space.

Emma smiled as she pulled the sheets off herself and set her feet into the soft slippers that had been laid out in the room before she'd arrived. She intended to track down some breakfast to stop the rumble in her stomach then get to work.

The encounters from last night, first with Kira then with Moira, had sent her mind spinning with recipes and flavors she could use to accommodate those who might not want to indulge in alcoholic beverages, and tea seemed to be the perfect choice for a base ingredient.

All this thinking about tea is making me thirsty. Demon Box hummed to life as Emma got out of bed and began getting dressed.

"Do you have to constantly be in my thoughts?" Emma asked. "Some things I don't exactly intend for you to hear."

Believe me, I know. Sass dripped from Demon Box's thoughts. *It's not like I want to be privy to all the saucy details you think about your friend out there either.*

Emma blushed. How much did Demon Box hear?

Far more than I'd like, it chirped. *If there was a way to shut off that valve without powering down, I absolutely would. You think I drone on and on? You should hear yourself when you think about Liam. Oh, what nice eyes he has, I wonder what he looks like with his shirt off, I wonder how big his . . .*

"Okay! I get the picture," said Emma. "I'll try to keep my thoughts in check from now on."

Just don't think them so loudly.

Emma paused. How could she control the volume of her thoughts?

Not everything I think gets projected out, Demon Box continued, obviously having heard her question. *If it did, you would be absolutely overwhelmed. Imagine if you could hear the computations that opening a portal requires? All the variables and functions I have to sort through to home in on a world and open a gateway long enough that we can both travel through safely. You only hear what I want you to hear.*

Emma hadn't thought of that before. "Two years of traveling together and you're only telling me about this now?"

I have my secrets too, you know.

"Yes, well, speaking of secrets," said Emma. "I think last night's performance absolves Ha'dran and Gloria of any arson suspicions, don't you think?"

Hmm. The phrasing was nearly identical to what I overheard. Do you think he was going over the details of his tale?

"I'm positive that's all it was."

What of the talk of Tarvo?

Emma thought for a moment. "They've lived together for a long time. I can imagine they'd get on each other's nerves from time to time. I don't think that alone is a reason to be suspicious of them."

Well, something is causing those malfunctions. I'm still suspicious.

"Why am I not surprised?"

You saw what happened to the espresso machine. What happens if I start malfunctioning next!

"You are already," she said. "Which reminds me. Once we get settled in here, we should really look into getting you fixed. We are attached to a world filled with technology."

If I survive that long.

Emma rolled her eyes. "If you want, I can leave you down in the bar again. Today, I'm headed to find a tea shop in Liam's world. I need to get some ingredients for drinks. This bar seems to be stocked for alcohol, but other beverages, not so much."

Oh, it's 'Liam's world' now, is it? Well, I imagine you're not complaining about spending a bit more time with Loverboy.

"Oh stop, he's not the same Liam I left behind. Besides, I don't think he has any interest in me."

You meat bags are all alike.

"Thanks. Maybe I'll leave you in the room so you can drone on to yourself."

Pfft. Then don't blame me if those scheming dwarves burn the place down while you're sipping tea.

"Do you really think it's possible to burn down a magical pub that exists outside of time and space?"

Demon Box whirred for a moment. *Perhaps you're right. Still, I'd feel better knowing their intentions.*

"I'm starting to think it's about time we let the rest of the crew know you exist, so it's not up to me to keep you company."

Demon Box sat quiet for a moment. *Perhaps that would give me a chance to stretch my legs. But maybe we should hold tight for a little longer, just to be sure.*

Emma was surprised to find O'Sullivan's empty when she came out of the storage room. The stillness caught her off guard. She'd half expected to see Kathy hunched over the bar, poring over the numbers from the previous evening, or James pacing in that quiet, brooding way of his, stewing over whether to keep running the magical pub or abandon it for whatever life he'd been living before.

The thought of James turning his back on The Pint and Portal saddened her in a way she hadn't anticipated. She slowed. *What would I do if this place closed?*

She hadn't allowed herself to think about it before, not really. Even though she'd been there a short amount of time, The Pint and Portal had become more than a job to her. It was the closest thing to a home she'd had in years, and for the first time in what felt like forever, she'd found a space where people didn't merely tolerate her—they leaned on each other, helped each other, and trusted her in return.

Plus, she couldn't imagine having to say goodbye to Liam again.

One thing was certain: she was done wandering from world to world. The Pint and Portal offered her something she hadn't even realized she'd been looking for—less adventure, more connection. A place where she could listen to the stories of travelers and adventurers without having to live them herself. A place where she could help others sort through their thoughts and struggles as she quietly tried to sort through her own.

Her conversation with Moira the night before tugged at her

memory. She'd actually enjoyed it despite the tension. It reminded her of the reasons she became a bartender in the first place. Connecting with people and helping them through their troubles.

That brought her thoughts back to James. Maybe he was the one she needed to have a talk with next.

Emma's gut tightened. If she wanted him to keep the portals open—if she wanted him to see what The Pint and Portal could be—she had to be honest with him. About herself. About her past. All of it.

The idea didn't comfort her. In fact, it unsettled her more than she cared to admit.

What if he didn't take it well? Moira could have convinced him of magic's danger. Her possessing magic could be one more reason to close the pub permanently.

Emma inhaled sharply, forcing herself to steady her thoughts. *I can't hide from my past forever.*

It was a risk she'd have to take. Maybe he'd surprise her.

She pushed open the front door to leave O'Sullivan's. Venturing out into this world on her own seemed somewhat strange. Despite visiting countless worlds over the last two years, she couldn't help but feel as though she was trespassing in this one. Like she was an intruder.

She hadn't needed permission to go anywhere in years—not since she was a Hunter trainee, over fifteen years ago. That version of her felt like a stranger now. Back then, she'd been bound by rules, orders, and expectations. After she left, she'd sworn she'd never let anyone control her again. She'd been a nomad ever since, drifting from world to world without attachments or plans.

At least, that's what she'd thought she would always be until she found The Pint and Portal.

The sensation might have had something to do with the fact

that this was one of those worlds with technology attached to it. Vehicles, electricity, and the like. The espresso machine would be a luxury for most of the worlds she'd visited. She never quite felt right venturing into them. Like she was an artifact out of place.

The morning sun warmed Emma's face as she closed her eyes, and she paused to draw in a deep breath of the fresh sea air. It carried a faint saltiness, mingled with the earthy scent of damp stone and a hint of baking bread from somewhere nearby. Despite its technological advancements, this version of Cuanmore still retained a quaint, almost timeless charm.

From what she'd seen—whether it was through Rudy, Liam, Adam, or even Moira—the villagers seemed to know one another, to look out for each other in a way that felt rare. It gave the town a sense of coziness that defied the cold sterility she often associated with more advanced worlds.

Maybe it was because this location still had some of its magic. She smiled at the thought. Usually magic and machines were independent of one another. It was rare to find a place where the two coexisted.

"Are you lost? Or just out to stretch your legs?" Liam's voice broke her out of her trance.

Emma couldn't help but smile as she opened her eyes and turned to face him. "Maybe a bit of both. I thought I'd check out that tea shop you mentioned last night. I also thought wandering around seemed like a nice way to start the day."

Liam's grin widened as he gestured down the road. "Come on," he said. "Why don't we head on over to the shop, then I can show you around town."

"That sounds lovely," Emma replied, falling into step beside him.

The cobblestone road stretched ahead of them, flanked by a mixture of timber-framed storefronts and squat stone buildings.

Their windows gleamed in the sunlight, and many of them were adorned with flower boxes overflowing with vibrant blooms. It was still early enough that the streets were still. Only the occasional resident went about their business in the morning light.

As they walked, Liam nodded toward a shop ahead, its timber-framed facade painted a soft cream, with dark wooden beams crisscrossing its face. "That's Rudy's bakery," he said, pointing.

A striped awning in pale green and white shaded the entrance, and beneath it, a chalkboard sign sat on the sidewalk. In bright, looping handwriting, the sign advertised the morning's special: almond strudel. Flower boxes beneath the windows brimmed with marigolds, petunias, and trailing ivy.

Through the glass panes, she could see the bakery's display cases brimming with fresh breads, golden pastries, and confections that looked perfectly delicious. The scent of warm sugar and fresh bread drifted out as a customer pushed open the door, and Emma's stomach growled in response.

"It smells incredible," she said. "Though I'm not surprised. The samples he's brought to the pub have been divine."

Liam nodded. "I bet you've never found a better bakery on any other world."

Emma smiled. "Now that sounds like a challenge."

Liam chuckled, gesturing toward the bakery's display window as they passed. "Though, I suppose you've seen bakeries like Rudy's on other worlds. Or maybe even better ones?"

Emma glanced at the colorful pastries piled behind the glass. "Better ones? I doubt it. But . . . different? Sure." She paused, considering the question. "Every world is different. There's always something unique about each one, something you don't expect."

Liam's grin widened as he slowed his pace, his curiosity clearly piqued. "What's it like? Visiting other worlds, I mean. It must be incredible, trying amazing foods, seeing how history might have played out differently."

Emma took a moment to think before she answered. "It is those things," she said. "But it was also very lonely."

"Lonely?" Liam's voice lifted in surprise. "I would have thought you would have had the chance to make an infinite number of friends."

"An infinite number of friends I'll never see again," she replied. "To be honest, I had a hard time making friends. It's hard to get to know people when you're constantly lost about how their world works. Do they have a king or a president, a tyrant or a benevolent leader? Do they have running water? Do they have ice cream or waffles, drink coffee or kappa? It can be overwhelming trying to keep up a simple conversation."

Liam nodded thoughtfully. "I guess I'd never have thought about it that way."

They walked in silence for a few moments, allowing the sounds of the village waking up to fill in the quiet.

"So . . . does that mean you might be sticking around for a while?"

A smile crossed Emma's lips. "As long as James is willing to keep me around."

The answer seemed to satisfy Liam, and he returned her smile.

They didn't travel much farther before Liam lifted an arm to point out a building that sat on the corner of the street. "Here we are. This is Isabelle's Tea House."

Isabelle's Tea House was about as cute of a building as Emma had ever seen. It could have been ripped out of a storybook and placed on the end of the block. The shop was surrounded by large oak trees clothed in lush green leaves. A large bay window wrapped around the outside, displaying jams, jellies, and tins of tea labeled with an array of varietals and blends.

Two small tables sat outside the building, each with a set of dainty teacups resting on top and a pair of red-cushioned chairs ready for the next guests.

"This place is adorable!" said Emma.

"Isabelle works hard to make everything magical," Liam said with a smile. "I'm always amazed at how effortless she makes things seem."

The two stepped inside, and Emma caught her breath. The interior of the shop was as whimsical as the outside. Shelves held many more containers of tea in a dizzying number of varietals, greenery decorated the shelves along with strands of lights and all sorts of decor.

Several more tables were set up around the shop, and Liam pulled out a chair at one of them and gestured for her to sit.

Emma did so and he tucked the chair back in. She could feel the warmth of his body behind her before he moved to take the seat opposite her.

"Welcome, welcome!" A woman with frizzy white hair and thick glasses came over to the table. She beamed at the sight of Emma.

"Liam!" She gripped one of Emma's hands, holding it in both of hers. The woman's skin was leathery, well worn, and likely often burned from scalding hot tea. "Who is this delightful colleen that you've brought with you? Look at that flaming red hair! And a powerful aura about her as well!"

"Isabelle, this is Emma," he said. "She's helping at O'Sullivan's as the barkeep."

Isabelle's eyes lit up with curiosity. "Ah, yes. Of course, of course." She gave Emma's hand an affectionate squeeze before releasing it. "You two make such a lovely couple."

Emma started, her face flushing. "Oh, we're not . . . We aren't together." She looked at Liam to get a sense of how he felt of the matter, but he was frustratingly nonchalant, and though there was a glimmer in his brown eyes, she couldn't get a read on his thoughts.

"What?" Isabelle clutched a hand to her chest. "Oh my. Well, it's not my place to pry."

She said it in a way that left Emma entirely unconvinced. Isabelle may not pry directly, but she had no doubt the woman would find her answers one way or another.

"Now then," Isabelle said, clasping her hands together, "why is it you lovely kids are here?"

Emma exhaled, grateful for the change in subject. "I'm looking for some teas that I can use for drink recipes. Particularly for drinks that don't have alcohol—mocktails. I'll need some chamomile tea for sure, but I'm hoping you have suggestions on others that might be appropriate."

Isabelle's face lit up. "Mocktails? Well, Timothy's son is sure making some changes at the old place, is he? They were desperately needed. And Liam, you're helping there as well?"

"Aye, ma'am. Just helping James get on his feet."

"You're a good lad. Always have been. Now then, about the tea you're after." Isabelle pressed a finger to her lips. "I'm afraid I don't know much about drink recipes. But I can show you a few blends, and you can decide if they'll work for what you have in mind."

"That sounds perfect," Emma said. "Show us what you've got."

"I'll be right back, lovely." Isabelle disappeared into the back of the shop, humming a song to herself that Emma didn't recognize.

"What a lovely place," Emma said, more to herself than to Liam.

"It certainly has its charm," Liam agreed with a smirk. Then he leaned toward her with his mischievous grin. "About what she said . . . about us. What do you think about that?"

Emma's heart lurched. She'd planned on ignoring the remark altogether. She hadn't expected Liam to bring it up.

"I . . ." She was at a loss for words.

"All right, here we are." Isabelle returned, oblivious to the scene she was interrupting. Emma breathed a sigh of relief. What was she supposed to say to *that*?

Isabelle poured a deep red liquid into the two teacups that sat on the table. "This is hibiscus tea. I don't know about mocktails, but I've always loved the color."

"I agree," said Emma. "The color of a drink is a big part of the experience, so depending on the flavor, this could work."

As Isabelle poured, aromas of cranberries and raspberries wafted around them.

Emma took a sip. The tea was unsurprisingly tart, but also fruity. There was a light floral note that added a surprising complexity.

Immediately, drink recipes began to run through her mind. She'd made enough alcoholic drinks that she thought she could use the flavors. Something with orange would pair well, but she believed lime and mint flavors would also complement it nicely.

"Yes, this is exactly what I had in mind. We'll take some of this. I'm also looking for something rather specific. You don't have a tea that is either blue or purple, would you?"

Isabelle thought about the request for only a moment. "I have just the thing." She ran behind the shop's counter in search of whatever it was she had in mind.

Emma did her best to avoid eye contact with Liam. Was he truly interested in her? It was what she wanted, but he didn't know who she was. Not truly. He was sweet, caring, and kind. He'd never accept her with all the horrible things she'd done.

They sat in silence for the moment, but she could feel Liam's eyes on her, waiting for her response to his previous question.

Thankfully, Isabelle returned before she had to.

"Now, this is a delicious tea that might be what you are looking for. I normally recommend adding a spot of honey, but it's probably best to try it on its own first so you're able to determine the flavor profiles."

Isabelle poured the liquid from the pot into two glasses set out on the counter.

"It's bright blue!" Liam said, clearly surprised by its color.

"That's not even the best part about this tea," Isabelle smiled. "Go ahead and try it and then I'll show you what I mean."

Intrigued, Emma lifted the tea and inhaled the steaming aromas wafting from it. The scent was subtle and a bit sour, though not unpleasant. She took a sip. The flavors were a bit earthy. The subtlety could work to her advantage. Using this tea as a base to a drink for the color alone meant she could manipulate its flavors with other ingredients.

"It doesn't taste like much," Liam said, a bit skeptical.

"Not on its own," Isabelle nodded. "Like I said, usually you add honey or something to bring a bit of sweetness to it. But let me show you why this tea could be a great choice for your drinks."

"What did you say the name of it was?" Liam asked as he took another sip.

"It's butterfly pea tea."

Liam choked, and if he hadn't already swallowed, Emma guessed he would have spat the drink out.

Emma's eyes widened, and she sat the drink down. She'd heard of drinks crafted from stranger things than butterfly pee, though she had to admit she was surprised it was such a bright blue color.

"Butterfly *what*?" Liam stuck out his tongue as though gagging at the thought, his tongue tinted with a hint of blue.

Isabelle laughed. "Butterfly P-E-A," she spelled. "It's a type of flower petal."

Liam face reddened as he let the explanation register, then he burst out laughing. "Oh, goodness. For a moment I thought you had us drinking blue insect piss."

Isabelle joined in the laughter. "Oh, heavens, no. There are some strange teas that are brewed out there, but this is simply flower petals. The flower gives it both the color and the subtle flavor."

Liam flushed with embarrassment. Emma took another sip to mask her own.

"Now, here's where things get interesting," said Isabelle. She reached below the counter and pulled out a small glass bottle. "If I add some tonic water, watch what happens."

She let a stream flow slowly from the bottle into the cup of blue tea, and before Emma's eyes, the liquid turned from blue to purple to a bright shade of pink.

"Magic," Emma whispered.

Isabelle raised an eyebrow. "It's not true magic, lovely, but it does make for a nice party trick. I imagine that, using this, you could come up with an impressive drink to wow your guests."

Emma thought for a moment. She'd used magic to make such transformations in the past, but it was always a gamble if the world she was on wasn't friendly to magic. This would be a much less risky way of impressing a potential patron.

She shuddered to think what Moira might do if she discovered her using magic to change the color of drinks.

"This is perfect! I'll take some of that as well. I'm sure I can create a recipe that will put this to good use."

"Excellent," Isabelle said with delight. "Now, you don't have to use tonic water. Any acidic drink or garnish will do. You can also use lemon or lime, and it will have the same effect."

They tried a few more teas, and Emma ended up with quite a variety that she could experiment with.

It was only then that Emma realized she had no way to pay

for her purchase, but thankfully, Liam happily paid for the tea at the expense of the bar.

Isabelle wrapped them into cute little packages and placed them in a bag for them to carry back with them.

"Come back here anytime—either of you," she said. "And Liam, don't let that one slip through your fingers!"

Emma blushed, thanked Isabelle, and quickly left the shop.

Hibiscus Citrus Cooler

Ingredients:

- 2 cups hibiscus tea, brewed and chilled
- 1/2 cup fresh orange juice
- 1/4 cup fresh lime juice
- 1 tablespoon honey or agave syrup (adjust to taste)
- 1/2 cup sparkling water or club soda
- Ice cubes
- Fresh mint leaves, for garnish
- Orange or lime slices, for garnish

Directions:

1. Brew 2 cups of hibiscus tea according to the package directions. Let it steep until it's a deep red color, then chill it in the refrigerator.
2. In a large pitcher, combine the chilled hibiscus tea, orange juice, lime juice, and honey or agave syrup. Stir until well mixed.
3. Fill glasses with ice cubes, then pour the hibiscus mixture until the glass is about ¾ full.
4. Add a splash of sparkling water to each glass for a bit of fizz. Stir gently.
5. Garnish with fresh mint leaves and a slice of orange or lime on the rim of each glass.

Moira's fears have become real, though not in the way we expected.

I'm still not convinced that there's any sort of correlation between the attacks on our worlds and the failings in the pub, but it's been enough to set Tim on edge.

Rudy is still adamant the events are unrelated, even as Tarvo returns to defend his world of dwarves. Needless to say, Rudy is devastated, but Tarvo won't let him travel back with him, saying it's too dangerous. It breaks my heart to see him have to say goodbye to the only man he's ever loved.

Ed's wife Sarah has returned to her world as well as there have been rumblings of Tíogar Mór sightings there also.

For now, I stand firm in this realm, holding out hope that this will all blow over. We can't possibly close up now; it's the gateway to many of our friends' home worlds, and they need hope now more than ever.

Moira has been vehemently adamant that we close things down, and I know Tim leans in that direction as well.

It's heartbreaking to even consider that as a possibility, meaning that doing so while Tarvo and Sarah are on the other side of their gateways might deny them a way to return. But I know that they would agree it'd be for the best. At least until the threat from their worlds has passed.

But we can't allow fear to win. This place is the one vestige of hope for so many people.

For now, the beer is still flowing, and patrons, as always, find solace here.

Emma

When it was time to open The Pint and Portal for its second night, Emma felt a little more prepared. Despite the few hiccups, opening night had gone rather well, and now she had a few more drink recipes under her belt. She'd been dreaming of potential cocktails and mocktails all day, both with tea and without, and she was eager to try them.

Almost the moment Liam pulled the switch to open the portals, Hal strolled in, casually taking his spot at the end of the bar. Emma inhaled sharply. She had also been trying to set aside her past prejudices when it came to the ogre and had conjured up something special to try and build a connection with him.

"Ale." The volume of the ogre's voice seemed a little less intimidating this evening.

"I've got a number of new drinks on the board tonight, Hal," Emma said, swallowing back her nervousness. "Would you like to try one of them?"

The green ogre raised his head, opening one eye wide and studying her. Emma wasn't sure if he was considering it or giving her the stink eye.

"I've got something called Swamp Water that I dreamed up last night. It was inspired by you."

Hal grunted. Emma could have sworn he was smirking.

"Ale," he said. His tone wasn't as gruff as it had been. There might have even been a touch of humor behind it.

Emma laughed. "You got it, buddy."

She grabbed the oversized mug that she'd used the night before and considered the types of beers she had on tap. There were the original beers they'd tried: The Sunset Pale Ale, the Coastal Shadows, as well as the original Night Stout. But Adam had also brought over a few more brews. The first were two different styles, his Emerald IPA and a Cuanmore Kölsch. There was a third that she specifically requested and was almost surprised he had. It was a non-alcoholic version of the stout that he called the Nocturne Zero. Just because someone didn't drink, it didn't mean they shouldn't be able to enjoy a good brew.

Last night, Hal had seemed to enjoy the Pale Ale, and she wondered if she should mix it up. The IPA was stronger, with far more hops and citrus notes. She figured the ogre might appreciate it, so she grabbed his extra-large glass and poured.

She lifted the mug with both hands and set it carefully on the bar top beside Hal.

"Something a little different from last night," she said. "You'll have to let me know what you think." Emma wondered how Adam would react if he knew his brews were being sampled and reviewed by an ogre.

The ogre nodded respectfully.

"Swamp water, you say?" came a voice behind her. "What's in it?"

Emma turned to see a younger gentleman sitting at the bar. He was dressed head to toe in a brown-gray robe decorated with vines and leaves. He had a short, fiery-red beard, and his hair was matted, but his eyes held a piercing glow that captured Emma's attention. He leaned on the bar, his staff propped beside him, a grin spreading at the thought of whatever description she was about to share.

But his eagerness couldn't mask the tiredness in his eyes.

"It's a bit of a tropical blend"—Emma pulled out a glass and set it on the bar—"with flavors of kiwi and pineapple. Want to try one?"

The man nodded. "It sounds delightful."

Emma, satisfied that she was going to be able to craft this cocktail for somebody, got to work. She'd peeled a few kiwis earlier in the day, hoping she'd get the chance to make this drink. She put them in a blender and let it run for a few seconds to get a nice puree. Then she poured the blend through a strainer, removing the chunkiest bits of fruit that didn't quite become liquid. She didn't want anyone having to chew their drink.

In a shaker cup, she added ice then poured the strained puree over top. She added pineapple juice, coconut rum, vodka, and a splash of lime juice. For color, she grabbed a small scoop of spirulina powder and added it to the mixture, before closing the cup and shaking it vigorously.

As she shook the mixture, she reached out ever so slightly with her magic, instructing the gin and rum to blend seamlessly with the other ingredients, highlighting the tropical flavors enough so that it turned out extra special.

The man watched with wide eyes as she added an ice globe to his glass and poured the green mixture over it. She grabbed a sprig of mint and popped it on top before sliding the glass across the bar.

"One Swamp Water." She grinned.

"Marvelous!" the man exclaimed. He eyed the green beverage, holding it up to the light, then took a sip. "My, for something called 'swamp water,' this is sure refreshing."

Hal who had been quiet until then grunted. He lifted a colossal hand and pointed at the young man. "I'll try."

Emma couldn't mask the grin on her face. If she could break through the ogre's stoic exterior, if she could befriend him, maybe it would be a step on the journey of moving on from her past. It wouldn't erase what she'd done—nothing ever could—but maybe it would prove she was no longer the person she once had been.

Determined, she repeated the process of crafting the cocktail, this time doubling the recipe. She assumed an ogre's alcohol tolerance was far higher than that of an average-sized person, but the real challenge was the glass. Even with a larger one, the drink would seem comically small in Hal's massive green hand—more like a shot than a proper cocktail.

When she placed the drink in front of him, the vibrant green liquid barely filled a fraction of his enormous grip. Hal lifted the glass to his lips, took a slow sip, then smiled.

A toothy grin split his face, revealing crooked teeth that jutted out at odd angles, their edges uneven and yellowed. In any other setting, Emma might have found the display horrifying, but here, in the dim light of The Pint and Portal, it didn't quite feel that way.

She forced herself to take a deep breath, steadying the flicker of unease that still sat in the back of her mind. Hal's smile was sincere. That much was apparent. And so, she pushed down the old prejudices that whispered in her ear, the ones she hadn't realized she was still carrying. This wouldn't be easy, but she was willing to do the work. She'd start by being appreciative that Hal was enjoying his drink.

"I think the magic added a unique flair." The young man winked.

Gloria suddenly appeared beside the man, causing Emma's heart to race. She didn't want the dwarf to know her secret, at least not yet.

"Three pints of stout for the table of humans in the back," Gloria said, oblivious to the man's comment. Emma breathed a sigh of relief as the dwarf continued. "You might want to go talk to them. They seem as though they're a little out of their element here."

Aren't we all.

She put the cloaked man's comment to the side for the moment. She'd have to wait for Gloria to leave before she could question it anyway. She grabbed three pint glasses and started pouring.

"It looks like we're going to have a busy night. If I get a chance, I'll make my way over there. What seems to be the issue?"

"I don't know if it's an issue, per se. But they seem like they stumbled off their farms and haven't seen a dwarf before."

"That's not really surprising," Emma said. "But I'll see what I can do. Where's James?" She took a quick glance around the pub.

"He's around. But you seem to have more experience with the type of world these folk are from. I thought you'd make them feel more at ease."

"Got ya," Emma said. "Let me finish up here and I'll come say hi." She put the three stouts on a tray and handed it to her.

"Thanks." Gloria grabbed the tray and was off.

Emma turned her attention to the man who sat before her, eyeing his appearance, his attire, and the staff that rested beside him. It was all coming together.

She inclined toward him, keeping her voice low. "You're a wizard?"

"Hmm? Druid, actually. But it seems you're something of a magic wielder yourself. I have to say you're the first mage I've encountered who balances spellcraft and bartending."

Emma resisted the urge to reach for the dagger beneath her cloak. She wasn't yet sure, but she felt the man was taunting her.

"Druid, wizard, mage," she said. "It's all the same."

The man pursed his lips. "Not entirely, though some may see it that way. Mages usually wield the elements: fire, water, wind, and the like. Wizards are scholars and typically stay indoors. Us druids, we protect the natural order of things."

Emma couldn't help but smirk. "So, like plants and animals?"

The druid snorted. "Well . . . yes, but lately it's been a little more involved than that. It appears the fabric of space and time have been . . . off balance."

"What's your name?" Emma asked.

"You can call me Nethramir," he replied. "I'm afraid I arrived here by accident. Though, I welcome a brief respite."

"I'm fairly new here," she said. "But from what I've seen, nobody arrives here by accident. I take it that it's not a good time for magic users in your realm?"

"Not such a good time for anyone," he replied. "A great shadow has overtaken my world. I was tasked with overseeing a group of young lads in search of a set of magic stones that might restore balance. I'm unsure if they'll have what it takes, but the prophecies were very clear about the time and place the chosen one would be born. I must trust the ancient texts."

"Why is it that we trust what the ancients said?" Emma asked, leaning on the bar. "Everyone always talks about ancient wisdom. Hell, this place and its wards were supposedly created by the magic of the ancients. We put so much faith in people who were likely as clueless as we are."

Nethramir nodded and raised an eyebrow. "This place was formed by an ancient magic, indeed. But the wards . . . those are much more recent. I'd say a couple decades."

"Decades?" Emma repeated. That didn't agree with what she'd been told. "How can you tell?"

The druid lifted his arms, his gray robe fanning out as he did so. "I'm a guardian of time and space. I not only sense magic, I can also determine when it was crafted. How do you think I knew you added magic to the ogre's drink?" He tapped his nose and leaned forward, a sparkle in his eye.

"That information isn't exactly common knowledge around these parts." Emma kept her voice low. "I'd prefer to keep it that way for the time being."

"Understood." Nethramir leaned back on his stool. "My apologies, I didn't mean to offend. But I'd be careful with that, there are others who can sense magic as well. The truth will come to light eventually."

Emma sighed. "It's not that simple. My past is a bit . . . unsavory."

"Doing the right thing is seldom easy," said Nethramir, "but hiding the truth often causes us more heartache than necessary."

"Yeah, yeah, O wise one." Emma couldn't keep the sass from her voice. She did refrain from rolling her eyes—barely. "So how did you happen to find the gateway that brought you here?"

"One of the lads brought with them an orb they said had been in their village for centuries. They thought it might be one of the talismans we needed. It was not, but I recognized the markings on it from a doorframe that had been built into the wall of our keep. Its purpose had been long forgotten. Very peculiar that it led here. A tavern with visitors from many realms. I must say it was a pleasant surprise."

"What had you expected?" Emma smirked.

Nethramir took a sip of his drink then chuckled. "Well, I suppose I don't know. Perhaps a hidden chamber of artifacts or secrets. Not this."

"This place has plenty of its own secrets, if that's what you're after."

Out of the corner of her eye, Emma noticed the portal from O'Sullivan's warble shut. James walked in with a tired look on his face. That man would need to get some more rest if he was going to continue to run two pubs with any efficiency.

But she could tell there was something else that was bothering him.

The druid tipped his glass toward her. "If you're any indication, then it does indeed."

Emma smirked. "That's not quite what I meant but . . . Actually, that gives me an idea."

"Oh?" Nethramir asked.

Before she could answer, James approached the bar. They hadn't even been open for two nights, and already James' eyes had bags under them. She could sense the pressure he was under to keep things running, and it was a mystery to her why he'd felt the need to jump into opening things up so quickly.

"How is everything going over here?" he asked.

"I think quite well," Emma replied. "But we're just getting warmed up." She nodded to the druid. "James, I'd like you to meet Nethramir. He's a druid, and apparently he can detect certain things about magic."

James stuck out a hand. "It's nice to meet you. I'm James, the owner of The Pint and Portal."

"Splendid!" said the druid. "I must say your barkeep is exceptional. A fine mixologist, and a highly skilled conversationalist."

"Is that so?" James gave Emma a sly smirk. "I have to admit, we've been so busy that I haven't spent as much time chatting with her as I'd like."

"Oh, a shame," said Nethramir. "She's quite insightful. And she's got a knack for crafting cocktails like nobody I've ever seen. There's certainly a magic to her craft."

Emma shot the druid a warning glare. The man was being intentionally coy about her ability.

"I've only heard good things from our patrons," James said, oblivious to Emma's scowl.

"James," said Emma, cutting in before Nethramir could say anything further. "I think the druid might be able to give us some answers to one of the questions we had earlier."

James raised a puzzled eyebrow, clearly unsure of what she was referring to. "Oh. Is that so?"

Emma turned her attention back to the druid. "Nethramir, how much about magic are you able to decipher? If we provided you with something that we believe had been influenced by magic, would you be able to give us any details about it?"

"It depends on what it is," he said thoughtfully.

Emma grabbed a glass and pulled on the tap from Adam's Nocturne Speciale brew. "We received a stout from a local brewer. It gave us visions when we drank some."

The druid leaned forward. "Is he a magician brewer?"

"I've known this man since we were kids," James said. "He's no magician."

"Hmm." Nethramir stroked his red beard as he pondered. "You know, there are natural hallucinogens that could cause such an experience. Mushrooms, plants, herbs, all sorts of compounds."

James nodded in agreement.

"If it was just the visions, I'd possibly accept that," said Emma.

She cast a wayward eye to James. She supposed he was bound to find out sooner than later.

"Please don't say anything to Liam," she said. She remembered Moira's visceral reaction to the thought of magic users coming through the gateways. "Or Moira . . . Not yet. But as Nethramir has already determined, I have a bit of a magical ability myself. Alcohol speaks to me and I'm able to manipulate it in the drinks I make. It's part of the reason why my cocktails are as good as they are, the alcohol tells me what it needs."

Emma paused momentarily to try and gauge James' face for a reaction, but he didn't flinch. Perhaps after meeting dwarves, ogres, and gnomes, a little bit of magical mixology was hardly a stretch.

She was more worried about him finding out what she did *before* she discovered her talents.

"Anyway," she continued, "I can't sense anything from this stout at all. It's as if it's blocking my magic somehow. I've never come across anything like it, and I don't think a non-magical ingredient could impose that kind of block."

She slid the glass across the bar. Nethramir inspected the glass, gave it a sniff, then looked at it again. He lifted his hand over top of it and waved it in a circular fashion. The beverage began to swirl, mimicking his movement.

Nethramir grunted as he studied the glass before him. "You're right, there is indeed magic here," he said. "The user *has* done something to mask what type of magic they used. I cannot tell if it's an ingredient, a spell, or something else entirely."

"Is it dangerous?" James asked.

"You've had some, haven't you? You seem to be standing upright and in one piece. But there's no telling if it's put you under some enchantment or other spell."

James frowned. "Great."

Emma sighed. "I guess we need to confront Adam. I can't serve this knowing there's some unknown magic attached to it."

"Agreed," said James. "Those dwarves last night seemed to think there's a beer here with a magic ingredient that a magic caster brewed. I don't know what Adam's up to, but we'll head back there tomorrow. One more mystery to solve in this endless puzzle of a bar."

"Did you want to try drinking that?" Emma asked Nethramir.

"I don't make a habit of toying with unknown magic," he said. "Especially one that's gone through such a great effort to mask itself."

"Fair enough," said Emma. "I can't say I blame you."

As Emma turned to dump the drink, she felt the hint of a breeze brush past her ear, and a thud in the wall behind her. She whipped her head toward the origin of the noise. A dagger was lodged into a wooden post, still shaking back and forth from the momentum of being flung.

"What the . . .?" She ducked instinctively and snatched her own dagger from its sheath in a single motion. The weight of the blade sharpened her focus as her eyes darted toward the direction the attack had come from.

The room seemed to hold its breath. Then, breaking the silence, a woman's voice rang out.

"Witch hunter!" she spat. "A curse on your soul and on your house for a thousand years!"

Liam and Ha'dran had already rushed to either side of the woman, grabbing an arm each, restraining her from doing any more damage. She was middle-aged, with straggly hair and a peasant's cloak pulled around her.

A pouch hung by her side with the hilts of three other daggers visible.

The restraint didn't stop her from spitting on the floor again. "Vile woman! She stole my daughters! None of us are safe with her here! You must pay for your crimes!"

Several gasps came from around the room. Emma sighed and sheathed her own dagger before lifting open palms toward the woman.

"That's not who I am," she spoke the words to herself as much as anyone else. "At least, not anymore."

Ingredients:

- 4 ounces fresh pineapple juice
- Kiwi puree (well strained)
- 1 ounce coconut rum
- 1 ounce vodka
- A few drops of spirulina or liquid chlorophyll (optional, for color)
- Crushed or cubed icc
- Fresh mint, for garnish

Directions:

1. Blend a peeled kiwi until smooth. It's highly recommended to strain for a smoother texture.
2. In a shaker with ice, combine the pineapple juice, kiwi puree, coconut rum, vodka, lime juice, and spirulina or chlorophyll. Shake well.
3. Fill a glass with crushed ice and strain the green mixture over it.
4. Garnish with fresh mint.

Mocktail Version

Follow the above recipe with the following substitutions:

- Substitute Coconut Water for Coconut Rum
- Substitute White Grape or Pear Juice for Vodka

James

The next morning, James made it his first order of business to pay Adam a visit, a swarm of unanswered questions caught in his mind like a violent storm.

It was one thing to learn that Emma possessed magic—it was unexpected but believable. But Adam? James had grown up with him, had spent days in the schoolyard with him, played rugby and hurling with him. The man was many things, but magician wasn't one of them.

He couldn't believe it. He wouldn't.

He needed to learn more about the Nocturne Speciale and uncover whatever was happening with the visions that both he and Emma had experienced. Even if the answers were unbelievable.

There's a magical pub in the back of my closet. Nothing should be unbelievable at this point.

The bartender strolled next to him as they walked through Cuanmore's empty streets. It was mid-morning, and the town streets felt emptier than they normally would this time of day.

Crisp air nipped at James' face, and he pulled his wool jacket tighter around himself, the ocean breeze cutting through the fabric.

Emma, however, seemed unfazed by the chill. She walked

casually with her hands tucked in her pockets as though cold didn't touch her. The flush in her cheeks was the only indication that she felt the chill at all.

The two walked in silence for a few minutes as James tried to parse out the words he needed to say. Surveying this bartender who had become such an important person to himself and The Pint and Portal, he realized this was the first time the two of them had been alone.

Suddenly the vast number of questions he had seemed overwhelming. Where did he begin? He was quickly realizing he barely knew the bartender. What had Emma's life looked like before she arrived through the gateway? Who was this woman who carried daggers, mixed amazing cocktails, and supposedly held some sort of magic?

"So are we going to talk about last night?" he asked. "Or are you planning on keeping your secrets to yourself?"

After the altercation the previous night, Emma had taken leave to her room, apparently dazed by the entire encounter. Liam and Tarvo escorted the woman back to her portal, informed her that sort of behavior wasn't welcome at The Pint and Portal, and instructed her not to return. The encounter left the pub buzzing with questions, but with Emma's absence the talk was nothing more than idle speculation. Of course, she had a right to keep her past to herself, but it would be nice if he'd had some warning of such a dramatic display being a possibility.

The gateways lead to an infinite number of worlds, he reminded himself. *I need to remember that absolutely anything is a possibility.*

"Do you need to know all my secrets?" She cocked an eyebrow with a smirk.

"Well . . . no, not *all* your secrets," James replied. "But a patron at *my* bar did toss a knife at your head while accusing you of being a witch hunter right after you said you use magic to mix your drinks. I know I'm new to the whole magic thing, but doesn't that seem a little contradictory? And I'd like to know if I can expect more assassination attempts in our future."

Emma sighed. "I suppose it's a fair question. I would have said something sooner, but I didn't know how you'd react."

James let out a laugh. "I mean, how do you figure I should react to my head bartender being on the receiving end of an assassination attempt? In the list of strange things that have happened this week, what's one more?"

Emma nodded. "It's a bit of a long story."

"We've got all the time we need. Why don't we take the scenic route? There's a trail that will take us to the ocean lookout. The sea air will be good for us."

That seemed to put Emma at ease, her shoulders releasing some of the tension they were holding. "That sounds nice."

James took a turn that would lead them toward the coast. It had been some time since he'd explored the town himself, perhaps wandering through the cobbled streets of the village would be good for him as well. As they walked past the stone cottages draped in ivy and shopfronts painted in cheerful hues, he couldn't help the wave of nostalgia that overtook him.

Is this really the place I've been trying to get away from? Compared to the bustling streets of Vancouver, there was a kind of peace here. The air was remarkably cleaner, the streets far less crowded, and rather than having their faces buried in their phones, the few people they passed gave them an enthusiastic smile along with a wave. It wasn't quite the fantasy world of the dwarves, druids, or ogres, but despite the chaos happening within the pub and in his life, here he felt like he could breathe.

"Why don't you start with your world," James said after a time. "And how magic fits into all of this."

Emma took a deep breath. "In my world, most of what you call Europe is one territory we call Lancastria and is under the rule of one king. The history of how that happened isn't really as relevant as the fact that our king hated magic. So much so that he put an incredible number of resources into attempting to snuff it out entirely. It was something many of the citizens feared."

James could imagine if people in his world found out magic was real, many of them would be afraid of it as well. "Why did the king hate magic so much?"

Emma paused briefly before answering. "I'm sure there was a root cause for it all, but in the end, magic was different. In my world, much as in every world I've visited since I left, those who are different are an easy target to blame. It was easy to gain support for an anti-magic campaign when one could point to literal monsters and claim that was what all magic was like. Those who didn't have magic were taught to fear it. Those who had magic feared for their lives as any wrong move, any accusation, meant certain death."

"It was a crime for someone to possess magic?"

Emma nodded. "The king didn't really categorize it as a crime, though that was how it was treated. Magic was called a curse. We were taught it could spread, so my job was to cut it out before it could."

James had to admit he was struggling to keep up a bit. He had so many questions. "Your job . . . was to rid your kingdom of magic. So that woman was right, you *are* a witch hunter?"

"I was," Emma admitted. "For most of my life. As I child, I lived on the street. I'd learned how to fight and how to take care of myself. At a young age, I was recruited and trained as a member of what we called the Hunters of the Cursed. Like the name says, we hunted magical creatures. Monsters born of magic, mostly. But our mandate was to rid the world of *all* magic. Often that meant arresting magic users."

A hunter of magic working in a magical pub. James wondered, if he kept The Pint and Portal open, if there'd come a time when nothing could surprise him anymore. He doubted it. "But obviously, you don't think that way anymore?"

Emma shook her head. "I know now that aside from being an evil task, it was an impossible one."

"Impossible? How?" James asked. "It sounds as if they had developed quite a campaign to seeing it destroyed."

"Saying you want to rid the world of magic is like saying you want to rid it of fire, or water. It's not a force that can be stopped. Sure, you can stomp it down or dam it up. You can keep it at bay for a time, but at some point, it will burst through and find its way."

They'd reached the lookout now. Far below, ocean waves crashed upon the rocky surface of the island. James paused, his gaze drawn to the relentless motion of the water as it smashed against the cliffs, working its way into the cracks before receding, only to surge forward again moments later. Beside him, Emma stood silently, her cloak flapping in the breeze and slapping against her calves and the blades she carried.

"Let me guess," James said after a time, "magic found its way to you, and you had to take a good look at who you were, and what you were doing with your life?"

Emma smirked. "It sounds like quite the fairytale, doesn't it? My entire world came crashing down in one single night. I had to decide if I was indeed cursed or if my entire worldview was wrong."

"I imagine that wasn't easy to accept after a lifetime fighting against it?"

Emma chuckled softly. "It was both easy and incredibly difficult. Self-preservation kicked in and I abandoned my post. Ran away to the clear other side of the kingdom—to right here in Cuanmore, in fact. If I hadn't, I would have likely been executed. But to believe I wasn't cursed? No, that took far longer, and I didn't do it alone either."

James nodded. It sounded like Emma had been on quite a

journey of self-discovery. "So this magic of yours . . . what does it do?"

Emma adjusted her cloak against the wind. "As I mentioned last night, I have a power that connects with alcohol. I can speak with it to enhance its properties, reverse spoiled wine, or enhance flavors in the drinks I mix. I had always wanted to be a bartender. When I learned I had this power, I realized why that had felt like my true calling."

James let out a short burst of air through his nostrils. "True calling . . ." He spoke the thought out loud, though it wasn't complete. "I wish I knew what my true calling was."

"What do you mean?" Emma said. "You have The Pint and Portal. I've traveled more than anyone, and I've never seen anyone possess such an incredible gift."

James let his gaze wander the vast stretch of ocean before them and let out a sigh. "It's not that it isn't remarkable . . . it's just . . . I've spent my whole life trying to leave Cuanmore. I've always felt trapped here in a life that was perfectly adequate but never truly mine. I set out to explore the world, have adventures and make something of myself. Coming back to it now feels like I've failed. Even though the pub is more amazing than I'd ever imagined possible, it wasn't something I chose for myself, you know? It was kind of dropped on me."

"You know," Emma said wryly, "you keep talking as if you had no choice in this matter. You don't *have* to stay here. You don't have to keep the pub open."

James exhaled. "I do though. If I don't run O'Sullivan's for a year, neither Kathy nor I receive our inheritance. You've seen how busy she is with her firm, she's hardly ever around the pub. She's got other responsibilities."

"Have you asked Kathy about what she thinks? Because I don't think she'd blame you for not wanting to do this."

"And go where?" he asked. "I don't have any job prospects, and I have nowhere else to go."

"You have nowhere *easy* left to go," said Emma. "But there's nothing stopping you from leaving this town and going anywhere else in the world."

James paused for a moment to consider what Emma was saying. She was right, he hadn't been held here by anyone other than himself. If he thought about it, he knew what was truly keeping him there.

"I don't want to let anyone down," he admitted, as much to himself as to her. "Kathy, my parents, you."

"Me?" Emma asked.

"If I don't keep The Pint and Portal open, where will you and the dwarves go? Back to the devastated world you came from? That's not right either."

"We'd figure something out," Emma said, then inhaled sharply, "But I do appreciate that you've allowed us to stay. Don't get me wrong, being a bartender at Pint and Portal is like a dream come true. But in the end, if you want to leave, it's within your ability. My original point still stands, the only one standing in the way of you leaving is you."

James let out a long exhale. Emma wasn't wrong but somehow it didn't seem all that simple. The crashing of the waves on the rocks below felt as though they were beating over him, wearing him down the longer he stayed put.

"What was it that made you want to get away in the first place?" Emma asked.

James thought back to his childhood and had to wonder if the feeling of moving on had always been a part of who he was. "My mother would always tell me stories of grand adventures," he said after some thought. "Of heroes who had left their small villages to save the world, to create something, to live an amazing life. I always thought that would be me, that I could be the hero in one of those stories, and I knew it could never happen if I stayed here. Cuanmore is a sleepy town that's got nothing more than a few shops and a view looking out to an endless sea. It always felt so ordinary."

Emma rested a hand on James' shoulder. "All of that has changed. You literally have access to any world you could ever imagine. Sometimes our preconceptions of the world evolve as we grow older. Sometimes they have to. And that's okay. I've explored more than probably anyone else there is. First, I traveled from town to town in my kingdom, but now I regret almost everything I did during that entire time. Then I traveled from one world to the next. I've experienced some incredible magic, encountered some amazing people. After a while I realized I was missing something."

James snorted, unconvinced. He looked back at the village —the family-run shops and small apartments that littered the streets. The town still *felt* the same. It still seemed ordinary. Maybe even more so compared to the worlds belonging to the patrons of The Pint and Portal. "Yeah? What was that."

"Somewhere to return to when I grew tired of being on the move," she said. "People who truly care about me, and a place to call home."

"You got to leave though," James said. "You got to escape your life and go on a grand adventure. You've seen and done things, have grand stories to tell. What have I done? I crossed an ocean, yeah, but for what? To sit at a desk behind a computer all day only to come crawling back."

"You think that's what I did?" Emma laughed. "Embarked on some great adventure? I was running away! That woman in there didn't throw a dagger at my head for no reason. I've done some truly horrible things in my life and regret them all. I've spent the last two years trying to outrun my past. Now, for the first time I think I've realized it can't be done. And I have nowhere to return to. No place I call home. A pub like Pint and Portal? It's that piece I've been missing."

James stood in silence, unsure of what to say.

"Don't give me that look. You don't have to feel sorry for me. I made the choices I did. I know I acted under false information, but I still destroyed a lot of people's lives. There's a debt on my soul that I'll never be able to repay."

James inhaled deeply, trying to process what Emma was saying. No matter what, she still hadn't been stuck in one place. She'd still lived a life fit for stories. Not stuck in a pub, only able to hear about the adventures of others.

"So, if it feels like home, I suppose you'll be staying for a while."

Emma's gaze grew distant as she surveyed the town, but James didn't believe she was looking at anything in particular.

"I suppose that depends at least partially on you. Even if you decide to keep things running, I guess part of me has been worried you'd force me to leave once you found out who I truly am. But otherwise, I think I could stick around here for a long time, depending on how certain circumstances play out."

"By circumstances you mean Liam?"

Emma shot him a startled look.

James continued. "I see the way you look at him, and the way he looks at you."

Emma bit her lip. "I think he was about to ask me out yesterday. We were interrupted and then I made sure he didn't get another chance."

"What's stopping you? Liam's one of the best guys I know. If you tell him, I'm sure he'll understand. Plus, after last night, I'm sure the thought's already crossed his mind. It'd be better if he heard the full story from you."

"It's one thing to have an employee with a past," she said. "It's another to find out something like that about someone you're romantically invested in."

"I think Liam would surprise you if you gave him a chance. He's been the least fazed by everything that's happened here. I don't know if a little bit of drink magic and a troubled past will scare him away."

"There's more to it than that," she said. "But it's something I won't discuss until I've chatted with him first. If I do at all . . ."

As mysterious as that sounded, James didn't think Emma should let it stop her.

"I've known Liam a long time. I've never seen him look at someone like he looks at you."

Emma's face twisted in disbelief. "He's never been interested anyone?"

"I wouldn't say that exactly. He's had girlfriends. Mind you, I've been away for a bit, but as far as I've known, none of them have made his eyes light up the way they do when he sees you. It's so strange. It's not like him to get so caught up with someone he's just met. But he seems familiar around you. Like you've known each other your entire lives."

Emma cleared her throat and lifted a hand to her bright red hair. "Yes, well . . . I have a way with people sometimes."

James was unconvinced, but he wouldn't press her into sharing something she was uncomfortable with.

"I'm surprised he's never married," she continued, "or settled down with anyone. He seems like such a nice guy."

"You'll never meet a better fellow than him," James agreed.

"That's what I'm afraid of. He might be too good for someone like me."

"Don't sell yourself short," James said. "People can change. I don't know the half of what you've been through, but it sounds like you've grown."

"It doesn't change who I was. The things I've done."

All those lessons in storytelling had at least taught him one thing. "What's the point of a hero's journey if there's no redemption at the end?" he asked.

Emma scoffed. "I'm no hero."

James couldn't help but smile at the advice of a thousand

character-storyboarding sessions resonating in his mind. "Everybody's the hero of their own story. And every decision you've made has brought you to this point. Right now, in this universe. Look, I can't know what it's like to go through what you have, but I've always believed that everyone deserves a second chance."

Emma shrugged off the statement, but from the distant look in her eyes, James could tell she was mulling over his words.

"As far as not settling down goes," James continued, "Liam's spent a lot of time helping Moira keep the deli going. He never knew his dad, and I think, right or wrong, he's always felt like it's his job to be the man of the house. The fact that he was willing to leave it to help manage the pub makes me think he believes things are running smoothly enough without him now."

"Moira." Emma snapped back into focus. "She seems so against magic. What would she think about . . ."

"I wouldn't worry about her." James dismissed the objection. "She's rough around the edges, but she's a kind soul. Where do you think Liam gets it from?"

Emma nodded, though the distance in her eyes told James she was still not fully convinced.

"Come on," he said. "We should probably pay Adam that visit."

They wound their way back through the village streets, taking their time before arriving at the brewery. It was still early in the day, so Adam wouldn't be in the shop, he'd be at his home, which was attached to the brewery. A small blue cottage that had been built into the side of the larger warehouse where the beer was crafted and stored.

James breathed in the salty air and tried to gather up some conjecture of what he was going to say. Talking to Emma about magic was one thing. She'd been around it her entire life and spoke of it like breathing air or pouring drinks. Even then it made his stomach uneasy.

But if he were going to continue running a magical pub, he supposed he would have to get over those unsettling nerves.

Shite, I'm really considering hanging on to this place, aren't I?

He had a feeling whatever Adam was about to tell him was going to make his decision painfully clear, in one direction or another.

He stepped up to the door and turned to Emma. "Let's see if he's home."

James

"I feel a bit funny about going to his private home like this," said Emma.

Despite her previous trepidation about Liam, she now stood with stoic confidence. Silent and as still as stone, she blended into her surroundings so completely that if James hadn't known she was standing there he might not have seen her at all. It was a disconcerting feeling, considering she was standing right next to him. There was little doubt in his mind that, regardless of how she felt about it, she'd been good at what she'd done.

"Adam won't mind," he said, shaking off the unease. "He told us to drop by anytime. Most folks here would pull us in for breakfast and not let us leave until tea!"

James knocked on the door hesitantly. He might not have been worried about dropping by, but he was about to accuse one of his childhood friends of possessing magic. Up until a few days ago, what would he have thought if the roles were reversed? He'd probably think the person needed some psychiatric help.

He held his hand above the door for a moment. What if this *was* all a hallucination? Perhaps this was how his subconscious was processing the grief of losing his father and his job and the shock of inheriting the family business.

Witch hunters? Portals to other worlds? All his childhood stories coming to life? A sudden surge of panic coursed through him. Maybe this *was* what it was like to completely lose it. *Bleedin' hell, I hope not.*

The door swung open, ripping James from his musing, and revealing Adam looking at them slightly bewildered. His red hair was a mess, standing out at all ends like he hadn't had a chance to comb it yet. He wore chocolate-brown overalls, an olive-green shirt, and matching work boots. The thick, woody smell of hops wafted through the front door.

"Heya, lads. This is a pleasant surprise! I was just going to head into the brewery and get some work done before the sales room opens."

"Sorry for barging in on you, friend," said James. "We wanted to have the craic about your beer and were hoping you can help us out a bit."

"Yeah, for sure!" Adam lit up with an eager grin. "Why don't you come on back with me? You can see where the magic happens."

James nearly choked when he heard the word 'magic' before realizing it was meant as a figure of speech. He scratched the back of his head, trying to mask his surprise.

"That sounds really good," said James. "I'm game."

"Great!" said Adam, waving them inside. "We can get there through the shop."

If James thought the smells of hops and barely were strong coming from the house, they were overpowering when the door to the fermentation rooms opened.

Bins filled with ingredients were stacked high adjacent to the wall, and tall metal bins decorated the room, each with another variation of beer being prepared.

"We've got a number of products getting ready," said Adam. "Most of these will be canned and shipped out to Dublin. We get a lot of sales off site. Most of the rest will be filled into kegs and shipped to nearby pubs and restaurants, including O'Sullivan's."

James only then realized he had never been in the back of a brewery before. The air smelled like warm bread and citrus, the faint hum of machinery blending with the occasional clink of metal. He wasn't even sure what questions he should be asking.

"Let me pour you something," said Adam, grabbing a few glasses off a shelf. "I've got the Night Stout, as well as the Kölsch that I dropped by your place last night."

"I haven't had a chance to try the Kölsch yet," said James. "What's that one like?"

"Oh, it's a great beer—light, crisp, and super refreshing. It's kind of a mix between an ale and a lager. You get this little hint of fruit, like pear or apple, but nothing too strong. The malt's nice and bready, and the hops add just a touch of herbal bitterness. Honestly, it's one of those beers you can drink anytime. I'll pour you one. How about you, Emma?"

"It's a bit earlier than I usually have a beer," Emma said. "But I haven't tried it either, and it'd be good if I could describe it to our customers."

As Adam poured, James let his eyes wander toward the towering steel tanks lining the wall. "So, uh, this is a bit embarrassing to ask, but what exactly am I looking at here?"

Adam chuckled. "First time in a brewery, then? Those are fermentation tanks. This is where the wort—basically unfermented beer—sits while the yeast does its thing."

"Yeast," James repeated, nodding. "And it eats sugar and makes alcohol, right?"

"Exactly!" Adam grinned. "Yeast eats the sugar in the wort and spits out alcohol and CO_2. That's fermentation in a nutshell. But," he added, gesturing toward the tanks, "it's not as simple as tossing everything in and hoping for the best. You've got to have full control over what's going on. Temperature, timing, and ingredients, it all matters."

Emma leaned against the wall, arms crossed, a faint smirk on her face. "You grew up in a pub, yet you don't know how beer's made?"

"Hey, I know how to *drink* beer," James shot back, grinning. "That counts for something, right?"

"Sure, if your goal is to keep Adam in business." Emma winked.

Adam shook his head, laughing. "I mean, I've got no problem with that. But it's always good to know your product. With beer there are mainly a handful of ingredients to consider: malted barley, hops, water, and yeast. The rest is about how you combine them." Adam handed the poured drinks to them before grabbing a small handful of dried green cones from a nearby bin. He held them out. "Smell these."

James leaned in and sniffed. The aroma was sharp and bright, like citrus peel with a hint of pine. "Wow. That's . . . intense."

"Those are Citra hops," Adam explained. "They give off a lot of tropical fruit and citrus notes. Great for IPAs. But if I used something like Fuggle or Saaz, the flavor would be completely different—earthier, more herbal."

James glanced at the tanks again. He was truly curious and surprised he'd never held enough interest to learn all this before. "So how long does it take to make a batch?"

"Depends on the style," Adam replied. "Something like a pale ale? Maybe two to three weeks, start to finish. But if you're brewing a lager, you're looking at six to eight weeks minimum. Lagers ferment colder and slower, which is why they're so crisp and clean."

As fascinating as it all was, James knew they weren't there to chat about beer all day.

"What about the Nocturne Speciale?"

"Ah!" Adam touched his nose with a glint in his eye. "That one's a secret."

James exchanged an uneasy glance with Emma.

"I'm afraid we have to protest," Emma said. "I don't know if I'm comfortable serving this beer without knowing what kind of magic you've used to craft it."

This time James did choke, nearly spitting out the mouthful of Kölsch he'd sipped.

Adam crinkled his forehead.

James raised his hand and stepped between the two of them. "I think I better take this one, Emma."

He reached into his coat and pulled out his mother's journal. He handed it to Adam, and the brewer began to flip the pages, his brow creasing ever deeper as he did so.

"There's a bit more to my inheritance than O'Sullivan's. I'm hoping you can maybe give us some insight."

He gestured to a seat behind the bar. "You might want to sit down for this one."

Adam looked skeptical, but he did as he was asked, and James went on to tell him everything. From The Pint and Portal to the dwarves, to the dagger being thrown at Emma's head the night before. He pointed to the journal.

"That's all the information either of my parents left me. My mother wrote this before she passed. But pages are missing." He flipped the book onto the counter. "It also mentions your parents as being a part of it all."

Adam picked up the journal and leafed through it slowly. His eyes skimming the words as he went. He'd yet to say anything.

"I know this is a lot to take in," James continued. "But there's been some weird magic happening at the pub, and well, like Emma said, there's been some sort of magic infused into the Nocturne Speciale."

Adam's brow furrowed. "You think there's *magic* . . . in my beer?" The brewer, understandably, studied the both of them like they had a few screws loose.

"There's something else we didn't mention. When we did the tasting here the other day, Emma and I had visions after we tried the Speciale. It was more than the nostalgia you had mentioned. It was as if we had been teleported to another location. Living through memories that have never happened. It was more than just a dream, it was as if we were really there."

Adam's mouth hung open as he stood there in a daze. James wasn't sure if the man believed him, or if he was in complete shock.

"From *my* beer?" he repeated. "You're codding me, aren't you?"

"We had a druid come into the bar last night, and he claimed it had been infused with some sort of magic, but he couldn't tell us any more than that."

"A druid?" Adam said incredulously. "In your pub? And he said . . . There has to be some sort of mistake . . ."

"There isn't," Emma said, taking a breath before continuing. "I know what Nethramir was saying is true because I possess a bit of magic myself, and . . . I can usually sense drinks. They talk to me. Your other beers talk to me. But the Speciale is completely silent, as though there's a wall holding me back."

Adam's mouth hung open as his gaze shifted between the two of them.

"Did your dad ever mention The Pint and Portal? Or any of this?" James asked.

Adam shook his head. "Bleedin' hell, he didn't." It took him another moment to sort through whatever thoughts he was processing until finally he said, "But that doesn't mean I don't have answers for you. Come with me."

Adam led them into a back room of the brewery, they passed bags of hops, barley, wheat, and other ingredients that lined the shelves. They continued until they reached a solid metal door. Adam reached into his pocket, pulled out a set of keys, and unlocked the door before ushering them in.

"None of my staff know about this," he said once the door was shut behind them. "I've never told anyone, actually."

There was nothing that immediately stood out as special about the room. A typical office space with a desk and office chair in the center. A filing cabinet had been pushed into the corner, and paintings hung on the wall.

At least, nothing seemed out of the ordinary until he took a good look at one of the paintings. The image depicted a very familiar scene. To anyone else it would have seemed like a whimsical piece of art. It was clearly a pub, but James recognized the spot and the angle instantly. It was a scene from within The Pint and Portal, depicting the bar top with a full shelf of liquor bottles stacked up against the wall behind it.

But that wasn't the part that caught his eye. Seated at the bar, so clear and well illustrated that it could have been painted live the night before, was a muscular, green ogre.

"Hal?"

Adam looked up, his concentration broken. He followed James' gaze to the painting.

"You've seen my mom's painting before?" he asked.

James snorted. "No. I've met the ogre."

"You've met . . ." Adam's mouth moved but no words came out. He shook himself off from whatever thought he had about it. "Never mind."

A set of lockers was stacked up against the wall behind the desk. Adam shuffled the keys on the ring he'd pulled out of his pocket and moved to unlock them, sighing as he went.

"Now, you'll have to believe me, I don't know where this came from," he said as he swung open one of the locker doors. "I found these after Da passed."

Adam pulled out a small red cloth sack, along with a few pieces of paper. He dropped the sack on the table.

James peeled open the bag, revealing its contents. What lay inside were like no mushrooms he'd ever seen before. They had the texture and coloring of common brown mushrooms, but their shape wasn't the round shape of button mushrooms or the jagged shape of oyster mushrooms. The closest thing he could compare them to were morels, the fungal delights found buried in the forest floor. Except these were uniformly shaped, bulbous on one end and tapered on the other—like tear drops.

"He called them Morac Mushrooms. Turns out he was growing them in a room in the back."

James grabbed one and weighed the fungus in his hand. *Tears of the Gods.*

Their shape confirmed his suspicions that these were, in fact, the mystical items T'og and his group of dwarves had been searching for.

"The dwarves and the druid also seemed to think the brewmaster who made the beer must have also been magic." He raised an eyebrow. "You don't happen to be a sorcerer as well?"

Adam lifted his palms. "Man, I'm still trying to decide whether to call a doctor to have your head examined. If it wasn't you, James, I'd think you were crazy. I still wonder if you're having a good laugh at my expense. I mean, these are just mushrooms, I have no way to tell if they're magic or hallucinogenic."

"But you used them. You must have known they were safe, at least. What made you think to add them to beer?" Emma asked.

Adam sighed. "My da left a recipe."

He pulled out a small envelope that had been tucked on the side of the bag and handed it to James. "I'm so sorry, James. I had no idea . . . If I did . . . I would have brought it over to your dad right away."

Inside the envelope were several slips of paper, and James instantly recognized them for what they were. They were slightly more wrinkled, with a few more stains and markings, but the paper was the same, and the writing on them matched his mother's. They had been part of her journal.

There were two pages. On the first page was clearly the brewing recipe Adam referred to. Most of it made no sense to James, but he did notice the inclusion of "Morac Mushrooms."

The second page interested James more.

It's hard to know what to make of the magical mushrooms that Edward has managed to procure. He's keeping their origin a secret, as if any of the rest of us are going to bound off in a quest to gather some mushrooms. I admit there's something compelling about them, but on their own, I don't believe they're worth his fascination with them.

Moira, of course, is desperate to be rid of them. So convinced that Tíogar Mór might be able to sense them, that these were the mystical items they were after on however many worlds they have conquered. Their mere presence in the pub has seemed to set her on edge.

However, reason dictates her fears are unfounded. It isn't as if smells and spores can travel between dimensions, and even if they did, it would be all but impossible to pinpoint their origin.

Edward, on the other hand, has come alive with them. He's been so focused on crafting the perfect recipe that he's almost neglected the rest of his operation. The brew, he claims, will be his crowning achievement, and if he's able to work his magic into the beer, perhaps he can craft something that will be calming to our guests. Another way for them to escape the horrors of their worlds.

We've all experienced the mushrooms' calming effects, though Timothy and Michael claim they saw visions. Perhaps there's a slight hallucinogenic property to them, or maybe they truly are magic. Who's to say.

All I know is, if he can create a brew to help our patrons forget their troubles, if only momentarily, I'm all for it.

Emma

The Pint and Portal sat empty as Emma busied herself tidying behind the bar. Demon Box rested on the counter behind her, and the portal back to O'Sullivan's hummed softly, but otherwise she was alone with her thoughts.

And she desperately tried to keep them occupied with drink recipes and other worlds while she waited for the first round of patrons to emerge from the portals, trying to quell the butterflies that still flapped through her gut. All the while, she did her best to convince herself that the anxious feelings she was experiencing were the byproduct of a dagger whizzing by her head the last time she stood in that exact spot.

Because it couldn't be that.

After all, it hadn't been the first time someone had aimed a dagger at her temple—though, she had hoped that part of her life was behind her. It certainly hadn't been something she'd expected to happen behind the bar of a cozy tavern.

If she were honest, she knew that was the least of what was rolling around in her mind.

I've never seen him look at someone like he looks at you.

That was a lot of pressure to put on her, and she still hadn't sorted out how she felt about Liam yet. Magic or not, there was no way someone as kindhearted as Liam would be willing to settle for someone like her.

Cursed.

No, not cursed. She'd gotten over that label long ago. It was the slur she'd used against magic users back when she tracked them, arrested them. Before she discovered she herself held magic. Before she realized that magic was just as much a part of most worlds as the air she breathed, or the water that made life possible. She knew magic was like anything else—neither good nor evil.

But *she* had done a lot of evil deeds, long before she ever knew she possessed magic. Her version of Liam had rejected her once already. She didn't know if she could handle going through that again.

The portals stood quiet for the moment. She knew Liam would be flipping the switch soon, and the peace that filled the space would be replaced by the cheer and wonder of returning guests.

James was still at O'Sullivan's with Adam. The brewer was eager to see this magical pub, but also so nervous that he insisted on having a couple pints first to loosen up his nerves.

What would it be like to encounter magic for the first time?

She couldn't imagine.

Are you still moaning about your feelings? Demon Box piped up. She'd brought the device down from her room earlier and left it behind the bar. But it hadn't said anything to her since.

"You've been uncharacteristically quiet," she said.

I haven't had much to say. Stuck in our room. Stuck in this pub. At least it's more entertaining than the closet the professor had me housed in for seven years. Sit alone for long enough, you start getting accustomed to your own thoughts.

"Oh, really?" Emma smirked. "I would have thought you'd be annoyed with yourself by now."

Who says I'm not?

"Well, I won't ask you to be quiet any longer. I'll be telling Liam tonight about my past, and I think that he should learn about you as well."

Demon Box whirred for a moment, lights frantically dancing on the panels of its surface. Emma braced herself for a cheeky comment.

What if . . . what if they threaten to smash me? Those dwarf axes would tear me apart!

Emma paused. Demon Box was always complaining that it had to remain silent. She must have scared it earlier. Whenever she'd asked it to remain quiet, it always did so begrudgingly.

Just because I'm scared to tell people who I really am doesn't mean I like it. It thought. It's no different than you and your magic. The wrong people find out and we get attacked, disassembled, or worse.

Emma nodded, directing her thoughts instead of speaking out loud. *For some reason I thought you were fearless.*

It's easy to assume that a talking box is without emotion. Like I'm nothing more than an annoying toaster.

Emma laughed and said out loud. "Oh, you make toast now?"

"Who's making toast?" Liam had stepped through the portal's maw. She'd been so engrossed in her conversation with Demon Box she hadn't heard the warble of the gateway. He looked around, clearly confused that Emma appeared to be talking to herself.

"Is Gloria hiding back there?" he asked.

Emma sighed. "No. She isn't. I was talking to . . . ." She didn't know where to start. "Are James and Adam still in O'Sullivan's?" she asked instead.

Liam crossed his arms over his chest. "You're changing the topic. Tell me, what's going on?"

Emma cursed under her breath. "You're right. The truth is, I haven't been completely honest with you about who I am."

"I'd hardly call talking to yourself a big deal. I do it all the time. Unless this is somehow about toast . . ."

Emma lifted a palm. "Just listen. I have something I need to tell you, and you might want to have a seat. It's going to be a lot to take in."

Liam eyed her with suspicion, but he didn't argue. He pulled up a stool beside the bar and lifted his hands slightly. "I'm all ears."

Emma grabbed Demon Box and set him on top of the bar.

"This is Demon Box," she said.

Liam cocked his head slightly. "You've named the device that allowed you travel between worlds?"

"That's not the half of it," she said. "Demon Box, why don't you take it from here?"

"It's nice to finally meet you, Liam." Demon Box's panels lit up as it spoke. "At least, to be able to speak to you. In reality, we've been hanging around each other all week."

Liam directed an unconvinced glance toward the device then to Emma. She could have sworn he was holding back a smirk. "So, your computer talks. You are full of surprises."

Emma sighed. "That's just the start. It's not only that it talks, it's also sentient. I can communicate with it . . . telepathically."

The skepticism on Liam's face grew. "Okay . . ." he said. "That's certainly a surprise. But of all the things that have happened this week, this hardly ranks as one of the weirdest. Why didn't you just tell me?"

Emma blew a puff of air between her lips. "That's not exactly something a sane person typically confesses. But I'm just getting warmed up. Let me pour you a drink. You might need it." She grabbed a pint glass, filled it with the Cuanmore Harbour Pale Ale, and slid it across the bar.

She took a deep breath and proceeded to tell Liam her story, holding back on the parts that involved him, but going over everything else. How she became a Hunter of the Cursed at an early age, how she traveled the kingdom hunting magic users and monsters. And how she regretted all of it.

"It really hit me when Hal came in," she said. "I've *fought* ogres. They were regarded as monsters. But Hal is loved by everyone here. A gentle giant. And we fought them, *I* fought them, only because they looked different than us."

The tears flowed freely now; Emma couldn't hold them back any longer. She'd pushed down all the guilt, all the shame for so long. Once it started surfacing, it didn't stop.

"All of the witches and magic users we arrested. We tore families apart, and for what? So the king could sow division among his people? So he could claim he was acting for their benefit, when really, he was committing atrocities? What kind of legacy is that? What blot did I leave on my world? The woman who threw the dagger at my head was only one in a long line of people I've wronged. People I've hurt. How much trauma have I caused? And there are other worlds where I never left, where some version of me is still doing it!"

"Hey, hey, hey." Liam worked his way around the bar until he stood beside her. He rested a warm and comforting hand on her shoulder. "You didn't know. You'd been raised to believe that what you were doing was right. Hell, you were only a kid when they took you in. They indoctrinated you to believe something that wasn't true. It's not your fault. Not wholly anyway."

"I know, I just . . ." Emma tried to speak between sobs. She stepped in close to him as he wrapped his arms around her. She pressed her face into his chest.

"We can only do our best with the circumstances we're given." Liam said. "Everyone deserves a chance at redemption."

James had said something similar. But for some reason, Liam speaking the words triggered something in her memory—

something from a long time ago. Words *her* version of Liam had said to her. Suddenly she realized what was happening, what she was doing. This wasn't fair to this Liam.

She pushed herself out of his embrace and stepped back, shaking her head.

Liam continued, unshaken by her action. "Emma, you have been nothing but warm and supportive since you've arrived here. You've helped James run this bar that exists outside of reality. You've been kind to gnomes, ogres, dwarves, and humans alike. You've gone out of your way to create drink recipes for those who don't drink. You've even somehow calmed my mum's nerves over reopening this pub. After you talked to her the other night, she seemed much more at ease about everything."

Emma sniffed as she fought to regain her composure. "I didn't know that."

"She'd probably not admit it, but I've noticed the way she talks about the place. How her shoulders are more relaxed. She mentioned she had a lovely chat with you, and I knew it had to be the reason. She's still apprehensive, but I think less so."

"Did she tell you what we talked about? About why she's nervous about the portals?"

"Other than she's not a fan of magic? No. Why? Did she say anything else? Does she know you have magic?"

Emma shook her head. "She doesn't know. But James and I did make an interesting discovery. Once he arrives, we can fill you in on the details . . ."

Liam lifted a hand to her face and cupped her chin, his deep brown eyes drinking hers in. "I'd like it more if he didn't show up. Not yet."

Emma swallowed as her heart threatened to burst from her chest. Liam leaned in, and she caught herself parting her lips, letting out a breath she'd been holding.

She placed a hand on his chest and froze.

We can only do our best with the circumstances we're given.

"No, wait." She barely got the words out.

To his credit, Liam stopped, his lips only an inch from hers. "What's wrong?" he asked, pulling back.

"I . . ." Emma hesitated, taking another step away. "Don't take this the wrong way. I *want* this. Far more than you can imagine. But you need to know everything before you decide that you truly want me too."

Liam stepped back, with that kind but questioning look on his face.

"You know how the multiverse works, right?" she asked.

Liam nodded slowly. "I've watched enough Star Trek to get the gist. Every choice leads to an alternate reality . . . something like that?"

Emma swallowed. "Yes, that's it precisely. Which means that in other worlds, like the one the dagger thrower arrived from, there are other versions of me, ones where I never left, and where I'm still hunting magic users."

"Yes, you just told me that, but you can't help—" Liam stopped abruptly as Emma raised a finger to his lips.

She caught her breath. They were so much softer than she had imagined them being. These were not the lips of the man she had kissed decades ago, and this was not the same man. But that was the point of this, wasn't it? His face was the same, his humor was the same, and yet at the same time, a million different decisions had made this man unique, kind, considerate, and willing to help those he cared about without question.

"In my world, there was another Liam," she said. "Another man who bore your face, but in reality . . . some things about him were the same, others very different. We were . . . close."

"Oh?" Liam's face darkened. What pieces he was putting together, Emma could only guess at, but she didn't like the expression building on his face. "I see."

She had to tell him the rest before he could leap to his own conclusions. "Both of us had been left as orphans very young. With that Liam, I scrounged the streets. We protected one another and had each other's backs. Eventually, we were both recruited by the Hunters. Everything I've told you about—our hunts, the quest against magic—that version of Liam was with me for all of it."

Liam's gaze had grown distant, his hands fidgeting on his drink as he tried to work things out. "And you loved him?" It was barely a question. The man was smart enough to puzzle the pieces together. His lips tightened.

He paused only for a moment, his eyes meeting hers in an unspoken exchange. Emma grasped for the words. She needed to say something . . . anything. But he took her silence as confirmation.

"I understand." Liam set his mug down on the bar and stood, turning to leave through the portal back to O'Sullivan's.

"No, Liam. That's not what I—"

"I may be a nice guy. In the past, I've allowed women to walk all over me. But I'm old enough to know that I'm not willing to try and live up to a fantasy version of myself. I'm not a monster hunter, I'm not a fighter. I'm not this man you imagine me to be. And I don't want to live a life in his shadow. I'm sorry, Emma."

For the second time that night she fought tears that threatened to make an appearance. "Liam, no. That's not . . ."

The words disappeared as she said them. He'd repeated back to her the very fears she held. But it wasn't like that . . . was it? She couldn't accept that she was only in love with a memory.

The portal warbled, halting Liam in his escape. James and Adam strolled through the gateway, both unaware of the situation they were walking into.

James was carefully reassuring his friend, while Adam had the wide-eyed stare of a child seeing something for the very first time. His jaw was slack and his hands were outstretched as if he might run into some unseen obstacle.

"It's true!" he said, catching sight of Emma and Liam. He pointed toward them. "That's the bar from Mom's painting!"

"Wait until the ogre shows up," James said dryly.

James glanced toward Emma and froze, his gaze catching on her tear-streaked face. His brow furrowed as he shifted his attention to Liam. Liam, however, had already eased his stance, his expression betraying no hint of their conversation.

Adam walked toward the bar with a cautious gait, gazing around the pub in disbelief. "I can't believe it," he said as he tried to take it all in. "It's been back here this whole time?"

James had a smirk on his face as if his own reaction hadn't mirrored Adam's when he'd first entered the room himself.

Adam looked up then with sudden clarity, the fog behind his eyes lifted. "And they knew! My parents knew and didn't tell me."

"Join the club," James remarked. "My folks, Moira, Rudy, they all used to run this place. None of us knew."

"But why?" Adam asked.

"Rudy said it was to protect us," James said. "But I'm guessing there's more to it. We have to keep searching for more clues." James turned his gaze to Liam. "Since Rudy's been busy, we're going to have to confront your mom. I think it's time we get some more answers. Be sure she comes by tonight."

Emma

The first portal of the evening shimmered into existence, its edges crackling faintly with light. Four dragon riders emerged, their cloaks billowing as they stepped onto the worn wooden floor, Kira at the head of the group.

"Kira!" Emma called out. "You came back."

The rider smiled, giving a polite nod as she and her companions strode toward the bar, moving as though the weight of the world had finally lifted from their shoulders. Gloria, ever eager to greet guests, intercepted them halfway, gesturing excitedly toward a table near the hearth. The dragon riders barely spared her a glance.

The dwarf turned toward Emma with a questioning look, her hands still mid-gesture. Emma caught her eye from across the room, smiled, and mouthed, *It's okay*. Gloria hesitated then nodded, though she looked none too pleased about the brush-off.

As the riders approached, Emma couldn't help but notice the streaks of dirt and sweat on their faces.

"It's been a harrowing few days," Kira admitted as she caught Emma's worried glance. "But I wanted to show Hector this place before we flew home. I'm sure it will be included in the tales told around the fire for years to come, and I don't want him to feel left out."

Emma stuck out her hand. "Pleasure to meet you, Hector. I'm glad you're okay."

The rider looked down at her hand, eyebrows drawn together in a quizzical look. He met her gaze and leaned forward in a short bow.

"Pleasure's all mine, miss. Kira's been telling me about your mighty fine pub here, and well, I have to say it's everything she said it was. If your drinks are even half as impressive, I'll bet they can soothe my weary body."

"How did they find you?" Emma asked.

"Sheer luck," Fredja said through gritted teeth. "Almost didn't."

Emma's smile faltered "What happened?"

"The Skraelith found us," Kira said.

"Skraelith?" Emma repeated. "The wyvern riders?"

Kira nodded. "They'd kidnapped Hector. They'd hoped to extract information about the Skyguard. Anything they could learn about our flight patterns, our safehouses. With that information they could have gained an edge on us."

"Aye." Hector's voice scratched as though he hadn't had a drop of water in weeks. "Nearly burned me alive, they did. Luckily, I managed to send out a cry for help just as our crew was passing by."

"It sounds like you've been through a lot." Emma reached for the jug of water she'd set out earlier. She grabbed four pint glasses and began filling them. She slid the first glass toward Hector, who took it with a trembling hand. "But I'm glad you found him."

"It was almost too late," Hector said after a long drink. The other three were thirstily gulping down their water as though they hadn't had a drop since they'd left the pub a week ago.

"But I'm a fighter," Hector continued. "And I swore I'd never go down by one of those wily bastards."

Emma didn't know the first thing about Skraelith, or how a world came to have a war between dragon and wyvern riders, but she wanted to know more.

"I'd love to learn more about your world," Emma said, leaning against the bar. "But you've been through hell. Let me offer you something more than water. Gloria can open a couple of rooms upstairs so you can shower and clean up. And if you decide you want a soft bed for the night, we can provide that too."

Kira raised a hand in polite protest. "We don't wish to be an inconvenience."

There was a longing in Kira's eyes that Emma was all too familiar with. How many nights had she spent on the cold ground wishing for a warm bath? Or a few minutes of warmth and comfort?

Emma reached out and grabbed the Sky Rider's hand. Kira eyed the gesture in confusion.

"I insist," Emma said. "I've often felt like I was more dirt and grime than human being. A good shower will help you all feel like yourselves again. Once you're ready, I'll have drinks ready for you. I've been working on a new non-alcoholic drink recipe ever since you left."

Liam appeared at her side with perfect timing. "Gloria's got plenty to do down here," he said, nodding toward the busy dwarf. Another portal opened behind her, spilling a group of goblins into the pub. "I can show you to a couple of rooms."

Kira bowed with a flourish. "Thank you. We'll accept the offer to bathe, but a room for the night won't be necessary. We're used to sleeping under the stars."

The party followed Liam up the stairs, leaving Emma to wonder if she'd ever know another rough night under the canopy of the sky, or if she'd grown old and soft.

She found herself surprised by the pang of sadness that came with the thought.

I, for one, will be grateful to never have to sleep out in the cold again, Demon Box chirped into her mind. *It's hard on my circuits.*

Emma huffed out a laugh, shaking her head. Her eyes lingered on Liam as he ascended the stairs, his broad shoulders disappearing into the shadows of the upper landing. She hadn't had a chance to talk to him since their last exchange, and the implications were eating her up inside.

Her fingers traced the edge of the bar rag she held to keep busy as she tried to still her thoughts.

I don't want to live a life in his shadow.

She couldn't blame him for thinking that way, but she didn't believe that was what this was. Maybe the sight of him had made her heart skip at first; however, there was more to it than that now. How could she convince him that it was him she was interested in, not the memory of another man who happened to share his face?

Liam deserved someone who was with him for who he was, not for the echoes of someone else. She didn't *want* to be drawn to him just because he looked like someone she used to love.

But what if she was wrong? What if she was clinging to the idea of him, onto some half-formed hope that he could fill the space she hadn't realized was still empty?

Emma shook her head and forced herself to focus. The pub was filling quickly now. A group of dwarves by the hearth burst into laughter, and a pair of goblins near the door were arguing over a map.

She inhaled deeply, grounding herself in the growing familiarity of The Pint and Portal. Whatever was or wasn't happening between her and Liam, she couldn't afford to get lost in it now. There were drinks to pour, conversations to overhear, and a hundred little tasks to keep her busy until the pub emptied out for the night.

Still, as she wiped the counter for what felt like the dozenth time, her gaze flicked toward the stairs again, and she couldn't help but wonder: *What would it take for him to believe me? To see that it's him I want and not a memory.*

Like clockwork, Hal took his regular seat, breaking her from her thoughts about Liam. Emma was more than a little surprised when the ogre ordered a Swamp Water instead of the regular ale.

"Be careful with those," Emma said as she crafted one and handed it over to him. "They'll sneak up on you."

Of course, she had no idea whether that was true for an ogre or not.

Hal simply grunted, and his lips curled into a smile, revealing the fangs protruding from his bottom gums.

"It's amazing that each of these groups finds this pub, nearly as soon as it's opened," she voiced the thought out loud. "Some of them are repeat guests, but most of them are finding us for the first time."

We're dealing with infinite possibilities, said Demon Box. *Yet somehow each person who has found their way seems meant to be here.*

Emma

Emma smiled when she saw the group of brewer dwarves enter the pub. They sat down at the same table as they had on previous nights and ordered another ale from Gloria. She'd had this discussion with James and Adam earlier, and they decided they could help these dwarves out.

She spotted Adam at a table close to the O'Sullivan's portal. The brewer seemed to be enjoying the people watching his seat afforded him, but his wide-eyed stare suggested he was still overwhelmed by the reality of the pub's existence and its fantastical patrons.

Emma set down the glass she'd been cleaning and made her way over to him. "Adam?" she asked as she drew closer. "Do you have the Morac Mushrooms with you?"

The question must have broken him out of whatever thought he'd been lost in, as he gave his head a slight shake and registered her presence right in front of him.

Still, it took him a moment to respond, but a flicker of recognition danced across his face. "Oh, yes. I've got them here, somewhere." He began digging through a bag he'd set under his seat. "Why do you ask?"

"Do you remember those dwarves we mentioned?" She nodded toward their table. "Well, they've just arrived."

"Are you sure this is the right decision?" Adam asked. "That note James' mother wrote seemed to suggest there's a chance they might be attracting those . . . evil . . . tiger . . . things."

Emma waved off the thought. "How long has it been since your father passed? You've been growing them in your back room this entire time and it's not been an issue. Even if these are what the Tíogar Mór are after, it's such a small quantity that it's not making a difference to anyone."

Adam nodded hesitantly, unable to argue with her logic.

"I'm going to pour these folks a few pints of the Nocturne Speciale. I'll meet you over there in a few minutes."

As she returned to the bar to pour the pints, Gloria was ready to fill their order.

"Dwarf table wants a round of ale," she said with a hint of annoyance in her voice. "They said they want something different than whatever they had last time. They can't remember the names of all the brews. Am I supposed to bloody well remember every pint that's served in here?"

Emma smirked. For a group of dwarves trying to find a certain brew, they sure were terrible at the process. "Don't worry about it. I've got something special for them that's definitely different than what they've had already. Adam and I are going to bring them over, so don't worry about their table for now."

Gloria shrugged. It meant one less table for her to serve, and she was off to help the next group of travelers.

Emma, for the first time since the pub opened, went to Adam's keg of mushroom-infused stout, poured the taps, and watched the liquid flow into the glass—dark and creamy. Still, she could sense nothing from it, her magic muted by the mushrooms.

She brought four mugs over to the table and greeted the

dwarves. Adam was already standing beside the table nervously, shifting his weight from one foot to the other.

"What's this?" T'og asked. "We ordered ale. This appears to be stout."

"My apologies," said Emma, "but I believe you will find the substitution agreeable."

She gestured toward Adam. "This is the brewer, Adam. He's crafted all the beers you've sampled."

A round of applause broke out among the dwarves. Adam crossed his arms above his chest, his cheeks turning several shades of red.

"We've discovered something since you last left," Emma continued, "and we wanted you to sample this and perhaps take some with you. It's on the house."

T'og raised an eyebrow skeptically but shrugged and reached for a glass. The other three followed. "Well, I'm not going to say no to a pint of stout, either," said one of his companions. "Especially not to one that's free!"

Almost in unison, the four dwarves raised their glasses to their lips and took long, deep drinks. Almost instantly, their eyes closed, and smiles lit their faces with a blissful expression.

Emma waited several moments until each of the dwarves' eyes opened. They each cast their gazes at one another in a shared realization of what had happened.

"By the goddess," one said. "Do you realize what you have given us?"

Emma smiled. Then she held up a Morac that she had tucked in her pocket for this occasion. "Tears of the Gods?"

Their mouths fell to the table.

"Then . . ." T'og began, "the stories were true!"

Emma lifted her hand. "We don't have many. I can give you some, hopefully enough to fulfill your quest."

The dwarf nodded eagerly. "Yes, yes. We only need a small sample. We only need to prove to the king that it is real."

The dwarf stood from his seat and gave a short bow. "Much thanks, m'lady," he said then repeated the action facing Adam. "And to you, master brewer. You do not know the great honor you have bestowed upon us. Our praises will be sung at the clan council, and we will receive much reward for proving the stories of the tears to be true. You have made this a possibility. So we thank you from the bottom of our hearts."

The other three dwarves also stood and gave short bows, mirroring T'og.

"I am also honored," T'og continued, "that you have allowed us to sample the tears. No one from our clan has done so since the time of our ancient ancestors, and even then, only the revered among them were so fortunate. I am more than humbled." The other dwarves made noises of agreement.

"We will ensure that your kindness is repaid. And we will speak highly of you in our realm. Emma of The Pint and Portal and Adam, the Master Brewer!"

Cheers erupted around the table.

Adam's face grew a deeper shade of red.

Emma chuckled and raised her hands. "That won't be necessary, fellas, but I do appreciate the gesture, and I appreciate your thanks. How much do you need? I will gather a small sample for you to take back when you leave here."

"We do not wish to appear greedy in our request, so we will only take a few. That should be enough to convince our scholars that this is the real thing."

"If you do need more," Adam said, clearing his throat. "Please come back and let us know."

The dwarves nodded again, reclaimed their seats, and resumed talking with smiles so large they could have lit up the entire room.

James

Despite most of the excitement being at The Pint and Portal, James was pleasantly surprised at how busy O'Sullivan's was. Patrons filled the seats, having good craic and a good laugh. Since The Pint and Portal opened, he hadn't spent much time in the pub he'd grown up knowing, and James smiled as he watched the patrons enjoying themselves.

He had spent some time at The Pint and Portal and everything seemed to be going right, so far. He could afford to take a bit of time to oversee his other pub. With everything that had happened, though, it was hard to keep his thoughts on this side of the portal. He did his best to focus on what was happening around him. But his thoughts kept drifting. James kept reminding himself that, so far, there had been no further malfunctions of equipment or power fluctuations, the dragon riders had been shown to their rooms to clean up, and Ha'dran was busy preparing for another captivating story. Everything was under control.

Adam walked in from The Pint and Portal, a huge grin on his face, looking around as he exited the storage room to ensure he wasn't attracting any undue attention. He pulled on his backpack, shifting its weight. "You should have seen the looks on the dwarves' faces!" Adam beamed as he approached. "They were falling all over themselves thanking me and Emma."

"It's nice to know the pub is helping others," James said. "Even if it's just a little thing."

"Little for us, maybe. They acted like we were offering them bars of gold."

"I guess sometimes we have to look a little closer to find what's important," said James. If a few mushrooms made a group of dwarves happy, who was he to judge?

"Seems like you've already turned things around in here as well," Adam said, nodding to the pub that was located firmly in their world. "I knew it would just take a bit of attention to the place or . . ." He lowered his voice and scanned the room nervously. "Or is it magic?"

James nearly scoffed until he realized he wasn't actually sure. If there was an ancient magic in the storeroom, who knew how else it affected the rest of the bar?

"To be honest, I don't know," James replied. "But if there is, it's not intentional, and it certainly didn't help Dad when he was running the place."

James wondered for a moment what the difference was. He didn't think he was doing anything special to promote O'Sullivan's. They'd cleaned up, repainted, and redecorated, but nothing they'd done was earth shattering.

He paused again, surveying the patrons. The laughter, the excitement.

It's like it was when I was growing up.

How many hours had he spent sitting in his room upstairs, wishing that he were anywhere else but here? Because despite the laughter, the excitement, the camaraderie, and friendships that were built and thrived in this pub, he always felt removed from it, just as he did now.

James caught his sister's eye from across the bar. Kathy must have been reading his thoughts because she lifted her eyebrows in a concerned stare. She too, looked around the pub, except a smile had crossed her face. A gleam of tears moistened her eyes.

He knew his sister well enough to know that she'd come to the same conclusion as he had. Unlike him, to Kathy, having a pub filled with love and laughter would be like coming home.

For him? James still wasn't convinced.

Sure, The Pint and Portal had made the prospect of owning this pub more exciting, more interesting. But he wanted adventure. He wanted to see things and travel himself. He didn't want to live vicariously through others, hearing tales of their stories and heroic journeys. Was that what his life would amount to?

"To be honest," said Adam, "I don't know if I thought we'd ever see it so busy in here again. You've done good, buddy." Adam clasped James' shoulder with a strong, supportive grip.

James cleared his throat. "Aye," he said. "It is good to see it so lively in here. My mother would have been pleased. I wonder what my dad would think."

Maybe his father would have been pleased as well. James was still unconvinced. Was it all worth it? Magical brews, portals to other planes. Ogres and dwarves. It was all real. But he wasn't sure if it was enough, especially if keeping the portals open meant that this world—his world—would be in danger.

The weight of his mother's journal sat in his pocket. The warnings that owning a magical pub wouldn't be easy: the power fluctuations, equipment malfunctions, threat of people attacking his staff, and not to mention the threat of Tíogar Mór that Moira was convinced was real.

He imagined someone stepping through the portal from a world at war with dwarves or ogres, the conflict spilling into their own. If they started fighting each other here, how could he possibly stop it? Moira's warnings about the wards failing echoed in his mind. If that happened, how would he ever protect the people he loved?

The sound of the front door opening interrupted James' thoughts, and he looked up in time to see William O'Malley come strolling through. Chest out, shoulders back, brows furrowed, the man appeared to be on a mission. James sighed, rolled his eyes, and turned to Adam, gesturing toward Mr. O'Malley, but keeping his voice low.

"This one has been looking to buy the pub," he said.

Adam nodded. "He's made me multiple offers over the years."

"Have you considered it?" James asked.

"To that old codger?" Adam snorted. "Never. Not even if I wanted nothing to do with the brewery ever again."

"You've never considered leaving? Going somewhere else for a while?"

Adam shrugged. "Not really. I like it here. I enjoy the friendship, the community. You don't find that anywhere else. You certainly won't find that in your big Canadian cities."

James nodded. It was true. His friend circle was much smaller back in Vancouver, and most of them he'd met through work. Here, it felt like others were watching his back, looking out for him. But was that enough? Returning not only meant he was resigning himself to the place he'd thought he'd left behind; it also meant giving up on everything he had worked so hard to achieve.

Laughter permeated everything in the room. Everyone else here seemed to be enjoying themselves, like they belonged. Why couldn't he?

"I was hoping I'd find you here tonight," said Mr. O'Malley as he approached. "If I didn't know better, I'd think you were avoiding me."

James lifted his hands, giving him the best fake smile he could muster. "No, no, not at all, Mr. O'Malley. It's just been busy. We've been trying to make a go of this. Like I told you before, it's what Dad would have wanted."

Mr. O'Malley pretended he didn't hear and turned to Adam. "And you, lad, what are you doing here? Trying to convince James to hold out on me like you have? You know, I see great potential in your brews, lad. I can pay handsomely. With me as owner, they'd have a dedicated pub to call home at The Cursed Dragon."

Adam cleared his throat, shuffled back a couple steps, and annoyance dripped from his expression as his eyebrow twitched.

"If I've told you once, I've told you a thousand times," Adam replied. "The brewery's all my father ever knew, and all his father ever knew. I'm happy to continue his legacy."

O'Malley grumbled under his breath but nodded in a hesitant acceptance before turning his attention to James. He stretched out his hand and held out a folded slip of paper.

"What's this?" James asked. He took the paper and opened it.

"That's my final offer," said Mr. O'Malley. "I know you don't want to be here. You would rather be on your way back to wherever it was you were. This town was never for you. You and I both know it."

James opened the paper and had to fight to keep his jaw from dropping to the tavern floor. As he stared, he tried to rein in his spiraling thoughts, trying his best to at least gather them into some semblance of a cohesive sentence.

What he was looking at was a substantial check. Multiples of what James would have expected to receive for the sale of the pub if he could sell it.

"Mr. O'Malley." James folded the check again and held it outstretched back to the rival pub owner. "You know that I can't sell the pub. Not yet."

"I know, I know," said O'Malley. "But consider this a

promise until you can. You maintain ownership of the pub. Run things as your father had—dry and dull and boring. You don't need all this excitement. You can head back to Canada and know that you and your sister will receive your inheritance. When the deadline comes a year from now, I'll take ownership and reopen this as a second location of The Cursed Dragon."

James swallowed. It was everything he had convinced himself to hang on to O'Sullivan's for—Kathy to get her share of inheritance, and a little bit of cash for him. He could get out of Cuanmore once and for all.

If he had held this check when he'd first arrived, there wouldn't have been a question. He would have shaken the bar owner's hand right there and then. His eyes drifted up to Kathy, who was carefully watching their exchange, then to Adam, who shifted his backpack.

Hell, a few minutes ago he had felt out of place here. But suddenly, with the prospect of being able to make this all go away, something shifted within him. He could sense Emma mixing drinks on the other side of the portal, sense that Liam was swooning over her, that the dwarves were busying them-selves and laughing among newfound friends, that Hal was quenching his thirst at the bar with a mighty pint of ale.

He knew that the Sky Riders were en route to their next destination, setting up their dragons in camp for the night so they could take a break from their adventuring, their search for their missing ally complete.

That somewhere in a distant land, some group of farm boys on a quest to save their world was about to stumble across a newfound gateway.

That a table of dwarves was elated to have found the magic ingredient that had been lost to their peoples for centuries and were already crafting songs about the pub where they found the revered Tears of the Gods.

He knew gnomes would be laughing, chittering away in

anticipation of receiving a few drinks, their squeals only understood by themselves.

And most of all, he knew that friendships had been forged and rekindled—Rudy and Tarvo, Emma and Liam, and all the other groups who had needed a break from their adventures in worlds he had never known existed a few weeks ago. People had been able to find a rest from their quests, all because The Pint and Portal had been reopened.

He also couldn't shake off everything that had gone wrong. The flickering power that his mother had warned was a sign that things were not going well, to the mushrooms in Adam's bag that might attract inter-dimensional warriors bent on destroying each world they encountered.

He thought of Moira and her hesitance to allow magic to cross barriers. Of Tarvo and his world destroyed by the Tíogar Mór.

Perhaps accepting O'Malley's offer would be the final way to do what his father had hoped to achieve by closing its doors, what Moira had hoped to do by her incessant pleas to shut the gateways—keep the magic at bay. Keeping threads of other dimensions out of their own and ensuring their world remained safe.

James looked again at the number in front of him. This offer seemed too good to be true, too exceptional, but it seemed to be exactly what he had wanted when he arrived.

"If I may ask a question," said James. "Why is it that you want this pub so badly?"

A grin formed on William O'Malley's face. "Well, I would have thought it would be obvious by now," he said. "Look around you. Look at what a little bit of proper management can do. You've done well, lad. I know you feel obligated to your father, but he's not here. And no amount of beer slinging is going to bring him back."

The directness of the statement took James aback. All he could do was blink in astonishment.

"I apologize if that seems harsh," O'Malley continued, "but it's true. You may think that this is an okay venture for you now, but will you feel that way in a year? Two years? Five? How long will you be content here? How long before that itch inside you grows and beckons you to leave again, seeking your own adventure? How long will it take before living in the shadow of your parents is no longer enough for you? I watched you grow up, boy. I know the spark that is in you to see worlds beyond this place. I've seen it too many times before. All the men and women that have come through these pubs over the years who were passing through. I can tell when the spirit of wanderlust has its grip on a man. I'm offering you the opportunity of freedom."

"Right," James said. "Out of the goodness of your heart?"

"Hey." O'Malley raised his hands in mock surrender. "I am an entrepreneur, but that's my nature. No doubt this is a fine opportunity for myself. The chance to run two successful pubs? To me, this is everything. It's what I love to do."

James hesitated. He had too many conflicting thoughts to know what to say.

"Hang on to that check for now," Mr. O'Malley said, apparently sensing James' hesitation. "I won't wait forever, but you think about it. Think on it over the weekend. I'll return on Monday. I would like you to make a decision by then. If you don't want to do this, I'll take my money and place it in another investment."

James' phone buzzed in his pocket. Relief flooded over him at having an easy way out of the conversation. "I've got to take this call, Mr. O'Malley. I'll let you know on Monday, one way or the other."

Mr. O'Malley nodded with a satisfied smile, apparently content to receive an answer that wasn't a sharp no.

A familiar name and number appeared on the phone's display, and the image of Trevor in front of the Vancouver skyline lit up the screen. Whatever the reason was for his colleague's sudden call, it was a welcome interruption.

He wound his way through the patrons, heading to the exit to get to a quiet space.

As he stepped outside, he glanced at O'Malley's check one more time. He blew out a puff of air in disbelief. Could the pub be worth this much to the man? What would happen to The Pint and Portal? They'd truly have to shutter it for good.

He quickly shoved the check into his pocket and answered the phone.

"Trevor, how are ya keeping?" he asked. As the door closed behind him, the noise of the pub echoed into the street.

"Good, James," came the voice on the other end. "How have you been, my friend? How's Ireland treating you?"

James ran a hand through his hair. "It's been challenging." That much at least was true.

"I can only imagine," said Trevor. "Hey, man, listen, I hate to bother you again. I know I told you that you would have lots of time over there with your family, but, well, we got a bite on one of our offers."

"Oh?" James asked, intrigued. "Already?"

"Yeah, surprised me too, but a game studio down in LA likes our work and wants to bring us on board. It's a big project. I'm talking multi-six figures for each of us."

James blinked in surprise and swallowed. That was an unbelievable sum for a single contract.

Not only that, it meant he no longer had the excuse to stick around Cuanmore.

Every objection to staying at the pub had eroded in a matter of minutes. But there was still something nagging him at the back of his mind.

"Wow, that's great," he managed. "When does the project start?"

"Yeah, so that's the thing." Trevor drew out the words as though unsure of how to relay the information. "They need us to start right away. They're asking if we can get going on Monday."

"Monday?" James said, "I can't be back by Monday."

"I know, I know," said Trevor, "and I told them that. I said that we're not in a position to begin Monday, but given the circumstances, we've got the green light to hold off until the first of the month."

James swallowed. That was only a couple of weeks away; it still wasn't much time.

Beside him, the pub door swung open as a couple stepped out, each with huge smiles painted across their faces. His gaze wandered past them and into O'Sullivan's.

It's like when we were kids.

Suddenly he wasn't sure if he was ready to leave this all behind.

James scoffed. One moment ago, he was wondering how he could stay here, and the next how he could leave. He shook his head. He didn't know what he wanted anymore.

He felt like he was going crazy.

"Listen, Trevor, I—I'm going to need some time to think about this before I give you an answer. I've made some commitments here, and I need to figure out what I'm going to do about those."

"Yeah, go ahead. Don't worry about it being in a couple weeks or whatever. You just let me know when you'll be back. I'm sure we'll make it work. Okay, buddy? I can fill in the gaps until you get here. But listen, I've got to go. Say hi to your family from me, and I hope it's all going okay."

The other end of the line went silent as Trevor hung up without James being able to say another word.

He scratched at the back of his head, his short hair rubbing against his fingertips. He should be excited. He should be thrilled.

He wasn't anything of the sort. If anything, he was more confused than ever.

Adventure. That was what he had always wanted, what he had dreamed of. It wasn't like Vancouver was some grand quest.

Maybe listening to stories could be just as much as an adventure. Certainly, sitting in a pub that was a hub between fantasy realms had to be more of an adventure than sitting behind a computer in Canada.

James snickered. It all seemed so ordinary now.

He pulled out O'Malley's check again, letting his gaze go over the hefty amount written on it. Adventure or not, it would be a lot of money to say no to.

So why am I having such a hard time saying yes?

Emma

By now Emma had grown accustomed to the opening and closing of portals as part of The Pint and Portal's background noise, so she had barely noticed the warble of the most recent one. Dozens of patrons were coming and going, and the sound had started to blend into the rest of the bar's activity.

But the sudden, unnatural silence that followed this time snapped her attention to it. The noise didn't simply die down, it vanished, causing a stillness that made the hair on the back of her neck stand on end.

It was only broken by the gasps of several patrons around the room, a few scraping chairs, and a clinking of glasses as patrons set their drinks down. Emma couldn't tell exactly where the sounds came from, but it didn't matter.

Her instincts kicked in, and she grabbed her daggers, one in each hand as she spun around, ready for another assault.

Only it wasn't an assassin.

It wasn't anything she'd ever seen before, but she knew instantly what it was.

Standing in front of the still-shimmering portal was a tiger, standing on two legs, dressed as a human, frozen where it stood.

Tíogar Mór.

The tiger-like figure didn't move. It stood frozen, its amber eyes warily scanning the room with a dangerous gaze, as though assessing whether he was predator or prey.

His fur was a deep orange color, streaked with white and black. He wore a tunic of dark leather, its surface marked with intricate patterns. Over it, armor plates reinforced his shoulders and forearms, the metal dulled from use. A medallion rested against his broad chest. The belt cinched around his waist bore an ornate buckle, and his posture was straight-backed and steady.

As though sensing the room he entered posed a threat, he turned and attempted to flee back through the portal from which it came, but the exit had already shut. Its orb hung dormant from the sleeve where it lay. Emma was quite certain the tiger did not realize the orb would need to be removed and reinserted for the portal to be reactivated.

Moira, who stood across bar, had contorted her body, posed to strike. "Tíogar Mór," she growled, as she lifted an arm toward the creature. If Emma didn't know any better, she could have sworn the woman was about to cast a spell.

The gesture nearly threw Emma off guard. Instinctually, she laid a hand on Moira's arm. "Wait."

"The wards have failed," Moira hissed. "We cannot let it in here."

"Just wait," Emma repeated.

"You don't understand if—"

"There's only one," Emma said gruffly. "Don't do anything rash."

Emma studied the newcomer carefully. She'd seen her fair share of predators on the hunt, as well as magical beasts on the run—running from capture, running from unfair laws, running from angry villagers—enough to know this tiger wasn't a threat. Despite the creature's massive size, the dazed look in his eyes told Emma he was more scared than threatening.

Several more blades unsheathed around her.

"This isn't right," she whispered. "Please don't do this."

Despite her voice being lowered, Liam was close enough to hear and turned to her. "He's one of them?" Liam asked, meaning the Tíogar Mór. "We can't let him hurt anyone."

"He won't," she said with as much confidence as she could muster. "Not unless he's provoked." Emma certainly hoped she was right.

"But you've heard the stories!" Liam's voice shook. "Of what they did to Tarvo's world."

"Yes, and I've heard stories of ogres as well! We can't let the mob attack this fellow just because of how he looks!"

Emma wouldn't allow herself to be responsible for that again. She refused.

Hal grunted. Liam's gaze shifted between them.

Moira had enough waiting, her arm started circling, muttering an incantation under her breath.

What in the bloody blazes!

"Stop!" Liam called out, his voice reverberating through the room. If he realized what his mother had been about to do, he didn't show it. Instead, his focus was on the dwarves, men, and others who held their swords at the ready. "There will be no violence in this place! Sheath your weapons."

A murmur of protest rippled throughout the pub, but nobody moved.

"Sheath them *now*!" Liam growled.

Several warriors did as they were commanded, and the dwarves also lowered their axes.

Tarvo stood beside the bar, both hands gripped on his ax and ready to pounce.

"Tarvo," Emma said softly. "It's okay."

Tarvo grunted without shifting his eyes. "It is never okay with these beasts. You would know that if you had seen my world."

"I *did* see your world," Emma hissed.

"Then you understand what they are capable of!"

She had to do something to help reduce the tension in the room.

For his own part, the tiger had retreated, his back to the wall, curled in a protective stance.

Cautiously, Emma made her way around the bar to stand in front of Tarvo. She raised her hands placatingly. "I've seen what *some* of these beasts can do. This one comes alone. I assure you, with the number of axes and blades in this room, if he tries anything, we can take care of him. But for now, trust me."

Tarvo looked at her briefly out of the corner of his eye and furrowed his brow. "I don't know if I can do that."

Emma took a cautious step forward. "Please," she said. "For me?"

Tarvo grumbled and took another nervous glance at the newcomer, who stood in the shadows, before relaxing his stance and lowering his ax.

"Let's just talk to him," Emma said. "The wards should have prevented those with ill intent from arriving."

"The wards are failing," Moira growled. "I've been trying to warn you . . ."

"This pub has stood for centuries without evil coming through those gates," Emma argued. "Hasn't it always been a haven for the lost? Perhaps that's all he is—lost."

Tarvo muttered, "I will believe it when I see it. And even then, I won't believe it. I've suffered too much. My world suffered too much at the hands of these . . . creatures."

"We can't judge his entire species because of the actions of a few. Please sit back down. Let me talk to him."

Tarvo grumbled, but reluctantly he sat, blade still in hand.

Confident she'd done as much as she could to diffuse things

given the circumstances, Emma made her way toward where the newcomer stood.

She strode across the bar, sure of her steps, intent on making this Tíogar Mór feel welcome, regardless of what the rest of the pub thought.

There were other dwarves, goblins, and men who still held their blades at the ready, but thankfully none had moved. None had tried to attack.

Movement beside her caught her eye, and she only then realized Liam had joined her. A smile crossed Emma's face as she felt some of the tension leave her. She wouldn't have to do this alone.

Liam, though uncertain, was willing to trust her.

"Please don't hurt me." The Tíogar retreated, lifting its arms as if to stop an attack. "I don't wish to hurt anyone."

Emma held up her empty palms as she slowed her approach. Liam mirrored her actions.

"No one here will hurt you," she said. "You have my word."

Liam glanced around the room as though he weren't so sure, and to be honest, neither was she. But they had to start somewhere.

"What is your name?" she asked.

"I'm Kai," he said nervously, as his eyes darted back and forth around the room. "And no offense, but I can see the mob of people behind you. They all look as though they would rather put a dagger in my heart than offer me a seat."

Emma nodded as she glanced back at the room behind her. "They're scared," she said. "They've had bad interactions with your kind in the past."

Kai lowered his arms, only slightly.

"So have I," he said. "I didn't mean to intrude. I found this strange glowing ball. I batted it around a few times and saw the space in the wall that appeared to be made for it. I inserted it and ended up here. I thought my luck had finally changed, but it appears I may have leapt into the fire."

Emma smiled. Cautiously, she lifted her arm, and moved two steps closer to Kai, closing the gap between them. "It's okay," she said. "There's no fire here. Only rest."

James

The weight of O'Malley's check pressed against James, as if it carried the gravity of an entire planet. Its pull was a relentless force urging him to take it out again for another look.

But he resisted.

Instead, James patted the pocket of his jacket to make sure it was still there. He didn't need to see the number scrawled on it to know what it said.

It was there, nestled right beside his mother's journal. Two worlds fighting over him right inside his pocket, tearing him in opposite directions.

James' hand lingered over it for a moment longer before he moved it away, shoving it into his lap as if it might stop the growing temptation.

Around them, O'Sullivan's was alive with clinking glasses and overlapping conversations, but it all faded into the background. The world outside of his mind felt so far away, distant and unimportant compared to the decision weighing on him.

Adam perched on a barstool beside him, quietly sipping from his own mug, content to sit in the silence that allowed James to process his roiling thoughts.

"You don't have to stay here with me, you know?" James said.

"What? Not a fan of my company?"

James chuckled. "You know it's not that. I just . . . you can head into The Pint and Portal if you'd rather be there."

Adam waved him off. "Pints are just as good in here."

"Company might be better though."

"Your entire world has been caught in a whirlwind this past week. I don't think I'm the one needing company."

"I think I rushed into this all too quickly." The realization took hold of him as he said the words. "I jumped into running two pubs when I didn't even want to run one. I jumped into an entire multiverse of problems when I hadn't dealt with the ones that brought me here to begin with."

James took another long pull of his drink. He had chosen this. He'd chosen all of this. Maybe as a distraction, a way of avoiding his father's death. Sure, ensuring his inheritance had been a part of it, but neither of those things felt like the entire reason.

Adam nodded. "Aye. Ya did," he said. "Though you didn't do it alone, Jamesy. And you still don't have to. You've got a whole group of people who are willing to help. I know. They helped me out when my da died too."

James bit his lip. "This feels like a larger ask than taking over the family business."

"True," Adam agreed. "But that just means you've got more folks helping you. Emma, Tarvo, and the rest of those dwarves all stepped up to help, even when they didn't have to."

James let out a heavy sigh. He supposed Adam did have a point. Something Emma said had been along similar lines.

I have nowhere to go back to. No place I call home. A pub like Pint and Portal? It's that piece I've been missing.

The thought reminded him of something his mother had written. James pulled out the journal and turned to the front page, ignoring Adam's bewildered looks.

A haven for the lost. A home for the found.

Lost or found—which one was he?

"You're considering O'Malley's offer, aren't you?" Adam cut in. "Despite everything else?"

"I don't know what I'm thinking anymore. When Kathy first told me I'd inherited this place, I wanted nothing more than to turn around and run back to Vancouver. I'd decided to stick around because I didn't want to lose our inheritance. We'd lost our only design contract, so I had nothing else going on. I had nowhere else to be. Now, O'Malley's offered me a large sum of money for it, and my work just called, telling me we landed a major contract. It's like the universe is playing a cruel joke on me."

"Do you mind me asking how much he offered?" Adam asked.

James took the check out and slid it along the bar toward Adam.

Adam glanced at the paper and let out a low whistle. "No wonder you're questioning things. That's a lot of cash."

"Both my dad and Moira didn't want anything to do with the place after my mom died. There are so many things we still don't understand. If leaving the gates open poses that much of a threat, do I take the chance? Maybe we'd all be better off if The Pint and Portal were closed for good."

Adam took another swig of his stout before setting his mug down. "I don't envy your position," he said. "But what I do know, is that there's nothing worth having in this world that doesn't come with a little risk. If you're unsure, here's the way I see it. You can always decide to sell the pub later on if it's not worthwhile. Hand it over to O'Malley now and that's it, you're not going to get it back. I think you're far better off hanging on until you know you're sure."

James inhaled deeply, trying to center himself. Logically, it all made sense; the reality still hit hard. Staying in Cuanmore meant investing his time and energy here. It wasn't just a decision; it was a commitment.

"What are you lads up to?" Rudy's familiar German accent cut through his thoughts, warm and booming as always.

James turned to see the burly baker approaching. Rudy's cheerful expression shifted the moment he got a good look at James.

"Whoa!" Rudy exclaimed. "Why the long face, lad? What's happened?"

James hadn't realized he was wearing his emotions so plainly. Quickly, he tried to shift his expression into something more neutral.

"Rudy, I didn't realize you were around," he said, forcing a smile.

"Had to run some errands," he said. "The bakery is running half staffed. I don't say that to make you feel bad, it's just how it is. I have to work twice as hard to keep things running.

"Either way, I'm glad you're here." James grabbed his mother's journal from the bar top and lifted it in front of him, giving it a shake. "I think it's time for us to have a bit of a chat about these Tíogar Mór, and The Pint and Portal."

"I suppose that's only fair." Rudy frowned and looked around. "We should probably move somewhere a little more private."

James glanced around. A young lad by the name of Seamus cleaned tables nearby. They couldn't be too careful.

"There's a booth in the corner," James said, tilting his head in the direction of the back of the pub. "Let's carry on over there."

James motioned for the bartender to pour Rudy a stout. It only took a moment for it to arrive and the three grabbed their glasses and moved to a more secluded wooden table. The pub was filled with patrons, but the volume and proximity to the other tables meant they'd be able to carry on a conversation without anyone eavesdropping.

As they sat, James picked up right where he left off. "I'm a slow reader, so I haven't gotten through everything yet. From some of the entries, it sounds like there was concern that the wards keeping danger out of the pub were failing. Is that true?"

Rudy sighed. "Moira has always been afraid of the wards failing. The pub and these portals have existed for longer than any records remember. There is and was no real reason to be concerned that they were. To be honest, until Moira brought it up, none of us had realized there were wards that *could* fail. We just thought they were a built-in feature of the place."

"Is that why Dad closed the pub after Mom died?"

"How far have you read in the journal?" Rudy asked.

"Not far," James admitted. "We've been quite busy."

"Do you mind if I see that?" Rudy asked.

James nodded and handed it to him.

"There are pages missing," Rudy said gruffly. "Did you find it like this?"

James nodded. "Adam had a couple of them related to using Morac Mushrooms to brew beer, but that didn't nearly account for all of them."

Rudy's brow furrowed as though concerned. He flipped toward the back of the journal, skimmed a few lines then handed the journal back to him.

"As for your dad closing the pub, like I mentioned before, Tim had never wanted to run The Pint and Portal to begin with. We'd lost your mother, Tarvo, Adam's mother, and others. Some due to accident, others went back to their own worlds to protect them."

"You were just okay knowing that you might never see Tarvo again? That seems particularly cruel."

Rudy's eyes glistened with an unshed tear. "Tarvo and I made that decision. I'm not a fighter, I'd only be putting myself in harm's way by going back, and he wouldn't have any talk of me going. He couldn't stay here while his world was in danger. It was the hardest thing I've ever had to do, but it was necessary. It was tough for all of us. Your father couldn't handle losing your mother. Yes, there was the risk of the Tíogar coming through, but for your dad, that was a secondary consideration."

James looked down at the page Rudy had turned to.

He didn't get too far, though, as the storage room door burst open, and Moira came barreling in. Her hair was disheveled as though she'd been tugging at it, and her eyes darted around the room wildly as though searching for something or someone.

A few patrons glanced her way, eyebrows raised, before turning back to their conversations. If they were curious about what she'd been doing in the storage room—or why she looked like she'd wrestled a cat into a bath—they didn't show it.

"Rudy!" she cried as she approached their table.

"It's happened. Just like I've said it would. The wards have failed. The Tíogor Mór have come through."

"Impossible!" Rudy replied. Despite that, he was on his feet and making his way toward the portal.

James slowly rolled out of his seat and grabbed his mother's journal. Adam followed. He eyed James nervously as they crossed the room. The last thing James wanted to do was to draw attention by having four of them suddenly sprint toward the storage room. But as he surveyed the crowd around them, he realized that nobody was paying them any mind whatsoever.

Maybe there was magic at play in O'Sullivan's as well, or maybe people in Cuanmore weren't as nosy as he remembered.

It's definitely magic, he thought. He wondered if somewhere in his mother's journal she'd talked about there being magic in O'Sullivan's too.

Regardless, they wound their way between the tables as quickly and as casually as possible.

They came out on the other side to find that Moira and

Rudy hadn't moved very far. They stood maybe three feet away from the portal's exit, both staring at the bar.

James followed their gaze. With its back turned toward them, seated at the bar, was most definitely a humanoid tiger.

"Is that . . .?" he started, but he didn't need the answer.

Despite not ever having seen one in real life, he knew exactly what he was looking at. He'd heard enough about them and had drawn them based on his mother's stories. He wanted to reach for his portfolio to double check the uncanny likeness between this fellow and the ones he'd been drawing since he was a boy—in his humble opinion, he'd done a bang-up job—however, he'd left it upstairs in his bedroom.

"Tíogar Mór," Rudy whispered. The baker's eyes went wide, and he started scanning the room. "Where's Tarvo?"

"Tarvo?" Moira asked incredulously. "Rudy, we have to *do* something about this."

Emma was behind the bar, smiling and having a conversation with the Tíogar. Liam stood behind her, arms crossed. He appeared a little more wary, but he was allowing himself to smile as well. James scanned the rest of the bar. Nearly every patron eyed the Tíogar warily.

James cleared his throat and started to make his way toward the bar.

"What are you going to do?" Moira hissed.

"I'm going to go talk to him," James answered.

"Talk to him?" Moira gasped, her hands flailing as though intending to physically hold him back. "James, we need to get rid of him!"

James spun on Moira so quickly that she jumped back, surprise washing over her face. "What has he done?" he asked.

"Nothing . . . yet. But I won't give him a chance to."

James lifted his mother's journal. "A haven for the lost. A home for the found. This is a safe place for all who find it. That hasn't changed. It won't as long as I'm here."

As long as I'm here . . .

Moira started to stutter a response, but James wasn't listening.

James pulled up a stool at the bar, a couple seats away from the Tíogar but only because the creature's frame was so large it was overtaking the seats alongside him.

"Welcome to The Pint and Portal," James said as he sat. Emma offered him a small smile, while Liam gave a grateful nod and quickly put some distance between them. "I'm James. I'm the owner here."

"Kai," the Tíogar said. His voice wasn't as deep as James had expected, and there was a bit of a growl behind it, but James didn't think it was meant to be threatening. Kai cast James a wary look. "Thank you, James, for welcoming me here. Emma has ensured me this is a safe place, despite the wariness of some of your other guests."

"If anyone gives you trouble, let me know." Not that he would exactly know what to do against a table of dwarves and their axes. "This is meant to be a safe place."

As he spoke the words, James realized how much he'd meant it.

Emma

The last portal had hummed to a close for the evening. Emma was quickly cleaning the last of the glasses that had been stacked up throughout the night, and Liam and Gloria were doing their last rounds of tidying.

Moira had left the pub in a fit after James sat down with Kai. Tarvo and Ha'dran went to their rooms early. And despite their offers to help, Emma had insisted James, Rudy, Adam, and Kathy retire for the night as well. Liam, Gloria, and she could handle what little work there was to end the night.

The three worked in silence. Emma was eager to be finished and return to her room to sleep. The last few days had been a whirlwind, and she hoped to catch up on some much-needed rest.

Liam was cleaning around the bar, picking up napkins and other refuse that had been left over from the patrons who'd sat around it.

"Thanks for your support with Kai," he said suddenly. "That was all rather embarrassing."

Emma stopped her cleaning for the moment. "It's me who should be thanking you. If you hadn't stepped in, I'm not sure people would have held back."

Liam laughed. "After the way you stood up to Tarvo? I don't think anyone was going to mess with you."

Emma pursed her lips. "Tarvo's more bark than bite. It's your mother I'm more worried about." She didn't mention how she was sure Moira had been about to use magic. It seemed too incredulous to be true.

Liam sighed. "Yeah, I'm going to have to have a word with Mum. She has seemed so anxious since the pub opened. I thought your talk with her had calmed her nerves, but that didn't seem to last. Especially with Kai showing up. She thinks the pub puts us all in some kind of danger."

"Rudy told James she's been worried about the wards as long as he's known her. She hasn't ever said anything to you about what encounters with magic or with the Tíogar Mór made her so nervous?"

Liam shook his head. "Whatever it was, she's not about to tell me about it. She's always been tight-lipped about her feelings. I was hoping she would open up to you about it."

"After last night, I wouldn't count on it. But I can try to talk to her, see what I can learn. We can't have someone feeling threatened simply for being who they are. I can't accept that, and I get the sense James wouldn't either."

Liam bit his lip as he drummed his fingers on the bar. "My mother or not, I won't accept it either. James trusted me enough to help him manage things the way his mother would have wanted, and that tagline didn't mean nothing. We're here as a place of refuge and rest. A talking tiger is hardly the strangest thing to have come walking through those gateways. I'm willing to bet there will be even stranger-looking folk who come through. We have to be open minded here."

"I think I'm going to go up to my room now," Gloria said. The dwarf wiped a bead of sweat from her forehead with the back of her arm. "I'm completely wiped."

Emma smiled. "You're doing great out there," she said. "You're really getting the hang of this."

"I'm having a great time," Gloria said, her smile beaming wide, revealing jagged teeth. "Who knew there'd be so many interesting folk out there?"

"That's certainly a different tune than when we first met," Emma laughed.

Gloria lifted a hand to her chin as she stood thoughtfully for a moment. "I suppose it is. But then again, not having to fight for survival every day tends to change a person's perspective."

"I suppose that's true." Emma nodded. She had hardly thought about it until now. She'd so often been on the hunt that she'd hardly ever stopped to consider what it was like to be the hunted.

"For what it's worth," Gloria said, "I don't think there's anyone who hated the Tíogar Mór more than me. But this place has helped me to realize that everyone is on their own journey. I'm a little uneasy around Kai, but I don't think it's fair to be openly hostile toward him as some of the others have been. We all deserve a chance to exist without living in fear because of who we are."

Emma thought back to their first encounter and how terrified Gloria was of the creatures who had ravaged her world. She understood why the dwarf would be uneasy and that this was a big step for her.

"Thank you for that," said Emma. "I know it's not easy when you've been through so much."

Emma could have sworn Gloria blushed. "All I can say is I'm grateful that you stumbled into our lives and brought us to this place. I'm sorry I was so hostile toward you at the beginning."

Emma smiled. "You were doing your best to survive. Sometimes that's all we can do."

A small smile crossed Gloria's face. She nodded then made

her way up the stairs to her room, leaving Emma and Liam to close out the pub.

"For being a monster hunter," Liam said as he pushed a chair under its table, "you're really empathetic toward people's journeys."

Emma looked at him from behind the bar. "What do you mean?"

Liam chuckled. "You know exactly what I mean. With Gloria now, and with Kai earlier. It's like you see people for who they are, or even who they *could* be, instead of who they were or who others judge them to be."

Emma shrugged. "I have to believe people can change. I have to believe there's room for people to make mistakes."

Liam rested his elbows on the bar and leaned forward. "Most people don't think that way."

"Most people don't have to account for their own past sins like I do." Emma let out a long slow breath as she stepped in front of Liam. "If there's no redemption for them, it means there's no redemption for me either."

Emma's gaze went unfocused as her own words hit home. The memory of the dagger whizzing past her as someone yelled 'witch hunter' replaying itself in her mind. "Maybe I'm just naive."

Liam reached across the bar and grabbed her hand. The warmth of his fingers sent waves of electricity through her. "There's no shame in wanting to see the best in people. For believing people can change."

Emma cleared her throat. "Listen, about our conversation the other day . . . about us . . . I'm sorry I never told you about—"

Liam put a finger to her lips. "You don't have anything to apologize for. If anything, I'm sorry for the way I reacted. It . . . you did surprise me, but that wasn't fair to you."

"I can understand where you were coming from, though. If I'm completely honest, I was scared of the same thing myself.

But the more I think about you, about us . . . Liam, I genuinely like you. Not because you look like the man I grew so attached to. You're willing to look out for your friends. You bend over backward to help people out. Do you know how rare that is?"

Liam shook his head, letting out a faint laugh. "You don't know how rare it is to see the best in people. You're so understanding. How is it even possible that you're real?"

Emma lifted a hand to cup his cheek. "I keep asking myself the same thing about you. We don't have to rush into this. I'm not planning on going anywhere. Maybe we can get to know each other better?"

He leaned in toward her, ever so slightly. "I'd like that," he said. Then that familiar mischievous look glinted in his eye. "I'd also like to kiss you."

A playful grin crossed Emma's face, as she reached out and grabbed Liam by the shirt collar, pulling him across the bar top. She leaned into him, her lips finding his.

For a moment, it felt like the world had slowed, the distant hum of the pub and the dirty dishes in the sink fading into nothingness. It was just them.

When they parted, Liam exhaled a quiet laugh, his forehead resting against hers. "Well. . . that's one way to ease into things," he said.

Emma smiled. "I think you were the one who said I'm full of surprises."

Liam chuckled, his breath brushing against her cheek. "I bet this beats having a dagger tossed at your head."

She released her grip on his collar and stepped back slightly, her hand lingering on his chest for a moment before falling to her side. "I should warn you, this might not be easy. Getting involved with me might present challenges."

Liam raised an eyebrow. "I think we've established that already. Do you mean because of the witch hunter thing? If what you said about the multiverse is true, there might be just as many people unhappy with me as they are with you."

Emma paused. She hadn't thought of that before. There would be no reason why it wasn't equally as likely.

"That's . . . not exactly what I meant."

Liam pulled himself onto a barstool, the glint in his eye never leaving. "I'm willing to work through whatever it is. Unless you're thinking you're going to start hopping worlds again, because I think I'm firmly planted in this one."

"That's not it at all." Emma laughed. "Liam, I've spent so much of my life running, fighting, keeping people at a distance. I've never really had the chance to let someone in before. I don't really know how any of this works."

Liam's smile could have melted her right there and then. "Then we'll figure it out together."

James

When James wandered into The Pint and Portal the next evening, he was surprised to see Kai in the same seat. The rest of the pub seemed a little more at ease with his presence. Except for Moira, who was sitting in the corner seat stewing.

James ignored the woman for the time being. All her talk of the wards failing and the danger of Kai's presence was starting to grate on him. So far, it had mostly been Moira and Gloria running the floor. Liam, Emma, and he had been filling in the gaps where they could, but it wasn't a long-term solution. Especially since he didn't think Moira was going to be able to keep working the floor. Not if she was going to be outwardly hostile toward their patrons.

He would have to find more help. Ha'dran had tried, but he ended up breaking more glasses than he delivered. He was a much better storyteller, and James was more than satisfied to have him perform and entertain.

If they *were* going to stick around, he needed to figure out a better living arrangement for Tarvo, Gloria, and Ha'dran. Despite their apparent contentment to stay within the pub's magical walls, they couldn't remain there forever.

"Nice to see you made it back," James said as he approached the Tíogar. "I was worried we scared you off."

Kai turned and gave James a full toothy grin. If James had just encountered Kai in the middle of the woods, he would have been terrified of his long sharp fangs and glowing eyes. Still, he had to swallow. It wasn't that he was worried about Kai, but taming eons' worth of primal instincts was certainly another matter. His heart raced, but he was sure he'd get used to the man's tiger-like appearance in time.

"I have to admit," said Kai, "I never would have come back if it wasn't for your kindness and that of Liam and Emma. Despite the reaction I received when I first arrived, I've never felt safer anywhere else."

The statement almost made James want to cry. The bar had threatened to skewer him the moment he arrived, and this was where he felt the safest? He wondered what Kai's home world must look like.

"What are you drinking?" James asked, nodding to his rocks glass. The drink was a golden color and gave off a distinct aroma of ginger and lime.

"Emma called it a 'Tiogar's Refuge,'" Kai said. "I was hesitant at first, but it's quite good."

"She has a knack for that sort of thing," James said, looking to his bartender. Emma smiled as she looked up and made eye contact.

"What's in it?" James asked. "It smells incredible."

"Spiced rum, mezcal, honey, lime juice, and ginger beer," Emma replied as she poured a pint of stout for another patron. "Want me to make you one?"

"Yes please," he replied. "And make sure you show Liam how to make these as well."

Emma nodded, handing the pint to Gloria and gesturing for Liam to watch her in action as she made James' drink.

"I'm glad you decided to come back," James said. "Again, I have to apologize for the initial reception you received. Some here have had . . . unpleasant experiences. But that's not fair to you."

"I understand," Kai grunted, his paw reaching around the glass. "They're vicious beasts. But I'm not like them, you know."

James blinked. "Like who?"

"The warriors your people are afraid of. They're a tribe called the Bhak'at. It's foolish to think all of my kind are like them."

It was a term James hadn't heard before, but there was no mistaking the disdain in Kai's voice. "You're right, that it isn't fair. Certainly not all humans are kind, and I wouldn't want to be judged by the actions of the worst of us. You're running from them, aren't you?"

Kai let out a low growl. "Running? No. I'm trying to stop them."

James got the sense that if he was ever going to learn more about the Tíogar Mór, this was his chance. "Some of the people here have had their worlds invaded by these warriors. You say you're trying to stop that?"

"Not alone, of course," said Kai. "I'm part of an underground resistance movement."

"What are they after anyway? Why are they invading other worlds?"

Kai snorted. "They see themselves as apex predators. First, they destroyed our own world. It used to be an oasis, you know, filled with lush jungles, incredible waterfalls, and millions of species. The Bhak'at took control, developed advanced and destructive technologies, and within a matter of years, turned it into a living hellscape. That wasn't enough for them. Their scientists then discovered a way to jump dimensions. They saw it as a way to escape the destruction they caused. As these things go, instead of learning from their mistakes, they're out to conquer any other world they can find. They tear it to the ground, trying to satisfy some primal urge. It's barbaric."

A tickle danced along the back of James' neck. He instinctively swatted at it, expecting a bug or something had flown past him. However, the sensation didn't stop, and he realized there was a breeze passing over him.

He looked around for its source—someone walking by briskly, or something of that nature—but there was nothing there.

He shrugged it off. Just another one of the oddities that had occurred in the pub since they'd opened.

"These attacks, it had nothing to do with the Bhak'at looking for a certain type of mushroom?"

They had given the mushrooms to the dwarves under the impression that they were likely safe, but this was his chance to be sure.

Kai raised an eyebrow. "Mushrooms?" He snorted. "What would they want with a mushroom?"

James used two fingers to gesture at Emma. The bartender caught his meaning without him having to say a word. She reached for a pint glass and filled it with a pull of the Nocturne Speciale.

James placed his mother's notebook on the bar top.

"Someone had a theory that's what they might be after," James said. "But you don't believe that's the reason?"

"We're carnivores." Kai's teeth caught a glint from the pub lights as he smiled. "Mushrooms aren't really our thing."

The breeze picked up now, enough to ruffle James' hair. Again, he looked around. It didn't seem as though too many in the pub had noticed. Other than Liam who James caught scanning the room suspiciously.

Emma brought a pint of the stout over to the bar. "Give this a try," she said.

Kai sniffed at the brew suspiciously before picking it up and taking a sip.

His cheeks puffed, and his throat twitched. Kai lifted a finger to his lips as he nearly spat the drink back out. Instead, he reluctantly swallowed before pushing the thing away.

"By the ancestors, that is a vile drink!" His tongue flicked in and out of his mouth as though trying to get the taste out of it. Finally, he picked up the remaining bit of Tíogar's Refuge in his glass and downed it.

Kai looked at Emma. "Could I get some water, please?"

If he and his kind had been after those mushrooms, James was sure he would have sensed it in the beer. Maybe it was too diluted. He had to be sure.

"Adam," he called over to his friend, who quickly appeared by his side.

"What is it?" he asked.

"Do you have any more of those mushrooms on you?"

Adam happily pulled a few from his backpack and set them on the bar in front of James. "Sure do."

James nudged Kai again. "These are the mushrooms I mentioned," he said. "Still not ringing a bell?"

Kai looked down at the three small tear drop shaped fungi, picked them up with a swipe of his paw, and pulled them in close to his nose, taking a short, sharp sniff.

His nose wrinkled, causing his whiskers to twitch. He looked no more impressed than he had with the beer.

"I'm sorry," Kai said, "but I don't think any Tíogar Mór would think twice about these things. Never mind invade a world over them."

Emma set down the Tíogar's Refuge James ordered.

"Could you top him off as well?" James nodded to Kai's empty glass.

Emma rolled her eyes as she set a second drink down. "I'm miles ahead of you, James."

That was one theory out the window at least. But he still had some questions.

Kai's fur shifted in the breeze, and James realized the wind he'd noticed earlier had steadily increased. He shot a concerned look at Emma. She'd noticed it as well, and started to move napkins, spices, and other lightweight items off the counter to beneath the bar so that they wouldn't blow away.

James glanced around nervously.

It's just like what Mom had written in her journal.

"I hope you don't mind me asking these questions," James said. "I don't mean to offend; this is the first time we've had the chance to speak with a Tíogar. If you're fighting against the Bhak'at, it's important for us to learn what we can."

Kai held up a paw. "No need to explain. I'm happy to help."

James breathed a sigh of relief. "I just have one more question for you. Some of our people are afraid that the Bhak'at might be looking to drain magic from this place. Mysterious things keep occurring, like this breeze that's happening now. Things in here have been acting unusual. Some say it's because the pub's magic is becoming unbalanced. Is this something the Bhak'at are capable of?"

The Tíogar thought for a moment then lifted a paw behind his ear and scratched. "I don't think so," he said. "We are not a magic species. Everything the Bhak'at have done has been through technological achievements. I'm sorry to disappoint you, but if this place is built with magic, I don't know if there is a way Tíogar could harness it without physically taking it over."

"I wouldn't say I'm disappointed . . ." James started, but out of the corner of his eye he noticed one of the portals opening. He looked in its direction in time to witness five more Tíogar Mór step through.

His stomach dropped. "Friends of yours?" he asked.

Kai didn't have a chance to answer as the pub descended into chaos.

Tíogar's Refuge

Ingredients

- 1 ½ ounce spiced rum
- 1/2 ounce mezcal
- 1/2 ounce honey or simple syrup
- 1/2 ounce lime juice
- 2 dashes of Angostura bitters
- Ginger beer (to top)
- Lime wheel (for garnish)

Directions:

1. In a shaker, combine spiced rum, mezcal, honey syrup, lime juice, and bitters with ice. Shake until well chilled.
2. Strain into a rocks glass over fresh ice.
3. Top with ginger beer and gently stir.
4. Garnish with a lime wheel.

Emma

Wind howled through the pub with such ferocity that Emma felt as though the walls themselves might tear apart. Glasses rattled violently on the tables, their contents sloshing over the rims, while half-drunk cups of ale and wine teetered dangerously close to the edge of whatever surface they sat on. The wooden beams overhead groaned as if they, too, were struggling to withstand the storm. Emma braced herself against the counter, worried that at any second, the entire room might be swept away.

Frightened patrons clung to their cloaks, their drinks, and each other as the gale's force only seemed to grow. Chairs skidded across the floor, overturned by the sheer strength of the wind. A plate shattered somewhere near the back of the room, the sound barely audible over the deafening roar.

"What's happening?" Emma yelled, her voice cutting through the chaos.

James stood from his seat. Beside him, Kai stood rigid, his paws splayed wide for balance, his ears flattened against his head.

The portal behind the new Tíogar Mór visitors winked shut while the portal to O'Sullivan's vibrated violently, the swirling light within warping and stretching as if caught in some invisible force.

"I don't know," James shouted as he fought to be heard over the noise.

A quick survey of the rest of the pub revealed most of it was falling apart. Tables were sliding across the floor; chairs toppled and spun. A gnome, with his brightly colored hat in hand, was running next to the bar. His short legs churned furiously, but he wasn't moving forward. Trapped in place by the strength of the wind, he was desperately trying to cling to something solid.

Hal, who hadn't seemed all that affected by what was going on, grunted, though Emma could barely hear it. The ogre bent down, wrapping one massive hand around the gnome, and lifted him effortlessly. He placed the small creature onto the bar like setting down a glass, using his hand to shield the little man from the gale force winds so he could rest.

Emma exhaled a breath of relief and turned her attention to the other gnomes. They were huddled in their booth, pressed tightly against each other in the corner. The wooden walls offered some protection, and they clung to the edge of the table, their faces pale but determined. For now, they were safe.

The rest of the patrons weren't faring much better. Some clutched their belongings, trying to keep their weapons or bags from flying away. Others held onto their drinks as though losing them would somehow make the situation worse.

A few fumbled with their orbs, their hands shaking as they moved toward the platforms in a desperate attempt to summon their portals.

"They can't seriously be thinking they're going to try to open their portals now, can they?" As if responding to the thought, the portal to O'Sullivan's, still open from the latest arrival, warbled and groaned.

"Something is very wrong," she thought aloud.

There's no doubt this is magic. Demon Box suddenly shifted into her thoughts. *This isn't the work of any technology.*

Emma admitted she'd had the same thought.

Before she could say anything more, the wind died down. The portal stabilized, its swirling light returning to a steady rhythm.

"Liam, can you close the gateways until we know what's going on?" James asked, his voice filled with a sudden determination and authority. "And pull the orb from O'Sullivan's as well. I don't want anyone getting hurt."

Liam nodded and immediately moved to do as he was asked.

"I'll tell you what's going on!" cried Moira. "It's them!" Moira waved a bony finger in the direction of the newcomers, her voice trembling. "I knew this day would come! Tíogar Mór coming here, trying to spread their destruction by using our portals. I swore I'd protect this pub, and protect it I will!"

The five Tíogar stood mortified, their feline eyes focused. Their arms went wide in unison, a couple lifted their hands placatingly.

Emma stood aghast. What thoughts must be running through their heads?

Beside her, Kai growled, his teeth bared, but he stood where he was for the moment.

Mutters and curses echoed throughout the pub.

Moira lifted her second hand and elongated her fingers as she started to circle her arms, muttering to herself.

"She's going to cast a spell!" Emma heard herself cry out the words in disbelief. Before she could think, before she could process what she was doing, Emma vaulted over the counter, her boots hitting the floor hard as she raced toward Moira. Sparks of electricity danced along the older woman's fingertips.

The three lead Tíogar Mór had lowered their bodies to the ground, curled in a predatory crouch. Thankfully, despite

Moira's cry, nobody else in the pub moved toward them. Some held their weapons at the ready, but most were watching, waiting to see how the scene unfolded.

Electricity crackled in the air as Emma closed the distance between herself and Moira.

"My wards have failed," Moira cried, her eyes never leaving the newcomers. "I can't let them take this place! I can't let them do what they did to my world."

As they collided, Emma's momentum carried Moira backward, and Emma found herself on top, pinning the older woman down. The crackling energy in the air faded, the wind died down and the faint sparks on Moira's hands fizzled.

The room went completely still. The patrons having all but forgotten the newcomers, stared at the two women sitting on the floor, one on top of the other.

Moira's chest heaved as she stared up at Emma, her furious expression slowly giving way to one of exhaustion. "I can't let them take it," she whispered again.

Emma's heart ached at the raw emotion in those words. Still, she didn't let go. "They're not going to take anything. They're not here to hurt anyone," she said firmly. "I know you're scared, but this isn't the way."

Moira's eyes flicked toward the Tíogar Mór, who were still crouched low. Slowly, they straightened, their hands still raised in a gesture of peace, their movements cautious now that the immediate threat seemed to have passed.

"You don't know what they did to our world . . ." Moira said.

"I saw what they did to Tarvo's," Emma replied. "That was enough. But these Tíogar here weren't the ones responsible for that. You can't project the sins of a few onto an entire species."

She looked at those around her—some had returned to their seats and were shifting uncomfortably at what had just unfolded. Some were still staring at them. Kai had joined the

Tíogar Mór who had just arrived, whispering in hushed tones that she couldn't hear.

Still, she didn't think Moira should be any more of a spectacle than she already was. She made eye contact with James who was standing just as dumbfounded as anyone else in the room. "I think it'd be best if everyone returned to their seats," she said.

James blinked in surprise at the statement, but he scanned the room and realized the audience still surrounding them. "She's right," he said, addressing the room. "Everyone, please return to your tables. Next round is on the house."

A cheer erupted from a dwarf near the bar, quickly followed by laughter from the dwarf's still-seated friends. The tension in the room dissolved as the guests slowly made their way back to their seats, the silence from moments before replaced by the familiar buzz of conversation.

Liam stood only a few feet away. His brows furrowed as his gaze lay intently on his mother.

As the other patrons returned to their seats, he cleared his throat. "Mum . . ." he began but his eyes carried an uncertain look. "What . . . was that?"

Moira didn't answer. She sat up slowly, her head drooping.

"Moira?" Emma said softly. The older woman didn't look at her.

Instead, Moira pushed herself to her knees then to her feet. She cleared her throat and dusted herself off, her back straightening as she turned to face her son. "I didn't want you to find out this way." Moisture filled her eyes. "In fact, I never wanted you find out."

"Find out *what*, exactly?" There was an edge to Liam's voice, tension as he braced himself for what he'd no doubt already begun to piece together.

"We should probably give you two some privacy," Emma said as she stood.

"No." Liam reached out and grabbed her hand. His eyes found hers, wide as though pleading for her to stay. Whatever Moira was about to share, he was terrified of it.

Emma squeezed Liam's hand. If he needed her here for this, she was more than willing.

If Moira had any objections to her staying, or any thoughts around her son holding the bartender's hand, she didn't let it show. Perhaps she was too lost in her own thoughts to notice.

"I'm a witch, Liam."

Liam's grip on Emma's hand tightened, but he remained silent.

"I'm able to manipulate the weather—wind and electricity, mostly. I've tried to hide it ever since we came to this place."

Liam paused, and Emma could only guess his thoughts were racing faster than hers.

"What do you mean 'since we came to this place?'" he asked.

Moira lifted her eyes toward him and inhaled deeply. "The world you grew up in isn't ours, Liam. I was one of them, once." She gestured to the pub behind him. "One of those who was in search of refuge."

Liam froze. Emma wasn't even sure if he was blinking. He just stood in silence for several moments as he studied his mother.

"Why didn't you tell me?" Liam asked.

Moira let out a weary chuckle. "There was no reason for you to know. You were too young to remember, and when Tim closed this pub, I never thought we'd have to deal with magic again. I never would have believed James would come back to start all this up again."

"So the winds? The power? All the little things that have gone wrong were just you trying to . . . trying to what? Convince us to close the pub?"

Moira sighed, her shoulders slumping. "I knew James was

on the fence about opening this place. I thought if I could convince you of the danger . . ." Her eyes darted toward the group of Tíogar Mór who were now being thoroughly entertained by Ha'dran and one of his tales. "You'd reconsider keeping it open."

It was James' turn to step in. He crossed his arms, clearly not impressed by the turn of events. "So what was all that about the wards failing? You were terrified yesterday when Kai came in."

Suddenly, the pieces began to click together. The conversation she had with Nethramir a couple of nights ago replayed in her mind.

The wards . . . those are much more recent.

"You created the wards." Emma spoke the words as she thought them. "You've been so worried about the wards failing because you were the one who set them up."

Moira looked at her with a wide-eyed stare.

"Moira!" Rudy said as he stepped up to join the conversation. "Is that true?

"Yes, it's true!" Moira said, her tone harsher, edging toward angry. "You, Shay, and Michael didn't take the threat seriously!" Moira was frantic now, her fingers tugging at her hair.

Rudy stepped toward her, his hands up placatingly. "Like we said then, the ancients knew what they were doing. They'd never let harm come to this place before, there's no reason to think their magic would fail us now. "

"I had to ensure there were safeguards in place," Moira cried. "They took my world, everything I loved. I couldn't let them take this too. I couldn't let them take my son." She burst into uncontrollable sobs, and Liam moved to her side, resting a hand on her shoulder and looking very much like he didn't know what to do.

But James wasn't through his line of questioning yet. "So the wards aren't failing?" said James. "You were the one causing everything? The wind, the espresso machine, the lights?" He pulled out his mother's journal and held it up. "You did the same thing back then, too, didn't you? Then you blamed the Morac Mushrooms for attracting the Tíogar Mór, and you made it seem like the magic behind the portals was failing."

Moira cast her gaze to the floor. "I wanted to protect you. I didn't want the same thing to happen to your world that happened to mine."

James pursed his lips and stepped forward. "Why are there pages missing, Moira?"

Moira's eyes shamefully rose to meet his. "Your mother eventually figured it out. She had her entire thought process mapped out, so I took out enough pages to tell the story in the way I wanted it to play out. Apparently, it wasn't enough."

Emma could see anger rising on James' face. She couldn't say she blamed him. These were his mother's personal thoughts, part of the legacy she'd left to James and Kathy.

"We tried to tell you back then, Moira," Rudy said. "This has been a safe haven for centuries. It's what brought us all here to begin with. If anyone's made this place unsafe, it was you."

Even Emma cringed at the accusation. Moira's eyes widened as realization overtook her face. "I didn't mean to . . ." The words caught in her throat as she spoke them.

"Your good intentions don't make up for your accusations against those Tíogar."

Moira cast a worried glance over to the table where the Tíogar sat. They seemed to have put the incident behind them. Emma knew, though, that people of any type were often good at burying how they truly felt.

"Liam, please bring her back to O'Sullivan's," James said. "I think the rest of us need to ensure everyone feels safe here."

Emma let out a quiet breath as she caught Liam's expression. She could tell he was still trying to come to terms with the avalanche he'd just learned. His mother was a witch, she'd caused everything that had happened . . . and he wasn't from this world.

He'd need someone to lean on, now more than ever.

She stepped forward, her hand resting on his arm. He glanced at her, and for a moment, their eyes met. There was something unspoken in his gaze, something that made her heart skip a beat.

Trust.

"We'll figure this out," she said. "I can come with you if you need."

Some of the tension lifted from his shoulders. "I appreciate that, but I think I'm going to need to talk with my mother, alone."

Liam leaned in and placed his lips on hers, and she allowed herself to melt into him. He pulled away too quickly. "Later I might need you to help me talk this out."

Emma smiled. "I'd love to."

James

As the last patrons left, James reset the main lever to prevent new portals from opening. All-in-all, the evening had progressed rather well after Moira left and the Tíogar Mór were allowed to feel comfortable in the space.

Kathy and Liam had appeared from O'Sullivan's, leaving Moira behind to contend with whatever Liam had told her. Ha'dran and Gloria were busy cleaning tables and bringing mugs to the counter—Ha'dran had only dropped one so far.

Rudy, Tarvo, and Adam were standing next to the bar as he approached, sharing a laugh with Emma and Demon Box—who was relishing its newfound freedom to speak openly among them.

"And then I said," Demon Box chirped, finishing some tale as James walked up to join them, "'Have you tried turning the portal off and on again?'"

The group groaned in unison while Demon Box let out a satisfied hum. "What? It was a good one!"

James couldn't help but chuckle despite missing the set up. "Are we sure letting it talk was a good idea?"

Emma smirked. "No, but I've grown used to it. And though I might regret admitting it, I kind of like having it around."

"Kind of?" said Demon Box. "Emma, you wound me! I've bent space and time for you, and all I get is 'kind of?'"

Emma laughed along with the rest of the group. "Don't worry," she said, "I plan on keeping you around for a while. There's still time for you to grow on me."

"Oh, be still my beating heart! Er . . . circuits? To be honest, I'm not sure what's actually powering the bus here."

James smiled and leaned against the bar, tuning out the rest of Demon Box's theatrics.

"You did well today," Rudy said as he pulled up beside him. The baker clasped a large hand on James' shoulder. "Your parents would have been proud of how you handled things."

James' heart sunk at the words. He should have been thrilled. He should have been proud. But all he felt was confused.

After everything they'd been through, how could he still be uncertain? O'Malley's check still sat in his pocket, a rope tugging at his heart.

"I'm not sure if that's true," he said. "I'm don't think I'm cut out for this."

Rudy smiled as he leaned against the bar. "You know, your father once said the very same thing to me."

"And he decided to shutter it. Maybe I'm more like him than I thought."

"Other than your lack of confidence, the two of you are nothing alike." Rudy's eyes widened as he realized what he'd said. "No offense, of course. Your dad was a wonderful man. As are you."

"None taken," James said.

"My point is," Rudy continued, "when he put his mind to it, he did a damn fine job with this place, and I know you will, too. But your dad was only here at all because of your mother. His heart wasn't in it, and he had a tough time handling the memories."

James sighed. He shoved a hand into the pocket of his jacket, and wrapped it around the check, pulling it out. "My job called me earlier; said I can return whenever I want."

"Oh?" Rudy asked with a single eyebrow raised, though James could have sworn the baker hardly seemed surprised.

"I've spent my entire life trying to run away," James continued, unfolding the paper and taking another glance at the numbers. "Even with The Pint and Portal, I didn't think it was enough. I didn't want to hear tales of someone else's adventures; I wanted to live them."

"And nobody would blame you," Rudy said. "I think after tonight, any of us would understand you not wanting to put energy into something you aren't passionate about."

James let his gaze wander over the people who had spent the last weeks with him, those he had let into his life, who had offered nothing but their unwavering support—not only for him, but for his family's legacy, and for each other.

"I've been given everything I'd need to turn my back and leave," he said. "There are no more excuses to keep me around, except . . ."

He paused, letting his thoughts settle as he continued to scan the room. It felt like the first time everyone was in the same place since they'd opened.

Rudy and Tarvo, Emma and Liam—his mother had been right, relationships had been kindled, and people reunited because the pub had become a part of their lives.

Then there were Ha'dran and Gloria; through story and camaraderie and entertaining their guests, the two dwarves seemed to have found a renewed sense of purpose. Gloria, especially, had grown more personable since she'd arrived, and when Ha'dran wasn't on stage telling his tales, he was delighting and engaging patrons at their tables.

There were those who'd accidentally entered this venture beside him. Liam for sure, but also Kathy and Adam. They'd had their lives blown wide open and their concepts of reality challenged.

A smile formed across his face as he watched each of these people who had become an integral part of his life so quickly. Each of them enjoying themselves. Enjoying each other. Enjoying the place that had so quickly grown to feel like home.

Home.

James looked around at the empty tables, the quiet wall where portals would open and close, the stairs leading up to the rooms where Emma and the dwarves had been staying.

When had he grown to think of this as his home? Not just as a place connected to where he had grown up, but actually home.

It hit him then. He wasn't in this alone. Those around the bar had already gone above and beyond. The patrons coming and going, who, despite being on their own journeys, were willing to be there for one another. They were willing to come back night after night and enjoy each other's company. No matter what hardship they'd come from or what devastation had been wrought on their own worlds.

James looked up at Rudy and met the baker's eyes.

"Except?" Liam asked, still waiting for James to complete his thought.

James hadn't realized his friend had been listening to their discussion.

"Except, I don't think I want to leave." The thought grabbed James as he spoke the words. "I've been so worried about being stuck in Cuanmore, that I almost missed the adventure this is. I was worried that listening to stories of other worlds wouldn't be enough. But look at everything that's happened this week."

It was then that James realized the rest of his companions had been listening as well.

Liam rested a hand on James' shoulder. Adam, who had taken a stool beside him, placed a hand on his other one.

"We've got you, buddy," said Liam.

"Does that mean you're planning on sticking around?" asked Kathy, with more than a hint of hope in her voice.

James unfolded the check Mr. O'Malley had given him. There was only one thing he could do now. He knew where he belonged. "It does," he said. With a prominent rip, James tore the check into two pieces. "I know you all have other obligations, so I don't expect you to stick around here. But I am so grateful for everything you've done to help get us this far."

Emma's grin stretched from one side of her face to the other. "I don't want to speak for all of us, but as far as I'm concerned, we're all in this together. I, for one, am here as long as you'll have me. What James' mom wrote in that journal is a motto I'll proudly stand behind."

She put her hand out over the bar top, her palm facing down. "To The Pint and Portal—a haven for the lost, a home for the found. What greater cause could there be? I'm willing to stick around if you'll let me. Who else is with me?"

Liam didn't hesitate, he put his hand on top of Emma's. "I'm in. You have my support." His gaze flicked from Emma to James. "Both of you do."

James couldn't help but catch the subtle smile that crossed Emma's lips. The spark in her eyes as Liam's skin touched hers.

Liam gave her a knowing grin before addressing the others. "Who else?"

"Tarvo believes in the power of this place," said Ha'dran, "and that's enough for me." The dwarf laid a hairy hand atop Liam's.

At the mention of his name, Tarvo nearly choked. Not to be outdone, he scrambled over to the bar and put his hand over Ha'dran's. "Damn right I believe in this place. I always have and

I always will. James, my support of you has never wavered. Rudy was right, your folks would be proud."

Adam set his mug on the counter before adding his hand to the pile. "Well, I may not know as much as you folks, but count me in. My parents obviously saw something in this place. And to be completely honest, this is the coolest thing that's ever happened to me. As long as this place stays open, Cuanmore Harbor Brewing will be more than happy to supply it with a variety of craft beers."

"I'm in too." Kathy stuck her hand in.

Gloria added hers next, as did Rudy.

That left James staring at the hands of his friends before him.

He had to fight to keep himself from tearing up, but he managed to steady himself.

"You all are bleedin' ridiculous."

Grins painted across many of their faces as they looked at James and then at each other.

"I have to admit," Demon Box chirped. "I'd prefer if I had some wine to go with all this cheese."

Everything James had ever done before had been on his own. Hours locked in his room drawing. Leaving to find a new career and path forward. More hours locked behind a keyboard.

Something else tugged at him that he only now realized he'd been missing all this time. Something he had been chasing but hadn't been able to put into words.

Purpose.

He'd left Cuanmore in search of it. Had dreamed of epic quests and heroic battles. He'd designed games with quests and missions as grand as any of the ones that had arrived on his doorstep through the portal. None of it had filled that void he'd been missing.

"Kathy, you were wrong before." The moment of clarity struck him so hard that he had to voice it out loud.

"I doubt it," said Kathy with a laugh.

"You had said this was a place where I could hear stories of adventures. Where I could live vicariously through those who came through those portals."

"Aye, I did," she said. "And you can still have that. You've heard the tales from some of these folks, they're all heroes in their own worlds."

James smiled. "But don't you see? Being a part of this pub, we're still part of the adventure. We get to be the main characters of this place, of The Pint and Portal. Who knows what stories we'll be part of next?"

Ha'dran nodded. Liam scratched his chin with his free hand and appeared thoughtful.

"But most of all," James continued, "I'm happy to get the chance to share it with all of you."

A chirp from a few feet away grabbed his attention, and he noticed the panels on Demon Box's casing light up.

"And let's not forget Demon Box." James grinned as he picked up the box and placed it under Emma's hand. "You're in this too, buddy."

"I'm . . . speechless . . . You don't know how much it means to me to be included!"

"You've been a part of Emma's family for a while now; that means you're part of ours too."

James added his hand to the top of the stack.

"To The Pint and Portal! A haven for the lost, and a home for the found."

There's a strange kind of magic in this place—one I've come to understand has little to do with the portals or the threads of power that weave through the walls. Those things may make The Pint and Portal unique, but they aren't what make it special. The true magic lies in the people who pass through its doors.

Tim used to tell me this place was too much to handle. He'd say it with a laugh, of course, though I always knew a part of him meant it. Part of him probably still does. And yet, every time we've considered walking away, something would happen to remind us why we stayed.

It wasn't the stories of grand quests or the glimpses of worlds beyond our own that kept us here (though those are thrilling in their own right). It was and has always been the connections. The way a stranger from one world could sit across from a stranger from another and feel like they'd found a friend, or something more. Heaven knows there has been more than one relationship forged in this place. I've realized that it's more than that; it's the way laughter finds a way to fill the room after a day of heartbreak. The way people who have lost everything can find a shoulder to cry on, a moment of purpose, or simply a place to rest.

Tim feels it too, even if he hasn't always understood the importance of this place. What we've built here is far more important than the threats that loom out there. The worlds beyond those portals are vast, dangerous, and often cruel. But here? Here, we can create something that's good.

I've also been thinking a lot about Moira lately. If only we could break through to her. I learned her secret the other day and how terrified she is of people finding out. I'd like to tell her she doesn't need to hide. That her magic is just another thread in the tapestry of this place, no more or less extraordinary than the stories our patrons bring with them. For now, I'll keep my opinions to myself, I know it's not my place. Some secrets are meant to be shared in their own time.

And still I don't know whether she's more scared of her secret getting out or of the potential danger that might come through those gateways. I know now that she doesn't need to worry about either. But her past has been filled with such tragedy; I can't say I blame her.

Perhaps time will heal those wounds. For now, all I can do is offer assurances that we'll continue to stand beside her.

She's still part of this family, whether she realizes it or not.

Speaking of family, I've also come to realize it isn't only something you're born into. It's something you choose and something you build. The Pint and Portal has taught me that over and over again. It taught me that even when the world feels fractured, even when you feel like you don't belong anywhere, there's always a place where you can be found.

Perhaps that's the legacy of this place. Not the portals or magic or the realization that there are infinite possibilities that spring from every interaction that we make; no, what makes The Pint and Portal truly special is that we can be a place where people of all types find acceptance and rest. Letting them share their burdens and their joys. Giving them a moment to breathe, to laugh, to feel like they're home.

Isn't that its own kind of magic?

No matter what lies beyond those doors, I know this: what we've created here matters. It's worth protecting. It's worth holding onto.

For however long we're given, this will be our haven. This will be our home.

***

Want more cozy fantasy?
Want to know more about how Rudy and
Tarvo met?

Coming Late 2025

A cozy fantasy filled with warm hearths, wary hearts, and truly magical strudel.

Rudy has never felt like he quite measured up. He's just a quiet baker with a big heart, a rolling pin, and a knack for pastries.

But when a mysterious portal hidden in a neighboring pub pulls him from his quiet routine into the realm of Hybarn, Rudy finds himself far from the comforts of his kitchen and right in the middle of a brewing rebellion.

The dwarves have never seen a human before, and they

don't trust what they don't understand. Especially not with a tyrant king waging war on magic. Rudy isn't looking to be a hero, though. He just wants to help, one warm loaf, one kind word, and one fresh-baked strudel at a time.

Among the skeptical warriors is Tarvo, a brooding dwarf with battle scars and a past he won't discuss. As Rudy bakes his way into the heart of the community, Tarvo begins to lower his guard. Together, they discover that even in the darkest times, comfort can be found in baked goods, quiet company... and perhaps something deeper.

Flour & Forge is a heartwarming cozy fantasy about finding belonging, stepping beyond our comfort zones, the magic of simple joys, and the healing power of fresh bread and forged bonds. Perfect for fans of Legends & Lattes, Can't Spell Treason Without Tea, and anyone who believes pastry can change the world.

ACKNOWLEDGMENTS

Like most of my stories, The Greatest Pub in the Multiverse first came to me as a spark of an idea - what if there was a pub connected to the multiverse? What would that look like?

I had no idea that it would send me into the world of cozy fantasy. Even though I published The Bartender Between Worlds first, this was the first idea. But it was a rough journey getting this novel out in final form. I rewrote the first third of the novel at least three times, and even when it was close to what you've read it still took a lot of reworking to get to where it is today.

I love the multiverse I've created though and I can't wait to journey with you to other iterations of this world.

I'd like to thank you, the reader, for believing in me and trusting me with your time to get this far. I know there is a never ending pile of stories to read, and yet you chose to pick this one up and spend your time with me. It still blows me away that my words are reaching thousands of readers around the world.

To my wife, Nettie. Thank you once again for providing such incredible artwork for this book. Thank you for your patience as I spend so much of my free time at the keyboard, working to make this dream a reality. I am lucky to have someone who supports and believes in me.

Thank you to Natalie Cammarata for the developmental edits and the fun commentary you provided in your notes. It made the editing process that much more enjoyable and I appreciate the time you spent on it.

Aime Lund, I've relied on you for Proofreading for the majority of my books now. I appreciate the Copy Editing & Proofreading that you do. Thank you for diving into the details and going above and beyond, and doing it in record time. You are truly gifted in your work.

To the Miblart team. You once again exceeded my expectations with this cover. Thank you for the work you continue to do to help bring more readers to my books.

Thank you to Shakira Shute, the amazing narrator for the audiobook editions of both this book and The Bartender Between Worlds. I will never stop saying that I've hit the narrator jackpot when you responded to the audition query. I also want to thank Audiobook Empire for matching the two of us together.

Liz Delton, Thank you so much for designing the Special Edition cover. It looks incredible!

I can not possibly try to name each and every person that has been a part of my journey as I'm sure to forget someone. Please know, if you have been in conversation with me, supported me, interviewed me, been interviewed by me, retweeted, reposted, rethreaded, reviewed, or given a long-distance high-five in this direction, you are appreciated and I thank you for the positive energy and vibes.

Last, but by no means least, I need to thank the incredible 233 backers of the Kickstarter campaign for this book. With the help of these amazing readers I was able to not only fund this book entirely, but also create a phenomenal limited special edition in addition to producing the audiobook version. These supporters showed me that this author dream is something I can make a reality and I thank you from the bottom of my heart. You'll never truly know what your support has meant to me.

Listed in alphabetical order of first name:

Adam Arvidsson, Adam Brown, Adi Adrel, Adrian Keen, Adva Shaviv, AK Momster, Alexandra Corrsin, Alexandre Pirot, Alexis W, Alice Blette, Allee Snyder, Alyn Troy, Amanda Balter, Amanda Corbin, Amanda Eschmeyer, Amber Melican, Amber Toro, Anders M. Ytterdahl, Angela Haas, Angelica Graves, Anja Peerdeman, Annie Kavanagh, Arwyn Cunningham, Astrid, Ayomide, Belle Bredehoft, Big Bad John, Bill Dixon, Bill Kohn, Boe Kelley, Brecht Sucaet, Brett Adams, Brian H., Caledonia, Carl Spitzer, Carol MacLennan-Gonzales, Carolee S, Carolyn Dunk, Cassie Newall, Cat, Catherine Holmes, Cathleen Atela, Celia Jones, Charlotte U. Pleym, Chase McGlinchey, Cherelle H, Chris Roeszler, Christina Jackson, Christine Andres, Christy S, Conall Fisher, Corey Dalman, Cortney Babcock, D.J. Desmond, Daniel E. Coolbaugh, Dave Litsky, David DeHaan, David Holzborn, Dead Fish Books, Dean Lambert, Dean R Whitehead, Debra May, Dexter Ellis, Diane Hansebout, Diego Riley, Dion Doege, Dominic Chiavassa, Dominique, Donna Bull, E. A. Hendryx, Eddie Joo, Eileen Holmes, Elfrida Svensson, Elizabeth Semkiu, Elizabeth Simpson, Emily Rousell, Emma Adams, Emma Brown, Emma Flaws, Eric R. Asher, Erin Veeneman, Fallenzap, Figmentsdreams, Frank Rosellen, Gabrielle Wright, Gary Olsen, Gianna Christopher, Horatio Astor, Hugo Essink, J Mills, J.D.L. Rosell, J.P. Rindfleisch IX, Jaime Ricciardi, James, Jan B, Jana M Evensong, Jason Pulham, Jax, JED, Jen Morton, Jenna Levitski, Jennifer Osterman, Jesper Kaudern, Jessica Hoyal, Jessica Staub, Jessie Gary, Jessie Lee, John Blankenship, John Fritz, John Gilligan, John Idlor, John O, John P Curtin, John W Ladley, Jordan Stiles, Josefine B., Judy McClain, K Raine, Kaitlyn Sexton, Kaitlyn VanderPloeg, Karen Chong, Katalin Laczina, Kate Toner, Kathy Friesen, Kelly Knight, Kelly McMahon, Kent M Smith, Kenyon Wensing, Kevin Scott, Kimberly, Kimberly Grymes, Kris, Kristen Altmann,

Krystal Bohannan, Kyle G Wilkinson, L Gase, Lady A Taylor, Laura Pomerantz, Leah Barr, Leticia Henriksen, Lianne Watkins, Lilith Sylvia Daisy Mühlberg, Lori Wolbrueck, Lorien Cord, Lovis Geier, Luke Lorah, Mackenzie Alexander, Magda, Manny Rana, Margaret Menzies, MaryAnne Armstrong, Matt Goodall, Melissa T, Merriwen Broadstrike, Michael Hoddersen, Michael Johnson, Michael Reilly, Michelle Glover, Michelle LaCrosse, Microwave_131, Mike Dubost, Misha Rose Pantoja, Morgan, Myriam Fengler, Mystique, Nancy B. Yeem Natalie Munford, Natasha Savoie, Nava Starling, Nicholas W Fuller, Nick Mandujano III, Nicole Gatto, Niki Kuhlman, Nikki Malakoff, OudjesEric, Pamela Franson, Paola, Paul Smith, Paula Roszina, Per M. Jensen, Peter "Tonour" Basak, Peter Allen, Rachel Lowe, Rachel Simpson, Randy Mack, Renae, rhea macchione, Richard A Sawyer, Richard Novak, Richie Hedges, Riley J Lohr, Risa Scranton, Rob Cifaldi, Rob Steinberger, Robyn Moore, Rocco Levitas, RogerM, Rosa Thill, Rosalie Weyer, Rowan Stone, Russell Fisk, Ryan Todd, Sabra Phillips, Samantha Bartell, Samantha Newberry, Sara Liming, Sarah Niebergall, Sarah R., Sarah S., Scott R., Sean Elliott, Sebastian, Sharon Lawrence, Shawn Lapetino, Shay Dinur, Silvia Amber, Starflakes, Starr Z Davies, Stella N, Stéphan Beauchamp, Stephenie Morales, Steven Byrd, Susan Wilson, SushiMango, Suzanne van der Heide, Sven Rodrigues-Wagner, Syl Wyant, T.L Stone, Tabitha Mashburn, Tania, Tanya Young, TheMightyKitsune, Tinsley Family, Tom Belanger, Travis Lynch, Trevor Jerome, Tuskanini, Tyler Cheek, Valerie Sizemore, Vicki Hsu, Victoria P, Mrs. Waz, Whitney Beaugh, Wineke Sloos, Wizard Flight, wonderlost, Zaqueen, Z.S. Diamanti, Zephyr Mini